DEVIL'S LEDGER

AN INTERNATIONAL BANKING
SPY THRILLER

A LOUISE MOSCOW NOVEL
BOOK 3

AWARD-WINNING BESTSELLING AUTHOR
LORRAINE EVANOFF

DEVIL'S LEDGER
AN INTERNATIONAL BANKING SPY THRILLER

To my husband Robert Lane Levy

ACKNOWLEDGMENTS

Thank you, Patrick McDonald, for your affirmations and editing, your invaluable feedback was a gamechanger. Many thanks to: Dr. Jim Stott, LuAnn Kulpaka and Karen Widess for your eagle-eye proofreading and kind encouragement; Stirling Levine for your martial arts wisdom; Haakon Koski for your amazing illustration skills; my family and friends for your enthusiastic support. A special thank you to my mom, Jude Baker, for your brilliant insight into the meaning of life.

"Yet in that bulb, those sapless scales,
The lily wraps her silver vest,
Till vernal suns and vernal gales
Shall kiss once more her fragrant breast."

~ *Mary Tighe*

PROLOGUE

November 16, 2009, Moscow, Russia

Magnitsky scribbled a quote from Solzhenitsyn's *One Day in the Life of Ivan Denisovich*. "Can a man who is warm understand one who is freezing?" The sound of approaching bootsteps echoed in the prison corridor and keys jingled. Magnitsky shivered, doubled over in pain, holding onto hope that he would finally be treated for gall stones and pancreatitis brought on by dismal conditions, frigid temperatures, impure food, and abysmal sanitation. He was being intentionally and inhumanely denied medical attention, but he never gave up on the possibility that a single soul might show mercy. One never knew when humanity might rear its beautiful head. Alas, that would not be the case for Magnitsky. In a final homage to Solzhenitsyn, he scrawled on the page, "Day 358, bell to bell." Then was dragged away.

Sacrifice was ingrained in Sergei Magnitsky's DNA. Nearly every Russian had read Aleksandr Solzhenitsyn's experiences in the forced-labor camps of *The Gulag Archipelago*. Like most of Russia and its western allies, Magnitsky had wanted to believe that was all in the past and viewed the 1940s Gulag as an anomaly. Solzhenitsyn viewed it as a systemic failure of Soviet political culture, an inevitable outcome of the leftist Bolshevik party established by Lenin, who, like all authoritarians once in power, enforced tight control over his populace, lest they lose sight of the party's objective and adopt opposing beliefs. Solzhenitsyn had warned that, although many inhumane practices had ceased, the basic structure of the Gulag system had survived, and it could be revived and expanded by future tyrants.

Solzhenitsyn's narrative of prison survival dictated Sergei Magnitsky's faith and gave him strength while incarcerated. Their accounts, while vastly different, were also ominously similar. Both had been political prisoners, Solzhenitsyn in the Lubyanka Prison, Magnitsky in Moscow's Butyrka Prison. Both had been relatively young, Solzhenitsyn age 27, and Magnitsky age 35. Solzhenitsyn had entrusted his story to an attorney he met in prison.[1]

Fellow Butyrka prisoners had entrusted their stories to Magnitsky – himself an attorney. But while Solzhenitsyn would never have been allowed to write down his experiences and had to commit them to memory, Magnitsky took copious notes providing fastidious detail of his detention. Both men had been inhumanely treated and isolated from their families under squalid conditions.

The parallels were greater than the differences and Magnitsky knew that it was likely that he represented the last vestige of freedom from Putin's tyranny. That is why Magnitsky held steadfast to his legacy as a soldier of truth. Future generations would look to him as a lone pillar upholding truth under the mass of lies. No other political prisoner of his era had held on as long as Magnitsky had. The courts, the military, bankers, and politicians had succumbed to Putin's abuse of power. After his corrupt rise to the presidency following the break-up of the former Soviet Union, one either obeyed Putin or faced the dire consequences of public humiliation, destitution, or even death. The deaths were numerous, and while ostensibly by natural or accidental causes, at the same time left no doubt as to the consequences of those who did not comply with Putin's commands. Putin had turned Russia into a mafia state.

Magnitsky was arrested for the crime of telling the truth. He refused to falsely testify on charges of tax fraud against his American client, Bill Browder, owner of the successful investment fund, Hermitage Capital. While preparing to defend Browder against false charges, his investigation turned up evidence that two criminals Artem Kuznetsov and Pavel Karpov, had been running a scam to fraudulently acquire companies by filing fake change of ownership documents with the State. They would then use the resulting proof of ownership to sell off the companies at huge profits. The two criminals used the scheme to acquire fake ownership of Hermitage and process a fraudulent request for a massive $230 million tax refund on manufactured losses. The same tax fraud for which Russian authorities had charged Browder. All under the auspices of President Putin.

After almost a year to the day in detention enduring abuse by guards to get him to "confess," Magnitsky's resolve had only grown stronger. Against his family's pleas and at the risk of his business, he persisted. His was a higher cause, bolstered by the bravery of others like Solzhenitsyn before him, all of whom had known what they were up against from the start. His abusers' intentions were clear from the moment he was arrested. They would lie, cheat, and misrepresent the facts. They would stack the courts in their favor.

Magnitsky died in prison on November 16, 2009, the real cause of which is still not fully known. But his investigation provided evidence that made its way to international intelligence communities. Evidence of Putin's international money laundering scheme to fund the development of arsenals to attack neighboring territories, including chemical weapons, to further feed an insatiable hunger for power.

Browder would eventually dedicate his autobiography *Red Notice,* "To Sergei Magnitsky, the bravest man I've ever known."

PART I

ONE

May 25, 2010, Valley of Kashmir, India

It felt like a 500-pound weight on his chest. His lungs were on fire and Jean-Philippe struggled to breathe. But the suffering would be worth the reward. *It had better be.* Silently, he counted ten steps. Then started again, *one, two, three…*

Thousands of devotees made the annual trek to the Amarnath Cave Temple in Kashmir. Many took the longer but less challenging route from Pahalgam. Others took the northern route from Baltal along the river Amaravati, which originates from the Amarnath Glacier. It is shorter, about 10 miles, but has a very steep gradient and is quite difficult to climb. That was the route Jean-Philippe had opted for. Although more challenging, he completed the trek in record time, just under three days, while carrying his own provisions. He now feared collapsing on the brink of reaching his destination.[2]

The annual Amaranth Yatra pilgrimage begins when the iced stalagmite located at the altitude of 12,756 feet reaches the maximum of its waxing phase through the summer months, taking the shape of a great phallus or *Lingam*. It ends on Shraavana Purnima Day, August 2nd. The *Shiva Lingam* is worshipped as a symbol of the Hindu deity Shiva. The symbolic 'temple' is cited in ancient Hindu texts dating back 5,000 years. The pilgrimage is often deadly. Of the millions of yatra pilgrims over the years, hundreds have died, many not physically fit enough for the arduous climb, high elevations, and adverse weather, others from road accidents, and still others from terrorist attacks.

Father Jean-Philippe and fellow monk, Father Gregory, had decided to make the trek in May to avoid the crowds and fully enjoy the physical and meditative benefits. Jean-Philippe had the ulterior motive of being as physically isolated as possible on Louise Moscow's birthday May 25th. Instead of their traditional full cassock of the Fathers of Mercy, they wore layers of local woolens, silks, and linens for warmth. They had also ditched their traditional wide-brimmed black Saturno hats and wrapped their heads in colorful local fabrics.

"Impressionnant!" Father Gregory exclaimed in French.

Jean-Philippe remained doubled over, still catching his breath. "I'm too old for this shit," he muttered in French to his friend who was ten years younger.

He finally stood up and took in the natural wonder. The majestic snow-capped Himalayas formed the backdrop of one of the most sacred pilgrimage sites of Hinduism, the cave temple of Amarnath, which stood about 150 feet high and 90 feet long. Inside the cave was a pure-white ice mound in the form of a Shiv lingam. Manmade objects decorated the cave, including a golden trident, or *trishul*, draped in ceremonious red fabric. The ice stalagmite had already begun waxing, along with a nearby formation representing the Parvati goddess of fertility.

Still early in the season, the formation wasn't at its peak size, which waxes from May to August as the Glacier melts and the water flows through the cave, reaching a maximum height of more than six feet on the full moon day of Shravan in early August. The main attraction is the world's largest natural Shivling, representing the male and female reproductive organs, the upper part resembling the phallus and the base resembling the vulva. This ice-lingam was considered the sacred Lord Shiva lingam.

"It really does resemble a Shiva lingam," Father Gregory said. "Am I blushing?"

"Worshipping the lingam is a once-in-a-lifetime experience of great religious significance," Jean-Philippe replied.

For their international espionage work they had both disavowed carnal pleasures and became monks, the side effect of chastity heightening their sense of humor.

"God bless the holy sex organ." Father Gregory reached into his pocket and took out two lengths of red string purchased from a peddler they had deemed the neediest along the journey. He handed one of the threads to Jean-Philippe and they each tied their threads to the crude barriers. "What shall we wish for?"

"A ride back down the mountain," Jean-Philippe quipped, in a rare moment of acerbity. Suddenly the sound of a helicopter drew their attention upwards.

"Remarkable," Father Gregory said, staring in awe of Jean-Philippe.

"Don't look at me!" Jean-Philippe eyed the chopper. "That's an H125 rescue transport."

"It has United States Military markings," Father Gregory observed. "I'm pretty sure they've come for you, and not me."

Two temple guards murmured excitedly to each other, and several Sherpas and campers watched in amazement as the chopper alit in the expansive area that would normally serve as basecamp during the mass pilgrimage at the center of walkways leading to the cave.

"Jean-Philippe de Villeneuve!" a voice over the bullhorn said. "Get in, now!" Jean-Philippe recognized FBI agent Michael Fuentes leaning out the open gunner door from his mass of dark curly hair. They both bolted toward the aircraft.

"Michael, what are you doing here?" Jean-Philippe asked.

"We need you at Langley!"

Jean-Philippe hesitated. "What about Father Gregory?"

"Where he goes, I go!" Father Gregory seconded.

"Climb aboard, both of you! Let's go!"

Once safely strapped in, Jean-Philippe studied the impressive Airbus H125, built to withstand high-altitudes, high winds, and uneven or snowy landing areas. The aircraft had state-of-the-art oxygen equipment, was lightweight and easy to refuel.

"Welcome aboard." Michael shook their hands.

"Nice ride," Jean-Philippe replied in English with a French accent. "Thanks for the lift. Did you say Langley? Why is the FBI doing transport for the CIA?"

"Haven't you heard?" Michael said with a dimpled smile. "I switched to the dark side and joined the CIA. It was part of my deal when they nominated me to recruit Louise."

"Louise is now CIA?" Jean-Philippe asked. "What do they want me for?"

"The CIA needs a deep cover, and you came highly recommended."

"By whom?"

"By me!" Michael gave another dimpled smile.

"Where Jean-Philippe goes I go," Father Gregory added, half joking.

Michael thought about it for a moment. "That's not a bad idea. Do you speak Russian?"

"Konechno!"

"Will Louise be involved?" Jean-Philippe asked.

"She's on her own deep cover assignment at this time."

"In Burgundy?"

"You probably know as well as anyone, J.P.," Michael chided.

"As long as she's happy," Jean-Philippe muttered wistfully.

TWO

September 7, 2012, Burgundy, France

It was weird being both happy and restless. Louise gazed over her rustic estate in the morning mist, the sheltering peach orchards to the north, the rolling hills to the south, with layers of purple morning shadows mimicking the now dormant lavender fields.

Having passed another liminal point of her life, this stage seemed to suit her. Perhaps it was the downhill fiftieth birthday she had accepted halfheartedly earlier that year. Unlike her fortieth which hadn't felt any different, or her thirtieth when she had just felt grateful to be out of her twenties, turning fifty had been a wake-up call, and she found equanimity. She could still pass for at least ten years younger, but that meant passing for forty-something, much different than passing for twenty- or thirty-something. Still, she felt physically and mentally stronger than ever, evoking the Agnès Varda line in Le Bonheur, *Happiness is a beautiful fruit that tastes of cruelty.*

The calming scent of dry lavender wafted over the 400-year-old cottage. It had been an indulgence, but if she had to pick an undercover career, it might as well be cultivating her own crops, if only for subject matter of her photography and painting hobbies. Lavender was better suited to the more southern region of Provence, France, but her instincts told her the soil here would be conducive. Her decision ended up being a profitable little side business. Surrounded by peach groves, her lavender was imbued with a smooth sweetness, unmatched by that of Provence and her "vintage" had gained demanding customers.

The tuxedo cat rubbed against her calf as the more talkative ginger cat meowed softly, lying in the shade of a large rosemary bush.

"Vous-avez faim, mes petits minous? Are you hungry my little kitty cats?"

She went inside, fetched the kibble, and refilled their bowls near the small shelter she had her neighbor build for the feral cats. Each cat had clipped ears, having been fixed. When she was home, she left the door open and allowed them to roam freely inside. They were outdoor cats and well taken care of by her community of neighbors, making them ideal pets for when she traveled on assignment. She refilled their water dish and set the potted catnip plant nearby.

"Voila un peu de herbe à chat. Bon appétit."

She had been concerned about giving catnip to cats living in the wild lest they become disoriented. But she had done some research and learned that catnip was found in nature and therefore naturally therapeutic for them. And their response was delightfully entertaining.

She picked up the lavender-filled trug and laid out bundles on the outdoor table for packaging. Her life was once again a fairy tale, or maybe more like a romance novel without the romance. The prospect of becoming a stereotypical *cat lady* didn't thrill her either. Those thoughts started to darken her mood, but she reminded herself of the prior real-life nightmares she had endured and felt some gratitude. She always had her trusty bicycle to transport her away to charming local destinations and *change her train of thought,* as the French say. She placed the trug on the farm table, washed her hands and slung her bag over her shoulder.

In her sundress, a cashmere pull-over, and rubber Hunter boots, she peddled down the pulverized granite driveway, past the narrow ancient stone pool at the end of which water trickled from a scallop shell fountain. Steam rose invitingly from the crystal-clear bathing pond, but she rode on, passing the neighboring orchard with hundred-year-old peach trees, the scent of dry lavender and the hum of bees in the air, quickly lifting her mood.

She rode along the Saône River of the Côte Chalonnaise wine region, named after the town of Chalon-sur-Saône, where she had lived for almost ten years since leaving her Caribbean Island paradise. Being on the river had made the town an important trading center of the Celts in Gaul times and later of the ancient Romans, with wine and olive oil being the main commodities traded along the river.

She arrived at the open-air market around the Town Hall, or *Hôtel de Ville,* and racked her bike. Although the farmers' market was open every morning, it always varied. Vendors and goods changed daily. Massive bouquets of sunflowers one day and bundles of lavender the next. The ubiquitous local Dijon mustard, escargots, and cornichons were always on display. She sniffed a peach that probably came from the very orchard where she lived. Her tiny estate being a protected landmark among the groves.

"Bonjour, Antoine," she greeted her farmer neighbor who was tending to his stand.

"Ah, te-voila, Lulu, bien dormi?" They exchanged the regional four cheek kisses.

"Oui, tres bien, merci." She selected various stone fruits and placed them in her bag without paying. "On prend un café?"

Antoine left his assistant to take over the stand and they went to the adjacent bistro and ordered coffee and baked goods. Antoine leaned back and sipped the delicious café au lait.

"Life is good, non?"

"It is indeed." Louise couldn't argue.

As if on cue, Antoine opened the daily newspaper, Le Monde, and the front page immediately caught her eye. Her heart skipped a beat and the world literally brightened as the sun broke through a cloud. Antoine noticed her expression.

"Qu'est-ce qu'il y a?"

Louise didn't hear him, absentmindedly pulling his newspaper closer to read the detail under the headline in French: *Magnitsky Accountability Act Passes First Hurdle in U.S.*

The news unearthed many questions that Louise had suppressed since the turmoil ten years ago when murderous thugs almost killed her. After she had closed the case that had been terrorizing the Burgundy region for decades, two unresolved questions continued to nag at her. First, what had happened to the insiders who had been abusing confidential client banking information to perpetuate their sex trafficking ring? Second, what role had Russia played? She found herself perpetually looking for news reports, taking mental notes, then dutifully adding them to her archives. She tracked anything that seemed relevant, clipping articles for her paper archives, and copying-and-pasting articles she found online into a proliferating Word document.

"Ah, I see you've noticed the Magnitsky headline," Antoine said in an English-French accent, signaling spy language mode. "It took you long enough."

Louise snapped out of her daze and sipped her café au lait. "The coffee helps."

In the agrarian Burgundy region local farmers came to know each other. When Louise had first encountered Antoine in his natural habitat of the farmers' market, although grizzled and unassuming, she sensed something about him. It was amazing how many former spies she had met over the years lurking in the general populace. Her ex-fiancé Jean-Philippe, the Italian stylist in Paris, and the former MI-6 who was her fishing guide, or *ghillie,* on vacation in Scotland. Even while in witness protection under her CIA-issued secret identity or *legend,* as Karen Baker in a Chicago suburb, a plumber she had hired turned out to be a former undercover detective.

Louise had been discreet and gradually gained Antoine's trust, but he had remained tight-lipped beyond reason. Still, when it came to Louise's well-being, he never hesitated to open the secret vault of information. Antoine knew and respected Louise's former fiancé, Jean-Philippe de Villeneuve, although they had never worked in the same division of the French CIA known as the DGSE. Nonetheless, being Jean-Philippe's ex had been reason enough for him to take her under his wing.

For Louise, after ten years of relative peace, she sensed old ghosts were rematerializing, dormant energies were back in flux, unsolved mysteries were resurfacing. She would soon be hearing from her father, George Moscow, and her college sweetheart Michael Fuentes, who happened to be an FBI-turned-CIA agent. She could feel it.

"You are a good friend, Antoine."

"And you are a good person, Louise."

Yes, too good, she thought. After a blissful childhood, her eyes had opened in her adult life. Working a high-level job in international high finance, then being forced into undercover work as a spook for various countries and agencies will do that to a person. But the genie of corruption was out of the bottle and refused to be sucked back in. If she hadn't so deeply trusted her early-career employers, the executive officers of Bank of Credit and Commerce International (BCCI), and experienced their venality first-hand, she may never have learned that the greedy will stop at nothing, even murder, to retain power and their ill-gotten gains.

"Louise," Antoine said, intruding her thoughts.

The fog lifted, and Louise laughed. "Yes, I'm a good person in a dubious world."

"It is as if you were put on earth to figure out the meaning of life," Antoine said. "You are truly a hopeless case.

"That never stopped me from trying." Louise tore off the end of her croissant, spread butter and apricot jam on it, dipped the edge into her café au lait and chomped into it. "I guarantee you, Antoine, someone will be calling me within 24 hours to put me on a case."

"They're not fools. This is your domain, Lulu," he said, referring to the Magnitsky matter.

"Many shoes are about to drop," Louise muttered. "…out of windows and helicopters."

"Lulu," Antoine distracted her from her reverie. "Would you like a head start?"

"Um, yes please."

He flipped his newspaper to the page he had been reading and pointed to an article bylined: *World's Oldest Bank, Banca Monte dei Paschi di Siena Under Investigation in Connection with Deutsche Bank.*

THREE

September 7, 2012, Burgundy, France

Louise peddled back to her cottage, thoughts racing and extra-sensory instincts tingling. Seeing the headline in the newspaper, the bud of her fixation had blossomed since being recruited to the CIA. This would be the turning point of the last ten years spent lying low and flying under the radar. The virtues of rural life were not as satisfying for Louise of late, and she was readying herself for the next opportunity to dig in the dirt. The world of undercover operations and spy craft, even with the accompanying adrenalin rush, was a long game of planting seeds and tending to the soil. Louise had been ripe for the picking.

After she had wrapped up her affairs on the witness protection island in the Caribbean almost ten years ago and gave the Tiki bar that she owned to her former bodyguard Big Steve, she moved to Burgundy and set up her farm and household. She had also invested in a restaurant anchored by the culinary magic of Magali, who, along with her brother Matthieu, had sheltered her during her investigation that had wrapped up in April 2002. She had spent considerable time helping to get the eatery off the ground while settling into her cottage and preparing her land for lavender fields. She hung out at the bistro often, even doing wait duties on busy nights. The locals had come to know her as a sort of silent boss à la Rick's Café American from Casablanca, with Magali even joking that she'd become her own best customer.

Two years had gone blissfully and rapidly by. Then, she was contacted by the CIA at the end of 2004 and recruited into a branch for special services. Their banking investigation division had been weakened under the Bush administration, and the current CIA Director wanted her specifically to shore up the resulting hot bed of corruption. Because of her expertise, the agency wanted to make her role official.

So, starting in early 2005, Louise spent several months of the year training at Langley and the rest of the time based in Burgundy. Magali covered for her part-of-the-year gap by telling locals that Louise had several other business interests, so when she returned it was as if she'd never been away. She had worked out her schedule to arouse the least amount of suspicion regarding her comings-and-goings, and her cover as a farm and restaurant entrepreneur had been perfect. The CIA had given her carte blanche on specializing her training and technology, provided she spend part of the year at the agency organizing investigations and continuing her remote operations throughout the year.

She focused most of her attention on languages, research, and self-defense, especially after having been on the receiving end of some brutal attacks during her past investigations. Louise studied Krav Maga,[3] a martial art developed because the size of the practitioner doesn't matter, and the strength and flexibility she had developed through her intense yoga practice had made the self-defense moves come naturally. By the end of her fourth year, she had earned a black belt, and impressed her traditional instructors, including the one she had found nearby in Burgundy, with her exacting attention to technique.

She also brushed up on her newly acquired Russian language skills, which she had taught herself as a sanity exercise while sequestered on the island. When the CIA tested her, they found that Louise had an inherent intellectual knack for picking up foreign languages quickly. Working at the Agency linguistic labs, Louise picked up all three Russian territorial dialects, and added a working knowledge of nearby in-country Slavic languages.

Вы не можете избежать того, что должно произойти, Louise thought as she turned onto the road to her cottage. The Russian proverb: *You can't escape what is about to happen.*

During all that outside training, Louise had also excelled in the banking division at the Agency with a ferocity, which told the Director he'd made the right decision. She organized case files and was authorized to assign agents to begin the process of infiltration, all while waiting for a case that she would personally take on.

Technology had also caught up to her, as she parked the bike outside her home. The Agency had been very accommodating in setting up her links to the outside world. The spare bedroom she had converted to a communications nerve center featured a direct meeting link to her team at Langley, as well as a security clearance, satellite Internet, and enough computing power to process a warehouse full of hardcopy archives. The satellite dish was discreetly concealed on the water tower in the lavender field.

When an overnight guest had inadvertently walked into her set-up, all he said was, "Êtes-vous Batman?" No, she wasn't Batman, but sometimes she felt that power.

Louise went to her 'spare bedroom' and fired up her coms system. She wanted to open the files she'd amassed on Sergei Magnitsky. It had been almost three years since Magnitsky's death on November 16, 2009, either murdered by Russian officials or a heart attack, depending on the news source. What would come to be known as *The Magnitsky Act* had passed its first hurdle toward becoming law and was headed to The United States House of Representatives.

As Louise pulled up the pertinent information, she reflected on why the world didn't demand full transparency of the underpinnings of international banking. The fealty of government officials only reinforced the corruption, all because for most people, banking was boring. For most, the thought of understanding finance or accounting put the *numb* back into numbers. But for Louise, it was utterly fascinating. The technical creativity involved in funneling trillions of dollars to the offshore dark economy was mind-blowing.

She had made it her personal goal to solve the mystery behind banking corruption. She knew there had to be a common denominator behind the lawlessness. It wasn't just greed. She might be considered naïve and idealistic at best, or crazy at worst. But it was equivalent to trying to solve the meaning of life. Meeting God. Louise was convinced there was a thread that could be pulled to unravel the entire centuries-old scheme.

From what she had gathered during her research into the vast corruption in Russia, with the wall coming down in 1989, and the break-up of the former Soviet Union in 1991, for the first time, Russian citizens had been given private ownership of their public institutions. To put it simplistically, it was as though the Russian government had given every Russian citizen one share of stock for each public organization formerly owned and run by the Government. Whether intended or not, the consequences were a free-for-all stock grab, whereby those with the means literally offered every Russian citizen cash in exchange for their single share of stock. Each share was meaningless on its own, but if consolidated resulted in majority ownership of former Soviet institutions, from fossil fuel, power and electric, to commerce, to banks, for pennies on the dollar of its real value. On the world market, those entities, which were insanely undervalued, when sold to high-paying foreign parties, brought huge returns on a relatively minor investment. Thusly was born the Russian Oligarch. One had to believe that this scheme had been orchestrated and coordinated in advance. It had been a long game by none other than former KGB officer, Vladimir Putin.

Louise had anticipated that the 2008 recession and collapse of global banking would bring her out of seclusion at some point. But the world of high finance has a well-documented lag in response time to corruption. As strict as regulations may have been, the rules were constantly pushed to the limit and under-resourced regulators took months or years to catch up. The onset of the financial collapse happened in May 2008 at the end of the George W. Bush administration. Sergei Magnitsky died in November 2009. It wasn't until three years later that Louise gained access to regulators' investigations, which had barely begun to make a dent in the corruption. It was all coming to a head in 2012. So, 2013 promised to be the year of banking scandals.

Louise browsed the Internet and pulled the same headline Antoine had showed her. The oldest bank in the world, Banca Monte dei Paschi di Siena, or MPS, was founded in 1472, two decades before Columbus sailed to what would become America. She perused images of the bank's Siena, Italy, headquarters, which occupied an ancient stone palace, its walls bedecked with medieval and Renaissance masterpieces. According to the article, for almost 530 years, it had existed peacefully, becoming a pillar to the Tuscan community. Its charitable foundation doled out hundreds of millions of dollars a year to the local university, sports teams, museums, and other local causes, an annual amount larger than the city's annual budget.

Then in 2002, MPS had approached Deutsche Bank to take advantage of the booming global economy and purchase derivatives. The goal had been to free up cash so MPS could participate in a wave of mergers remaking the Italian banking industry.[4] However, in 2008, when the global stock markets went haywire, MPS suffered huge losses and Deutsche bank issued more derivatives in a scheme to allow MPS to conceal crippling losses from the previous derivatives, for a hefty fee, making it a huge moneymaker for Deutsche. The oldest bank in the world had become an international pyramid scheme. If her suspicions were correct, a new investigation would be a vast undertaking requiring reinforcements.

She decided to call on her old friend, Frédéric LaFontaine, a genius financial software guru who had made so much money in tech that his permanent address was a luxury yacht. He knew both the financial inner circle and the inner workings. What better way to remain under the radar than at sea? LaFontaine was so stealthy she suspected he was part of the spy club but was never able to confirm it.

She was deep into her research when the distinctive ping of her phone startled her. It was from Michael, her first love in college, and an ally in her pursuit of the truth for the last twenty years. He was an FBI-turned-CIA operative, and one of the few connections to her past she was still close to. She expected the digital missive to be an answer to a question she had sent about a case, but it was...

"Have you heard from Mary lately?"

Louise had a visceral response of panic, and auto-dialed Michael's number. He picked up on the first ring.

"Somehow I knew I would be hearing from you," Louise said without introduction.

"You must have been sending me mental *Bat Signals* from Burgundy," he replied.

Ha, she thought, currently in her own bat cave.

"That's what I love about you, Lulu." Michael used her nickname to play up their camaraderie. "No matter how removed you are from the real world out there in your paradise, you have a sixth sense. Some might consider you a control freak."

"Some might call me paranoid. Is my mom all right?"

"I don't know, is she?"

"Why did you ask if I had heard from her lately?"

"My mom asked."

Their mothers were best friends.

"I'll book a flight now."

"It's your call."

"I'll be there tomorrow."

The reason for her panic was that she had been having problems reaching her childhood home. Calls and texts to her mom Mary and her father George had gone unanswered. It was one of the things causing her recent restlessness, and her call with Michael had just cemented her decision to go home.

She booked a business class ticket on the first flight out of Paris-Charles de Gaulle Airport the next afternoon. She prepared her house for an indefinite stay in New York, then packed her carryon with basic black clothing and vital sundries and went to bed.

The next morning, she arrived early at the bistro that she partially owned along with her vineyard owner friends, brother-sister team, Matthieu and Magali. She entered to find Magali's son, Luke, whom she had known since he was about two years old, and who was now pre-teen. He was diligently sweeping the floors.

"Bonjour mon ange. Maman te met au travail?"

"I'm working to earn money for Christmas presents!" Luke replied with an adorable French accent.

"Bravo, Luke, your English is excellent!" Louise was truly impressed.

"Thanks to you, Aunt Lulu!" His curly blond hair fell across his ocean blue eyes, almost identical to when he was a toddler, only taller. She beamed with pride.

"Bonjour Lulu!" Magali said, carrying a tray of freshly baked croissants from the kitchen. "Tu veux un café et un croissant?"

"Yes, a quick café au lait and a croissant would be perfect. I have to catch a flight to New York." Louise gestured toward Luke. "My interpreter will translate for you." Louise smiled as Luke repeated in French for him *maman*.

"Merci, Luke." Magali winked at Louise having understood her in English. But she played along, very proud of her son too. She whipped up a café au lait, and placed it along with a croissant, butter, and jam in front of Louise, who took a seat at the zinc-top bar.

Louise ritualistically sipped her café and crunched into the croissant. "I'm going to miss this while I'm gone."

"Voted best croissant in Burgundy!" Luke exclaimed.

"The best in the world if you ask me!" Louise said.

"A new adventure?" Magali whispered to Louise while polishing the bar top.

"I'm going home to check on my mom."

Magali gave the universal maternal look of concern and reassurance as

Louise finished her breakfast.

"Don't worry, I'll cover for you, partner," Magali said.

"Merci, ma belle. It's probably nothing. I'll let you know." She leaned over and gave Magali four cheek kisses. "How's your big brother, Matthieu?"

"He has his hands full with the vineyards."

"Give him my best." Louise hopped off the bar stool and exchanged four cheek kisses with Luke. "Bye, love you, bye!"

She sped away, arriving moments later at the SNCF train station where she left her car in the long-term parking. After a three-and-a-half-hour train ride, she had just a three-minute walk to Charles de Gaulle airport. She took off and landed at JFK, having gained six hours with the time difference, and was in a rental car driving up the Hudson River Valley the same afternoon.

September 9, 2012, New York

The drive from JFK to her parents' home in Westchester County had the familiar feeling of time travel. Just yesterday she was among the calming scents of her lavender fields and today the Manhattan skyline was shrinking in her rearview as she sped north. Taking the scenic route, she merged onto U.S. 9 north, the placid Hudson River on her left. As she passed Yonkers with its lush foliage people enjoyed the lingering post-Labor Day sunset on the glistening river. It was tempting to stop but she didn't want to lose any time with her mother. While hoping her anxiety was unnecessary, she knew something was up, or Michael wouldn't have contacted her.

She soon approached the legendary town of Sleepy Hollow evoking a sense of foreboding and continued east on Phelps Way through Rockefeller State Park Preserve. The thickets of trees and historic landmarks reminded her of the eerie Forest of Fontainebleau at the edge of the ancient artist village of Barbizon, France.

She had last seen her mom for her 50th birthday in May, when she traveled with her childhood friends to her Burgundy cottage. At the time she was convinced something was amiss with her mother, despite her denials. Mary seemed to have aged prematurely, was less spry, not her usual bubbly self. She tried not to push her mom too hard, chalking it up to normal limitations of aging and Louise needing to adjust expectations.

Pulling up to her family home Louise felt a mix of relief and dread. Approaching the back door, the scent of baking and cooking coming from the half-open kitchen window was eerily absent. Louise tried the knob, which was unlocked. She pushed the door open and entered.

"Mom? Dad?"

Louise hadn't notified them of her impromptu visit, wanting to surprise them. So, it was reasonable to assume they might be out running errands. It was just after 2:00 p.m. on Sunday, so they could be shopping for dinner and the week ahead. The stairs groaned as she climbed to her parents' second-floor bedroom. Approaching the door that stood slightly ajar, she could hear Mary's gentle snoring. It was difficult to conceive of her mother as elderly. Louise was born when Mary turned thirty, so she could always easily do the math adding thirty to her own age. Her mom was now an octogenarian. Given the era, they had their one and only child relatively late in life, unplanned. Her father's career as a prosecutor for the New York District Attorney in charge of white-collar fraud wasn't conducive to family life. But theirs was a bond of love and when the surprise pregnancy happened, they embraced it.

She hated to wake her mom, so she put her bag in her old bedroom and freshened up. It was a long drive back and forth to Manhattan, but seeing Michael was part of the reasons she came. She sat on the bed and texted him.

CLAM CHOWDER IN ONE HOUR?

She immediately got a reply. *ROGER WILLCO.*

"Lulu?" Mary's voice was hoarse. She looked a wreck standing in the doorway.

"Surprise!" Louise said, using jazz hands. She stood and came over to give her mom a big hug and walked her back to her bedroom.

"I didn't hear you come in. I've been so tired lately." Indeed, Mary appeared to have aged even more since she had last seen her.

"You're probably acclimating to the cooler fall temperatures," she lied. She helped Mary back into bed and covered her with no resistance and gave her a kiss on the cheek.

"What are you doing here?" Mary asked weakly. "Did your father summon you?"

"No…" Louise replied, smirking at the word *summon*. "Neither you nor Dad have picked up your phones when I called. Also, Michael contacted me about you."

"I'm not answering the phone." Mary turned away. "I...I don't know about your father."

Louise filed this new information away and would take it up with both her parents later.

"I'm going to run out and see Michael for a little while. Do you need me to pick anything up?" But Mary had already dozed off.

Louise grabbed her bag and fished out her car keys. As she ran down the stairs she almost collided with George Moscow.

"Dad!" Louise wasn't expecting the encounter and was caught off guard.

"Louise? What's happening? What are you doing here?"

"Michael called me and said mom would probably appreciate me visiting. Neither of you was answering your phones. What is that all about?"

George paused, a bit too long for such an easy question. "Things have become...complicated with your mother and me. I didn't feel like discussing it with you. We'd been so used to being out of touch that it was easier just to continue status quo."

He had always used military terms to try to keep her in line. It had never worked. "I am disappointed, especially seeing her in such a weakened condition. We'll talk later. I'm running late." Louise brushed past him toward the door.

"Where are you going?"

"To meet with Michael. Do you want me to cancel? I can make you something to eat if you like. It doesn't look like mom will be up for cooking dinner."

"Don't worry about it. Go see Michael. I'm heading into a conference call now." He kissed her on the forehead. "We'll continue this conversation when you get back."

"Okay. Can I get you anything while I'm out?"

"No, I'll order in."

"Really? You're sure?"

"Yes. Say hello to Michael for me."

Louise was confused and a bit annoyed. The one thing Mary was adamantly against was take-out food. But she didn't have time for questions and left to meet Michael.

Arriving at their usual New York City meeting place, Manhattan's historic Grand Central Oyster Bar, Louise was ten minutes late and a bit frazzled. But to Michael she was beautiful. Her look was traveler-chic, hair up in a chignon, no make-up or jewelry, slim-fitting black turtleneck, comfortable partly faded jeans, and Dr. Martins black Mono 1460 Boots, her go-to shit-kickers. She was a bad-ass beauty. Michael rose from his seat at the soup counter to greet her.

"Do I know you, young lady? I was waiting for an old friend, a woman of a certain age, but you're welcome to join me until she gets here."

"Wow, you're really not good at compliments." Louise kissed him on both cheeks out of habit, which he went along with, despite wanting the customary American smack on the lips.

"Can I help it if it's hard to fathom you being a 50-year-old?"

"Women are young at any age, haven't you heard?"

He managed to cop a squeeze of her biceps. "You're still buff, I see."

The chef at the soup bar placed Michael's order on the counter in front of them, two steaming bowls of classic clam chowder, and then tipped his imaginary cap. Louise smiled, nodded appreciatively, and picked up her bowl. They walked to an empty table in the corner and sat down facing each other.

"It's amazing, you just get more beautiful," Michael said.

"Again, with the age thing? I get it, the Big 5-0." She took a deep breath. "I need a drink." On cue, the server arrived, and Michael ordered two vodka martinis, dry, up, olive.

"Can I help it if I'm your biggest fan? You never age and here I have gray hair."

"You've had gray hair since you were twenty. Besides, it looks good on you. It's so unfair. Crow's feet and gray hair only make men look better."

"Well, you have nothing to worry about. You'll age gracefully until 100."

"I'm not so sure after seeing my mom," Louise confided. "She seems to have aged 10 years in just the past six months. Is that possible?"

"A lot of factors could have caused that."

"But you have a particular one in mind?"

"As you have surmised, something is up."

"Gee, what could have tipped me off. Something being…"

"George. And it seems to be taking a toll on Mary."

"My dad looked a little piqued," Louise said, trying a spoonful of the chowder. "Then, he said something so strange. I just shrugged it off, but it's still bothering me."

"What did he say?"

"That he would order in."

"*Order in*? Like dinner?"

"Exactly."

"I don't get it. How is that strange?" Michael asked.

"Mary would be insulted if we ever ordered in. It was just never done in our house."

"Even pizza?"

"Especially not pizza. She makes the best pizza I've ever eaten."

"Better than Italy?"

"Italy is a close second."

"That doesn't surprise me. Mary's cooking is one of life's true pleasures."

They both sipped their martinis and ate their chowder.

Suddenly, in unison they both said, "So what did you want to see me about?"

"What? You called me, remember?" Louise said.

"You texted me, *chowder in an hour*, remember?"

Louise put down her spoon. "Goddammit, Michael. It really pisses me off when you mess with my head. *You* called me first." Michael continued to eat his soup, stalling for time. She glared at him refusing to eat.

"Eat your soup," he said.

"Come on, Michael, what the hell is going on? Does it have to do with the Magnitsky bill passing the first hurdle?"

"No…Yes… In a way." He set down his spoon. "It has to do with Deutsche Bank."

"Aren't they all related? I've been looking into the case and Deutsche Bank is knee deep in all of these Russian money laundering deals."

"You're always one step ahead of everyone."

She resumed eating her soup and sipped the martini, the vodka pairing beautifully with the clam chowder. "Actually, I was about to contact you about Monte dei Paschi Bank."

"Ahh, yes. The world's oldest bank that just disclosed that it's flat broke because of questionable derivatives purchased through Deutsche Bank."

"That's the one. I saw the article about it yesterday in Le Monde."

"Deutsche Bank is linked to all these cases including the one your dad is involved with."

"So, let me guess. My dad wants me to go under cover and investigate."

"Your dad is not prosecuting the case *against* the Russian company. He's *defending* it."

Louise blanched. "Excuse me?"

There was a long silence.

"Louise, we need your help."

"*We*? The FBI? Or the CIA?"

"Yes."

"Let me get this straight. The FBI and the CIA want me to investigate corrupt Russian oligarchs, the Central Bank of Germany, *and* my own *father*?"

Michael remained silent. This was hurting him as much as it was Louise. George Moscow had been like a father to him ever since he and Louise were an item in college.

"Louise, you are in the best position to look into this. You live in Europe. You're a financial wizard."

"Flattery? Really?" Michael's next tactic was a dimpled smile. Louise smirked. "The problem for me is that something doesn't quite add up."

"You could explain debits and credits to an eight-year-old," Michael said. "I get it. You should be a professor. But we need your help now."

"Does it involve fixing the Black Economy? Because that's top on my bucket list."

"It will be a start. It will also give you a chance to get back at your father for tricking you into the BCCI investigation."

Ever since Louise had been hired by the middle eastern bank BCCI back in 1989, which turned out to be a massive and deadly international money laundering network where her father had a direct hand in getting her hired as an unsuspecting mole, risking her life, a wedge had been driven between them. "There are a few leads I could follow. What's the situation?"

"It's classified."

Louise was losing patience. "So, what am I doing here?"

"Remember that enlistment oath you took before you began training at Langley?"

"To support and defend the Constitution of the United States against all enemies, foreign and domestic," Louise recited.

"Yes, that oath. If I read you in, you can't tell anyone. Do you understand?"

"Of course, I understand. The training reinforced that vow."

"Good. Because as hard as it may be to imagine, there is an unprecedented amount of infiltration into the U.S. by Russia."

"You mean, like, Russian assets?"

"Unprecedented and very close to the top."

Louise shook her head as though shaking dust off her brain. "Wait, you're saying there are members of our government that might be working for Russia?"

"Top officials and close to home."

Louise went on the defensive, her eyes cold and her facial expression neutral. CIA training had prepared her for the worst, but she didn't expect anything this bad. "Michael, if you're suggesting that I will be investigating my own father as a Russian asset…"

"Just see where the trail leads. But only if you're 100 percent up for it."

Louise was tired from jetlag and the martini. This was surreal. Her gut reaction was to flip the table upside down and spill the soup and drinks all over Michael. But she just sat there reminding herself to stay calm, her weakest character trait. She had never really overcome the sense of her father's betrayal during the BCCI case. He had taken advantage of their relationship to place her in a compromised position for the sole purpose of catching his culprit. Now she might have to spy on her own father to see if he was taking advantage of his position to betray his country. It was too much.

Louise got up, almost knocking over her drink. "I have to go."

Michael stood up blocking her. "Louise, you cannot say anything to George."

"I can't promise that."

"You have to. Remember your oath, betraying that oath would be a felony." She pushed past him. Michael placed some money on the table and followed her all the way to her car in silence, knowing the brisk walk would help calm her down. She got in her car and rolled down the window, staring straight ahead hands on the steering wheel. Finally, she looked up at him.

"Okay, I'll do it," Louise said, a glimmer in her eye.

The house was strangely quiet when Louise returned. The lack of the familiar sounds of pots and pans on the stove or dishes being washed, the constant background noise that Mary had provided as she was growing up, was something she could not get used to. The silence gave a sense of foreboding, conjuring up memories of her last major case in Burgundy in 2001. Like the lurking evil that now tainted her perceptions of the pictur-esque and historically rich region of Burgundy, France, after she exposed the murderous sex trafficking ring. Even her mother Mary had been connected to that case in her young adulthood. Louise now saw her own home in a whole different light.

A light streamed from the slightly open door of her father's office, and she peeked her head in. Her father was lying on his back, arms folded on his chest like a corpse, on a small unmade bed that he had set up in his office. *Her parents were no longer sleeping in the same bed.* Heartbroken, Louise started to pull the door closed.

"Back so soon?" she heard her father say and poked her head back in.

"Yes, I'm a little jet-lagged so we cut it short. Sorry to disturb you."

"Come on in, Lulu," he said, getting up and waving for her to sit across from him at his desk. George was a Harvard Law School graduate, but he looked more like a button man for the mob than an intellectual. He was six feet tall, and over two hundred pounds, with hooded eyes and a nose that appeared to have been broken at least once. Street smart and tough, he talked out of the side of his mouth, but never said anything confidential or incriminating. He had been a New York City detective in charge of white-collar fraud for decades and had been instrumental in taking down the international bank, BCCI, with the help of his daughter, Louise. Talking with George Moscow was like consulting the Delphi oracle, you received a veiled revelation of truth, and tried to decipher what it meant.[5] George had left public service and gone into private practice recently, which seemed to coincide with the timing of their trouble at home.

"You set up a bed in your office?" Louise cleared her throat to keep her voice from cracking.

"Long hours on this case. It's been hard on your mother."

They both wore masterful poker faces not giving away what either one knew.

"It never bothered her before," Louise said, trying to sound supportive. It was the best way to get a potential witness to relax, at least according to her training at Langley.

"I've never been this busy before."

"Is there anything I can do to help?" Such the caring daughter.

"Thanks sweetheart. It's almost over now." It sounded more ominous than he must have intended. "There are some leftovers in the kitchen. Chicken soup from the deli."

"That actually sounds good. Can I get you anything?"

He got up and kissed her forehead. "No, I'm good, sweetie. Get some sleep."

"Good night." She backed out of the door and went to the kitchen to prepare some soup. Her stomach was in knots. This was the absolute worst-case scenario and caught her completely off guard. Louise heated up two bowls of soup and brought a serving tray up to her mom. She pushed the door open. The light was on, but Mary was dozing. Her sleeping position looked so awkward, on her side, her face turned upward, mouth slightly open, pale complexion. Louise paused silently watching for signs of breathing. Mary's shoulder rose with the next inhale, and Louise exhaled.

"Mom," Louise whispered, setting the tray on the side table.

Mary stirred, wiping a little drool from her mouth. "Hi, Lulu. What time is it?"

"It's almost nine."

Mary popped upright. "In the morning?"

"No, it's nighttime. You must be starving." Louise moved the tray onto the bed. "Here. Eat some chicken noodle soup that dad picked up."

Mary looked both crestfallen and hungry for the soup. They ate in silence. No deli soup could compare to Mary's homemade chicken soup with dense chunky hand-cut noodles. But this soup still offered comforting warmth and aromas. Louise hesitated to get into a conversation about what was going on with her parents. It was late, and Mary's eyes told her enough for now. She ate the last spoonful and placed her bowl on the tray and Mary did the same. Louise put the tray on the side table and gave her mom a big, long hug.

"Get some rest. See you in the morning."

"Good night, sweetheart," Mary said, lying back down. She was asleep before Louise picked up the tray and left.

Louise sensed the other shoe would soon drop on Michael's assignment, so she took the initiative, turning on her laptop and doing a Google search of the Italian Monte dei Paschi di Siena bank known in the finance world as MPS. The world's oldest surviving bank's origins dated to 1472 in the Tuscan city of Siena from which it derived its name. At the time, Siena was a Republic, and the bank was created to offer loans to "poor or miserable or needy persons."

In the intervening 540 years, the bank and the city of Siena had become intertwined. In 1624, the Grand Duke of Medici resolution insured all accounts held at MPS using the proceeds from his pasturelands of the southwestern Tuscan maritime coastal land, or *Maremma*, laying the foundations of deposit protection programs still used today in banking systems worldwide.

For centuries, the bank had a reputation of being well managed, making no risky investments, while remaining generous to the community. The bank funded local businesses, charities, sports teams, and events such as the famous Palio Di Siena horse race. According to a Siena adage, all Sienese currently worked for, aspired to work for, or were already drawing their pensions from the bank.[6]

But now, the situation had become dire, due to the amount of corruption and incompetence that had been going on within MPS. After the 2008 global economic collapse, and some very risky investments made by the MPS president, Giuseppe Mussari, in 2009 the bank began incurring huge losses. Estimates of the losses ranged from five-hundred to seven-hundred-fifty million Euros. [20] In order to hide the losses in the bank's financial statements, Mussari entered into derivative contracts with Deutsche Bank and the Japanese bank, Nomura. These underhanded operations were never communicated to the bank's own auditors or to Italy's Central Bank, Banca d'Italia.

To Louise, something didn't add up. It was time to gain first-hand knowledge, instead of whatever crumbs reporters could get on the record from insiders. Getting information from her father was never going to happen. He was already tightlipped beyond reason and would be more so in one of his ongoing cases, especially if he was working for the wrong side. But Louise was determined to connect the dots.

She decided another meeting with Michael would be the first step before approaching her financial insiders, and it couldn't be in a public place. Just as she was about to text Michael their code word, she received a one-word text on her mobile phone: *FOLIAGE*

FOUR

September 10, 2012, New York

According to their established protocol, on the morning immediately following a text of their code word, FOLIAGE, they agreed to make their way to a pre-arranged secret meeting spot in the Catskills.

Michael and Louise had first met when she was an undergrad at Princeton, after which she went on to earn her Harvard MBA. Michael had graduated from West Point and was promptly recruited by the FBI, not only for his academic achievements but also for his language skills. He had grown up in Rome with a Chilean mother and Spanish father, and went to university in Paris, so he spoke four languages fluently. It was at Princeton they had come up with their quaint code word, *FOLIAGE*, and their protocol for a clandestine emergency meeting that required specific evasive maneuvers, *en route*. Little did they know, they would come to rely on their jejune spy craft for decades to come.

Defying their established protocols, Louise did not take the train to Poughkeepsie and hire a rental car from there. Instead, she used her CIA training in evasive tactics making sure she was not being followed. She would not drive straight to the meeting point. Instead, she would take a long meandering *surveillance detection route,* known as SDR. This would allow her to identify cars or people who keep popping up over time and distance. For example, if she saw a man in a black beret carrying a baguette twice on the same street, he could just be walking in the same direction. But if she saw him on two different streets miles or hours apart, she might have spotted a tail, known as a *surveillant*.

After an hour of driving evasively, she was confident there was no tail. Louise made her way up the Hudson River, opting for the more picturesque route north along the east bank, then to the west bank of the Hudson River. Giving a nod of acknowledgment as she passed Poughkeepsie, she continued a few miles before veering west toward the Catskill Mountains to the

Ashokan Reservoir. She got out leaving her purse, locking the car, and putting the key in the front pocket of her jeans. She walked down the path to the reservoir where she found Michael waiting, arms folded, toe tapping, next to an upside-down rowboat.

"Been waiting long?" Louise snarked. "It's your fault I was trained in evasive tactics."

"Little help? I'm not as young as I used to be."

"Good thing I wore my mom's Hunter boots."

Louise helped Michael flip the rowboat and launch it into the reservoir. Michael grabbed the oars that were strapped inside and inserted the oarlocks into the pivot points. Louise waded shin deep then climbed aboard. Michael jumped in and took the oars.

"Who knew our secret spot would become our FBI Live Drop?"

"There are no coincidences," Michael replied, mock-cryptically.

"If there were no coincidences, *that* would be an amazing coincidence," Louise replied.

She inhaled, taking in the view of the stunning fall colors and Michael rowing, tiny beads of sweat on his brow, a lock of dark hair falling across his hazel eyes. He completed the picture with a dimpled smile.

"Like what you see?"

"It's very pleasant," Louise admitted. "Can't we just stay like this forever?"

Michael rested the oars in the boat, the sound of swishing water giving way to peaceful silence. A distant wild turkey call and falling leaves rustling in the gentle breeze as they floated in the middle of the man-made lake. They drifted to a portion of the reservoir that had always haunted and amazed Louise. The body of water looked entirely natural but had in fact been a valley town that was filled with water after the building of the dam. With the morning light now hitting the crystal-clear waters she felt like a bird soaring over ancient ruins. The seasonally low depth permitted a rooftop to break the surface, the sun's rays revealing the entire edifice of a reluctantly abandoned home below the surface.

"Isn't it strange how things are connected?" Louise mused, breaking the silence. "The Magnitsky case involving the largest hedge-fund in Russia, Hermitage Capital, founded by Bill Browder was originally funded by the murdered philanthropist Ekram M. Almasi, who just happened to be the last case my father assigned to me."

"The evidence of the case is overwhelming," Michael said. "Russian criminals masqueraded as officers of Browder's Hermitage Capital and stole a $230 million tax refund. Putin expects the world to believe that such a complicated scheme was pulled off by a convicted murderer, Vova Mikhailov, who worked in a sawmill, and a convicted burglar Vasili Kozlov. Obviously coached, they falsely testified to have gotten their instructions for the theft from Magnitsky himself. In exchange they were sentenced to only five-years in prison."

"And were allowed to live," Louise snarked. "Three other accused accomplices are now dead from KGB-style causes," Louise added. "One died of a heart attack *before* the crime even took place, so I imagine he refused to cooperate. Another fell from his balcony, and a third plummeted out of a penthouse window."

"That's how it works. All deaths feasibly accidental, but at the same time, a clear warning to anyone who dares defy Putin. Pure KGB Playbook," Michael said. "I'm impressed but not surprised at your depth of knowledge already. Now it's my turn to impress."

"That's what I'm here for," Louise said, taking out a thermal travel mug of coffee from inside her jacket. She took a sip and passed it to Michael.

He took a soothing sip and began his briefing. "Sergei Magnitsky uncovered proof that the tax heist was an inside government job and notified authorities that criminals were preparing the theft three weeks *before* it happened. But the Russian police did nothing."

"Magnitsky knew they were planning the heist on Browder's company before it happened?" Louise asked.

"Correct. Magnitsky had the nerve to notify officials of criminals within the government, which was damning to Putin. So, in response, in June 2007, Interior Ministry police raided Browder's Moscow offices and confiscated Hermitage corporate seals and official corporate certificates of Hermitage's Russian subsidiaries, giving the holder of those documents corporate signing powers. Four months later Browder discovered that a convicted killer named Victor Markelov had used those same corporate documents to act in the name of Hermitage to file for a $230 million tax refund, the exact amount Hermitage had paid in taxes on $1 billion in profits that it had reported for tax year 2006."

"The road to hell is paved with good intentions," Louise said sarcastically. Michael took another sip of coffee then handed her the thermos.

"Magnitsky and Browder didn't back down. Hermitage notified authorities of the tax fraud, but no investigation was opened until February 2008. Magnitsky did his own investigating and found that the hijacked Hermitage subsidiaries had been re-registered in the tax district run by co-conspirator Olga Stepanova. The $230 million refund Markelov filed for was based on fake losses, which Stepanova approved *the same day*. The largest tax refund in Russian history was approved on Christmas Eve for a *convicted murderer*, with no questions asked. Before Russian authorities even began their investigation, the $230 million had already been wired to newly opened bank accounts and then disappeared."

"Way too easy," Louise said.

"When the banks were questioned about tracing the funds, Irina Dudukina of Deutsche Bank said that the records had been in a truck that exploded in 2008. Credit Suisse records showed $20 million flowing through various bank accounts of dummy corporations in Panama and Cyprus. Browder contends that their informant said the $20 million was used to pay off Olga Stepanova for aiding the tax scam."

"It all seems so sloppy, but they got away with it," Louise said.

"Now this is where it gets personal."

"You mean, involving my father?" Louise offered him the thermos, which he accepted, taking a sip as he chose his words.

"Your father is defending a Russian named Desya Karev, who is the owner of Myloden Holdings, against charges of money laundering. The US is seeking to seize $20 million in Manhattan real estate and bank accounts from Myloden and its related companies."

"Myloden is the company that Sergei Magnitsky discovered was laundering some of the $230 million," Louise interjected.

"Yes. Browder's attorney, Reggie Masters, sought to have your father and his firm Baxter Humiston removed from the case, claiming conflict of interest, and accusing him of using information obtained during a prior case."

"What prior case?" Louise asked.

"Browder had previously retained George Moscow to file subpoenas to obtain documents regarding a company that had no relationship to Hermitage Capital or Myloden Holdings. Masters accused your father of inappropriately using that previous case to send Browder 'abusive' and 'intimidating' subpoenas that could damage him in other related proceedings."

"That seems out of character for my dad."

"Yes, I was there in the courtroom during the hearing. At one point, your dad pounded the table and stood up, furious at Masters. He remains adamant that his Myloden case is unrelated to Browder's previous case. But they're at a stalemate right now with Browder refusing to respond to the subpoenas, arguing that your dad had access to privileged information about him. But that's not even the worst of it."

"Worse than my dad defending a murderous Russian oligarch?"

"There is intel that Magnitsky discovered explosive evidence behind Putin's motivations for the money laundering."

"Evidence of what?"

"Something like George W. Bush's claims against Iraq that started that never-ending war." Michael passed the coffee back to Louise.

"I need something stronger." She sat in stunned silence letting it sink in. "You're suggesting the dirty money was laundered on behalf of Putin to use for a secret Weapons of Mass Destruction program?"

"Affirmative. It was right after Magnitsky made those accusations that he was arrested in Russia and eventually beaten to death by prison guards. Now, your dad is accusing Browder of refusing to act as a witness in the New York case because it could expose discrepancies in Browder's *concocted* tax scam story, to use his word."

"*Concocted* story!?" Louise was beyond disappointed. She was furious. "I've been following Browder's case from the beginning and no one with any integrity believes his story is *concocted*. Why would George side with Russian oligarchs, of all people?"

"That is the nut we're trying to crack. It's quite a turn of events."

"Saying it's *suspicious* that my father would flip to the Russians is putting it mildly."

"Louise, you understand this is your most dangerous assignment. Getting you into the training program at Langley wasn't just for shits and giggles. We need you to be fully prepared for what's coming. It's not too late to back away."

"Going after my father isn't a problem for me, if that's what you're worried about."

"It's not just your father. As it turns out, your bad blood with George might work in our favor. It gives you the perfect cover to go after our real target."

"Who's the real target?"

"This guy is a master of the Russian Dark Arts. He already knows about your past rift with your father. You're the perfect lure, for lack of a better word."

"So, you need me to be some kind of honeypot[7] to attract this *master of Russian Dark Arts* who is trying to gain access to my father, who himself has already flipped sides?"

"Yes, that's the genius of it. If our target believes you're working against your father, you're more valuable to him. This Russian doesn't care what side *he* is working for. His clients include both sides. He works for both Putin's closest allies, as well as his greatest foes."

"There really is no loyalty with these guys, is there?" Louise asked rhetorically.

"In Russia, loyalty is enforced by threats. That's why this case is so dangerous."

"So, who is this guy? Where do I find him? Russia?"

"That's the craziest part. He's now a citizen of the United States, the Russian-American lobbyist named Akari Raskalov."

"Can you send me a secure file on him?"

"That's the other kicker. This guy is obsessively anti-technology. For him, nothing is secure, and he would know."

"He trades in Kompromat," Louise said, astutely.

"Exactly. If you thought BCCI's Black Network was bad, this guy was behind violent corporate battles in Russia after the collapse of the Soviet Union, using *black public relations.*"

"*Chyorny P.R.,*" Louise said in Russian, having taught herself the language during her years in witness protection on an island in the Caribbean and perfected it at Langley.

"Stolen or fabricated documents are powerful weapons. The Soviet KGB technique you mentioned, *Kompromat,* collecting compromising information against political foes. They'll use any method from computer hacking to physical invasion of homes and offices."

"It's like the operation American Express used to discredit Ekram M. Almasi from my last banker's grave case.[8] Strange how these things keep turning back up like a bad penny."

"Very true. In fact, one of Raskalov's current clients, the Russian attorney Natacha Vershinina, is running a misinformation campaign to get

Congress to stop passage of the Magnitsky Act."

"So, he really does work for both sides."

"His client Ms. Vershinina is also part of the legal team representing Myloden."

"My father's firm is part of *that* legal team?" Louise was now all in against her father. "What is my leverage with Raskalov? All he cares about is money, right?"

"He'll work for the highest bidder," Michael confirmed.

"Will the CIA put up the funds?" Louise asked.

"The CIA will fund all your personal expenses. But we don't think it will be necessary to offer Raskalov money, per se."

"Well, the CIA definitely cannot afford my *in-kind* payment," Louise quipped.

"We think there's something even more valuable than money. Or your body." That got Louise to smirk. "Above all, nothing can be done over email, period. They will use anything to destroy a person's reputation and very convincingly so. Nothing can be written or sent digitally in any way. This will be a real test of your mental abilities."

"Is that why Langley put us through such intensive training in the Loci method of mnemonics?" Louise asked.

"Yes, your memory palace was built for a reason."

"It's like meditation. Personally, I prefer gut instinct, and those memory techniques do mess with that intuition. But I must admit, after a few months in training, it cleared my head and enhanced my mental sharpness."

"The Memory Palace has been used since ancient Rome and is responsible for some incredible memory feats,"[9] Michael concurred.

"So, what will I have to offer this *Master of the Dark Arts*?" Louise asked.

"You won't offer him anything. He will seek you out for information about your father."

Louise suddenly realized the severity of the situation. "He's looking for kompromat on my father?" She took a deep breath and composed herself. "Will he come to Burgundy?"

"He is currently in Siena researching kompromat on Monte dei Paschi executives."

"So, I'm going to Siena. How will I make my presence known?"

"You will go ostensibly for an investigation into the annual Palio horserace."

"The medieval-style bareback horserace with literally no rules?" Louise shook her head.

"There is one rule: No jockey may interfere with another jockey's reins."

"I stand corrected," Louise said.

"It is held each summer in front of tens of thousands of spectators in the middle of the tiny town center," Michael explained. "The winner gets a banner."

"A banner?" Louise said, suspicious.

"The winner also drinks wine from a baby bottle symbolizing rebirth."

"That part I can get behind." Louise finished off the coffee. "Oh, that reminds me! At Langley I took intensive Italian. Now I know why. The word *palio* means banner in Italian. Any more intel on the horserace?"

"Each jockey represents one of seventeen fiercely rivalrous districts, or *Contradas*, in Italian," Michael continued, with surprising enthusiasm. "Most Siena districts are named after animals: snail, porcupine, she-wolve, etc. Each *Contrada* has its own museum, church, public square with a fountain, traditions, its own banner. Although there are seventeen districts, there is only room for ten horses in each race. So, there are two races, one on July 2nd and the other on August 2nd. The winning neighborhood receives a special banner bearing the image of the Virgin Mary, in whose honor the races are held."

Louise stared at him, impressed. "That's oddly detailed information."

"The Devil is in the details."

"Please go on."

"Official betting is prohibited, but *allegiances* can be purchased for tens of thousands of euros. This is where your investigation can focus. There are secret negotiations, some suspect to fix the race. If a jockey misses an easy opportunity to get ahead at a turn, he may have been paid to fall back. In almost any other country this would lead to outrage among spectators. But in Siena, no one wishes to change a thing about the Palio."

"Why is that?"

"Italians admire people who profit from bending the rules. Look at Silvio Berlusconi, the former prime minister, who brushed off sex and corruption scandals. Benito Mussolini is said to have adored the Palio."

"So, as an investigator into the race, I will be very unpopular," Louise said. "Who will I be investigating on behalf of? An animal rights group?"

"We'll quietly release intel to the inner circle, that you are looking into

Paschi Bank's contributions to the Palio, so it will get to Raskalov. We'll also make sure he knows you're George Moscow's daughter. Pursuing you for kompromat will be irresistible to him."

"That's me, irresistible."

"Let's get to work training your brain tonight so you can fly back tomorrow."

"We can't stay here. We'll starve and freeze to death," Louise said. "And we can't do it at my parents' house for obvious reasons."

"Go home and freshen up then you come to my place. It's regularly swept for listening devices. I'll cook dinner."

"I'll bring the wine."

Louise stood outside the door of Michael's East Side Tudor City condo holding up two bottles of wine. "I wasn't sure if the dinner paired with white or red, so I brought both."

"Let's start with sparkling water and get to work. Then we'll see what feels the most rewarding afterwards. Come on in."

"Your place is very mannish," Louise said, taking off her jacket.

"It's your first time here, I'll show you around." He quickly walked a few feet to the galley kitchen on the left, placed the white wine in the fridge and the red in the small wine rack. "This is the kitchen." He turned back and stepped into the main area. "Dining room-slash-office." He motioned to the far corner. "Comfortable fold out sofa bed sectional and large TV."

"No bedroom?"

"I bought this studio ten years ago." He walked across the TV area to a door that led to another apartment. "When the adjacent condo came on the market, I bought it and busted through the wall to have a bedroom. I suppose that is a pretty 'mannish' thing to do."

"It's very cozy. Wonderful neighborhood."

"Not much of a view, but very nice quiet residential area." He clapped his hands indicating it was time to work. They sat at his large dining table that also served as a desk. He cracked open one of the books on a stack. "Here we have the amazing history of the Tuscany region of Italy." Then he took another book. "Here is the history of Siena, focusing on Monte dei Paschi Bank."

Using the Memory Palace method, Michael and Louise went through the grueling task of memorizing an array of critical names, places, code words, and phone numbers with a mental walk-through of rooms in an imaginary palace in her mind. By the time they finished Louise had a vivid picture of all the information.

She rubbed her eyes. "I feel like I've lived in Tuscany for years."

"You'll do great. You'll see how much this information will help you when you're there. It's a very important mission. Probably the most important."

"You really seem to have taken this case to heart."

"I know how hard this might be for you, Louise. I'll be here for you no matter what." He got up. "Drink?"

She got up and followed him to the kitchen. "What's for dinner?"

"Butter lettuce salad with oven-roasted rosemary chicken and potatoes. Shall we start with the white wine?"

"Excellent choice, chef."

He popped the cork and poured two glasses. Then he proficiently stacked all the books and papers on the side, while Louise set the table. He took the prepared lettuce from the fridge and tossed a salad with Dijon vinaigrette, then opened the oven and plated the food.

"Wow, I'm impressed. This looks and smells delicious."

They clinked glasses. "To Louise Moscow. The most beautiful spy ever known to man."

"To your impeccable taste." Louise smiled at her own joke.

"You're so modest." Famished, they devoured the meal and chatted about old memories. They cleared the table and Michael offered a simple sweet for dessert. "A little dark chocolate?"

"Maybe open that bottle of red for a short nightcap?"

He opened the bottle, poured two large red wine glasses, and they clinked.

"To our friendship."

"It's wonderful how our friendship has evolved, Michael."

"Stay the night?" He gave her a more subtle dimpled smile than usual, but the sultry hazel eyes were the selling point.

She washed down a bite of chocolate with the lovely Pinot Noir she had brought. "After this meal, I think you're stuck with me until the morning. But I'll take the sofa, okay?"

"Nonsense. You take the bed. The housekeeper just changed the sheets. You'll be very comfortable there. I'm going to stay up a little bit longer anyway. There's a fresh tee shirt on the bed and a brand-new toothbrush in the en-suite. Make yourself comfortable. I'll tuck you in."

"I hate being a foregone conclusion." She headed to the bedroom.

"Thomas Crown Affair. Great movie."

He loaded the dishwasher then went in to check on Louise. She had already tucked herself in and was drifting off to sleep. He sat next to her.

"Sorry I'm so tired," she said, barely able to keep her eyes open.

"Sleep well." He kissed her on the cheek and went back to the sofa.

The next morning, with her proverbial marching orders, Louise was ready to head back to Burgundy en-route to Tuscany. But first, she needed to have a serious sit-down with Mary before her departure, to make sure she was safe and properly cared for. Also, selfishly, a long chat might shed some light on George, and his current project.

She drove up to her parents' house by 8:30. The curtains were drawn, and it was gloomy inside even though the sun was shining outside. Her father's car wasn't in the drive or garage, but she double checked his office anyway to make sure he wasn't home. She threw open all the curtains, went up and started filling the tub in her parents' bathroom. She sat on the bed and brushed the hair from her mother's face.

"Mom, it's almost nine o'clock. Come on. I started a bath for you."

Mary stirred, struggling to open her eyes. Louise had never seen her so thin. It was alarming. She rifled through the nightstand and the medicine chest for evidence of a medical condition but found none. She turned off the bath water and sprinkled in some Epsom salts along with some fresh sprigs from the herb garden on the windowsill. At least her father, or someone, had been keeping the houseplants and garden watered. She returned to the bed where Mary was now sitting on the edge with her feet on the floor. Louise helped her to her feet, and they walked to the bathroom.

"Relax in the tub for a half hour and I'll put some clothes out for you."

Louise chose some comfortable but bright colored clothes from the closet and placed them on the bed. She opened the door to the bathroom and saw Mary looking relaxed and cute with her gray hair pulled up in a ponytail and some color back in her cheeks. She opened her eyes and saw Louise.

"I'm starved."

Louise smiled. "Let's eat!"

They drove to the quaint town center of nearby Pleasantville. Louise had always enjoyed visiting the small, funky-artsy town, it was the opposite of the black-and-white conformity of the movie with the same name. Walking down the tree-lined streets of the Old Village was the perfect attempt to ease Mary out of the house and back into society. The town had a bit of celebrity status. New York Times Crossword puzzle editor Will Shortz held an annual tournament there. Plus, film industry and political types were known to frequent the town. Bill Clinton was often spotted jogging past the train station.

Mary knew the way and they headed straight into the Pleasantville Diner and plopped down at a booth. The server brought two cups of their famous coffee.

"Haven't seen you in a while, Mary."

"Hi, Sue. Yes, I'm semi-retired."

"Retired from what? Socializing?" They exchanged a giggle. "The usual, Mary?"

Mary nodded yes and looked at Louise.

"Make it two," Louise said.

Sue winked at Louise then went to put in the order. Mary added sweetener and cream to her coffee, sipped, and closed her eyes, satisfied. She opened them to Louise's glare.

"Semi-retired? What is that supposed to mean?"

"Do you see me cooking or cleaning anymore?"

"Fair enough. That doesn't mean it's not weird."

"People change."

"You don't," Louise countered.

"If your father can change, I can change."

That was another odd thing to say, Louise thought. Mary, for all her domestic charms, had always been a fighter. One thing Louise didn't have to worry about was someone taking advantage of Mary. But it was obvious something had changed…and Louise suspected it probably had something to do with George.

Louise leaned in for privacy. "Mom, remember that extreme reaction you had ten years ago when I told you I was working in Burgundy, France, on a case? You clammed up and continued to carry a deep dark secret. But after that case was resolved, you were back to your old self, as if something had been freed in you."

Mary pursed her lips in her way, making them almost turn white. She didn't like to be reminded of her involvement in that history, even though she was better after the case was solved. Louise had been instrumental in putting the pieces together, but it was a matter of pride.

"One doesn't go around squawking about being kidnapped by a sex trafficking ring," Mary finally said.

"No one is asking you to, Mom. I just mean, something else is going on now. It seems like you've given up. It's not like you to be so fatalistic. Accepting whatever this new chapter of your life is. Especially if you don't like it. You're usually a fighter." She stopped talking as Sue the server returned and placed their orders on the table.

"Waffles and scrambled eggs. Enjoy!" Mary dug in, really savoring the first bite.

"I'm happy to see you eating. You're so skinny," Louise said, realizing it was something her mom would say. She ate and had to admit the food was delicious. They finished eating before addressing the subject again. Sue refilled their coffees and took their empty plates.

Louise decided to take a risk and changed the direction of the conversation. "Mom, the way your health has deteriorated doesn't make sense to me. Is there something you're not telling me about you and Dad? This is no way for your long marriage to play out."

Mary blanched. "Did your father say something?"

Louise regretted suggesting it. "No, dad didn't say anything. You know he doesn't talk about personal feelings with me. Mom, no matter what, I just want you to be happy. Do you want to move to France and live with me? You'd love it. Lavender and sunflower fields for miles."

Mary reached across the table and took Louise's hand. "That sounds wonderful, darling. But please don't worry about me. Everything will work out."

Louise wasn't convinced, but at least she had gotten Mary out of bed and talking. After leaving the diner, they took a short walk in the park, then headed home.

Louise helped Mary get into bed before breaking the news. "Tonight, I'm flying back to Burgundy, Mom."

"Okay, sweetheart. It was so nice of you to come check on your mommy." Mary sounded condescending. On top of that, Louise was disappointed that she gave no protest about her leaving. It really wasn't like her. But she had done all she could for now. As soon as she got further along in her investigation she would come back and check on Mary. For now, she had confirmed that Mary was suffering from her father's recent alienation. He was breaking her heart and she was mourning their marriage.

"I'll try to make it back for Christmas."

"Don't make a fuss if you can't. It's doubtful we'll do anything this year." Mary saw from Louise's reaction that her rejection of the traditional holiday celebrations really hurt.

What happened next was truly perplexing to Louise, as she ruminated on her lost Christmas holidays. Mary propped herself up, as if an electric shock had gone through her prone body. Louise was transfixed by this sudden transformation, and she stood to help. Mary waved her off and got out of bed. Her mother walked to the corner of the room, retrieved a step stool, opened the bedroom closet, and reached up to grab something off the top shelf. She replaced the step stool, gave a cloth-bound notebook to Louise, and went back to the comfort of her bed. Her effort to complete the task had taken everything out of her.

"You'll find all your answers in there," Mary said, her voice suddenly very soft.

Louise stood up and began to thumb through the pages. It was a journal, meticulously kept with a date for each entry. At first glance, it all seemed to be about George, and the change in their relationship.

"Lulu!" her mother exclaimed. Louise turned around, completely shocked by the nature of her mother's cry. It sounded like a siren wailing. Louise had wandered about six feet away looking through the journal. Her mother had completely sat up in bed, her eyes like saucers.

"Mom!" was the only sound that came from Louise's throat, as she approached the bed. Mary had settled backward, a panicked look in her face. Her body went limp again.

"Tell your father I love him," Mary uttered, as Louise took her in her arms.

With that, Mary Pokorny Moscow died in Louise's arms.

❧

Louise was sitting at the kitchen table, uncharacteristically drinking some of George's prime bourbon. She had managed to call her father at his Manhattan office to tell him that his wife…her mother…was dead. She then had to deal with the man's anguished sobbing on the other end of the line. After describing all the circumstances of Mary's demise, Louise sensed her father was in no condition to drive, so before they hung up, she told her father she was ordering a car for him. She sat quietly waiting for him to get home, sipping her drink, and embracing her internal bereavement. Mary's journal was safely packed away in her bag, and Mary's body was still upstairs in the bedroom.

Louise had tried to revive her mother using CPR, but her mother had died peacefully almost instantly. She had called 9-1-1 on the bedroom phone, described the situation, and dutifully answered all the dispatcher's questions. The ambulance seemed to take forever and no time to get to the house, but all the techniques they used to revive her mother were also for naught. It was Louise who told them to stop, and to leave her body in the bed. She and her father would take care of funeral arrangements. She signed all the emergency medical papers and called George after the paramedics left.

The Town Car pulled up in the driveway, and Louise watched with red-rimmed eyes as her father crawled out of the back. She was relieved she happened to be at home and with Mary when her mother had passed, but she was still in a state of shock that would last a long while. George entered the house, his face a reflection of Louise's own grief, and they embraced in a long and sobbing hug, the only remaining survivors in their small family unit.

"Where is she?" George finally asked, wiping away his tears.

"Upstairs in the bed you used to share," Louise managed to say.

They somehow made it up the stairs together and entered the bedroom. Mary was lying on her back, her eyes closed, peaceful. Louise had arranged the body after the paramedics had worked on her. George went to her and embraced the body that was once his wife, a new set of body-wracking sobs surging through him.

"I will leave you with her last words," Louise said over the din of his wailing. George went frighteningly quiet, turned around and looked mournfully at her. "'Tell your father I love him.'" Like a spasm, another mournful sound escaped from George. She let it subside, and simply said, "Take your time. I'll make the final arrangements."

Like the closing scene of a movie, Louise walked to the door as George turned his attention back to Mary. The room seemed to surreally mimic a 'God's eye view' camera shot as, with a distortedly wide angle, a small man and wife together for the last time, getting smaller in the middle of it all, as the point of view seemed to rise higher than any ceiling could go.

Louise's daydream finished with a long fade to black as she closed the door and the final credits rolled in her mind.

FIVE

The night of her mother's burial, before falling into a fitful sleep, Louise had set her alarm for 7:00 o'clock. One of two recurring dreams had returned that night, the one where she lost either the engagement ring given to her by Jean-Philippe, or the scarab given to her by her father. This time it was the latter for obvious reasons. Upon waking, she was always so relieved to find both safely on the chain around her neck.

Hoping that her father would sleep in after the stress of the two days of events, she quietly got up, repacked her bag, and checked with the airline to confirm her rescheduled flight to Paris later that evening was departing on time. She then called Michael and told him her plan to resume business as usual. When he protested that she needed to stay longer and take a mental health break, she assured him there was no need. Her psyche training in emotional trauma had taught her it was not good to drastically change life plans after the loss of a loved one. She had information now, information she never wanted, but she had to process it and confront her father with it. Then she needed to go home and begin the next chapter of her life.

"I agreed to the assignment. It's exactly what I need now," she told her old friend and fellow CIA agent. "Be ready for my next call."

She moved silently down the hall and checked on George. He was still sleeping, no doubt fitfully, rung out over the whirlwind of the last few days, as was she. She wondered, given the information in Mary's journal, if he had been crying crocodile tears for his late wife, but it sure looked real to her. They'd been married for over 50 years. Could it have been tears of guilt?

She went down to prepare breakfast, having stocked the fridge after Mary had moved on to a better place, a simple French style omelet. Once the coffee was brewing, she heard stirrings from George's study. She prepared herself for what could possibly be the most difficult conversation she would ever have with her father, potentially precipitating a break in their relationship. At the same time, he could be a source of information, even intel, that could help her to put Michael's assignment in context. She had to choose her words carefully.

"Good morning. How are you feeling?" Louise asked as George ambled into the kitchen.

"Believe it or not, I'm feeling okay. I didn't participate much in the toasts that your uncle Ray and cousin Mary were offering."

"Yes, I dodged that bullet as well," Louise said. "They kept telling me how much they regretted not visiting. It seems that people don't realize what they have until it's gone."

George was silent, contemplating Louise's last bit of philosophy. He finally offered, "What's for breakfast?"

"Spécialité de la maison," Louise demurely replied. "Omelet filled with Boursin cheese and sliced baguette, a recipe from my restaurant."

"Oh yes, how is that cover working out for you?"

"Like Rick's Café Americain in Casablanca. I'm Rick, of course. It's become one of the most popular eateries in Burgundy. Everyone comes to Magali's!" Louise wasn't sure where she was going with this. But sensing an opening as she served the omelet, baguette, butter, jam, and coffee, she decided to broach what she really wanted to talk about with George. "Speaking of covert ops, how's it going in the private law sector?"

George looked up in surprise. "Anything in particular you would like me to disclose, Ms. CIA agent?"

Louise didn't expect that response. "You know that Michael recruited me. You're lucky I was authorized to read you in about it. They seem to know a lot about you over at Langley."

George grunted as if to say, *Ha!* But he didn't say anything else.

Louise tossed Mary's journal in the middle of a table, as if submitting surprise evidence in a bad courtroom movie.

"Mom had been keeping a journal."

George didn't know whether to reach for the notebook or pretend it didn't exist. *Deny, deny, deny.* He decided to let it be.

"Your Mother started to become ill much sooner than you know. I doubt there is anything in that journal that has an ounce of truth. Her perception was tainted by her resentment for me."

Louise controlled her anger and calmly said, "Mom knew you better than anyone on earth. She started the journal because she felt you disconnecting and wanted to figure out how to save her marriage. It seems perhaps

I got the spy gene from her. She knew how to gather intel."

"What intel?" George demanded. He reached for the journal, but Louise was quicker and snapped it up.

"Oh no," the daughter told the father. "You don't deserve to read this."

"Okay fine!" George's voice was rising. "What's your point?"

"Are you a Russian asset?"

The question hung in the air like the indelible scent of the fresh-brewed coffee. If Louise was playing verbal poker with George, she couldn't detect a tell in his face. He was stone cold.

"The firm does work for a Russian monetary fund, you and your buddies at Langley should know that." George chose his next words carefully. "Define *asset*."

Louise glowered. "Here's a definition, Dad. Replace the 'et' in asset with 'hole.'"

"Nice mouth." George was shifting to his button-man for the mob mode. "Did you kiss your mother with that mouth?"

Louise wanted to take her plate of eggs and toss it into her father's smug face. "You … leave…her…out…of…this." Louise spit out the words, barely containing her anger.

"I never wanted her in!" George said too loudly. Birds that had been roosting outside the kitchen window suddenly took flight.

Louise held up the journal. "I spy a spy and I've got my eye on you," she said coldly. "If I find one word of this journal is true, indictment for treason will be the least of your worries."

George contemplated tearing the book away from his daughter but didn't have the heart. Why were they having this discussion the day after the funeral? He brought things back to earth.

"Does this have anything to do with what Michael recruited you for? Maybe your next case?" he asked, much calmer than before.

"I don't know," Louise had to admit. But all evidence was pointing toward her father's involvement. After a beat, she added, "I'm leaving today."

Even George was surprised at what he said next. "I think that's best."

Louise was speed-dialing practically as the words came out of her father's mouth.

"Michael, it's time to go," she said as soon as he answered. To her father she said, "I'm leaving. Michael is meeting me at the airport before I leave. You can clean up the mess. Something I think you're used to doing."

George stared at his congealing breakfast as Louise gathered her luggage, placing her mother's journal in the front flap. As she stood at the door preparing to leave, they stared at each other, not knowing what to do. Louise broke the tension. She couldn't help it. They had been through so much in the past week and had buried a loved-one just yesterday.

She walked over and kissed her father on the cheek.

George gave her a steely-eyed glance. "Judas, must you betray me with a kiss?"

Louise just shook her head. It was as if her life had suddenly been cleaved in two, half before Mary's death, and another half starting now. Hearing Michael coming up the driveway, she exited to the darker other side.

SIX

September 12, 2012, Burgundy, France

Upon returning to her cottage, the first thing Louise did was place Mary's journal in a secure hiding place. She went to bed early and spent the next day unpacking, doing laundry, and organizing the house. She checked on the cats and visited the bistro, then packed for an extended trip leaving the next day. Something had been eating at her since the confrontation with her father. Although Michael had forbidden it, Louise went to her secure communications room to do a quick search on the Internet for information about her father and the so-called *Master of the Dark Arts*, Akari Raskalov. She was stunned to see how little information there was other than what they themselves had made public in the form of brief corporate bios. She did a search of herself and Jean-Philippe as a comparison. It was jarring to see that there was vastly more information about each of them, albeit mostly from their pasts, both having been in voluntary exile for the better part of two decades. This showed the true power that her father and the *Master of the Dark Arts* wielded. Any information about 'George Moscow' or 'Akari Raskalov' posted to the Internet by a third party was systematically scrubbed by professional security agents. *He who controls the information controls the world.* Out of curiosity, she Googled Vladimir Putin and was equally stunned to see the limited amount of controlled information was readily available about him on the Internet as well.

Despite having grown up in the same home as George Moscow, her father had been so secretive all her life, she was just realizing how little she knew about him. Her trust in him had been blind faith and he had tested that to the limits many times. If anyone knew how to keep information from the public, it was her father. With his grasp of criminal law, she suspected he could feasibly conceal corrupt activity from the public and never be caught, analogous to a forensic cleaner able to commit the perfect crime and make evidence of a murder disappear. Michael's admonishments echoed in her mind, and she shut down her computer indefinitely. It would be interesting to experience life offline, a digital detox.

The next day, she hopped on the flight from Burgundy to Florence. In her rental car, she went through the usual *surveillance detection route* (SDR) until she was confident that she had made it out of Florence without a tail and headed down route E35 for the 55-mile drive to Siena. Despite Michael and the FBI discretely leaking news of her arrival in Siena, she would still run an SDR and take mental notes to identify surveillants. But now she would be encouraging it.

She checked into her hotel, grabbed a cappuccino to-go and went out to walk the cobblestones of the medieval Tuscan town and see what kind of characters turned up. She had barely walked a block toward the central square, Piazza del Campo, before discerning three pursuers. According to her training, surveillants work in teams of up to seven or eight, so it was possible she would spot more. To draw them out, she made a quick pivot left and crossed the street. Then she turned right barely dodging oncoming traffic, all while pretending to look in her bag. Observing via the reflection in the store front window, she saw a man in a suit-and-tie she deemed a banker walking toward her. Evading eye contact, he made a sudden stop and checked his watch then turned right waiting to cross the street. Louise dashed ahead of a moving car, and *Banker Guy* took a step then jumped back onto the curb to avoid being hit. *Banker Guy* resumed crossing the street at an angle from her. He could have passed for any random business-man, but his sudden change of direction might have given him away as a tail.

She pulled a lip balm out of her purse and stopped in front of a shop window to apply it while checking for more surveillants. Another suspicious character caught Louise's eye. Judging by her style, the woman could have passed for either a supermodel or a schoolmarm. She was tall and thin, with full lips and wavy brown hair cut in a blunt chin length bob. She wore an elegant scarf around her neck, thick-framed glasses, chunky but stylish all-weather boots, and a chic backpack as she window-shopped, presumably for more earthy-chic attire. She was in her late twenties early thirties. Louise took her time with her lip balm and then fixed her own hair, which she was vainly alarmed to see had become disheveled. She observed *Schoolmarm* abruptly turn on her heals and head in the opposite direction, thus switching off with another surveillant Louise had identified, an inebriated older man in an overcoat carrying a flask, which he swigged occasionally. Louise resumed walking, noting if he stopped when she did or turned away when faced toward him. His acting was impressive, Louise thought, no one would have suspected he was a spy. But having previously spotted him on the other side of town when she first arrived, she knew it was highly unlikely a local indigent could travel across town by foot or waste a coin on a bus. Sloppy work on his part.

Louise felt *in the zone*. Perhaps it was the relatively small city with a population of about 50,000, most residents having lived their whole lives there. The quaint medieval route had become like a video game with spies suddenly popping out of doorways or alleys, morphing from one form to another. She couldn't record anything digitally, but this video game format worked well in her 'Memory Palace' to track the various characters. She even assigned avatars to their names. She was getting distracted by her own thoughts and pulled herself back to the SDR.

So far, she had *Schoolmarm* and *Indigent Guy* confirmed. *Banker Guy* wasn't a sure thing yet, but a fourth player entered the game, *Smarmy Guy*, making himself plain as day. She had first noticed him outside the hotel at the sweet little espresso bar she discovered. The barista made the best foam art she had ever seen, and it was also delicious. His simple caricature of her in the foam was so good she felt guilty drinking it. As she was leaving, *Smarmy Guy* held the door open for her and gave her a cartoonish double eyebrow flash, crooked smile, slimy head waggle. It was almost too genuine to be an act, so she had shrugged it off at the time. But as she resumed her SDR, she spotted him walking toward her. He gave her the exact same expression as earlier, and she couldn't help laughing. She kept walking but turned to catch him watching her. If he had turned back to pursue her, she would have known he was not a surveillant. But since he had not done so, he had given himself away. No respectable Italian man would walk away from a woman acknowledging him. That made three confirmed.

Contrary to normal protocol where she would want to neutralize and evade the threats, Louise would use these agents to send a message back to Raskalov, or whoever: *Louise was in town*. Meanwhile, needing more information, and having no access to the Internet, Louise decided to read every article available in the local and international news reports in search of clues. She stopped at a kiosk and purchased several French and English language broadsheets, politically left and right leaning, including the New York Times, the Wall Street Journal, Le Monde, Le Figaro, and even the satirical Le Canard Enchaîné. From the U.K. the pink-paged Financial Times.

Louise crossed the Piazza del Campo, stopping to admire the famous Gaia fountain. Michael had walked her through the most important landmarks of Siena before their dinner at his place. She had looked forward to visiting the fountain built in 1342. It was a wonder of hydraulic engineering with water brought through underground aqueducts from 25 miles away. According to their research of Siena, the fountain brought so much joy it was given the name *Gaia,* or joyous. But there was also another theory about the name. Gaius was one of the most common names in Roman history, the feminine of which was Gaia. It became part of a traditional Roman wedding ceremony, spoken by the bride, *as you are Gaius, I am Gaia*, the word Gaia connoting *bride*, the fountain was therefore dedicated to the *Bride of God*, patron of Siena, the *Virgin Mary*. The fountain featured a relief of Madonna and Child. This subject had taken Louise full circle to her ex-fiancé, Jean-Philippe, who had converted to a monk with the Fathers of Mercy who were devoted to protecting the Virgin Mary. Louise was partial to the *Bride of God* interpretation.

She took a seat at a nearby outdoor café bearing the fountain's name, *Fonte Gaia*. Placing the newspapers on the rattan chair next to her, she ordered an Earl Grey tea, and began to search each paper, filling her Memory Palace with anything of interest. Of all the papers, the most important would be the local Siena News. Having taken an intensive course in Italian she understood enough to look for key words of the local crime section. But Siena had less crime news than most cities proving the city streets incredibly safe. She then perused the English and French language papers, but nothing set off any alarms. She stacked them neatly on the empty bistro chair next to her, sipped her tea, closing her eyes as she savored the comforting flowery flavor and let out a heavy sigh.

"Mi scusi."

She opened her eyes and saw the face behind the voice. An Italian man who could have been anywhere from early forties to mid-fifties. *Damn, men age well*, she thought.

Not wanting to encourage conversation, she spoke English. "Sorry, my Italian isn't very good." He stared at her showing no sign of understanding. Her first impression of him was bookish, disheveled curly hair, round glasses, and supple lips, just her type. He reminded her of Jean-Philippe, the compassionate sparkle in his eyes sending a tingle throughout the entire heart shaped area from her hips down to her knees, evoking a sudden sense of dread. She half hoped he was a surveillant so she wouldn't be tempted into an impulsive Italian romance.

He spoke again. "Giornales? Finito?"

Realizing he was only interested in the discarded newspapers she said, "Certo. Prendere."

"Parli italiano?"

"No. Poco," she lied, pinching her fingers together indicating that she only spoke very little Italian. He blushed and nodded awkwardly then bent down to pick up the papers.

"Grazie mille," he said respectfully.

To her surprise, he didn't just take the Italian papers but all the papers. Was he going to scrub them for her fingerprints? Normally she might panic, but in this case, she was *inviting* spies to follow her and, in turn, eventually lead her to the Russian American lobbyist, Akari Raskalov. It was a topsy turvy world, indeed. Still, something inside her didn't want him to be a spy, he was no *Smarmy Guy.*

Before walking away, she noticed he stopped to read one of the articles on the front page of Le Figaro, giving her the impression that he spoke French, and an opening.

"Vous parlez Francais?" Louise asked, but he just stared at her, confused. Then he realized she noticed he was looking at the French paper and responded.

"Ah! No, non parlo francese." Then he pointed enthusiastically at a word and showed her the page. "San Francesco d'Assisi, quattro ottobre!" He was pointing to the logline for the approaching national holiday on October 4th for St. Francis of Assisi, patron saint of Italy. She had read about it with Michael. Each year, the town of Assisi in the Umbria province welcomes a different Italian region who donates oil for the lamp in the crypt of Saint Francis.

"Ciao, Francesco, come stai!" The server arrived with a cappuccino and placed it on *Francesco's* table. But Louise had noticed that the bookish Italian hadn't ordered anything.

"Ciao, Fabrizio." They exchanged greetings then the server, whose name was apparently *Fabrizio*, came to Louise's table.

"Un altro tè?" he asked.

Shaking her head, she smiled and replied, "No grazie." Fabrizio dashed off to another customer as she poured the rest of the tea from the pot into her cup and took a sip. Fabrizio's words echoed in her mind. He had called the bookish Italian *Francesco*. It was interesting that his name was the same as Saint Francis of Assisi and she saw another opportunity to engage.

"Anche il tuo nome è Francesco?" Louise asked if he was also Francis like the saint.

"Si! Sono Francesco. Come ti chiami?"

"Sono Louise," she replied. "Piacere di conoscerti."

The server, Fabrizio, returned to her table. "Basta?" he said, asking if she had finished.

"Si, finito, grazie."

Fabrizio began clearing her table when a young Italian couple walked past the café.

"Ciao, Francesco!" They exchanged cheek kisses then continued walking on. Francesco finished his coffee and gathered up Louise's donated journals. "Bene. Devo andare, gli animali hanno fame." If she understood him correctly, he said *the animals were hungry*. "Ti piacerebbe incontrarli?" It sounded like he was asking if she would like to *meet the animals*.

His charms were irresistible. She looked at the server, Fabrizio, who put her bill on the table and nodded enthusiastically and said, "Francesco e molto bravo." For emphasis he repeated in heavily accented English, "Frrrancesco is a grrreat guy!"

Francesco seemed to be well-known and liked by the locals giving her the perfect opportunity to safely assimilate into the community.

"Certo, perchè no," she said, accepting Francesco's offer.

She paid her tab and they started to walk away. Louise suddenly realized she might be putting him at risk of spies learning where he lived. On the other hand, the locals already knew him, so it was probably no secret. Sure enough, she spotted *Indigent Guy*, walking toward them. The fact that neither showed any recognition of each other as they passed was an indication that either *Indigent Guy* was not local or that they were working together. Louise would know sooner or later.

After walking about a mile, they arrived at what appeared to be an ancient farmhouse on the edge of town. The exterior was classic stone and mortar with a clay roof, wood and iron trim, and fencing. Tall pointy cypress trees delineated the property and simple pergolas of thatched roof atop wooden posts dotted the pastures providing shade alongside ancient olive groves. The patio was covered by a more formal pergola of natural logs and wood beams, all overgrown with ivy. The pebbles crackled under their feet and the scent of an overgrown basil bush welcoming them outside the door was almost identical to hers in Burgundy. As they approached, two cats gently rubbed against Francesco's legs, and he reached down to scratch their ears. The tuxedo cat came over to rub against Louise's boots and she also gave it ear scratches. The ginger cat looked on purring calmly and Louise could tell they were comfortable with her.

"A loro piaci!"

"Yes! They like me!" Louise agreed. "Forse annusare i miei gatti." She explained that they must smell her feral cats. "I feed the strays. Nutro gatti selvati…" She tried to think of the word for *feral*, making claws with her hands and growling.

Francesco smiled. "Gattino selvaggio. Anche tu sei una gattara!"

"Yes." Louise laughed and pointed to herself. "I'm a crazy cat lady."

"Brava! Entra!"

Louise followed him inside the picture-book home, with original wood beams, stucco walls, and terra cotta floors. Eclectic antique furniture set in the afternoon sun through locally printed linen curtains, the scent of herbs and fresh ground coffee beans gave it a welcoming feel. They passed straight through and went out the back door to the magical estate.

The L-shaped farmhouse created a natural courtyard. The immediate acreage was a converted vineyard, the former vine posts now serving as enclosures sheltering all manner of animals. Baby goats hopped and jumped on makeshift ramps, chickens and roosters hunted and pecked, a symphony of barking, cackling, braying and other farm noises had a soothing effect on Louise's psyche. Francesco piled her donated newspapers into a bin to be used for various farm animal purposes. Before throwing in the French paper, Le Figaro, he pointed to the headline.

"Quattro ottobre," he said, reminding her of the approaching festival of Saint Francis of Assisi on October 4th. But the way he glanced at the front page again convinced her there was something else that interested him. He turned toward the farm with the wave of his hand. "Ecco i miei fratelli e sorelle!" he said, introducing the animals as his *brothers and sisters*.

He started by giving them an uplifting sermon, much like the patron saint of Italy, Saint Francis of Assisi was known to have done. Then he began refilling their feeders and watering troughs, Louise lending a hand. In the nearby pasture, Louise saw sheep and cows leave their grazing and head to the barn for the feeding. Further out, she could see the remaining vineyard extending over the rolling Tuscan hillside. Paradise tended to by a modern-day Saint Francis.

She asked if all the animals were rescues. "Hai salvati tutti?"

"Sì! Tutti salvati da abusi o abbondoni."

Louise's heart melted as Francesco explained how he had saved each animal from abuse or abandonment. Louise was now convinced that Francesco was not working for the *Master of the Dark Arts*, or corrupt bankers. He was certainly not a horse baron for the Palio horse race. In her research with Michael, she had learned about the inhumane treatment of the horses. Between 1970 and 2007, forty-eight horses had died after collisions on the tightly curved track.

Not seeing any horses, Louise asked about them too. "E i cavallie?"

"Seguimi." She followed him just past the barn to a large paddock, where several majestic horses grazed. "Salvato dal Palio," he said. That settled it, if Francesco had been rescuing horses injured in the Palio horserace, he was one of the good guys. Meeting Francesco had given her a little calm before a brewing storm, as she psyched herself up for an encounter with the *Master of the Dark Arts* on a mission to betray her own father.

Francesco seemed to sense her mood change from peaceful to preoccupied.

"Ecco la vigna Sangiovese!" Trying to brighten her spirits, he drew her attention to his vineyard of Sangiovese grapes. It was the perfect distraction. "Ti piace il Chianti?"

"*I love Chianti!*" Louise said enthusiastically in Italian.

"Andiamo."

They went back inside leaving the critters to their meal. After washing up, Francesco started a fire in the hearth. He uncorked one of his family Chiantis, with a pronounced pop.

"Riserva 2010," he said, pouring with one hand and doing a chef's kiss with his other. "Eccellente!" He gave Louise a glass and they clinked. "Cin cin!"

They both swirled, sniffed, sipped, aerated then swallowed. She noted the wine was light and drinkable like her beloved pinot noir. "*It's very young but delicious,*" she said in Italian.

Francesco prepared a snack of grapes, olives, almonds, and cheeses as he explained that Chiantis were only aged ten to fifteen years. Louise enjoyed the vintage aged only two years, smooth yet complex with a hint of dark black cherry. She looked at her watch, 15:30 according to European time, close enough to five o'clock. She had done enough work today and relaxed. She explored Francesco's decorative objects and mementos. On the side table next to the inviting down sofa was what appeared to be a very old bottle of Chianti in the traditional form with a rounded bottom and covered with a close-fitting straw basket. It had a worn-out label matching that of the Chianti she was currently drinking, but the year was 1306.

"*Ricasoli is your family name?*" Louise asked in Italian, reading the label.

"Ah, sì." He pointed to himself. "Francesco Ricasoli." He set the platter of snacks on the coffee table, and they sat on the sofa in front of the fire. They clinked and he thanked her for helping feed the animals. "Grazia mille per il tuo aiuto."

There was always something liberating about communicating in her non-native language. It was like having a new personality free of the baggage of one's real life. It also involved intense listening, sight, scent, taste, touch, almost telepathy, and was very sensual. Over the years, Louise had kept her forays into carnal pleasures to a minimum. But, surprisingly, lately her recent hormonal adjustments seemed to have increased her sex drive.

The warmth from the fire and the magnetism of their bodies was irresistible. As with her work, Louise had always pushed herself beyond her comfort zone to transcend liminal boundaries, like a self-imposed *dépaysement*.[10] Coupled with her hormone changes, that tendency had become more intense. As though sensing her thoughts, he drained his wine glass, his lightly stubbled jaw line drawing her eye to his neck. She felt a flutter, a tingling in her nipples, the heft of her breasts against her clothing. He set down his glass then rubbed her shoulder and came closer to kiss her neck. His hands seemed to be drawn to her racing heart, the arousal moving down to her abdomen. He kissed her mouth and a flurry of heat washed over the entire area of her hips. He leaned in as Louise placed her glass on the side table. The spell was suddenly shattered as her hand knocked the ancient Chianti bottle from the table, landing with a thud on the Afghan rug.

Francesco looked deep into her eyes, his breath intoxicating. "Fiasco," he said.

Louise put both hands over her mouth, mortified. "Mi dispiace!"

Francesco dismissed it with a wave of his hand. "Non è un problema." He stood and picked up the unharmed bottle. Pointing to the traditional straw that it was wrapped in with a proud grin. "*Questo* si chiama *fiasco.*"

Louise blinked and then turned bright red with embarrassment. Realizing he was saying *fiasco* was the Italian word for the *basket* surrounding the Chianti bottle.

"*The fiasco is not a fiasco?*" she asked in Italian. They both burst out laughing. They sat down and Francesco explained the ancient tradition of the straw basket-weaving around the bulbous bottles to protect them during transport. It reminded her of the history of the Romans transporting wine and olive oil along the Saône River near her home in Burgundy, as evidenced by large clay amphoras unearthed from ancient Roman ruins in the region used for the same reason. *The Italians really took their wine and olive oil transportation seriously*, she thought.

She became lost in Francesco's kind eyes and sweet smile. A man with intelligence and humility was kryptonite to her. She settled back into the warmth of the sofa and their mutual attraction. He cupped her breasts and they kissed. Still mourning her mother and on an important mission, she felt it best to give herself some breathing room before romance. Louise checked her watch, 18:00, then she sweetly told him it was time for her to get back to the hotel.

"Dovrei andare."

"Ti accompagno." He insisted on walking her back to her hotel.

They arrived at her hotel, the Grand Hotel Continental, a UNESCO World Heritage site built in the 17th century, which she and Michael had specifically chosen for its many historic resources on the premises. As they entered the lobby the concierge personally greeted Francesco. She was once again impressed by his stature in the community.

"Ciao, Francesco!"

"Maurizio, come stai?"

They had a brief friendly chat in Italian and Louise was now convinced that she had made the ideal connection in Siena. She turned to Francesco to say good-bye.

"You know where to find me," she said in Italian, but her eyes said much more.

"Vieni ad Assisi per il 4 ottobre?" he asked.

"*I promise to come to Assisi for October 4th*," she replied in Italian.

They kissed and he respectfully made his exit.

Before going to her room, she perused several daily newspapers in the lobby then helped herself to a free copy of Le Figaro. She wanted to figure out what it was that had caught Francesco's attention. In addition to making Monte dei Paschi Bank connections, she was now very interested in the Francesco Ricasoli's family. She had much more research to do, and being restricted to non-Internet sources, she needed to access a library.

She approached the concierge. "Ciao, Maurizio. I heard you have a wonderful library. Is it possible for me to use it?"

"For a friend of Francesco, I'm happy to let you use our *wonderful* private library."

"Does it have periodicals?"

He leaned in confidentially. "Trust me we have everything you need. Sometimes, the Biblioteca Piccolomini borrows from *us*." She followed him down a hallway and through double doors into a vast chamber with two mezzanine levels. It was not as formal as what many consider the most beautiful library in the world, Biblioteca Piccolomini. But it was enchanting, crammed with books, periodicals, and artifacts on display. He motioned to a corner that featured a traditional periodical section complete with microfilm archives.

"This *is* wonderful." Louise was truly grateful.

"Just one rule, signorina Moscow, you mustn't make copies of anything, not even photographs. Also, nothing can be removed from this library."

"No problem. I just want to read."

"I'll leave you to work."

Having strict orders from Michael and now Maurizio not to record anything digitally, Louise filled her Memory Palace, collecting information as she perused the vast archives of periodicals. She moved on to the library that was organized using the universal Dewey Decimal system, including rare ancient books. She started with a quick research of Francesco's family winery based on the label she had committed to memory, supplementing her Memory Palace by jotting down the most salient points in her notebook. The Memory Palace was beginning to take on medieval characteristics.

LOUISE'S JOURNAL

The Ricasoli family story dates back to Baron Bettino Ricasoli who in
1872 wrote a letter addressed to Cesare Studiati, professor at the

University of Pisa. He wrote down the formula for what would be-
come Chianti Classico. The legend was that he had worked for over 30
years in search of the 'perfect wine.' The creation of the Chianti wine
formula had taken three decades of research. Called the 'Iron Baron'
he developed a precise sequence and a strict percentage of 7/10 San-
giovese, 2/10 Canaiolo, 1/10 Malvasia or Trebbiano.[11]

The family still owns the oldest winery in the region, the Brolio
Castle, dating back to the middle-ages. Bettino Ricasoli's great-
grandson, Francesco took over the family business in 1993.

"The research we do today has almost one thousand years behind
it." ~ Francesco

The archives featured photos of the ancient family vineyard and the
Brolio Castle. But Louise had not seen such a castle on Francesco's property.
So, if Francesco was running the winery out of a medieval castle, she had to
assume the farmhouse property was separate and designated for his animal
rescue. She didn't doubt it for a second. It was the perfect use of the family
estate. Satisfied with her new intel about Francesco, she moved on to her
next subject.

The oldest bank in the world, Monte dei Paschi di Siena Bank, commonly referred to as MPS, would have a whole section for itself, or so she
assumed. But, after a thorough and determined search of the Dewey
Decimal System and the microfilm collections, she was disheartened to find
that no ancient writings on the origins of MPS had been catalogued or
scanned. Not one to give up, she ventured through the cramped but
sprawling library until she found a darkly lit section of the bookshelves
marked in Italian, *Ancient Archives of Siena.* Within the 400 square foot
space, the amount of history was remarkable. She felt like a kid in a candy
store, eyes wide as she looked at well-preserved manuscripts of all sizes and
covers, from colorful to plain, dating as far back as the Renaissance.

It would be challenging, but it was a once-in-a-lifetime opportunity to
access this information. Louise began the task of speed-reading pages for
anything of interest, intermittently referring to a massive Italian-to-English
dictionary as needed. She had her work cut out for her. From her initial
assessment, she would need to spend at least a week to get a proper grasp of
the bank's history.

Maurizio appeared. "Mi dispiace, signorina Moscow. But I must close the library now. You're welcome to come back tomorrow."

Louise suddenly realized the time and that she was starving. "This has been so helpful. I'd love to come back tomorrow. Is the restaurant still serving?"

"Of course. I'll show you to a nice table."

Louise was still carrying the French newspaper Le Figaro. Dinner and a glass of wine would give her fresh eyes to read it. She ordered Tuscan comfort food, the Siena specialty of *ribollita*, a slow-cooked dense, soup-like mixture of bread, beans, and vegetables and, of course, a Chianti Classico. The season turning cooler, it was the perfect bedtime meal. She delved into Le Figaro, most of the sensationalized headlines cringeworthy and of little value. *What did Francesco notice?*

She ordered dessert, the local traditional panforte made of honey, dried fruit, nuts, spices, and pepper and a chamomile tea, then resumed reading. After rereading the front page several times, she became frustrated not being able to figure out what had caught Francesco's eye. Perhaps it *was* just the Festival of Saint Francis of Assisi. The server approached her table.

"Would you like anything else, signorina?"

She looked up from the paper and shook her head. "No grazie."

In her peripheral vision she perceived another dinner guest discretely watching her. His face seemed familiar, but she turned away not wanting to be rude. She rubbed her eyes and returned her gaze to the cover of Le Figaro one more time, in a final effort to allow her subliminal mind to take over. Suddenly two front page photos came into focus. They had been taken during the March 2012 G20 summit in Cannes of the French president, Nicolas Sarkozy, surrounded by officials, discussing his 2012 election strategy. He claimed his policies were 'not dictated by bankers,' attempting to appeal to voters on the left and the right, despite being a member of the right-leaning Republican party himself. Louise smirked at the first photo, Sarkozy characteristically and undiplomatically scowling while shaking the hand of German Chancellor, Angela Merkel. In the second photo he was smiling warmly shaking the hand of conservative UK Prime Minister, David Cameron.

None of it struck Louise as unusual. But what she did notice next was what must have caught Francesco's eye. There was a conspicuous man in the background of both photos. She suddenly realized it resembled the man in the restaurant! She looked up at the table where the man had been, but it was now empty and completely cleared of dinnerware. Had she imagined him? Perhaps she had read the page so many times she projected him? Or, more likely, had she just had her first encounter with the *Master of the Dark Arts*, Akari Raskalov?

"Signorina?"

She blinked and realized the server had been waiting for her reply.

"Il conto, per favore."

He placed the leather case on the table and Louise signed for the meal. She went to her room, brushed her teeth, and laid down, exhausted. Still, she had so many questions. If Francesco recognized the man in the photo, and if that same man she had seen at dinner was Akari Raskalov, did that mean Francesco knew him? Was Francesco working for intelligence or in some official capacity? Her exhaustion overpowered her speculation and she fell asleep.

Louise bolted upright in bed, heart racing. It was unmistakably night sweats, but not the hormonal variety. A loud bang echoed in her mind. The sound of waves crashing. One of her recurring dreams. In this one, she was high above, but the massive surf grew, each wave building higher than the last, threatening her, until it was clear the next would be unsurmountable no matter how high she climbed. The tsunami came crashing down with a deafening boom.

There was a knock at her door. She tossed the covers aside and got out of bed. Through the peephole no one was visible. She got dressed and went down to the concierge, Maurizio, with yesterday's copy of the French paper, Le Figaro.

"Good morning, Maurizio."

"Buongiorno, signorina Moscow. I hope you slept well?"

"More or less."

"Oh? Is the room to your liking? Would you like to move?"

"The room is wonderful. I just..." She searched for the words. "I'm wondering if you can help me. I was waiting for a friend last night, but I missed him. The only photo I have of him is here." She showed him the front page of Le Figaro pointing to the photo of the man she thought she saw at dinner. Maurizio's expression gave nothing away, a trained professional in discretion.

"Signorina, if I see this man, would you like me to transmit a message?" He picked up the hotel stationary and a pen to write.

"No, thank you. I'm going for a walk then I'd like to go back to the library, okay?"

"Absolutely. A presto."

SEVEN

September 19, 2012, Siena, Italy

Louise returned from her morning walk, but it was now day seven of her non-digital investigation into Monte dei Paschi Bank. To maintain her mental sharpness, and to keep her muscles from melting into fat, she had begun a morning routine consisting of yoga, meditation, Tai Chi, and floor exercises including push-ups, crunches, and jump rope. Then, a walk to get coffee and back to the library. Normally any routine was bad for espionage work, but the *Master of the Dark Arts*, Akari Raskalov, still had not made himself known to her, so she made herself easy to find.

With coffee in hand, she arrived back at the hotel. But the hotel library archives although impressive with centuries of historical books, memoirs, and periodicals, had run its course, at least for now. She had barely made a dent yet, but nothing she had read so far about MPS provided clues into suspicious activity. She knew it was past time for something to happen and had been expecting to hear from her link to the underworld. Or as she liked to call it, the *underwater world*. During her last investigation that began on her Caribbean Island hideaway, Louise had become the protégée of a mysterious *man without a country*, Frédéric LaFontaine, who lived a lawless life on the high seas.

LaFontaine called it *The Wild Wet*, where laws that governed international waters were antiquated and arcane, and – much like offshore banking – intentionally so. Most vessels in the shipping trade are registered in small corrupt countries like Liberia and Panama to avoid oversight and regulation from more fastidious governments, like offshore companies. On this latest assignment, Louise had been waiting for LaFontaine to send her a discrete means of contact, as was his protocol. But nothing had prepared her for this.

She arrived at the hotel entrance from her morning walk, the doorman greeting her with a friendly smile. But just as she was about to go in, the sound of horse hooves on cobblestones made her turn back. Far from a knight in shining armor, she saw a man on horseback, colors flying, in full Contrada uniform. The sky-blue and white fabric, with an image of a white wave on his chest, give him away as LaFontaine's messenger, but only to her.

"Ciao, ragazzi!" the horseman shouted.

"Ma, cosa fai, Giuliano?!" the doorman shouted, using the Italian hand gesture, thumb pressed against fingers, waving in the air. "You startled our poor guest," he added, referring to Louise. The doorman clearly knew the horseman, who must have been a local.

"Che bella!" the horseman said, turning on the charm, a little over-the-top. Louise suppressed a laugh at the antics of this character. "Come ti chiami?" he asked.

"Madonna santa!" the doorman huffed. "Mi dispiace, signorina. He is so *rude*. He comes every morning to torment me! Crazy Onda Contrada! Basta!" He pounded his fist against the inside of his bent elbow in the universally understood gesture for *fuck you!*

Louise replied to the doorman whom she had come to know by his name. "It's okay, Oscar." She turned to the horseman. "Ciao, Giuliano. Sono Louise."

The horseman reached down to shake her hand and Louise reached up and took it, feeling him give her a note from LaFontaine.

Giuliano looked her directly in the eyes and winked, an intelligent twinkle belied his goofy act. "I'm here every morning, signorina."

She pulled her hand away concealing the note in her closed fist. She understood his verbal message to mean he would come by every morning for delivery of messages either to or from LaFontaine. Then in a spectacular equestrian display, he directed the horse to rear up and waved good-bye.

"*The color of Heaven, the force of the Sea!*" he said in Italian. Louise took it as the motto for the Wave Contrada.

"Mortacci tua!" the doorman shouted, clearly riled. If Louise understood him correctly, he said, *your feeble ancestors!* She assumed he was from a rival contrada.

She turned to Oscar and asked, "Onda is your rival?"

"Si, signorina, Torre has been the rival of Onda since 1559, and *forever.*" In one final act of defiance, he violently flicked his fingers under his chin and out toward the horseman as he rode away. Then he regained his composure, stood in military pose, and politely opened the door for Louise.

She nodded appreciatively and went inside.

Anxious to read the message from LaFontaine, she went to her room and opened the tightly folded paper. LaFontaine had arranged to dock his yacht in Porto di Talamone on the west coast between Florence and Rome. He would be there by the time she received the note, so she wasted no time.

She packed a bag and was on the picturesque drive to reach the coastal Tuscan town within two hours of meeting the horseman. Her plan was to leave her rental car at the port, cruise the Mediterranean for a couple days and be back in time to join Franceso at the Festival of Saint Francis in Assisi. Louise passed the fabled Natural Park of Maremma, which was the site of stunning coastal pastures. One of these days she was going to be a normal tourist and stop to enjoy the scenery. The entire area with natural thermal baths and world-class beaches begged to be explored. But not today.

As she approached the port, LaFontaine's extraordinary yacht stood out among the local cruisers and sailboats docked in the marina. She parked and left her car for the duration.

"Ciao bello!" Louise called to Frédéric who was waiting on deck. She walked up the gang plank and they exchanged cheek kisses.

"Bellissima, Louise Moscow! It's wonderful to have you aboard once again."

"It's wonderful to be back on board, captain." The deckhand took her overnight bag and they adjourned to the aft deck. To avoid further scrutiny of his mammoth vessel, LaFontaine signaled for his First Officer to head out to sea. LaFontaine was the captain but relinquished duties to the second in command so he could enjoy time at sea.

Frédéric LaFontaine stood on the deck of the only home he'd known for the past fourteen years. The boat was free to roam in the international waters of the world, one of the privileges of his considerable wealth. He owned the formula to a software program that had revolutionized banking, and the profits he had accumulated could take care of several generations of LaFontaines, if he would ever get around to fathering an heir.

The wealthy elite disdainfully called him 'Bruce Wayne' behind his back because of his altruism, especially exposing the corruption of oligarchs and people in positions of power. The haters despised him but couldn't touch him, given the nature of his financial knowledge – backdoor access to all secrets in the electronic vaults – plus he was nimble, having no fixed address at sea.[12]

"Is there anything I can do for you at this time, Lulu?" he asked, noting her exhaustion.

Being back at sea taking in the scenic Tuscan coastline, Louise just wanted a moment to decompress. She curled up on one of the comfortable sofas in front of the large fire feature. Covering herself with a cashmere throw, she sank into the ample cushions and took a deep breath.

"Do you mind if I just take in the sunset and relax for a bit?"

As if on cue, the deckhand popped the cork of a perfectly chilled Veuve Cliquot. LaFontaine let out his signature laugh, as distinct as ever, like a bird call, but even heartier than she had remembered, an indication of a man who had found the key to happiness.

"Your wish is my command," LaFontaine said, filling two champagne flutes. He handed one to her and raised his to clink.

"To paradise," Louise mused.

"To paradise. Speaking of which, you must explore this region. There is so much history here, even before the Romans. As are all important ports, so much fascinating political drama."

"Drama is right," Louise said mostly to herself, thinking of her own mother and father. LaFontaine left her to her thoughts until she was ready. He signaled to his First Officer wide open throttle until they reached open waters. Soon, another champagne cork popped, and the sun dipped below the horizon leaving the sky in that mysterious twilight interval of haunted apparitions, mermaids, and ghost ships. The golden glow of the fire crackled, the flames and candle lanterns arranged around the deck the only light source. A few hours later, they were about sixty miles south on the Tyrrhenian Sea between Naples and Sardinia. They spent the voyage immersed in deep conversation, catching up on the past years and lifechanging events. The scent of cinders and sea air made the moment even more mystical.

"Frédéric, am I hallucinating?" Louise asked, rubbing her weary eyes.

At the same time the deckhand approached LaFontaine. "Capitaine, il y a un navire perdu." He confirmed what Louise was seeing.

"An abandoned ship?" Louise asked.

"It happens more often than you might think," LaFontaine replied. "At any given moment, there are 50,000 vessels crisscrossing the oceans, all essentially undetectable. Most of the time, these boats are registered to offshore shell companies and, after they have served their purpose, are simply abandoned and left to rot."

"50,000 vessels?" Louise asked in amazement.

Most are equipped with a rudimentary satellite-based GPS called Automatic Identification System. In 2002, AIS was required standard equipment on all new ships and retrofitted on older ships by 2008. But it is easy to disable the AIS and the vessels quickly fall off the radar, then simply vanish."

"The Outlaw Sea," Louise said, referring to the book by William Langewiesche.

"The open sea is the *Wild West* or as I prefer the *Wild Wet*." LaFontaine laughed at his old joke and Louise gave an approving smile. "Most of these abandoned boats are completely corroded, degrading the environment, some even leaking petroleum products. Sadly, unlike the Internet or porn industries, shipping is notoriously slow to adapt to new technologies. It seems companies prefer to keep the oceans vast and unknowable."

"It's horrible to think what they might be hiding."

"There are several developers working on software to maintain an overview of the entire world's ocean transport system, tracking where ships have been and what they are carrying. Whoever cracks that market will become a god. Right now, Scott Borgerson's tech company CargoMetrics Technologies is the closest. Borgerson could be in a position to help the environment but that doesn't seem to be his goal."

"So, he's just another greedy corporate scavenger." Louise shook her head.

"He is also the secret fiancé of the British socialite Ghislaine Maxwell."

Louise perked up at the mention of the name. "Ghislaine Maxwell, whose father mysteriously died in what could be considered another banker's grave?"

"Yes, his death could be considered a *banker's grave*."

"He was the business partner of the American child sex trafficker, Jeffrey Epstein."

"Precisely. Ghislaine Maxwell has intimate connections to the world's oligarchs. The attraction between Scott Borgerson and Ghislaine Maxwell is probably not just romantic. As Henry Kissinger said, power is the ultimate aphrodisiac." This last notion shook Louise. Was this the simple answer to her father's betrayal? She thought not.

The First Officer sidled the boat starboard of the abandoned 62-foot yacht, the name *Driftwood* fittingly emblazoned on the hull. They all moved to LaFontaine's lower deck to get a better look. The vessel appeared to be seaworthy but must have been adrift for some time. The First Officer aligned the two swim platforms and the crew tied to the vessel as LaFontaine weighed his options.

"We should check if anyone onboard needs urgent care before calling the Coast Guard," LaFontaine finally commanded.

"On monte à bord, capitaine?"

"Mettez-la sous les projecteurs!" LaFontaine ordered them to turn on the large spotlight. It was as bright as daylight fully revealing the vessel like a magic trick.

"We could practically scuba dive under it with that light," Louise commented.

LaFontaine did not give his signature guffaw, instead remaining completely silent, a signal that he was watching for the slightest movement.

Suddenly Louise noticed two men wielding firearms enter from the shadows, so stealthily they might have been ninjas or former secret service. Louise's defense instincts literally kicked in and she made her move. Pushing Frédéric safely aside, she swiftly delivered several Krav Maga strikes, and within seconds the first man lay on deck holding his crotch in agony. The second man was quicker, as she delivered several strategically placed blows to his vulnerable parts, he defended himself with MMA moves.

"Louise! Stop!" she heard a familiar voice shout. But recognizing the man a split second too late, she ruthlessly poked him in the throat. The familiar American voice choked out, "Louise, it's me!"

"Charlie?" Louise relaxed in non-defensive mode. She was mortified having inflicted injury on the two allies. She offered her hand to Jack and helped him up. "So sorry you guys. Charlie, what the hell are you doing here?"

"I work for Frédéric!" He coughed. "Where the hell did you learn to fight like that?"

"Langley," Louise replied. "I refused firearms training and as a compromise I had to reach the highest-level martial arts training in Krav Maga."

"It paid off," Frédéric said. "Nicely done." Seeing Charlie, he added, "Sorry, Charlie."

Charlie limped toward them then cringed. "What's that smell?"

LaFontaine signaled for silence and to move closer but not board the other vessel yet. Then a breeze wafted in their direction, and everyone caught a whiff of the putrid scent.

"It could be dead fish," Charlie said as he and his now-recovered colleague, Jack, stepped carefully onto the other boat's platform and shined their flashlights into the galley and bridge. No sign of life. They inched toward the steps leading down to the berth where the stench grew stronger. Charlie stopped and turned away, taking a cloth from his pocket to cover his nose. Jack did the same. Suddenly Charlie stopped, noticing someone on the floor in the galley. He shone a light revealing a terrified girl holding a bloody butcher knife. She put her hand over her eyes against the flashlight and began crying uncontrollably.

"It's okay," Charlie said gently, lowering his weapon. "We're here to help you." He tended to the girl who was about thirteen and wearing nothing but a wet towel. He easily coaxed the knife from her hand and checked her for injuries. She had clearly been abused, ligature marks on her wrists and ankles. "You're a fighter. Good girl," Charlie told her.

Jack radioed for the First Officer to call the Italian Coast Guard. Then wielding his weapon, he resumed investigating the cabins below deck. He only needed to open the master cabin to confirm the source of the stench. A dead man and woman covered in blood from multiple stab wounds.

"Is there anyone else on the boat?" Charlie asked. The girl had calmed down somewhat and raised two fingers and pointed to where Jack had gone.

Jack reappeared with an update. "Male and female victims, cause of death likely multiple stab wounds. The Italian Coast Guard are on the way."

Frédéric brought Charlie a thermal blanket to cover the girl. Charlie lifted her up in his arms and carried her onto LaFontaine's yacht.

"The authorities will want to question her. But it might be good to have Louise get her some clothes. We have extra supplies in the guest cabin."

Louise looked at the girl with compassion and strength in her eyes. The girl seemed to immediately trust her. Louise put out her hand and she took it, allowing Louise to take her to the guest cabin with an en-suite head. Louise seated the girl on the chair at the vanity while she found a pair of comfortable pajamas.

"I'm Louise. What's your name?" Louise kept the interaction simple. The girl just stared into the middle distance, unshed tears welling in her eyes. Louise took a knee in front of the girl and held the soft pajamas, robe, and slippers out to her.

"It's okay. You don't have to talk if you don't want to." Louise took a deep breath through her nose then exhaled through her mouth.

She did it two more times until it had the contagious effect of inducing a yawn and the girl inhaled deeply. On the exhale the tears came, and her lips quivered into sobs. "It's okay." Louise did another big inhale and exhale. She sat at eye level with the girl who finally took the pajamas. "I'll leave you to put these on." She pointed to the blood in the girl's hair and hands.

"The police will need to take samples for evidence. Can you stay strong for a little while longer and not wash this off?"

The girl looked alarmed.

"It's okay. I'll be with you the whole time." Still no response but she took another deep breath. "Good girl. I'll leave you here for five minutes, okay?" Louise held up her splayed hand then pointed to her wristwatch. "Five minutes." She walked out the door and closed it quietly.

Louise listened carefully through the door for the sound of running water or anything alarming. She heard rustling and then after five minutes she knocked. The door opened and the girl was wearing the pajamas, robe, and slippers Louise had given her. Louise held out her hand and the girl gripped it tightly. Louise led her back to the deck where the Italian Coast Guard were already waiting. Some of the crew was dealing with the scene of the killings. Two very kind looking medics were waiting for the girl.

The multilingual medics tried different languages to see some sign of understanding. The girl seemed most responsive to English but still refused to speak. The Italian Coast Guard officers swabbed her for evidence then let Louise take her to shower and wash her hair. Afterwards, they offered her hot chocolate and treats, which she devoured. Finally, she felt safe and lay down next to Louise on the sofa in front of the fire. Just as her eyelids became too heavy to stay open, in perfect American English she said, "Thank you, Louise."

The Coast Guard took her into their care, but Louise insisted on being kept informed of any updates and offered to help in any way to locate the girl's parents. They exchanged contact information and the Coast Guard left for the shore in Rome.

"Thank goodness we found her," Louise said. They sat at the bar of LaFontaine's saloon.

"What a courageous little girl," Charlie said.

"After everything we went through to bring down those international sex trafficking rings, it still goes on," Louise said.

"This was a rough one," Charlie admitted. "Most of my maritime assignments involve drug dealers. The only ones where I've dealt with children involved helping parents find their kids lost toys or lost kids to find their parents on a cruise ship port. This was soul crushing."

"Soul crushing indeed," Louise said. "These offshore entities are completely lawless."

"Well, I'm on board to do whatever it takes to make waves in their operations. Puns intended," Charlie said. LaFontaine poured champagne and they clinked glasses.

"I'll drink to that," Louise said.

"It seems like yesterday that Louise was in witness protection on a Caribbean Island, and I was the unknown entity regularly referring offshore clients to her for financial services." Charlie winked at Louise. "I got your back."

For all his humility, Charlie was formidable. The former Navy SEAL had helped fight the Hong Kong triads, he was an advanced certified pilot, skydiver, and open water scuba diver, who had shifted to private detective specializing in maritime crimes, mostly in the Atlantic. But when it came to international banking cases, he always referred the clients to Louise.

Louise recalled the old days. "You and Frédéric were my guardian angels. That investigation ended my exile, and I met you both. Charlie brought Frédéric into my life."

"Do you miss the island?" Charlie asked.

"Not so much. Would you? I mean if you left the Caribbean and moved to Europe?"

"The Caymans are my home sweet home."

"I do miss the beach and Big Steve," Louise said.

"He's livin' large and doing great. You'd be proud how he has kept up the Tiki Bar."

"I'll have to hitch a ride with Frédéric to go visit soon."

"Any time, ma belle," LaFontaine said. "Speaking of making waves, we should get some rest and regroup tomorrow to talk about your new case."

"Yes, I'm exhausted," Louise said, getting up and stretching. They exchanged cheek kisses and said good night. Louise adjourned to the luxurious berth that she had adopted as her floating home-away-from-home. The mattress was just right, the en suite head was larger than the master bath in her Burgundy home, all the comforts of a five-star hotel.

Another recurring water dream roiled her sleep. A massive crystal blue wave overtook her, but at the same time she felt no danger. She awoke refreshed, the view of the gleaming blue Mediterranean reminiscent of the dream washed away the nightmarish memories of the prior evening. She assumed the dream had been induced by the motion at sea. But it was so majestic and vivid she had to wonder if it had more portent. The location of the dreamscape seemed so specific, the point of view soaring over cliffs, the waves below churning, turning, like turquois glass topped with white spray against cerulean sky. The boat had traveled at a leisurely but steady velocity overnight and from the surroundings they appeared to have reached the coast of Naples around the front ankle of boot-shaped Italy.

After the horrific night, it was crucial to recalibrate her Chakras before delving into the case with Frédéric and Charlie. Dressed in yoga pants and sports bra, she went to the upper deck for morning Tai Chi. She found that coupling the ancient Chinese martial art that emphasized *Chi (air)* controlled by the mind, with her yoga and meditation, made for a well-rounded routine. Tai Chi stresses natural breathing, gradual movements, and smooth weight transitions. The practice maintains youthfulness because the powerful, yet gentle postures direct the Chi to various body parts, improving circulation. She called it *meditation in motion*.

About fifteen minutes into her routine, Charlie appeared on deck and joined in, following along effortlessly. Louise was impressed with his mastery of the art.

"I didn't know you did Tai Chi, Charlie."

"Going on forty years now. When did you take it up? I thought yoga was your thing."

"A few years ago, I added it to my routine. Tai Chi offers an amazing combination of self-defense, meditation, and healing."

"I couldn't agree more."

"I do the Hsu Fun Yuen 64-posture form," Louise added.

"Hsu Fun is fantastic. The standard Beijing 24-posture form is intentionally unimaginative. The Chinese government is very strict about what the masses are allowed. I just started with a new teacher Grandmaster Wai-Lun Choi."

"Do you mind if I follow along with you for a bit to see?"

"Of course."

Charlie began his postures offering verbal cues as Louise followed along.

His routine was like hers, but more powerful. They finished, put their palms together at their hearts and bowed their heads.

"I could use some coffee," Louise said.

"Your wish is my command." LaFontaine's regal laugh echoed, like an august and clement king, majestic and ceremonial. "I thought you'd enjoy breakfast up here with a 360-degree view."

"You thought right," Louise agreed.

The crew served continental breakfast on the upper deck, the setting exemplifying LaFontaine's omnipresence in the world. If there was an inner circle of secret knowledge, he was its prophet. As they ate breakfast, LaFontaine got down to business. "The Italian Coast Guard radioed this morning. They have made some progress identifying the girl. She was very lucky."

"*Lucky*, for lack of a better word," Louise said.

LaFontaine's expression showed regret for his own choice of words. "Not exactly luck, to be honest. We've been out here for some time combing the seas."

Louise softened, realizing she still held lingering outrage over her past investigation that dug up a murderous sex trafficking ring. "You mean, you knew the boat was here?"

"Yes, a couple days before picking you up, we encountered that boat and found it suspicious. The couple were overly cheerful, while the girl looked out of place and frightened. We noted their position and planned on circling back to reconnoiter."

"Oh, that's why we seemed off course. We were headed too far west for Naples." Louise noticed Charlie and LaFontaine exchange wry smiles. LaFontaine handed Charlie a dollar bill.

"Your sense of direction is still as sharp as an eagle, Louise," Charlie said, placing the bill in his shirt pocket.

Ignoring their antics, Louise refocused. "It seems land and sea still run rampant with child sex traffickers. If only you'd stopped when you first saw them, she wouldn't have had to…The horror of what she went through." Louise choked up.

"At the time, our suspicions were iffy at best, and they might have done something drastic. We took the safest precaution for everyone."

"It just makes me realize how widespread and entrenched the problem is. The worst part is that I have to focus on my current case instead of investigating whoever trafficked that child."

"They may not be mutual exclusive," Charlie chimed in. Louise glanced at LaFontaine who shrugged regretfully.

"Hélas, it's true," LaFontaine said, in his accented Franglais. "High-level financial crimes are often rooted in sex trafficking. That should not surprise you, Lulu."

"I'm not surprised," Louise replied. "But I'll always be shocked. Was it my imagination or did that the little girl sound American?"

"It's very likely she went through one of the orphanages on the Bailiwick of Jersey."

"Yes. The tax haven off the coast of France. The orphanage scandals a few years ago created a global media circus," Louise said ruefully.

"That little island is the world's biggest tax haven," LaFontaine said. "Even Apple parks money there to avoid taxation. The wealthy elites of Jersey have done everything in their power to cover up that scandal and remain completely invisible. Ministers who cover up the crimes are bestowed knighthoods by the Queen of England, while honest politicians and pesky foreign reporters are arrested. The country also grants residential status to Russian oligarchs."

"Is that how Akari Raskalov fits in?" Louise asked, wanting to make the connection.

"You might want a refill," LaFontaine said, taking a sip of café au lait before expounding on the subject.

"I'd love another café au lait," Louise said. The deck hand brought a fresh French press and pitcher of steamed milk and they all refilled.

"If you consider your father to be an oracle," LaFontaine began, "or that Abedi, your old boss at BCCI, had mystical powers, this guy rises many levels above, or below them, depending on your perspective. He is not to be trifled with. There is no room for error with that man."

"Louise, I know that look in your eye," Charlie said. "You can always rely on me as your curtain twitcher." She smirked at Charlie's reference to spies watching from windows. "But Frédéric and I cannot always be there to save you from your own impetuous actions."

"Don't worry, Charlie. I wouldn't put you at undue risk. I may still be impetuous in certain things, but at my age, I've come to take mortality more seriously."

"Good to know." Charlie slathered butter on a croissant and poured more café au lait.

"Now that we have that settled," LaFontaine resumed. "Louise, you must realize what you are dealing with. Someone like you will never understand greed and corruption on a visceral level. It's not in you."

"When I first started working at BCCI," Louise countered, "I admit I was fascinated by the lifestyle and being in the proximity of people with true wealth and power."

"But you were never hungry for it yourself," LaFontaine said. "You were intrigued, intellectually. That is all. Many become addicted to prominence and power to do whatever they want, to the point that they will compromise themselves. Raskalov is a man who is addicted to being close to the action. He thrives on bending people to his will. It is as simple as that. But what makes him insidious is that he also loves his anonymity. He shuns fame, contrary to someone like Donald Trump who feeds off adulation. Trump is a master at luring otherwise sensible people into his fantasy world and keeps them there by using the threat of banishment. It's a mafia mind. This explains the behavior of many of his sycophants enabling his crimes.[13] Raskalov is not that kind of person. He is in it for the shadowy conquest. *Playing God.*"

"Point taken," Louise said. "I'm still waiting for this *God* to approach me. But I don't know what else to do. I'm not even sure what he looks like."

"Recognizing him might be your greatest challenge." LaFontaine picked up a manilla folder and took out an eight-by-ten-inch photo. "Here's a recent photo of him in his natural appearance."

The color photo showed a burly man with a rubicund complexion, brown curly hair graying at the temples, and thick black rimmed glasses. He appeared to be sitting in a restaurant, not happy to be having his likeness captured.

"But he's a master of disguise," LaFontaine continued. "He could look like anyone, depending on where he is. If he's planning a trip to Afghanistan, he will grow a long beard and wear a skull cap to blend in with the Afghan elders. He's practically a shape shifter. He can speak several languages fluently. One thing that you *can* look for is his very gregarious nature. He's fast talking with a sharp sense of humor." Frédéric paused to sip his coffee. "I presume you have been warned never to communicate to anyone by email or phone?"

"Yes, because of his proclivity for hacking."

"Exactement," Frédéric said in French. "He is a former Soviet military counterintelligence officer in a unit of the Red Army after its 1979 invasion of Afghanistan. He honed his craft in the 1990's after Russia opened state-owned businesses to private ownership. He moved to Washington, DC for the express purpose of becoming a lobbyist specializing in opposition research. He brags about how easy it is to find tech-savvy professionals able to access just about any email account. Do not be surprised when you meet him if he chats about one of your emails he has read."

"Even my secured CIA server emails?"

"Tout à fait. He himself will tell you never to communicate by email about anything that you want to remain a secret. He is a master of *Chyorny P.R.*"

"*Black public relations*," Louise said, recalling the conversation with Michael.

"Oui. He is highly sought after for his expertise running negative campaigns. He warned all his friends and associates that nothing is secure, and nothing is sacred. Using fabricated or stolen documents he helps business owners damage rival businesses, or politicians to damage opponents, eliminating the need of physical threat, which he will still not hesitate to use."

"Kompromat," Louise said.

"He goes further than that. His negative campaigns can make the most honest businessman appear to be something horrible. He could make a Rabbi appear anti-Semitic."

She stared at the photo, now convinced it was the same man in the French newspaper, and the man watching her in the hotel restaurant. "Do you think he's working for my father?" Louise did not want to know the answer, but she had to ask.

"More likely against your father, in the sense that he would want him compromised. Also, I wouldn't be surprised if he already installed spyware on your computer via Russian hackers. He will deny it and swear he gets his information through fastidious research on behalf of his clients. He speaks openly about his so-called *services* to reporters. He even writes puff pieces on behalf of his clients that he gets published in major newspapers. But his hacking network can infiltrate corporate databases and obtain gigabytes of sensitive data including passport numbers, bank accounts, loan documents, emails, and other private information."

"And he works for both sides," Louise interjected.

"Absolument! He will infiltrate a close ally of Putin to obtain anti-Kremlin kompromat for one client. Then he will turn around and work in Putin's favor. Right this moment, Raskalov is lobbying heavily against the Magnitsky Act. He is very crafty and always one step ahead."

"So, how does all that tie to my father and Monte dei Paschi Bank of Siena?"

"That is where it gets interesting."

"It's just getting interesting now?" Louise looked like she might hyperventilate.

LaFontaine motioned to a deckhand. "Champagne?" Louise didn't say no, and the deckhand popped a cork on a bottle of Veuve Cliquot.

"Could I have a scotch and soda in a tall glass with one ice cube?" Charlie asked. The deckhand mixed the drink at the fully stocked upper deck bar and served it to him.

LaFontaine continued. "In order to understand greed, we must go back to the beginning. The world's oldest bank has something of a mystical past."

Louise looked skeptical. "Banking? Mystical?"

"Think about it," Frédéric said, "Money has always been the object of fascination."

"Because having a lot of it brings power," Louise concluded.

"I've always found treasures buried at sea to be very fascinating," Charlie quipped.

"You are both correct!" LaFontaine said, sounding like everyone's favorite college professor. "Traditionally, currency is three things: a unit of account, a store of value, and a means of payment. As an expression of sovereignty, coins bear the symbol of the country. Minerva's owl, the symbol of Athens, was one of the first expressions of state identity. But there is also a mysticism behind currency. Countries play on the symbol of sovereignty as a sign of divinity. The head of Philip of Macedon could be mistaken for that of Hercules. British and United States currency have embossed words like *In God We Trust*.

"Fyodor Dostoyevsky wrote about physical money being *coined freedom*, likening the value of a coin to an imprisoned man," Louise said. "He who cannot spend money to obtain material possessions can only dream of freedom."

"Greed is a prison," Charlie said.

"Exactly. That's what is so perplexing," Louise said.

"One theory is that humans have been removed from our original connection with the earth, our Pranav or Chi," LaFontaine said. "The first currency started in cradle of civilization, Mesopotamia, by the priest class. The Mesopotamian language used the same symbol for *cow* as for *money*. The word *Capital* refers to a *head* of cow. Even the word for *cowrie* shells which have been used as currency is believed to refer to a *cow*. This perception of monetization of nature and land shifted the entire human consciousness."

"Buddhist economics," Charlie chimed in.

"Buddhist economics?" Louise asked.

"Exactly." Frédéric LaFontaine explained, "Buddhist economics tries to return humans to valuing nature for what it is. Buddhism is *the here and now*, this moment is all there is. If we view economic systems as an extension of nature, we see money as something positive. However, if we view economics in terms of the *value* of all things in nature, such as land, or cattle, then we see money as antagonistic. It becomes a new form of communication. When money became a necessary part of human evolution in those terms, a separation of the mind and natural world was the result, which eventually created a separation from nature within human consciousness. Money takes on a mystical quality."

"Something to worship," Louise said.

"The Mesopotamian priest class were the first to have written language wielding great power over the masses," Charlie added. "That means for 6,000 years, since the beginning of civilization, that rift has been ingrained in humans.

"You have your work cut out for you, Lulu," LaFontaine said. "Greed is ingrained and there are nefarious forces at play."

"It does make sense," Louise said, like seeing an apparition. "Maybe it's just not ingrained in some of us. I just don't have that fascination."

Frédéric became serious and looked Louise directly in the eyes. He was almost unrecognizable. Even his French accent softened. "My intelligence indicates that violence against anti-Kremlin activists is increasing as Putin buttresses his power. You can expect more bankers' graves and political murders. My intel indicates that the Syrian civil war that began in 2011 will be inflamed by Putin causing hundreds of thousands or perhaps millions of Syrian civilians to flee to Europe with the intention to destabilize Europe. It is a long-game KGB tactic. An unstable Europe will help Putin invade other strategic territories."

"Russia could invade other territories?" Louise asked, skeptical.

"Of course. Crimea in Ukraine is crucial to Russian dominance. When the Baltic states, followed by Ukraine and Belarus declared independence from the Soviet Union in 1991, breaking into fifteen independent republics, it meant Russia would never again become a world power without re-taking control of Ukraine. It sits on the Black Sea, a critical Russian naval hub of geographical importance with access to the Mediterranean."

"Yes, I remember very well, being in Budapest, Hungary during the protests ending in the Berlin Wall coming down. But, again, what does this all have to do with my father and Monte dei Paschi Bank?"

"That's what you're going to find out," LaFontaine replied. "Keep in mind, you are not alone. International Intelligence agencies are working from all sides within the European Union. You are well positioned because you are your father's daughter and can gain unique access."

"Where have I heard that before?"

"Look at it this way, Louise," Charlie said. "If you had remained an investment banker at JP Morgan Chase in Manhattan and not aspired to become an incredibly savvy financial and technical expert, you would have missed all this excitement."

"Thanks, Charlie, but it's more like excrement than excitement. I have the feeling no matter what job I took I would have been sucked into the shit-storm."

"We will love you unconditionally, even if you retire and become a best-selling novelist," LaFontaine said. "Then you could do real damage."

"I have enough subject matter for several tomes." Louise got up, walked to the railing, and gazed over the Mediterranean. With the exception of a few modern vessels, the still-functioning vintage boats with their classic lines and weatherworn fisherman going about their daily routines, it could have been 1,000 years ago. "Such simple beauty."

LaFontaine stood by her side, providing a much-needed fatherly, or brotherly, presence. She searched his azure eyes, lucid with wisdom. No one ever discussed his age, he seemed ageless. A Bodhisattva.

"Lulu, follow your gut instinct, as always. Don't force it. We can only do the prep work and then let the magic happen. It's what *motivates* us that makes the difference."

"Thanks, Frédéric. That has always been my modus operandi and I have no intention of changing it now. It just feels like this is my most important and dangerous case ever. The pressure is on."

"I agree, it probably is the most dangerous, but it's the most crucial," LaFontaine said. "It will take a multi-pronged approach, but you will have back-up."

The vessel pulled into the port of Naples.

"May I take you on a quick tour of Naples?"

"I'd love to!" Louise said. "It's my first time."

They left Charlie to his own devices and LaFontaine took her for his favorite coffee in Napoli, followed by the best pizza, and ending with the best gelato. The whole time he briefed her on anything relevant she should know about the *Master of the Dark Arts*, Akari Raskalov.

"Your contact will be the communications director at Monte dei Paschi Bank," LaFontaine said. "I consider him a friend. But he has closed me off recently and frankly I'm worried about him. Do not get too close to him. Just report to me his whereabouts, maybe follow him, keep track of his daily activities."

Louise was committing the information to memory. "What's his name?" Then he said a name that shook her to her core.

"Dario Rossellini."

"Dario Rossellini, the Italian banker?"

"You know him?" Frédéric was stunned. His reconnaissance had not made any connections between Rossellini and Louise.

"If it's the same guy, yes. He was briefly a client at BCCI…" She faded off. There seemed to be more, but he didn't pursue it preferring to allow it to take a natural course.

"Make contact with him," LaFontaine said. "He will be the core of your investigation."

PART II

EIGHT

Siena, Italy, October 2, 2012

They cruised up the coast overnight and Louise reached Siena two days before the October 4th Feast of San Francesco. She couldn't wait to see her own Francesco. She organized and got a good night sleep.

The next morning, wearing a simple but alluring frock and strappy espadrille wedges, she walked to the café where they had first met. She was happily surprised to see Francesco having coffee and reading the newspaper. His look upon making eye contact with her melted her heart.

She approached and took a stack of newspapers out of her tote bag. "Porto i regali." *I come bearing gifts.* The words reminded her of the Latin phrase, *Beware of Greeks bearing gifts.* But Francesco seemed happy to see her. He stood excitedly to kiss her cheeks.

"Ciao, Bellissima!" She sat at his table and ordered a café latte and a delicious cone shaped puff pastry called a *cornetto* stuffed with homemade whipped cream. Her Italian was improving every day and it was easy to talk to him. One of those rare men who really looked her in the eyes and listened. His demeanor was peaceful and unaffected. She was curious about his astrological sign. Out of habit, she asked his birthday. "Quand'è il tuo compleanno?"

Instead of mocking her as most men might, Francesco wrinkled his brow and responded in all seriousness as though a question at a job interview. "Il 2 luglio."

July 2nd seemed too good to be true. Most of the important men in her life had been Libras, the same as her rising sign, which, according to her chart, was her second-best match. But her Venus was in Cancer, so Cancer was her *best* match. She smiled to herself. Then replied with the more obvious response. "*July 2nd is the first Palio Race!*" she said, in Italian.

Francesco nodded his head, but looked regretful, not a fan of the race.

"E tu? Quand'è il tuo compleanno?"

"*My birthday is May 25th,*" she replied.

Francesco seemed taken aback. He gazed at her, eyes sparkling, as though he had seen a seraph. Louise tilted her head and shrugged as if to ask, *what's wrong?*

He explained an important holiday fell on May 25th, the Feast of the Dedication of the Papal Basilica of Saint Francis of Assisi. His passion for Saint Francis of Assisi, his kindness toward animals, and his devotion to nature were inspiring, especially as she embarked on a deal with the devil.

Speaking of the devil, a dark figure traversed her peripheral vision. Even though she had only seen him once in person and in grainy photos, there was no mistaking him, it was the *Master of the Dark Arts*, Akari Raskalov. His silhouette seemed to float across the Piazza del Campo, past the fountain heading north toward the Banca Monte dei Paschi di Siena.

"Parola d'onore?" Francesco broke into her thoughts asking her to promise to go to Assisi with him for the October 4th Feast of Saint Francis celebrations.

"Sì, certo. Prometto." Louise renewed her promise to go to Assisi.

Satisfied, Francesco picked up the newspapers to leave. "Andiamo a casa?"

Louise contemplated his offer, wanting nothing more than to come home with him. But she told him she had to run some errands and could come to his house around five o'clock. That would give her time to try to find Raskalov. Or see if he would find her.

Francesco accepted her offer. "Ciao, a presto!"

They exchanged cheek kisses and went their separate ways.

Louise strolled in the direction of her hotel, window shopping at a lei-surely pace for the benefit of anyone following her. Through the reflection in the storefront windows, she spied *Indigent Guy* walking in the opposite direction. She observed Francesco place some change in the man's open hand. It was both heartwarming and disturbing. Studies have found that a person witnessing kindness toward others responds the same as if it were directed toward them. On the other hand, she could reasonably suspect that they were conspiring, and the coins were a signal.

No matter. The mark, or tail, depending how one looked at it, *Indigent Guy* staggered toward the supermarket ostensibly to buy another bottle with his new-found *means of payment*. Louise pivoted right toward Monte dei Paschi Bank and crossed the street to flush out any other tails. She saw *The*

Librarian walking absentmindedly while looking at her phone.

The third tail still hadn't shown himself, or perhaps Louise was losing her touch. That morning she hadn't spotted *Smarmy Guy* at her favorite café latte spot and wondered where he was. She quickly covered the 300 meters to Monte dei Paschi headquarters when she marked *Banker Guy* entering. Of course, he was an actual banker.

Despite Charlie's rebuke about recklessness, she walked into Monte dei Paschi with no plan. Her modus operandi was brazen improvisation. Not many could pull it off but being attuned to her surroundings and her instincts gave her the upper hand. Her style often threw others off their game and forced them to adjust their own strategy. As she entered MPS, she took out her passport and debit card and approached the teller.

"Buongiorno," the friendly teller smiled. She had large innocent yet intelligent brown eyes and a slightly mussed bouffant due to her thick wavy hair cut into an A-line bob.

"Buongiorno." Louise returned the smile and played tourist. "Do you speak English?"

Her American English accent caught the ear of the intended target, Akari Raskalov, who was chatting with one of the managers at a business banking desk. Louise felt his stare but continued her conversation.

"Yes, how can I help you?" the teller replied.

Louise changed to a whisper so as not to broadcast how much cash she would be carrying. "I'd like to withdraw more than the ATM allows. May I withdraw the equivalent of 1,000 US dollars in Euros?"

"Of course."

The teller efficiently completed the transaction and Louise started to walk out. The Russian turned to watch her leave and she saw her opportunity to stage a *meet-cute*. It ended up more bumbling than staged, as Louise fumbled with her phone trying to put her wallet and passport back into her bag. Her phone slipped, and everything toppled to the floor in a heap.

"Shit!" Louise exclaimed, then catching herself she looked around, blushing. In a flash Akari Raskalov was kneeling to help her. He held up his hands as if to say, *I'm not a thief.*

"May I help you?" He spoke in perfect non-British English, with a slight Russian accent.

"Thank you so much. Excuse my French."

"Are you just visiting Siena?" he asked.

"Yes. Tomorrow I'm going to the Feast of Saint Francis of Assisi."

"Wonderful tradition. Is it your first time here?"

"Is it that obvious?" Louise was thrown off, not expecting the villain to be so charismatic.

They stood and he offered his hand. "My name is Akari."

Since he only gave his first name, she took his cue. "Louise," she said, shaking his hand. Suddenly his cell phone rang.

He looked at the number and said, "Please excuse me. I must take this." Raskalov turned away to talk as Louise stalled by busying herself with her purse. Apparently, he was unaware that she understood Russian because he seemed to be speaking very candidly about what was surely a highly confidential subject matter. Apparently one of his clients was pissed off that his corporate rival still hadn't been destroyed. Nonetheless, her first impression of this master of disguise was a charmer. The feeling appeared to be mutual, as he hung up the phone with a glimmer in his eye.

"So sorry for the interruption. May I offer you a refreshment? There's a lovely café just ten minutes from here. One of my favorites in all of Italy."

Knowing his reputation for high living, Louise was intrigued and accompanied him to the unknown location. As they continued past the Piazza del Campo and the Fonte Gaia café, Louise started to wonder where he was taking her. The winding medieval road with its ancient edifices and cobblestones toyed with her sense of the time it took to arrive at their destination. But in exactly eleven minutes, less than half a mile, they entered a charming tea-room. The fact that tea was one of Putin's favorite *natural causes* of death was not lost on Louise. Still, the inviting parlor with its vaulted ceilings and stone fireplace, the aromatics of the world-class infusions and delectable-looking confections, was hard to resist. It was almost *to die for*.

They followed the owner to a cozy corner table that seemed to be reserved for Raskalov. The owner waited for their order without giving them a menu.

Raskalov asked Louise, "May I order for you?"

"Please do."

Impressed with his charms, but giving nothing away, she held a blank expression as Raskalov ordered rare teas and house-baked treats in Russian. From their interaction, she gathered the server was also the proprietor. After he left, they resumed their conversation.

"You are Russian?" Louise asked, innocently.

"Guilty as charged," he replied with dry Russian wit, holding up his hands in surrender.

This encounter was going to be a wild ride, Louise could feel it.

"So, Louise Moscow. I was reading one of your emails recently."

Louise had that burning sensation that courses through every capillary. Like the realization you clicked *reply all* before sending a confidential email. She knew her face was red, as she sent a mental *thank you* to Frédéric for his prescient warning. She often didn't know until it might otherwise have been too late how helpful Frédéric's guidance was. She quickly thought of a probing and mildly threatening comeback.

"Were you reading an email concerning one of my investigations? Let's see, an email would have to be after 1995. So, it could have been about anything from my infiltration of BCCI to the international human trafficking ring I uncovered."

He quirked a crooked smile and raised one eyebrow, reminding her of her Russian-American CIA friend, Vladimir Egger, who also had a crooked smile. But Vladimir's came off as sexy. Raskalov had charisma but it did not outweigh his ominous presence.

"You are a remarkable woman. Brave, beautiful, brilliant."

"Blushing," Louise countered.

"No need to be modest. It was quite a coincidence running into you, in fact." His stare pierced her soul as though he was the courtroom judge who could tell if she was lying.

"Let me guess. You don't believe in coincidences."

"Luck. Good fortune. Destiny. Fate. These can all be manipulated in one's favor."

"I'm more of a fly-by-the-seat-of-my-pants kind of gal."

"Julia Roberts in *Pretty Woman*," he shot back. "Great movie."

Yep, Louise liked this guy, or at least she liked his style.

The libations and treats were served. Everything looked and smelled mouthwatering. Louise helped herself, emotions having triggered hunger and thirst.

"I leave nothing to chance," he continued. "Through copious research I control every outcome. Then, when I feel I know everything, I go even deeper. Especially when it comes to hiring someone."

Nothing Frédéric or Michael had said could have prepared her for what she thought she just heard. "Are you offering me a job?"

"Good help is hard to find."

"You know a lot about me, but I don't know anything about you."

"What would you like to know? I was born in Russia, was a counterintelligence officer during the 1979 invasion of Afghanistan. My skills seemed a good fit for the lobbying industry in the United States, so I worked hard, obtained my U.S. citizenship and now provide intel to worthy clients."

"My training in ethics and finance seemed a good fit for banking," Louise wisecracked.

"Ethics are subjective," he countered.

"Not if you want to pass your college ethics course and certification exams."

"You voted for Ronald Reagan, but still regret doing so. Unlike many Americans, you are intelligent and open to new information and can change when provided convincing evidence. Once your younger self learned that the Republican trope of pulling oneself up by the bootstraps, or the work ethic, were nothing more than ploys to keep the underprivileged in their place you realized that Democrats really do work to make policy to help those less fortunate. You are the proverbial bleeding heart, Louise."

She was getting that burning sensation again. As a rule, she kept her political opinions to herself due to the diversity of clients and colleagues in banking. How did he know her deepest ideologies? There was perhaps a handful of people who knew this level of detail about her. One immediately came to mind, her father.

"Your change in political party has been a bone of contention between your father and you," he continued, as though reading her mind.

Louise chose her words very carefully. Her initial thought was that his job offer was an incredible opportunity. It would put her in a uniquely opportune yet dangerous position.

"If you know all of this about me, then you certainly know that working for a political lobbyist or a corporate spy would be against my principles."

"The Devil's in the details." He noticed the sudden look of recognition in her eyes as Michael's words echoed in her mind. "I just want to hire you for what you are already assigned to do: connecting with the communications director at Monte dei Paschi, Dario Rossellini. He has important information. Only now, you would be paid for it. Handsomely."

"You must also know that, for me, money is the lowest form of motivation."

"This I know," he said. "But I also know the one thing you cannot resist is solving problems. Making connections. Finding the answer."

Wow, this guy was good.

"It depends on the question," Louise said.

"I'll make you a deal. If you succeed in meeting Rossellini and if you gain any intel at all, *and* if you decide it is mutually beneficial for me to have that knowledge in terms of what I will use it for, I will pay you in exchange for the information. If you do not feel I can get the result you want with the information, you have no obligation to give it to me."

"Why don't you tell me what information you're looking for and what you are planning to do with it, and I'll tell you if I'm interested? Or is this a Schrödinger's Cat situation?"[14] *And who's to say that you won't torture me for the information once I get it?*

"I like you," he said, motioning for the bill. "Let me pick you up at your hotel tomorrow evening and take you to dinner."

Of course, he knows where I'm staying, she thought.

"I'm sorry but I have to leave tomorrow morning for the Feast of Assisi. I won't be back until at least October 8th."

Raskalov thought for a moment. "That works for me too. I have a short trip planned. Let's have dinner when you return after the 8th. We are much the same in spirit, Louise." Raskalov was trying to make her an ally. "We both search for clues and make connections. I keep it all right up here." He pointed to his temple. "Just like you."

"But I use my information for good," Louise said.

"No judgment is the way to enlightenment."

"You have an interesting interpretation of enlightenment."

Remembering her date with Francesco whose house was fifteen minutes away she looked at her watch. It was sixteen-forty-five. She made her excuses and got up to leave.

"I'll be in touch," Akari said.

"I look forward to it."

Her internal clock set long ago to banker's hours was still deeply ingrained and she arrived at Francesco's house right on time. The two kitties greeted her outside as she knocked on the front door. Francesco welcomed her inside. His warm prolonged hug reminded her of how much she needed the support of a good friend. He asked her to relax while he fed the animals, but she insisted on helping. She still wore her espadrilles wedges, so he pointed to a row of rubber Hunter boots, and she slipped on a pair her size. The physical exertion of the barnyard chores alleviated some of the pressure of her dangerous mission and its questionable cast of characters. She bonded with the critters and Francesco, his muscular physique and chiseled jawline awakening her animal instincts.

Leaving the menagerie to their meals, they went inside to feed themselves. First things first. Francesco poured a delightful Chianti. Louise enjoyed the scents, flavors and effects, the delicious wine further softening her edges. After a simple repast of spicy tomato and shrimp Fra Diavolo and salad, they relaxed in front of the fire with another glass of wine. Louise couldn't remember the last time she felt so relaxed. He could have his way with her, and he sensed it.

He took her glass and set their drinks down. He placed his hands firmly around her slender waist to easily maneuver her back against the armrest, in the position of dominance. Louise wanted him inside of her, but she took a deep calming breath. Not out of prudishness but more out of practicality, she sat up pushed him back against the sofa and assumed a more dominant position straddling him.

Yes, she wanted him inside of her. But another rule she had picked up from finance, something she called *strategic procrastination*, never fuck within the first week of meeting a man, and even then, think about it. A Vietnam army vet once corroborated her *strategic procrastination* tenet. During his service, he would ignore all incoming *hot requests* for at least one week. If it was important, they would call back several times, quickly. Otherwise, they are just reacting to some random demand from their boss.[15] The analogy was a little off the mark, but the reasoning applied. It was almost always better to delay.

She pressed her torso against his, then took off his glasses and kissed him deeply, feeling his mass against her pelvis making her quake. A hard cock was her kryptonite. She wanted him inside her, but the next best thing was inside her mouth. She might have been in the minority, but she loved giving head. She theorized that her oral fixation came from having been born with her thumb in her mouth. She had sucked her thumb until the third grade.

Wearing a dress gave him easy access. He cupped her and began gently rubbing his thumb side to side over her clitoris, raising her heartrate. She backed away and unzipped his jeans. She got on her knees then nimbly pulled his very lovely cock from his sexy boxers. She grasped it, surprised to discover he was circumcised, which should have been her first clue. Not allowing suspicion to distract her from passion, she took him in deeply, then pressed her tongue against his shaft, easing in and out and in, bringing him to orgasm, almost coming herself. She swallowed, hating to make a mess, then sat up and took a sip of the Chianti, mingling the family vintages. Then he lay back and she lay on his heaving chest. He kissed the top of her head sweetly and they drifted into a kind of ethereal half sleep.

Soft fur brushing her hand gently interrupted her reverie. The purring of the ginger cat mingled with the sound of Francesco's gentle breathing. She got up and helped herself to a glass of Pellegrino from the fridge then sat on the floor to play with the cat. Francesco serenely opened his eyes to see his two friends blissfully snuggling.

She only needed to make eye contact for him to understand it was time for her to leave. He walked her back to the hotel and they kissed good-bye.

Then she snapped right back into work mode, re-energized for her next move.

NINE

Knowing the horseman would be there every morning, Louise prepared a note for LaFontaine and timed her walk to be at the hotel entrance when he arrived. The message was a request for a new meeting on LaFontaine's yacht, this time, off the Adriatic coast since she wouldn't be far during the October 4th festival in Assisi.

Oscar the doorman was at his post when she returned with her daily café latte. Like clockwork, she heard horse hooves on cobblestones. The two rivals had their usual mutually antagonistic interaction. Then Louise shook Giuliani's hand, slipping him the note and he was off. How he got the message to LaFontaine was anybody's guess. It could have been carrier pigeon for all she knew. Louise asked the valet to bring her rental car around and went back to her room to finish packing. As a prominent participant of the festival, Francesco had already left early that morning to prepare his procession, giving her an excuse to take a separate car.

A half hour later, she rolled her small suitcase outside, loaded the car, and drove off toward Assisi. After about an hour she crossed the Tuscan border into the Umbria region, with vistas of the picturesque Lake Trasimeno and its azure waters surrounded by medieval castles and villages, including two islands topped with historic fairytale castles. Another half hour later she arrived at the hermitage where then *Friar* Francis first lived in search of solitude in 1210. As she approached the valley beneath Assisi, the grandiose baroque church of Saint Mary of the Angels soared skyward, like the Emerald City. Louise parked and entered to get first-hand experience of the extraordinary church before reuniting with Francesco in Assisi.

The mega church had been built around the original tiny chapel, which had been given to Friar Francis after he had asked the Pope's permission to start his own order. The juxtaposition, like a nesting doll within the larger church, was magical. Louise followed other visitors into the humble chapel and sat on the ancient pews marveling at the history it represented. Francis had founded the Franciscan Order to reform the decadence of church government, living simply without worldly goods, loving all creatures, a righteous reform that attracted a huge following.

She said a silent prayer of gratitude then got back on the road to Assisi. She checked into the hotel Nun Assisi Relais Spa Museum she had booked with the help of her Siena hotel concierge, Maurizio. The hotel was a brilliant restoration of the Santa Caterina Monastery built in 1275. Her room featured original roman frescos, exposed stone walls and a terrace that overlooked the medieval city and valley below. Louise was excited to learn that this converted monastery had been built on a location that ancient romans had devoted to the worship of water for over 2,000 years and consisted of ancient natural springs, much like her adoptive Burgundy.

She freshened up and set out to explore the historic city. In particular, she wanted to get a better understanding of Saint Francis by visiting the Basilica of St. Francis of Assisi. She meandered, guided only by the tower of the imposing basilica high above in the distance. As she approached, she immediately recognized the iconic religious habits of the Franciscan order worn by Friars headed to or from appointments, their simple brown robes tied with a white rope, reminded her of Jean-Philippe in his full monk cassock.

During her research she had learned that the monks' robes symbolized the tradition of Saint Francis to embrace a life of simple unattached poverty, as well as the destitution of the peasants who the Franciscans served in the 13th century. The robes of the Franciscan monks were made of cloth or old clothing donated by those same peasants who always wore undyed brown, the least expensive fabric of the time. Also, the simple corded rope known as a *cinture* worn around the waist had three knots symbolizing Poverty, Chastity, and Obedience, the three cornerstones of the Franciscan Order.

Whether it was Francesco's kindness and compassion, or the storybook church containing the tiny chapel, or the Medieval time capsule of the entire region, the Franciscan Order was having an immediate and profound effect on Louise, more than any other religion she had encountered throughout her life, despite having been influenced by Christian faiths of every denomination, starting with her own Catholic mother.

Until now, Louise had been more inclined spiritually toward Buddhism or agnostic spirituality. For her, anyone who believed they *knew* for certain the *one true God*, revealed their own arrogance, or a blind faith, which she was not ashamed to admit she lacked. Perhaps she was captivated by the Franciscan Order because she too had shunned the pursuit of material wealth.

She acknowledged the irony of having accumulated some wealth of her own. Although, she had always used her money for good, donating generously to important causes, investing it in the restoration of her historic Burgundy home, or the Tiki Bar that she had gifted to her friend and protector, Big Steve. She always donated generously to the arts and education. Of course, her work uncovering corruption in banking was done for the sake of justice, certainly not for money. Strangely, it seemed the more she gave away, the more she received.

"Saint Francis' miraculous history is well-known."

Jolted from her thoughts, Louise realized she had made her way to Basilica of St. Francis of Assisi and was standing inside the entrance. The voice spoke in English and reverberated throughout the church. She noticed a sign in the entrance, *Daily Services in English*. She saw the Minister General at the pulpit who continued his sermon:

"He had been known for his love of the Eucharist and of all living creatures. In 1223, Francis arranged for the first live Christmas nativity scene and thus Francis had become associated with the patronage of animals and the natural environment. It became a tradition for churches to hold ceremonies blessing animals on his feast day of October 4th. St. Francis then returned to the mountain of La Verna, now known as Mount Penna in Tuscany, a very lonely and savage place, good for someone wanting to do penance and live a life away from people. He had come for a forty-day fast in preparation of the Michaelmas.

"When he arrived on September 14, 1224, he was received by a multitude of singing birds that surrounded St. Francis, perching on his shoulders, on his arms, at his feet. While praying on the mountainside during the Feast of the Exaltation of the Cross, he had a vision of a seraphim and received the stigmata. He began to develop nails of hardened flesh which protruded from his hands and feet. He also began to form a wound in his side like that of Christ. Fellow Friar Leo, who was with Francis at the time, provided the first ever docu-

mented witness account of the phenomenon of stigmata. Saint Francis would be the second person, after St. Paul, to bear the wounds of Christ's Passion.

"But Francis suffered from the stigmata and a painful trachoma caused him to go blind. He received care in Siena to no avail. He was brought back here, where the Franciscan movement had begun, and feeling that the end of his life was approaching, Francis spent his final days dictating his spiritual testament. He died on the evening of Saturday, 3 October 1226, singing Psalm 141, Voce mea ad Dominum."

On cue, an operatic voice rang out, singing "Voce mea ad Dominum". A chorus of friars joined in stunning harmony. Louise was overcome with emotion hearing the singing friars. She moved closer approaching from the outer aisle so as not to disrupt the gathering. The song ended, and the audience burst into thunderous applause. When the clamor dissipated, the friar spoke, addressing the soloist.

"Thank you, Friar Alessandro." He turned to the parishioners. "We are blessed with the voice of the world renowned *Singing Friar* today. What a beautiful gift to this congregation."

The Singing Friar bowed to his fellow choir members and Louise noticed Francesco among them! The friars all took their seats for the remainder of the sermon. Louise sat at the end of the pew to wait for Francesco and listened to the rest of the Minister's sermon:

"Given the fame of Saint Francis and his miracles, Pope Gregory IX ordered his beatification and the building of a church in his honor. Simone di Pucciarello donated the land for the church, a hill at the west side of Assisi, known as the Hill of Hell, where previously criminals were put to death. Afterward, the hill became known as the Hill of Paradise. Francis would appreciate the renaming.

"On July 16, 1228, Francis was canonized by Pope Gregory IX, who laid the foundation stone of the new church the following day. Since the construction had begun at his order, the Pope declared the church to be the property of the Papacy and thus a Papal Basilica. The remains of Saint Francis were brought in a solemn procession to the Lower Basilica from its temporary burial place in the church of St. George, on Pentecost day May 25th, 1230."

Louise gasped loudly at the mention of her birthday, drawing the eyes of several in attendance, including Francesco, who realized for the first time she was there. He grinned at her, then turned and whispered something to the Singing Friar Alessandro who nodded serenely toward Louise. Even from afar, the Singing Friar appeared to have a childlike purity.

The Minister concluded the sermon, oblivious to their interaction.

"The basilica was designated a pilgrimage site eligible for the same graces and honor as a papal pilgrimage to the Holy Land. That was a radical change and served to highlight the esteem with which Francis was held."

"On the eve of the Feast of Saint Francis tomorrow October 4th, we honor this basilica, built into the side of a hill comprising two churches known as the Upper Church and the Lower Church, and a crypt where the remains of St. Francis are interred."

He made the sign of the cross and the friars crossed themselves. *"Let us pray to this sacred ground."*

Louise knelt and closed her eyes as the Father gave a blessing in Latin.

"Un angelo sulla terra."

There was no mistaking his voice. Louise lifted her eyes and saw Francesco silhouetted in the light from the stained-glass window, like Saint Francis. He knelt next to her until the end of the service, then exchanged cheek kisses.

"Ciao, Louise!" he whispered excitedly.

They rose and walked outside with the crowd of parishioners. Once they were away from church, he stopped and kissed her on the lips. Melting to his touch, she realized he was being respectful leaving the church before expressing his affection for her, which turned her on even more. These were the moments when Louise cursed her life as a spy. She promised herself to retire forever if she survived this latest case.

"Sono così felice che tu sia venuto."

"I'm happy I came too," Louise replied in Italian. *"I made a promise,"* she added, which felt like a wedding vow.

"Andiamo." He led her down a few twisty cobblestone streets until she wasn't sure she would have been able to find her way back. But the journey was so enchanting she didn't care. Finally, they stopped at Il Frantoio, a restaurant with a terrace overlooking the valley and some of the best food Louise had ever eaten. Francesco ordered a local organic wine and appetizers. They toasted and chatted. Louise felt she was speaking in tongues, sometimes finding words she had no idea she even knew. In addition to the intensive training at Langley, she had spent many years with Michael whose maternal language was Italian, and she had spent much time with his family, so Italian might have been more engrained than she realized. Whatever the reason, Louise had never felt so in her element. Francesco's tongue had loosened a bit too. He was excited about rumors that the first pope ever was considering taking the name of Saint Francis in 2013. It felt like there was magic in the air.

After two hours of playful conversation and laughter, they headed back to the hotel. The mystical surroundings, and the unpredictably winding old roads notwithstanding, Louise realized that Francesco had taken her on a circuitous route back to the hotel. He had used *evasive tactics*. That combined with Francesco recognizing Akari Raskalov in the French newspaper, she looked him in the eyes and understood that he knew that she knew that he knew. If he wasn't a trained spy, he was involved in the case somehow.

Unconsciously she had also been checking for anyone following them and concluded that Akari Raskalov had not kept someone tailing her, which in some ways alarmed her. But, for now, she would throw caution to the wind and enjoy the simple life and experience the Feast of Saint Francis of Assisi.

"Buona notte, bellissima," Francesco said, giving her cheek kisses. "Dormi bene."

Louise checked her watch, it was only 17:00, too early to say good night. But he explained that procession started before dawn, so he needed to go to bed early and be up by three o'clock.

"Capisco," Louise said. Exhausted from the drive and the day of exploration, she was tired too. They kissed good night and she went to her room and fell asleep.

᪥

Assisi, Italy, October 4, 2012

The sound of gentle knocking and her name being whispered made Louise stir. She opened her eyes to inky darkness with no idea where she was. *Who she was?* Awaking from a deep sleep was like being thrust into existence from the womb with no self-awareness before that moment. Then, reality came roaring back. She listened carefully and was relieved to recognize Francesco's voice. The clock said four o'clock and she groggily rose from the comfortable bed. She flipped on the light and opened the door.

"Buongiorno bella ragazza," Francesco said with a disarming smile. He wore what appeared to be traditional folk attire, a light-blue long-sleeved shirt over dark blue pants and a white scarf tied around his neck.

They exchanged cheek kisses and Louise invited him in with a wave. Her mind wasn't quite alert enough to conjure Italian words, so she gestured toward the Nespresso machine. As he prepared her coffee, she took clothes from the closet and went to the bathroom to get ready. She emerged refreshed, wearing jeans with a cashmere sweater over a loose cotton blouse. Francesco handed her a café latte in a paper cup, and she slipped on her Doc Martens.

"Andiamo alla Festa!"

They walked a few blocks, arriving as dawn illuminated what appeared to be the entire town wearing authentic medieval garb assembled near the steps of the 14th-century city hall. Regal banners of royal blue and red hung from all the buildings. Francesco kissed her cheek and told her to *look for the animals at the end* and left to make final preparations for his exhibit.

After a moment, the mile-long pageant began. Flanked by police officers, the mayor of Assisi solemnly led the procession to the Tomb of Saint Francis, accompanied by the mayor of Friuli Venezia Giulia, the Italian region bordering Austria, Slovenia, and the Adriatic, who would offer the traditional annual oil for the lamp at the entrance of the tomb. They were followed by town's children singing the *Canticle of the Creatures*, a religious song composed by Saint Francis. Then trumpeters playing Assisi's Anthem. Finally, the children's medieval drum corps dressed in bright medieval tunics and scarves of Assisi colors played their music for Saint Francis and then Francesco's live nativity scene. A local couple and their child dressed in nativity costumes walked the baby goat and the baby donkey. They followed the bearers carrying the statue depicting a friar comforting Christ on the crucifix, led by robed friars reciting prayers using a microphone while aids carried speakers for all to hear.

A tiger-orange sunrise silhouetted the ancient village and gradually revealed the morning fog, painting a mystical setting. The procession arrived at its destination for the final ceremony. Two cathedrals built into the side of a hill comprised the Upper and Lower Basilicas. The lower, completed in 1230, contains the crypt where the remains of St. Francis were interred. Next to the Basilicas is the Sacro Convento Friary, with the entire complex towering over the valley below like a fortress. The Minister General made the sign of the cross and the congregation followed.

"Let us pray to this sacred ground."

Louise had quickly researched Assisi in preparation for the trip. She took this moment to furtively observe the Friary that houses a vast library of medieval documents, codices, and incunables. It also has a museum with works of art donated by pilgrims through the centuries, as well as a valuable pieces from the Perkins' art collection. Louise wondered if the treasures were the reason for the police presence. But the entire congregation seemed devoted to the preserving and honoring the past, and she couldn't imagine nefarious forces among them.

The feast that followed was just that, in every way imaginable and tangible. Francesco's live nativity converted to a petting zoo delighting the children who had so fearlessly partaken in the solemn ritual at the tomb. The festivities with a cornucopia of food and libations served by townspeople in full traditional dress continued into the evening.

Francesco placed his animals safely back in their temporary stables for safe transport home, then accompanied Louise back to her hotel. They spent time in the spa decompressing in the healing waters. The ancient pool beneath the hotel was nestled between six limestone pillars of the first century A.D. The spa featured a circuit of four separate bathing rooms with varying temperatures and humidity.

Wholly spent, they adjourned to her suite and capped the night off with champagne. The look that Francesco gave her with the cherubs of the fresco presiding over them sent her into a higher realm of sentience. His mere touch gave her frissons as he undid her robe and she lay back. He reached around, placing his hands on her lower back, arching her to him. He softly took her nipple in his mouth, almost bringing her to orgasm. When they had finished, they were completely drained and fell asleep in each other's arms.

Louise hadn't thought it possible to feel this way about another man. But at the same time, she knew from the start that he was the kind of very traditional man that she could never be betrothed to. His would be a marriage to a local fair maiden of similar background. Louise was a Ruby Tuesday. Adrift on existential waves. She was convinced there was not a man on earth that could anchor her. She took comfort in the words of Buddhist monk, Thích Nhất Hạnh.

The wave does not have to die in order to become water. She is water.

Louise had divulged to her mother that she thought she could never love again. We are only allowed one true love and she had already had two, Michael and Jean-Philippe. Mary replied that Louise had already lived several lives in vastly different worlds and therefore the odds were that she could find a true love for *each* of those lives.

In the morning, Francesco had to leave early for the final Festival of Fire. Louise had to decline participating although it sounded like it would be epic. But she needed to get back to her secret life as a spy. He kissed her with the same sweet passion as the night before and was gone.

Being in Assisi, Louise was only 75 miles from the port city of Civitanova Marche on the Adriatic. It was an easy cruise for LaFontaine, who had navigated to Greece, according to a secret note received from the horseman the morning after she returned from their last cruise.

Louise drove her car east, arriving at the Adriatic in one-and-a-half hours. Not expecting such stunning azure waters and enticing beaches, she was reminded of her friend and protector Big Steve on her private island hideaway. Enjoying the view, she waited on the dock until the massive vessel maneuvered to a mooring and a Zodiac retrieved her.

Once aboard LaFontaine's yacht, Louise felt a sense of returning home safe. With the wind in her hair and Caterpillar C18 engines under the hull, Louise was back in her element. She had always loved the sea. In this case, the Adriatic en route to the Ionian. The max speed of 16 knots for that length vessel was impressive. It was an 85-foot motor yacht that looked like something out of a James Bond film. In fact, LaFontaine had christened it *Vague-A-Bond,* which was a multi-pronged play on words. Not only was it phonetically identical to the English word *vagabond*, but also *vague* meant *wave* in French, *à bond* meant leaping or surging, and *Bond* as in James Bond. The vessel had a powerful military-like exterior, suggesting superior mechanical capabilities, while providing sumptuous decks and interiors.[16]

They set out to sea and once at a distance from the coast and mobile signals, they sat by the fire, and Louise told LaFontaine and Charlie the news.

"Akari Raskalov offered me a job."

A deckhand poured champagne for Louise and Frédéric. Charlie sipped his gin and tonic, one ice cube, in a tall glass.

"Double agent?" Charlie guessed.

"Financial consultant?" LaFontaine speculated.

Louise shook her head no. "Both. Sort of a banking confidential informant."

Without hesitation LaFontaine said, "This is an opportunity of a lifetime. It would dovetail with your connections to Dario Rossellini."

"Dario Rossellini is precisely who Raskalov wants me to inform on."

"We should stick with your angle as an international financial consultant," LaFontaine said, still not aware of Louise's history with Rossellini, which she hadn't disclosed yet. "With your stellar reputation in finance, no one will question your motives. My idea is to give you paying client in search of entry into the derivatives market."

"It's a pleasure discussing the esoteric world of finance with you, Frédéric. There's no need to simplify complicated terminology or explain debits and credits."

"Finance was the first of my many careers," LaFontaine said.

"Is this where I go for a swim?" Charlie said.

"Sorry, Charlie. We'll talk slowly," Louise teased.

"Don't bother," Charlie said, sipping his drink, leaning back, and turning his face up toward the sun. "I'll absorb the information like my vitamin D, by osmosis."

"Let me get this straight, Frédéric. You're suggesting I pose as the consultant of a wealthy offshore investor looking to buy high-risk derivatives through the oldest bank in the world, which is practically defunct?"

LaFontaine let out a booming guffaw. It had been a while since she'd heard it and Louise was beginning to think nothing would make him laugh again.

"Nothing gets by you, Lulu." He beamed with pride at his protégée.

"You are correct. When you put it that way, someone wanting to get into derivatives with MPS would be highly suspicious at this point. But I thought of that and have an idea. Your offshore investor has a passion for horse racing and has become obsessed with the Palio Horserace. He wants to buy his way into the race in time for next year."

"He sounds perfectly deplorable."

"Or deplorably perfect," Charlie said.

"Exactly," LaFontaine concurred. "The perfect red herring."

"Let me guess. You have an actual person in mind."

"My psychic beauty, the Adriatic is the perfect place for you. Cyprus is where Aphrodite was born. In Greek, *aphro* means foam, as in sea foam, and *dite* means birth."

"The goddess of love was born from sea foam?" Louise pondered this. "That is ontologically brilliant," she concluded.

"N'est-ce pas?" LaFontaine replied. "And we are headed to meet your deplorable racehorse lover from Cyprus shortly. He will go back to Siena with you."

"Wait, didn't you introduce me in Siena as an anti-Palio Race activist?"

"That was just confidential buzz to get word out to Akari Raskalov of your arrival. Now that you have made contact, you can move on to the next phase. My Cyprian friend has enough legitimate wealth that Rossellini will be chomping at the bit to meet with you both."

Louise rolled her eyes at his fabulous pun. "Isn't Cyprus 3,000 miles from here? I need to get back to Siena as soon as possible to reunite with Raskalov."

"We're only going as far as Corfu where he has a place. If we cruise all night, we'll be there before sunrise and you'll both be back in Siena by noon the next day. After you make contact, your new *client* will then fly back home from Siena."

"I've been wanting to go to Corfu and the outer Greek islands for a long time," Louise said. "I'm excited to finally see the west coast of Greece, even if only for a few minutes."

"If I had known I would have taken you before!"

"This worked out perfectly," Louise said, always the optimist. "I still want to come back and explore someday. Did I ever tell you that I found a mysterious manuscript that has clues to where the Lost City of Atlantis is located? I think it suggests Atlantis was near Greece."

"It's more likely off the coast of Morocco," Charlie said.

"Really?" Louise said. "Well, I'd still like to come back and explore ancient Greece."

"Why not both?" LaFontaine laughed. "You can soon retire and live a life of leisure."

"After this job, that's my plan. I'm too old for this."

The hours flew by as they cruised down the Adriatic, reviewing details of the case.

"What should I be looking for when I meet Dario Rossellini?" Louise asked.

"You'll want to gauge his response to certain questions. My sources confirm that there is a serious internal cover up of illegal banking practices related to Deutsch Bank. It is expected that Monte dei Paschi is hiding losses incurred since the 2008 financial crisis. I'm not sure how yet, but you must expose the fraud going on there."

"How can I possibly gain access to their records?"

"You'll find a way as you always do," LaFontaine asserted. "Of course, I will give you a secret weapon."

Louise smiled. "You're my own personal Q from James Bond. What is it?"

LaFontaine checked his watch. "It's late, and we're all exhausted from the long strategizing session. Get some sleep and you will see in the morning."

The bellow of the foghorn and the caw of seagulls, along with the gentle rocking of the yacht decelerating into the harbor woke Louise. She sat up and stretched, the vertebrae of her spine cracking in satisfying succession. She rubbed her scalp then groggily looked out of the large porthole. The sunrise glistened on tranquil water that reflected the spire-shaped island of Palaiokastritsa, Corfu. The vessel cruised past the picturesque Monastery of Virgin Mary. She felt like Cleopatra invading the peaceful inhabitants who had lived undisturbed for centuries. They dropped anchor in the Bay of Ampelaki with a view of the Corfu Aquarium. Louise dressed and went above deck to meet Frédéric and Charlie for breakfast.

"Good morning. Aren't we docking to pick up your friend?" Louise asked.

"It's too shallow to dock so he is arriving by tender," Frédéric explained.

A gentle breeze tousled Louise's hair as she sipped a delicious café au lait and munched a fresh baguette with jam. The sudden roar of an engine broke the peaceful serenity as a 1,350 horsepower Mercedes-Benz SLS AMG Cigarette Boat zoomed up portside.

"Some *tender*," Louise snarked.

"The guy knows how to make an entrance," Charlie said.

LaFontaine laughed.

The Cypriot stepped spryly onto the Baja deck of the Vague-A-Bond, and they all gathered for a meet-and-greet.

"Kostas, my old friend! It's so great to see you." LaFontaine and Kostas hugged like brothers who hadn't seen each other since childhood. "Louise, Charlie, meet Kostas Ioannou."

Louise was taken aback. If LaFontaine had captivating blue eyes, Kostas had the greenest eyes she had ever seen. She didn't even know that eye color existed and wondered if he wore colored contact lenses but doubted it. She could tell from his demeanor this guy didn't waste time on vanity, sharing LaFontaine's ageless grace and comfortable but elegant taste in attire. It must come with the mysterious wealth.

"Louise, so happy to finally meet you. I feel like I already know you." Kostas kissed her cheeks.

"I feel like I already like you!" Louise said, covering for having only heard of him the day before. The yacht turned 180 degrees to head back up the coast of Italy and they spent the time relaxing and getting to know one another better. At sunset, they gathered around the fire for drinks and the conversation really took off.

"Kostas, how did you and Frédéric meet?" Louise asked.

"Alas, that is not my place to answer. You'll have to ask him that one."

From the look in Frédéric's eyes and lack of laughter, she moved on to another subject.

"Okay, I was trying to give you a softball question. But here's my real question. Why did Frédéric enlist you of all people to help me infiltrate Monte dei Paschi?"

"Frédéric warned me that you don't waste time."

"Well, I'm a very nosy kitty cat," she said, paraphrasing a line from the movie *Chinatown*. "Is there any special connection?"

"This will all come out eventually and it's really no secret. But my stock brokerage fund is heavily involved with Deutsch Bank money laundering scheme for Russia. My presence at your meeting with Dario Rossellini is intended to stir the pot."

Louise chose her words carefully, stalling for time to think. "Did you just admit to being involved in a money laundering scheme with Deutsch Bank?"

"Let me clarify. Technically, it isn't illegal."

"Go on."

"This is where I make my exit," Charlie said. "Good night, dear friends." They bid him good night.

"I'd like to hear this," Frédéric said, refilling their champagne glasses.

"Please, go on, Kostas. I'm taking mental notes."

"Well, for the past two years or so, every weekday morning, I receive a call from the equities desk of Deutsche Bank's Moscow headquarters from a young woman named Dina Maksutova, with an order to sell blue-chip Russian stock, usually equal to about 10 million US dollars, on behalf of my Russian client with a company based in Cyprus."

"Your stock brokerage firm is in Cyprus, so your client's company is offshore?"

"Exactly. Anyway, I sell this 10 million worth of Russian stock on the London market, in exchange for dollars, pounds, or Euros, knowing full well that, Dina Maksutova of Deutsche Bank has just fulfilled another *buy* order of the same stock in the same quantity, but with Russian rubles, on behalf of a different Russian company."

"Let me guess, the two companies are owned by the same person, your Russian client."

"Bingo, as you Americans like to say."

"That's textbook money laundering. So unimaginative, so blatant," Louise seethed.

"And very legal. It's called *mirror trading*. The Deutsch Bank mirror-trades are linked to a much larger capital flight practice nicknamed the *Moldovan Scheme*. It started in 2010 basically as a series of fake loans and debt agreements with UK-based companies to funnel billions out of Russia, routed through Moldova to a Latvian bank, hence the name. The Russian bank, Promsberbank, shareholders included Igor Putin, the cousin of the Russian President. It has nothing to do with making profits. It's about expatriating money."

"A nice way of saying money laundering," Louise said. "Like the Faraday Shields of Medieval alchemists. They worked hard to change metal into gold, which they never achieved. But the many discoveries in the process were even more precious than gold. In the case of money laundering, the magic of making dirty money in Russia disappear and reappear in another country in same amount but a different currency still owned by the same entity."

"Konvert in Russian," Kostas said.

"Konvert..." Louise repeated thoughtfully. "The Russian word for *envelope*."

"It's also the Russian word for *mirror trading*. That's why they need a broker, like me, to handle the deal," Kostas said. "It gives the appearance of legitimate simultaneous trades. It's risky though. Repeated trades are a clear indication of an effort to hide dirty money. And yet, billions of dollars have been funneled out of Russia this way."

"If Russia is trying to rebuild as a world power, why continue these illegitimate schemes?" Louise asked.

"The bigger question is why is Deutsche Bank helping them to do it?"

Louise nodded. "Deutsche Bank has a horrible past helping dictators. As Bogart's character Rick Blaine said in Casablanca, to the Deutsche Bank official trying to get into the casino. *Your cash is good at the bar. You're lucky the bar is open to you.*"

"He was probably snubbing Deutsche Bank for purchasing gold stolen from the Jewish people to help Hitler," Kostas said. "Your ability to make connections is excellent, Louise. Frédéric told me that you were manipulated into working for BCCI by your father."

That stung, but it was true. Now her father was once again forcing her into a dangerous job, albeit indirectly. "Well, as they say in the United States, fool me once shame on you..."

"We won't be fooled again." Kostas' reference to The Who lyric made her smile.

"Has your firm ever fallen under scrutiny from U.S. officials?" Louise asked.

"Yes. That's why I'm getting ahead of this *mirror trading* scandal. Cyprus may be an offshore territory, but we do business legally and despise being manipulated by criminals. Frontrunning, otherwise known as insider trading, which was legal in Russian until 2011, was considered a legitimate way to supplement one's income. Those have been replaced by over-the-counter trades and mirror-trades, just two examples of the thousands of tactics used by businesses with the help of brokers."

"More alchemy," Louise said. "I'll never understand why a broker would risk his integrity for money."

Kostas laughed. "Their *integrity* is not sold cheap. Before the 2008 global economic crash, Deutsche Bank Moscow traders were making two or three times more than their counterparts in London and New York. Clients are willing to pay handsomely for these questionable trades. The client is the architect of the scheme, and it is worth it to bribe someone inside the bank for the profits. Once the broker is hooked, he can be manipulated. They are not the criminal geniuses. Rather, they are more like the patsies."

Louise was impressed with Kostas' grasp of English. His vocabulary and use of idioms were extensive and he only had a soupcon of a Greek accent.

"Well, thank you both for your insights." Louise gave Frédéric cheek kisses, then Kostas. "I looked forward to working with you, Kostas. Goodnight."

Louise headed for bed, leaving the two men to further discuss their world dominance.

The next morning, they docked at Civitanova Marche, got their land legs, and bid farewell with handshakes and cheek kisses.

"It's like a movie scene. Two heroes walking off on a new adventure," LaFontaine said.

"We'll round up the usual suspects," she said.

With a glimmer in his eye, LaFontaine replied, "Louise, I think this is the beginning of a beautiful friendship…for all of us."

Louise and Kostas got in the car and drove off toward Siena.

TEN

On the drive, Louise wasted no time prying. "What is the name of your fund?"

Kostas gazed into the passenger side rearview mirror. "Hellenic Bank."

Louise raised her eyebrows. "I know this bank. It has a good reputation. It is a very recognizable and respected Cyprus bank." She had now come full circle. While working at BCCI, one of her wealthy clients used an offshore account at Hellenic Bank. She had not yet disclosed that the client was Dario Rossellini. *This is getting interesting*, she thought.

"Yes, as CEO and founder, I take pride in our reputation," Kostas said. "We were duped by a ring of greedy, power-hungry animals." His anger was palpable, who could blame him?

Louise avoided discussing her past relationship with Rossellini for now and just nodded, eyes always moving, watching the road ahead, side, rearview, while listening intently. When she drove, she was always on high alert, going into the left lane only to pass, a habit she had formed driving in France, *defensive aggressive*. She quickly approached a slower car ahead and flipped on her right turn signal, coasted left into the passing lane then sped past and moved back into the right lane. It was an odd custom to use the right turn signal to pass on the left, but she had embraced it. Kostas seemed unfazed by her driving style.

"The *Moldovan Scheme* you mentioned that started as a debt scam," Louise said. "Was that used by Deutsche Bank on Monte dei Pasci?"

"No, the Moldovan Scheme is also known as The Russian Laundromat," Kostas replied. "It involved moving billions in *real* currency out of Russia through payments of *fake* loans in a carousel borrowing scheme, whereby loans at one bank were paid off with loans from another."

"What kind of scam do you think happened at MPS?"

"It's likely refinancing bad investments with even worse derivative stock, for which Deutsche Bank charges a hefty fee."

"Do you think Rossellini was involved?"

"Rossellini is probably just another patsy, like me. Or worse, he's being coerced and exploited," Kostas replied.

After a couple hours, Louise merged onto the exit for Siena city limits and arrived at the Grand Hotel Continental a few minutes later. Kostas had reserved a suite and checked in.

"I'll leave you to settle in and we can regroup for dinner if that's okay," Louise said. "I'll ask Maurizio to reserve a table for us at the hotel restaurant Sapordivino for 20:00."

"Perfect."

Louise went to her room, to rest and meditate on a strategy. There were so many meetings she needed to organize but wasn't sure where to begin. How would Akari Raskalov know she was back in Siena? He would find her, but how would she make her return public? She decided that Monday morning she would walk to Monte dei Paschi Bank and try to schedule a meeting with Dario Rossellini in person.

For now, she did yoga to readjust her chakras after the many trips by car and boat, then meditated and freshened up for dinner.

The server uncorked a bottle of Chianti, Louise smiled to herself noticing the label to be that of Francesco's family Ricasoli. The wine poured like a burgundy ribbon into her glass.

"You look pensive," Kostas said, breaking into her thoughts.

She picked up the glass by the stem and swirled, observing the rich 'legs' flowing down the inside of the glass. She stuck her nose in and breathed in the cherry notes. Kostas performed a similar ritual then they clinked glasses and sipped. It was dry, light-bodied, and very drinkable. Louise savored the flavors before replying.

"It was a long week," she finally said. "I'm trying to step back and reset for connecting with Rossellini."

Now it was his turn to look pensive. Then his expression brightened. "At least we have time to strategize over the weekend."

"Good point, tomorrow being Sunday gives us a little breathing room. Have you stayed at this hotel before? It's important that we stay off the

Internet, but they have an impressive library here with centuries of historical archives and an extensive periodicals section."

"I was here long ago." His voice trailed off, then he breathed deeply. "Tonight, let's relax and enjoy some delicious dinner and conversation. Tomorrow we'll dive into the case."

Louise furtively scanned the room and sensed no ominous presence. "Cheers to that." During the quiet meal Kostas went into detail about his home country of Cyprus. "It sounds magical," Louise said.

"You must come visit. It would be my honor to give you a tour of my favorite places."

"Thank you, I'll take you up on that generous offer someday."

"It's a deal."

Louise finished her chamomile tea. "Well, I'm exhausted. See you in the morning?"

"Yes, I'll meet you for coffee in the library. Is nine too early?"

"That will be fine." They exchanged cheek kisses and went their separate ways.

Louise rarely slept past six in the morning. By eight o'clock she had already done her morning yoga meditation and went out for her favorite café latte from the little coffee bar next to the hotel. Maurizio was at the front desk and let her into the library making her wonder if the omnipresent concierge lived on the premises with a monitor aimed at the lobby to notify him of guests. She entered the library and asked him to show Kostas in as soon as he came down.

Her new modus operandi when she entered the crammed library was to pause and absorb the energy. It freed her mind and summoned the information to her instead of seeking it out. In college, her friend, a stunning dead-ringer for Mariel Hemingway who was a few years younger, was overly eager to pursue any potential beau and always made the first move, ending up chasing him off instead. Louise convinced her to remain still and let them come to her. The result was one beau after another approached her. It was hardly a fitting analogy, but the concept of not trying too hard seemed to work with solving problems too.

As she stood taking in the library's Mana,[17] Louise had not expected to be approached by the *Master of the Dark Arts* himself. He didn't so much approach as suddenly materialize in her peripheral vision from behind a bookshelf. *Did Maurizio let him in?* He took a seat at one end of the large reading table that had reading lamps every few feet. She began browsing the bookshelves, slowly making her way over to him. She plucked a book from a shelf and sat across from him at the opposite end of the table and turned on one of the lamps.

"Fancy meeting you here," Louise said. She opened the book and pretended to read.

"Did you enjoy your trip on the Adriatic?"

"Very much. It was enchanting, full of mystery. The best-kept-secret for vacationers."

"Indeed, it's one of my favorite places to disappear."

Louise remained aloof like random strangers in case someone entered. "Are you looking for some light reading? Or would you like me to recommend a book to help you sleep?"

"I sleep very well, thank you."

Cold as ice, Louise thought. His callousness was revolting. But pulling from her spy training at Langley, she took a breath and tempered her judgment.

"How was your trip?" she asked. His intense expression was at once surprising and encouraging. She sensed he was under pressure, vulnerable, not the smug persona he had portrayed at their last meeting. She refused to blink, remaining silent until he spoke. Finally, he looked at his watch. "Eight-forty-five." Clearly, he knew Kostas would be there shortly.

He rose and pretended to leaf through a periodical. Then he spoke pointedly. "Ms. Moscow, now that you are back in Siena, please move about freely. Don't be concerned about me. If there's anything you can help me with, I'll be sure to let you know. For now, just go about your life as though I *didn't exist*. That will be best for both of us."

Louise raised an eyebrow but remained impassive. Then she heard the key in the door and turned to see Maurizio letting Kostas into the library. She turned back to Raskalov, but he had disappeared. *Maybe Maurizio had not let him in.*

Louise stood and smiled. "Good morning, Kostas."

They exchanged cheek kisses and sat at the table where Raskalov had just been sitting. Her intuition told her that, for now, she could take Akari

Raskalov at his word and pretend he *didn't exist.* But she had paid her tuition for that intuition, attentively honing her skills, a lifetime of obsessing over details, connecting the dots, keeping her mind and senses sharp. It was now her superpower. She felt she could let her guard down, trust those with whom she had already established relationships, Francesco, Maurizio, and Kostas.

"Did you sleep well?" Kostas asked.

"Like clockwork," Louise replied. "After falling asleep quickly, I woke up seven hours later and did my morning routine, yoga, Tai Chi, and meditation."

"Excellent practice." Kostas sounded sincere. He struck her as a man of few words with vast experience and wisdom to impart. In contrast to LaFontaine, who was bubbly and talkative, Kostas had a subdued equanimity, a Zen master.

"Well, where should we begin?" Louise asked, taking two notepads and two pens out of her bag and handing one of each to Kostas.

He raised his eyebrows. "You came prepared."

"Always."

"Let's begin with a quick review," Kostas said quietly. "The trouble began when Monte dei Paschi Bank went public on the Italian Stock Exchange in June 1999. Up until that point, the bank had been *Paschi Bank* mostly involved in agriculture and local cultural Tuscan programs."

"*Paschi* is from the Italian word *pascoli* meaning pastures," Louise said. "Referring to the pastures of the *Maremma,* or marsh lands, which made up most of Tuscany, until it was farmed by cattle herders called *butteri.* The original wild, wild west *cowboys.*"

"You have a passion for making connections," Kostas said. "You like to understand everything around you. That is why you are so good at numbers."

"True. I don't like when things don't add up." Louise thought for a moment. "So, my idea was to introduce you to Dario Rossellini as a Cyprian banker looking to partner on a marketing campaign. Not only as a banker, but also as an ambassador for Cyprus, to attract tourism. Using the horseman and pastoral scenes of the Maremma and the Palio horseraces, mirroring them with similar scenes of Cyprus that you described to me at dinner last night." Louise took the notepad and wrote. "The log line could be...oh, I don't know...*Go East Young Man*, like a play on the old saying, *Go*

West Young Man, because Cyprus is *east*. It also harkens back to the old world of Monte dei Paschi. It could even use cinematography reminiscent of the great Italian spaghetti westerns starring Clint Eastwood of Sergio Leone."

Kosta tilted his head. "That's actually a great idea for a real marketing campaign. I often collaborate with the Cyprus government on tourism."

"Even better!" Louise said. "We definitely have *The Good, The Bad and The Ugly* out for *A Fist Full of Dollars*." Kostas smiled graciously at her joke. "We could use this to get a foot in the door with Rossellini. But, once we have him interested, what do we do?"

"I'm sure this will get Rossellini to invite us to dinner, which will give us the opportunity to gain insider information about what's really going on with MPS."

"Like *The Moldovan Scheme?*" Louise asked.

"Yes, but in this case, *The Deutsche Bank Derivatives Scheme*," Kostas clarified.

"Can you explain that?" Louise asked, holding her pen to paper to take notes.

"After going public in June 1999, MPS began aggressively expanding in all banking sectors, opening over 2,000 branches. The financing for that expansion was done through risky derivatives underwritten by Deutsche Bank. Frédéric told me to try to find the real nature of those derivative contracts might be."

"Then we'd better get started."

They delved into periodicals and books going back decades trying to uncover anything that might be relevant within the history of MPS, taking copious notes, stopping only for lunch and tea. Like a woman shopping for that one-of-a-kind piece of clothing, Louise searched every corner for that special treasure, patiently trying everything that looked promising, *you never know until you try it.* Louise let her eyes wander across the historical books in case anything jumped out. If something looked hidden or was shoved back, she scrabbled in and scrutinized it. That was how she came across an intriguing book about Monte dei Paschi Bank di Siena. It dated from the fourteen-hundreds but was in Italian. In the interest of time, she decided to *borrow* the book and ask Francesco to help translate it for her. She wrapped the book in her silk Hermes scarf and placed it into her purse without Kostas noticing.

"Let's take a break for today," Louise said. "Shall we meet for dinner?"

"That sounds fine," Kostas replied.

In addition to the ancient book, Louise had also found one of her favorite novels, *The Italian*, by Anne Radcliff as light reading in the local language to build her vocabulary. She went down to the concierge and discretely showed Maurizio the books in her bag.

"Ciao, Maurizio." Then she whispered in English for added privacy, "Is it okay if I borrow these two books for a couple days? I promise to take great care of them."

His eyes widened in fascination at the ancient book. "Secondo." He walked into the office and returned with a small box. "May I?"

"Of course." She handed him the 15th century book.

"Where did you find this?" he asked, turning the book over in his hands and admiring it.

"It was pushed back on the shelf in the historical archives."

"Incredible." He opened the box and placed the book inside where it fit perfectly. "This has a special lining and will protect the book."

"Oh, thank you. I'd like to have Francesco translate some of it for me."

"Certo. Francesco is a good guy. Please give him my best."

"Okay, I will. Ciao. Arrivederci."

It was late afternoon, feeding time for the animals, so Louise decided to visit Francesco. It was unlike her to contact any man unprompted. Her number one rule was *never contact a man unless he calls first*. But Francesco was no ordinary man. She walked to his farmhouse checking for any surveillants. She didn't see any so it was possible that Raskalov had indeed called them off in good faith, so she could go about her business as though he *didn't exist*.

Instead of through the front door, she came around to the back gate. She could hear farm animal noises and Francesco gently chatting as he filled each feeder.

"Can I help?" Louise asked.

Francesco smiled. "Bellissima! Che bella sorpresa!" They exchanged cheek kisses and Louise placed her bag aside.

"*Maurizio says hello*," she said in Italian.

"Ciao!" He seemed genuinely happy. She helped with the feeding and after all the troughs were filled Francesco said, "Finito! Aperitivo?"

She grabbed her bag, and they went inside. After washing up, he opened a Chianti and served up some appetizers placing them on the large kitchen farm table. They clinked glasses and silently snacked, having built up an appetite. After dessert of dried and fresh fruit, Louise took the box containing the ancient book from her bag and placed it on the table. He opened the box and admired the book's cover then carefully took it out of the box and flipped a few pages.

"Questo è molto antica."

"*Yes, very ancient,*" Louise said. "*About Banco Monte dei Paschi di Siena.*"

She carefully turned to the page that had caught her eye, where she had placed a scrap of paper. She pointed to a passage and asked, "Biblioteca segreta?" meaning *secret library.*

He looked closer until they were practically touching cheeks. The rising temperature was comforting after all their exertion and epicurean pleasures. He rubbed her back sensing she could use his soothing touch. She melted into his arms, and they just held each other for a moment.

"Dai. Cosa sta succedendo?"

"*Nothing's wrong. It's just my work,*" she confessed in Italian. She suddenly realized that she knew a lot about him, but they had never discussed her personal life.

He pointed to the book and then to her. "Il tuo lavoro?"

"*Yes. My work is investigating...*" she said in Italian, emphasizing by holding her hand up as though looking through a magnifying glass. "*Inchiesta.*"

He pointed to her and then mimicked putting a deerstalker cap on. "Sherlock Holmes!"

She shrugged as if saying, *sort of.* Then she pointed to the page that described a *secret library* illustrated with a simple sketch showing large shelves and a stained-glass window. "È vero?" It was a long shot, but Louise hoped if it *was true*, maybe he knew about it.

He thought for a moment then gave her a knowing look. "Ti porterò."

"*You'll take me there?*" Louise couldn't believe it. She checked her watch and realized she needed to get back to the hotel to meet Kostas for dinner. "Domani?"

"Assolutamente," he promised.

He walked her back to the hotel, and they agreed to meet at the Fonte Gaia café the next morning then they kissed good night.

Louise and Kostas enjoyed another quiet dinner in the elegant but homey hotel restaurant. She couldn't stop thinking about *the secret library*, but she didn't want to tell Kostas until she knew for sure. Instead, she said, "Let's meet at noon at the hotel library tomorrow."

Dressed in an all black pencil skirt, turtleneck, and boots, Louise took her early morning walk to Monte dei Paschi headquarters, which opened at the odd hour of eight-twenty. Keeping an eye out for her *friends*, sure enough, as she was about to enter the bank, *Smarmy Guy* held the door open for her. He gave her a provocative smile as she entered then continued walking down the street. So much for pretending that Akari Raskalov *didn't exist*. She approached one of the Business Banking desks.

"Buongiorno." The business banking manager, a young man perfectly coiffed and elegantly dressed in a suit and tie, stood and greeted her with a handshake.

"Buongiorno, I'd like to schedule an appointment with Dario Rosselli-ni," Louise said.

"Signor Rossellini will be flying back to Siena this afternoon."

"Oh. Is he on vacation?" Louise asked, trying to glean some intel.

"No, he's traveling for business in Germany. I believe he is available tomorrow afternoon." He motioned for her to sit then sat at his desk and checked the schedule on his computer. "May I ask what the meeting is regarding?" As soon as Louise replied he clicked the mouse to move the cursor and began typing.

"My name is Louise Moscow. I'm a banking consultant. My client owns a bank in Cyprus and is interested in collaborating with Monte di Paschi on a local marketing strategy centered around the Palio Horseraces."

Unfazed, he said, "Mr. Rossellini is available at 16:00, his last meeting of the day."

"That's perfect."

"A number where you can be reached?" Louise gave him the infor-mation and he typed it into the calendar. "You're all set. We will see you tomorrow afternoon."

♪🕭

Louise left MPS and walked to meet Francesco at their usual café. After breakfast, he took her by the hand and led her through the streets, the long shadows withering in the late morning sun. In about half a mile they walked through gates leading to an ancient ivy-covered edifice, as though stepping back in time. Words carved in stone indicated it was the Church of St. Augustine, but as they entered the courtyard, she gathered it was also a monastery.

The sanctuary appeared to be completely off the beaten path of tourists, a hidden treasure. The garden so serene, furry critters and birds roamed unintimidated by humans, at the center of which a fountain, where a monk fed a stray cat some kibble from his pocket.

As they approached Francesco said, "Buon giorno, Alessandro."

The monk's sparkling hazel eyes reminded her of Michael. His head cleanly buzz-cut and his beard fully grown but neatly trimmed. Louise balked, sensing she knew him. Then she realized he was the *Singing Monk* she had met at the Feast of Saint Francis in Assisi. His demeanor was warmly inviting and peaceful.

Francesco and Alessandro began a lively banter in hushed tones, which Louise didn't even try to follow. They must have been speaking regional slang mixed with ancient Roman or Latin that she could never pick up. Suddenly they went silent and turned to her.

"Andiamo!" Francesco said.

They walked out and Louise soon realized they were heading to Monte dei Paschi headquarters. They approached the 14th-century neo-Gothic Salimbeni Palace, which along with two adjacent palaces were still the property of the bank. Alessandro led them to the front entrance, but instead of going into the bank, they took a side passage, to a heavy antediluvian wooden door, which Alessandro unlocked with a large antique iron skeleton key. They entered what appeared to be a secret section of the palace.

They continued down a stone hallway, then arrived at another large wooden door. Alessandro opened it and let Louise inside.

"*Business offices?*" Louise asked in Italian. "*May I look around?*" Alessandro replied by bowing silently then turned on the lights. Francesco and Louise perused shelves and desks. "Father Alessandro," she said, looking him in the eyes and asked, "*If you truly care what happens to this bank it is in your best interest to take me to the other executive offices."*

Alessandro looked at Francesco, who simply said, "È molto importante."

Alessandro led them down more hallways, crossing through several rooms. The first was packed with priceless artwork and treasures dating from the Middle Ages when the bank was founded in 1472 and earlier. They continued through and ascended a wooden staircase leading to stone towers. Alessandro opened the door to a concealed alcove where a priceless Renaissance painting was casually sitting on a mantle. It seemed there were masterpieces strewn about all throughout the structure. He led them inside another room and closed the door.

Without hesitating, Louise shuffled through some papers on the large desk and saw mail addressed to Giuseppe Mussari.

"Is this the office of Monte dei Paschi president, Giuseppe Mussari?" she asked in Italian. Alessandro nodded solemnly. Louise immediately understood this was her opportunity to find the evidence that LaFontaine said they needed. She saw a display case that held several trinkets, one of which was an antique magnifying glass. She picked it up and held it in front of her eye.

"Sherlock Holmes!" Francesco said. They laughed in a moment of levity.

"Permesso?" Louise asked, indicating she'd like to look around. Alessandro seemed completely fine with Louise's investigation. She suspected Francesco had spoken to him last night after she left. She searched through the desk and cabinets careful not to disturb anything. Finally, under some papers and supplies she found an old safe.

"Apri per favore?" Louise asked if they could open it.

Alessandro looked at Francesco who nodded.

"È facile da ricordare," Alessandro replied. "Uno, due, tre, quattro."

Louise couldn't believe the combination to the safe was *one, two, three, four.* He opened it for her, and she pulled out a stack of official looking bank documents, clearly marked as contracts between MPS and Deutsche Bank. She took a small high-resolution spy camera from her bag and snapped several pictures making sure to capture the language.

Just then, the clock tower bell began to ring, startling Louise. She eyed Alessandro who nodded reassuringly, but they quickly closed everything back up and left.

Louise checked her watch to see it was just approaching noon. She apologized and thanked them then they went their separate ways.

Louise met with Kostas in the hotel library. She showed him the digital photos of the bank documents and they spent the afternoon continuing their research into MPS finances.

After a long eventful day, Louise was exhausted, and they had an important meeting tomorrow. They skipped tea and had an early dinner then said good night.

ELEVEN

Siena, Italy, October 9, 2012

Tuesday morning Louise was up with the sun. She did her usual routine and went down to Bar Bazar caffè for her favorite cappuccino foam art, this time the server crafting an exquisite caterpillar. Louise couldn't take her eyes off the image as she left, not noticing *Smarmy Guy* was holding the door for her. She smiled absentmindedly, but this time *Smarmy Guy* invaded her space and grabbed her upper arm almost spilling her coffee.

Suddenly, Kostas appeared out of nowhere. "Let her go and we won't have any trouble," Kostas said. *Smarmy Guy* played it cool for a moment putting his hands up, then he threw a sucker-punch at Kostas. Like a professional boxer, Kostas deftly blocked the punch then made solid contact with *Smarmy Guy's* nose. Leaving him with a trickle of blood running from his nostril and blinded by pain, Kostas escorted Louise quickly into the safety of the hotel lobby.

"Where did you learn to fight like that?" Louise asked.

"Boxing is my passion."

"I thought horses were your passion."

"They are. I agreed to Frédéric's request to help your investigation. But I had an ulterior motive. Because of my passion for horses, I'm here to stop them being used in the Palio race. My ultimate mission is to revert the Palio to the ancient tradition of *pugna* fighting instead the horse race." He held a boxing stance with his fists up, ready to fight, like a Cypriot Rocky.

I really like this guy! Louise thought.

Louise sipped her coffee then checked her watch. "Time to go see Dario Rossellini."

Dario Rossellini warmly greeted Louise and Kostas, speaking fluent English with a charming Italian accent.

"Louise Moscow. Welcome to Banca Monte dei Paschi di Siena." Dario Rossellini gave her cheek kisses then shook hands with Kostas. "What a pleasant surprise."

"It is for me as well, Dario," Louise said. "It's been a long time."

"You two know each other?" Kostas asked.

"We go way back." Rossellini and Louise just smiled at each other and left it at that. "Bene! Let me give you the VIP tour." Rossellini gave some history of the medieval structure as they walked through. "Banco Monte dei Paschi made its headquarters here in this 14th century Salimbeni Palace. The palace was built on top of 12th and 13th century structures and was renovated in the 20th century, restoring much of its original beauty."

The golden recessed lighting enhanced the ancient stone walls and unique ceiling made of dark wooden bowed beams, installed vertically forming an arch reminiscent of a ship's hull. There was something solemn about the interior. They walked through a medieval door that led to stunning arched hallways with ornate marble floors and colorful mosaic tiled ceilings.

They took an elevator that opened on the third level with more arched hallways leading to a large conference room with stone walls and a wood coffered ceiling. Two long wooden tables sat perpendicular to each other along adjacent walls each with six large, mullioned windows that diffused sunlight into the chamber. Both tables were flanked by large formal chairs were evocative of *The Last Supper*.

"This used to be a ballroom, now used for board meetings and conferences," Rossellini said.

"What a lovely view," Louise said, observing the piazza with a statue below.

They went up one more floor and entered a spacious room with a desk below an arched window that was slightly open letting in a refreshing breeze.

"This is my office. Not such a great view." The office looked out over a back alley.

"It's still a charming workspace," Louise said. "It's the most beautiful bank I've ever seen. Thank you for the tour."

"It is one of the nicer perks of working here. If you must work in finance…"

"At least work somewhere interesting," Louise said, finishing his thought.

They went back downstairs, and Rossellini led them out to the quiet Piazza Salimbeni that they had just seen from the windows above. Rossellini led them to the center of the courtyard where the statue atop an octagonal rise three steps high towered over them.

"This is our local archdeacon, the 18th century economist, Sallustio Bandini," Rossellini said, indicating the statue. "His writings are considered enlightened. He donated his private 3,000-book collection to the University of Siena under condition that it be made available to the public." This caught Louise's attention, but she refrained from mentioning *the secret library* she had visited the day before. Rossellini turned toward the bank, the six mullioned windows on the third level now visible from the outside. Each mullioned window comprised an arched element encasing three narrow, vertical windows. The floor above that one had six windows, which appeared comparatively smaller. Dario's office had a similar window facing the back. The building was topped off with symmetrically spaced turrets. It was graceful and elegant overlooking the well-maintained piazza paved with large granite squares.

"On March 4, 1472, the Republic of Siena approved the petition to establish the bank. That's why it's considered the oldest bank in the world still in continuous operation. It was founded on the Statute of Paschi of 1419, which was a law that regulated all agricultural activities in Maremma, or maritime lands of Tuscany.

"The marshlands where the *butteri* herded cattle on horseback," Louise said. "They were the original cowboys."

Rossellini's eyes sparkled and he tilted his head pensively. "I've never thought of it that way. But I think you are correct. The Palio Horse Race is like the wild west of Italy." His unpretentious nature, salt and pepper hair and genuine smile gave her hope that he was one of the good guys. He continued. "BMPS derives its name from the *Monte di Pietà* or *Mount of Piety.*"

"When you say, *mount of piety*, is there a spiritual meaning?"

"You ask very pointed questions, Louise. I appreciate your respect for history. Yes, *monte di pietà* is the Italian word for *pawnshop*. It literally translates to *Mount of Piety* and is a loan program used since the Renaissance period, so the less fortunate had access to loans with reasonable interest rates, like an institutional pawnbroker. Borrowers put up whatever valuables they had as collateral for a low-interest loan. It was conceived by the Catholic Church on the principle that the borrower would benefit, not the lender.

"The way it was set up required a collection of funds, or *a mount,* from donations by financially privileged people who had no expectation of repayment. Then, those in need would come to the *Monte di Pietà* and give an item of value in exchange for a monetary loan. The loan amount would be about two-thirds of the borrower's item value. The term of the loan would be one year. The profits from the modest interest rate were used to pay for the operation of *the mount.* The concept began here in Italy and spread to Catholic countries. The Nacional Monte de Piedad of Mexico established in the 1700s is still in operation."

Louise was flabbergasted. The oldest bank in the world had in fact begun as a benign institution that was not out for profits. Instead, it was established to help the less fortunate. She had spent her career in banking counting and investing other people's money only to realize the original purpose of banks was to grow the community, not amass wealth for the very few.

Even more surprising, Rossellini no longer seemed to be the banking executive she remembered, very reserved, reticent, the kind of client who came off as evasive. That had been the rift between Louise and Dario Rossellini when she worked with him as a BCCI client. Personally, she had found him fascinating, utterly charming, and genuine. But the dichotomy of his professional cageyness kept their relationship strictly business. This new side of Rossellini that she had never known, his enthusiasm and passion for the ancient institution, suggested a more holistic character. He continued to mystify her.

Rossellini waved his hand over the courtyard as though brushing stardust from Louise's eyes.

"This current form of BMPS dates to 1624. Siena was incorporated into Tuscany when the Grand Duke Ferinando II guaranteed Monte dei Paschi bank depositors with income from the state-owned Maremma. The deposit guarantee allowed the bank to consolidate and increase banking activities during the 17th and 18th centuries. By 1871, when Rome was officially designated the capital of Italy MPS expanded through the Italian peninsula offering new services including mortgage loans for the first time in Italy."

"Mortgage literally means *engaged until death,*" Louise said.

"You are quite the linguist," Kostas said.

"Banking can feel like a little death," Rossellini muttered.

"La petite mort," Louise said, referring to the French expression for the post orgasm moment that feels like a loss of consciousness or a *little death*. They stood in silence.

"The two most powerful temptations in the world are sex and money. So, Kostas, you are the owner of the Hellenic Bank in Cyprus?" Rossellini said, abruptly changing the subject.

"Yes, we are one of the offshore banks that has become very popular with Deutsch Bank Moscow. I thought it would be good to meet you and perhaps we can help each other. A joint marketing campaign to rebrand MPS and offshore banking."

"You are a client of Louise, which means you are an honest banker. I commend you. It is easy to bend the rules in our business. I will match your honesty. MPS is founded in altruism. It is majority owned by the non-profit organization Fondazione Monte dei Paschi di Siena that supports education, science, health, the arts, especially in Siena. Together we have been financing the Palio di Siena horserace for many years." He gestured toward the MPS headquarters. "There are much more tangible and intangible assets here than most realize. The headquarters house a priceless art collection and historical documents spanning centuries. None of which have been appraised. However, since 2009 the non-profit foundation's annual revenues decreased from 340 million euros to just over 62 million euros, requiring the foundation to suspend all endowments. So, you see, Kostas," Rossellini lamented, "even if we wanted to collaborate with you, we are in no position to venture into any new investments at this time."

Louise realized that there was a reason Rossellini was holding the meeting outside. It wasn't just to show them the historic palace façade, but also to avoid prying ears.

"We'd still like to invite you to dinner to discuss this in private," Louise proposed.

"Yes, even without a marketing collaboration, there is much to discuss," Kostas said.

Rossellini looked at his watch. "Dinner is a good idea. But having just returned from Germany, my wife will want me home for a night or two. Let me check my calendar and have my assistant contact you with some possible times."

"That's fine," Louise said.

"Shall we continue the tour?" Rossellini said, indicating the way back to the bank. They headed to the arched entrance with the great iron lattice gate the left half of which was currently open. Above the entrance, etched into the stone, were the words, *Monte dei Paschi.*

"Is that crest above the door and all the windows the bank logo?" Louise asked, referring to a ubiquitous silver oval. At the outer edge of the oval was a banner with the words *Montis Pascuorum.* In the bottom half of the oval was a bowl, which contained three oblong shapes rising up from the center, the middle one taller than two outer ones.

"Yes. Montis Pascuorum is Latin for Mountain of Pasture Lands."

The connections were all firing together like synapses in Louise's mind. Indeed, the origins of currency and of banking were founded in the land. Not only placing a value on the land itself, as the *landed gentry*, but as keepers of the land, the government overseeing the sanctity of that value. In this case, it had failed miserably. Monte di Paschi had brought the Italian Central bank and the country and possibly even the European Union down with it by not protecting its most fundamental values.

"Thank you for the tour, Dario," Louise said, shaking his hand. "I look forward to discussing further."

"Me too," Kostas said.

"My office will be in touch by tomorrow," Dario Rossellini said.

They said good-bye and parted ways.

Back in her hotel room freshening up before dinner, Louise's cell phone rang.

"Pronto."

"May I speak to Louise Moscow?" a woman said.

"This is Louise."

"Ah, buon giorno, Signorina Moscow. This is Dario Rossellini's assistant, Montserrat."

"Buon giorno, Monserrat."

"Mister Rossellini is looking forward to dinner with you and Mr. Kostas. Is eight o'clock tomorrow evening suitable?"

"That is perfect."

"Okay. We have booked signor Rossellini's usual table at Osteria La

Taverna di San Giuseppe."

"Grazie mille. Ciao."

At dinner Louise told Kostas about the dinner reservation and they toasted.

"To the small triumphs."

Louise and Kostas spent the day in the library researching in preparation for dinner with Dario Rossellini at Osteria La Taverna di San Giuseppe. There was nothing more powerful than knowing one's client, or in this case, one's potential informant.

That evening, they made the short but arduous ten-minute trek from the hotel up Via Giovani Dupré to the crest of the hill. The location was lively, with people on foot or on motorbike spluttering over the cobblestones of Siena's ancient town center. They entered the restaurant to find Dario Rossellini already chatting quietly with the owners. The warm reception, the aromas, and the relaxed but professional staff made the restaurant feel like a gourmet oasis.

"Welcome," Dario Rossellini greeted them with a smile. "These are the owners, father and son, Marco and Matteo."

"The family resemblance is unmistakable," Louise said, shaking hands.

"We are all family here," Marco said, not in any way hinting the mafia sense of family, but a real family, something Louise had come to appreciate about the entire town.

"I hope you are hungry," Matteo said. "This is not a place for dieters."

"After walking up the hill I'm famished," Louise said.

"Gravity will help you back down," Matteo said.

"It smells delicious," Kostas said.

"Your table is ready, right this way." They followed Marco through the restaurant past smiling patrons ruddy from the restaurant's Tuscan warmth and Chianti. The décor was like stepping back to the early 12th century, with a vaulted ceiling, exposed terracotta brick white-washed walls, the shelves of which were laden with Tuscan wines placed haphazardly from every angle. He seated them in a private corner. Candlelight combined with the glow of recessed ceiling lights, and scallop-shaped sconces added to the tasteful ambience.

Almost Shakespearean, the meal was served in well-rehearsed and perfectly timed multiple courses. The drama featured stellar flavors created by the Micheline-starred chef, showcasing fabulous local chianti, topped off by great dialogue.

"Another gem in this magical city," Louise said, hoping to finally get to know more about Dario. "Are you from Siena, Dario?"

"I like to think of Siena as my home," he replied, evasively. "The Sienese are a fiercely proud people. We have the proverbial chip on our shoulder. It is difficult to accept defeat, after centuries fighting our rival city."

"Rival city?" Louise asked.

"Florence is our ancient rival. We may have lost most of the battles, but we came out on top in terms of grace and elegance. The rose-colored brick, the location with its steep, twisting cobblestone roads, dignified churches, palaces, and grand public hillsides buildings, many consider Siena to be the most beautiful town in Italy. Have you visited the *duomo* yet?"

"No, but it is next on my agenda," Louise said.

"I never tire of visiting it. The Roman Emperor Augustus founded the city on this location about 2,000 years ago. But like most Tuscan hill towns, this area was first settled by Etruscans around 700 BC. They were an advanced tribe of people who changed central Italy through irrigation." He waved his hand as though indicating the entire Tuscan region. "This was all marshlands. The Etruscan tribe called Saina settled this hilltop and made the surrounding marshlands farmable. Augustus named it Saena Julia."

"So, you're saying that Siena was *not* founded by the mythical sons of one of the twins Romulus and Remus, who were abandoned on the Tiber River and nurtured by a she-wolf?" Louise asked, tongue-in-cheek.

Rossellini chuckled. "As always, you did your research, Louise. Yes, the official local lore for tourism uses the town's she-wolf emblem, but it is a holdover from that myth. But Siena was founded by Augustus heir to Julius Caesar named after the Saina tribe."

Louise took the opening to guide the conversation. "I have been reading the archives at my hotel. Mark Antony disputed Augustus' claim to Caesar's throne, as a political tactic."

"I see where you're headed. The form of slander made popular during the Roman Empire to discredit political opponents by accusing them of having inappropriate sexual affairs."

"Another Roman invention. Political dirty tricks that continue today."

"Taken to an art form by the Russians," Kostas added.

"The truth is, Julius Caesar had no legitimate children under Roman law and therefore adopted his grandnephew Octavius, making him his primary heir," Rossellini explained. "It wasn't until Octavius learned of the will, that he decided to accept Julius Caesar's political legacy and adopted his great-uncle's name, Gaius Julius Caesar. Then in 27 BC he assumed the name Augustus to completely distinguish himself from his uncle's name."

"And Augustus named Siena after the Saina tribe," Louise said.

"Correct," Rossellini said, continuing the history lesson. "But old Siena was far from main roads, and it wasn't until the Byzantine raids during the 4th century caused the Lombards to alter their trade routes to the north that Siena began to prosper as a trading post and from religious pilgrimages. But, between the Black Death of 1348, that killed more than half of the population, and the attacks by the marquis of Marignano in 1555, Siena had little opportunity to rebuild. As a result, much of the city has barely changed." He waved a hand over the restaurant setting. "Like this restaurant, visitors easily slip into the Middle Ages.

Kostas raised his glass. "To Siena." They clinked glasses.

"Another reason this is one of my favorite restaurants is because the owners protect the privacy of patrons. They regularly sweep for listening devices and vet all clientele. Any non-locals are required to complete a short questionnaire."

"Interesting," Louise said. "I've never made that connection before. But now that you mention it, almost every five-star restaurant that I've been to has this formality."

Dario nodded almost imperceptibly. "All that to say, we may speak freely here."

"Not like at the bank," Louise ventured. "You took us out to the piazza to chat."

"Perceptive as always, Louise." Dario remained silent giving them the floor to speak.

Kostas had kept his input to a minimum until now. "As you may know, Dario, we have something in common. We represent highly respected banks that are being taken advantage of by a corrupt and dangerous ring of powerful criminals with the backing of Russian officials."

Dario lowered his eyes at the trigger word. "Very powerful and very dangerous. Since 1994, when the largest private bank in Russia, Inkombank, was illegally taken over by the *boss of bosses*, Rolan Morozov, he gained access to the world banking and financial system."

Now Louise was triggered. "*The Brainy Don*," Louise said. "The Russian Jew who moved to Budapest and scammed his fellow Russian Jews trying to emigrate to the United States and Israel. He made deals to buy their assets and sell them for fair market value and forward the proceeds to the owners. But sold the assets and kept the proceeds. He served seven years in prison but when he was released, he went on to enjoy a successful career as a mob boss."

"Indeed, it pays to befriend the richest man in the world, Vladimir Putin," Kostas said.

"Gaining access to the world's banking and financial systems gave him power to manipulate many unsuspecting people into allowing the sex trafficking ring that I uncovered during my investigation of Ekram M. Almasi's murder."

"Another prominent name is Pavel Volkov who took over Ukraine's Nadra Bank. They comprise the upper echelon of organized crime," Rossellini added.

"They have full access to international banking systems," Louise repeated.

"Volkov's companies control most of the formerly state-run Ukrainian titanium assets and chemical plants. He is one of the largest investors in the power and chemical sectors across eastern Europe including Cyprus," Kostas added.

"That jibes with fears that Putin's real goal is weapons of mass destruction," Louise said.

"The *Iron Triangles* will stop at nothing," Rossellini said.

"Robert Mueller coined that term in his speech last year," Louise said.[18]

"I missed that. What speech?" Kostas asked.

"In January 2011, the director of the FBI, Robert Mueller, gave what is known as the *Iron Triangles* speech explaining how 21st century international organized crime works," Louise said. "Criminal enterprises are making billions through numerous mob operations ranging from ripping off United States Medicare programs, to copyright infringement, and cornering the market on natural gas, oil, precious metals and selling to the highest bidder. The crimes are complex and heinous. With no scruples whatsoever, they will do anything for a profit, including deliberately worsening climate change, supplying opposing sides with firearms during warfare and peddling nuclear weapons."

"They have infiltrated every aspect of global banking," Rossellini lamented.

"Absolutely," Louise continued. "Mueller's key point of the speech was how these groups infiltrate businesses, providing logistical support to hostile foreign powers and manipulating the highest levels of government. Mueller called it *Iron Triangles.*" Louise held up her hands to demonstrate. "There are three sides to the triangle: one side is the mafia, another is corrupt government officials, the third is crooked business leaders."

"Replace those sides with names," Rossellini said. He held up his hands, making sections in the air. "In Russia, Morozov is the mobster, Vladimir Putin is the corrupt government official, along with Sergei Lavrov, Sergei Kislyak, Konstantin Kosachev, and so on, and the crooked business leaders are Pavel Volkov, Igor Sechin, and other oligarchs."

"Many of them play all three roles," Louise added. "The point being, the three sides of an *Iron Triangle* work together, strengthening the other two sides to fuck everyone else over."

"Morozov is the mastermind behind the kind of tax refund schemes that ruined Bill Browder's Moscow investment company Hermitage Capital," Kostas replied. "By the time the authorities find out about the theft, the funds are offshore and it's too difficult to unravel the evidence. It's money laundering at massive government levels."

"Morozov's money laundering and pyramid schemes make the twenty-billion-dollar BCCI scandal look like a misdemeanor," Louise said. "After 21 years, the BCCI investigation finally just closed this year. Ekram M. Almasi was one of the founding members of Browder's Moscow fund," Louise said. He was right to be paranoid about Russian mobsters and keeping a small army of former Mossad bodyguards with him at all times."

"No one accepts his male nurse acted alone," Kostas said.

The floodgates opened and Rossellini couldn't help adding to the discussion. "Don't forget Refik Aslanov, the former Russian Minister of Commerce and Trade, then deputy director of Russia's Department of Hotel Management for seventeen years. After the capitalist transformation of Russia, he started his own private real estate development company, Rockbay Group, with Russian-American mobster Felix Sater and Donald Trump."

Louise rolled her eyes. It wasn't surprising that such a sleazy con man would be working directly with these criminals.

"That is not the most shocking or in your case eyeroll inducing part," Kostas said. "It's likely that Refik Aslanov is just a front man for Tayyip Erdoğan."

"The President of Turkey," Louise said.

"Exactly. Erdoğan along with Exxon executive Rex Tillerson, have stolen a trillion dollars of Middle East oil since 9-11. Trump along with Jeffrey Epstein and Felix Sater are tied to criminal organizations that supply ISIS with Stinger missiles and materials to make nuclear weapons. It is believed that Felix Sater is in fact an important FBI informant, but it remains to be seen whose side he is working for. Although his information has led to the conviction of many criminals including members of the Cosa Nostra organized crime families, and his crowning achievement of having helped the U.S. track down Osama bin Laden, some question if it's possible he will turn the FBI in favor of the powerful Russian Jewish mafia."

"It's funny how the Russian mob knew where Bin Laden was," Louise quipped.

"The Russian Jewish mafia dates back to Stalin's Gulag," Rossellini said. The conversation had taken on such an intensity that Dario's words were like an alarm bell. "Ironically, it was under Communism that the Russian Jewish Mafia became so powerful. After Lenin's death in the 1924, Stalin removed large populations of Jews from positions of power and sent them to the Gulag prisons and deported large numbers to Central Asia, primarily Uzbekistan. In the Gulag, Stalin allowed these Jewish officials to run the Gulag. It was the simplest way to control the millions of inmates across Russia. Under the harsh conditions these Jewish leaders bred the world's most dangerous criminals. Their prison roots are a legacy of brutality. They even have a history of tattoos with different meanings denoting rank, number of kills, torture."

"Twenty million Russians died in the Gulag," Louise said. "Not to diminish Hitler's genocide. But people often forget Stalin's atrocities."

"That brings us back to Dario's point," Kostas said. "One of the infamous Russian Jewish Mafia members that emigrated to the US was none other than Donald Trump's mentor, Roy Cohn. Trump had been a complete financial failure until 1991 when Cohn began funneling illegitimate profits stolen from the Russian economy, transferred to Mikhail Fridman's Alfa

Bank, and laundered into the legitimate US economy via Trump's real estate investments. The Russian Jewish Mafia owned Trump. The Suka is a double entendre, meaning 'rat' as in someone ratting out a colleague and becoming an informer, and it also means…"

"Bitch," Louise said, finishing Kostas' sentence.

"Correct," Kostas said. "A lackey doing someone else's bidding."

"Once indebted," Rossellini added, "if Trump betrayed Cohn he would soon learn the dual meaning. In the Gulags, the Suka *rat* met a horrific end."

"Is that why you went outside the bank to speak to us, Dario?" Louise asked.

Rossellini sipped his wine and breathed deeply. "Monte dei Paschi was lending money when Christopher Columbus was still dreaming of the shortest route to India. The bank had always been prudent but fell victim to the reckless cheap loans during the booming economy before 2008. The purchase of our rival bank in 2007, in our effort to expand across Italy, resulted in massive debts. Then the 2008 crash happened."

"Talk about horrible timing," Louise said.

"To get out of it, we compounded the problem with more poor decisions. MPS now has the worst financial trouble of any bank in Italy, with massive debt and a plunging share price. The fifty-five thousand residents of Siena view 'Daddy Monte' with a new sense of vulnerability. The non-profit and all Sienese owners will be forced to give up their majority ownership. The bank that helped define our identity for more than five centuries is slipping away from us. Almost one-hundred-fifty million dollars a year that went to the community from 1996 to 2010 has evaporated in the past two years. Nobody saw it coming. The mayor of Siena, Franco Ceccuzzi, was forced to resign this year after losing support over the handling of the city's interest in the bank's management."

"You can trust us, Dario," Louise said. "Tell us what happened."

"I believe there are very damning documents showing derivative contracts with Deutsche Bank used to disguise massive losses. A Deutsche Bank investment-banking employee quit in protest. After leaving the bank, he leaked hundreds of pages documenting the transactions to journalists and regulators. There's no hiding the losses any longer. It will be a huge scandal very soon. My role is not just a communications director. I wear many hats from crafting strategy to providing personal financial services to some clients."

Louise and Kostas exchanged a look, the documents she photographed were most likely the same documents Rossellini just described. "You can turn state's evidence and testify as a cooperating witness."

Dario looked defeated. "My fate is sealed."

Suddenly the lights dimmed to near pitch-black giving Louise a moment of panic. She felt a hand grip hers. Then candle flames appeared, and the entire room erupted into a heartfelt rendition of happy birthday for one of the customers. As her eyes adjusted to the light of birthday candles, Louise saw Dario's hand on hers.

He smiled at her reassuringly. "This is not just a place where bankers and tourists come to enjoy the best food in Siena. It's a second home to many locals."

"The best sign of a great restaurant is that locals eat there," Louise concurred.

"I'm so sorry for letting them down," Dario Rossellini said. "I should have spoken out much sooner, but my job is to keep up the façade. After centuries, corruption and bad management caused the bank's downfall." They went silent contemplating the tragedy of the bank.

Matteo approached. "We offer a private wine and cheese tasting for dessert."

"Offer accepted," Louise said, welcoming the change of mood.

They left the table and descended a small stone staircase in the back to a cavernous, subterranean Bacchant temple.

"This hall was hand chiseled by Etruscans three years before Christ. We now use it as a wine and cheese cellar," the young owner, Marco said.

The ancient cave walls were stacked to the ceiling with more than 600 bottles of well-aged wine. In the center, a large table displaying mounds of local cheeses and fruits resembled a renaissance painting and gave off a seductive aroma.

"This cellar used to be at ground level," the Matteo explained. "But through the ages as Siena was conquered, former construction was simply built over."

Marco resumed where his father left off. "This entire region is founded on Etruscan architecture built between about 900 and 27 BC. Ancient Roman civilization eventually absorbed Etruscan civilization. But the hallmark of their skills in stone, wood and other materials remain in temples, houses, tombs, and even the city walls, bridges, and roads. Most of the remaining examples are ruins of the original structure. But there are some tombs and temples such as this one that remain almost intact. As you can see, Etruscan architecture was heavily influenced by ancient Greek architecture, which was also still developing. Both influenced Roman architecture, as is clear from the Colosseum in Rome, which can be considered a variation of Etruscan architecture. By about 200 BC, the Romans began using Greek styling, while retaining Etruscan shapes and purposes in their buildings."

They ended their delicious Tuscan meal of rich bold flavors, balanced but simple, using the best local ingredients, with local cheeses, fruits, chocolates, and dessert wine. They bid farewell to the father and son and parted ways. Outside the restaurant Louise and Kostas also said goodnight to Dario Rossellini.

"We can't thank you enough for sharing this charming restaurant. It was one of the best meals I've ever had," Louise said. They exchanged cheek kisses. "Also, thank you for confiding in us, Dario. As I said, we are here to help you."

"I appreciate that," Dario said. "But it all seems out of my hands now. May I offer you a ride to your hotel?"

Kostas rubbed his belly. "I prefer to stretch my legs on the short down-hill walk back."

"Same here," Louise said. "Thank you again."

"Will I see you before you leave?" Dario asked Kostas.

"Yes, I'll be in town working on bringing the brawling tournaments back to replace the Palio Horse Race," Kostas said.

Dario looked at him like he was crazy. "You mean to bring back the ancient tradition of *pugna* fighting instead of the horse race?" Kostas raised his fists in a boxing stance, smiling. "And I thought I was quixotic."

"Me too." Louise laughed.

"If our plan to help save Monte dei Paschi works it will give me leverage to make some changes to the Palio Race," Kostas said.

"Kostas and I will work on that plan and will be in touch," Louise said.

Dario looked at them with a slight glimmer of hope. "I look forward to it."

With that, they left on a positive note for the fate of the bank. Louise and Kostas returned to their hotel and said good night.

TWELVE

Siena, Italy, October 10, 2012

Louise awoke with the sun dappling morning light into the exquisite suite. She had never had a *place* feel so much like a *person*. Although Paris, Burgundy, and her Caribbean Island each had its own distinct character, Siena, and its bank, Monte di Paschi, felt like actual characters with individual lives and personal drama living an epic tale. With the town and the bank in starring roles, it was like reading a play and rooting for both the protagonist and the antagonist. Not a spoiled child who had been given too much too soon, or a socially ambitious woman (or man) marrying into wealth and family name. Neither seemed fitting analogies. Siena was like a prize fighter after holding the world champion title, then losing it, and then winning it back. But now the legend was being mismanaged, dogged by greed, ego, and gullibility. From experience, Louise knew Monte di Paschi bank was the victim and not the villain. There were always dark forces that worked against anything that was sacred.

With a renewed sense of hope, she dressed and prepared a note for LaFontaine's messenger letting him know that she had the photographic evidence. Then she went down just in time to find the quirky horseman pissing off Oscar the doorman. She shook his hand, the message thus as good as delivered. It was amazing when her scrappy plans came together. As if on cue, Kostas appeared, and they went for coffee at the Bar Bazar to discuss their next move.

"Let's divide and conquer for a few days," Louise said. "You keep reaching out to investors for MPS, and I'll start drafting a financial restructuring of MPS, using various levels of your investment funding. We can touch base in a few days."

"Sounds good. That will also give me time to work on my personal project of the Palio Horserace." He put his fists up in the boxing stance.

She smiled and they exchanged cheek kisses good-bye. She went to her hotel room and re-packed her *go-bag* which was always ready in case of emergency. She heard a swishing sound and picked up a sealed envelope that had been pushed under the door. It was from Dario Rossellini.

She went down to the concierge. "Maurizio, I noticed you're almost always available. Which I appreciate." He smiled knowingly. "But if I ever need to leave unexpectedly, is there a self-check-out where I can leave the key if necessary?"

He pointed to an antique box mounted on the wall near the check-in desk. "We have your credit card on file, so you can just place the key in that box."

"Perfect. Oh, could I have afternoon tea served in the library at 16:00 today?"

"Nessun problema."

"Grazie mille."

She left the hotel to finally take the opportunity to visit the Siena Cathedral and its famous Duomo. She walked the short distance past the Piazza del Campo and up the hill to the gothic Cathedral that had taken almost forty years to build beginning in 1215. Its exterior was breathtaking. Black and white being the official colors of Siena, the cathedral's alternating black and white marble gave it distinctive stripes.

She went through the narthex entering what felt like an entire city street. The floorplan was in the shape of the Latin cross, the long central nave, with two grand transepts crossing in front of the sanctuary and altar area, was like walking down a boulevard. She looked up to appreciate the magnificent 'Rose' stained-glass window, then turned left at the first transept to enter the famous Piccolomini Library where she admired the massive collection of well-preserved ancient manuscripts and paintings by Pisano, Donatello, and Michelangelo.

She had barely visited a fraction of the cathedral when she realized it was almost time to meet Dario Rossellini at the location given in the note that was slid under her door. Being especially fond of frescoes, before leaving, she stopped briefly to admire the recently discovered and restored wall paintings under the narthex. Then she went outside and turned left walking a few meters and turned to face the Cathedral to see the surreal vision.

"You found the *unfinished wall*." She turned to see Dario Rossellini looking very fit and distinguished. "Would you like to see the best views of Siena?" he asked, boyishly.

"I'd love to."

She followed him into the Opera Museum at the back of the Cathedral to the entrance of the famous *Unfinished Wall*. It was a popular tourist attraction for anyone willing to climb the stairs.

"The wall was built to expand the Cathedral in 1348," Dario explained. "But the Black Plague swept through the city and all work stopped. This is one of the purest examples of the city being frozen in time and a testament to Sienese power and ambition. The wall can be climbed by these narrow stairs for a view of the city. Shall we?"

"Absolutely!"

They made the steep climb three floors up the ancient steps nestled within the wall and emerged on top of the structure with panoramic views of Siena.

"The view is dizzying," Louise said. "There's the Piazza del Campo." She pointed at the point of reference standing atop the narrow wall with no barriers. "It feels almost like flying."

"It offers a very unique perspective."

"And so secluded." Louise didn't waste a minute. "You could tell me anything."

Dario looked out over the picture-perfect Tuscan countryside and an-cient structures. "It's similar to looking at the stars in heaven, a reminder of how small and insignificant we are." His silent anguish was palpable. Louise felt powerless to help him.

"Dario, I found the evidence that you might be able to use to protect yourself." She showed him the series of photos of the documents on her spy camera. "These are in the vault in Mussari's old office. You can lead the authorities to these documents. It will give you leverage."

He turned to her. "You have already helped me just by being here. Someone I can trust." He reached out and took her hand and she felt him slip her a note. "Thank you, Louise."

She refused to let go of his hand for fear of what he was planning to do. If he intended to jump, he would have to take her with him. Finally, he gave a childlike grin. "Andiamo!" Then he pulled her back toward the stairs and they walked down. At the bottom he gave her cheek kisses. "You are a good friend, Louise." Then he walked away. Louise plunged her hand still clenching the note deep into her pocket and headed back to her hotel in time for afternoon tea.

Louise had gotten into the habit of having afternoon tea in the hotel library and reading through the historic archives. The raw emotion of the encounter with Rossellini had given her an appetite, but it was still a half hour before her tea would be served. She settled into the cozy nook where she could enjoy the delightful house-made delicacies and tea, an Italian version of the English tradition. The reading nook provided excellent lighting and even a magnifying glass for weary eyes. The nook also provided privacy for reading sensitive information.

She took out the note and scanned the message conferred to her by Dario Rossellini. It seemed to be cryptic clues that she would need to decipher. She was in the right place to research clues into the world's oldest bank. She went over to a section of the library where she had found dusty archives that established Monte dei Paschi di Siena as the oldest bank in the world and retrieved several manuscripts then returned to her reading nook.

Confirming what was already discussed, she read how a *Mount of Piety* was founded by order of the Magistrature of the Republic of Siena in 1472 based on the 1419 law *Statuto dei Paschi*, that regulated agricultural and pastoral activities in Maremma. The bank headquarters had remained in the same palace for over 540 years. In 1624, Siena was incorporated into the Grand Duchy of Tuscany and the Grand Duke Ferdinando II guaranteed bank depositors the income from the state-owned pastures, or *paschi*, pronounced *paski* with a hard *C*. Over the centuries the bank consolidated and expanded throughout the Italian peninsula, initiating new financial services, including the first mortgages in Italy.

She set aside the early texts and perused current financial trade papers, which had been intensely reporting on the bank's strife. In 1995, the bank was transformed from a statutory corporation to a limited liability company called Banca Monte dei Paschi di Siena. At the same time, the non-profit Fonddazione Monte dei Paschi di Siena was established to continue the bank's charitable functions and to be its largest single shareholder.

In 1999 Banca Monte dei Paschi di Siena was listed on the Italian Stock Exchange and became known to traders as BMPS or just MPS. From 2000 to 2006 MPS intensified commercial expansion acquiring regional banks and developing products in other sectors. Banca MPS became the fourth largest Italian commercial and retail bank with 2,000 branches, 26,000 employees and 5.1 million customers in Italy, as well as branches abroad. To finance this expansion, the bank invested in derivatives through Deutsche Bank. This was where the photos Louise had taken of the loan documents in the safe would come into play. If she or Dario Rossellini made the documents public, all hell would break loose.

Louise wrote on her notepad with her left hand as she flipped pages with her right.

"Your due diligence is impressive."

Louise recognized the mildly guttural Russian accent as that of the *Master of the Dark Arts*, Akari Raskalov. Without hesitation, she deftly slid Rossellini's note between the pages of an old book, closed the cover, and set it aside.

"You're just in time to join me for tea," she said.

"Afternoon tea is one of my favorite indulgences."

"Yes, I know," she said, throwing his own tactic back at him.

"They have a wonderful selection here."

He sat in the armchair across from her as though it were a throne, the antique oak coffee table a barrier between them. On cue, a male server wheeled in a cart containing a silver tea set, two fine china cups, and matching traditional tiered snack tower.

"Mr. Kostas will not be joining you today?" the server asked in a musical Italian accent.

"No, Kostas had an appointment," Louise replied. "But my friend will be joining me."

"Va bene." The server proficiently arranged the loose-leaf tea in the teapot strainers, placed the teacups on saucers before each of them, and the tower of delights ranging from savory crustless finger sandwiches to sweet biscotti in the middle of the oak table. Before exiting he turned over an antique hourglass. "Cinque minuti."

"Grazie."

They both stared in silence at the hourglass waiting five minutes for the tea to steep. Louise took the opportunity to get up and put the old textbook with Rossellini's note back on the shelf. She sat down just as the hourglass emptied and poured tea into both cups. She handed one to Raskalov and chose a cucumber and cream cheese finger sandwich for herself. She took a bite and spoke, finally breaking the silence.

"I'd almost given up on you." She picked up the cup of hot tea and blew on it. "What brings you back?"

He picked up his tea and blew on it. "Timing is everything in the quest for information."

"Timing is everything in the quest for kompromat," Louise paraphrased.

He watched her sip the tea and that was the last thing she remembered.

Russia, October 11, 2012

When Louise came back to consciousness, her brain was working like it had been processed through a kaleidoscope. To quiet her mind, and to quiet herself – the first human instinct was to scream in terror – she somehow was able to concentrate on her CIA training, where one portion was specifically designed for hostage situations. It was all about buying time and gathering information. To lift the fog in her head and body, she was grateful to be able to wiggle her toes. Then she took the time to assess where she was.

She was strapped to a gurney in a moving vehicle. She could distinctly hear voices speaking in Russian, casual conversation, as if two buddies were on a road trip. *They don't know that I speak the language,* Louise thought, which is a useful advantage for buying time and intel. One of the voices she recognized…Akari Raskalov. She must be an important trophy of Kompromat if the *Master of the Dark Arts* was personally escorting her somewhere. But where? She was sweating, her stomach was churning from whatever they had sedated her with, but she would remain silent and determine her location.

Raskalov was lost in his own thoughts riding in the front of the van. He was always relieved when a 'situation of capture' was completed. After Louise had fallen under the powerful sedative infused in the tea when she had stepped away to put the book back on the shelf, he gave the signal and one of his security team portraying the server in official uniform entered from the back. They moved Louise into the fetal position and placed her on the shelf under the tea cart, pulling the floor-length tablecloth over completely concealing her.

The server wheeled the cart through the kitchen and into the laundry area of the hotel, which was right off the back service entrance. Outside the laundry bay, an official looking van, Azienda di Lavanderia di Siena, or Siena

Laundry Company, was waiting. Making sure the area was clear, which included disarming a nearby security camera, Louise was deftly lifted into the back of the van, the inside outfitted like an ambulance. The medic on the team was there to place her on an IV which would flow nutrients, and the ability to keep her sedated.

Then one of Raskalov's detail, known as the *Translator*, pilfered Louise's hotel room key, and her rental car key. He went to her room and packed her things, then casually walked through the lobby, and deposited the room key in the box at the front desk, along with a pre-written note that Louise Moscow was checking out and instructing them to tell anyone who inquired that she had to go back to Burgundy for a business emergency.

Then he called the phone number on the plastic rental car key chain and posed as the hotel valet, asking them to send an employee to retrieve the vehicle from the hotel. He then asked the real valet to bring the car around, posing as the agent for the rental car company he had just called. Since the valet staff dealt with the car service virtually every day, they didn't think to ask for I.D. The *Translator* retrieved the car and took it just outside the hotel valet area. When he spied the rental car van, he approached and handed off the car key as if, again, he worked for the hotel. They had just bought themselves at least a week of cold trail. The *Translator* strolled away awaiting his next instructions from Raskalov.

Meanwhile, the laundry van drove off headed for the international airport in Florence, ironically named Amerigo Vespucci, after America's eponymous merchant explorer. A Dassault Falcon 7X, part of Putin's personal fleet of aircraft, was standing by with more of Raskalov's security detail. Upon the van's arrival, now stripped of its laundry company identity, Louise was secured into the luxurious jet's cabin by the medic, then Raskalov and his detail boarded.

"куда мы направляемся?" the pilot asked, *where are we going?*

"Санкт-Петербург," replied Raskalov.

They were taking Louise to Saint Petersburg – previously known as Leningrad – to a secret prison especially authorized by Vladimir Putin to get information from detainees.

"Какие ваши любимые рестораны в Санкт-Петербурге?" the driver asked

Raskalov, *what are your favorite restaurants in St. Petersburg?*

They finally gave it away, Louise thought, as Raskalov and the driver continued their casual conversation.

Louise recalled some insight from training. *Food is always a common way to get intel.* She was on Russian soil now, no doubt transferred via private plane from the Florence airport. Her brain mentally ticked off the possible places they might be taking her, in her somewhat limited knowledge of the city. When she had done a deep dive into the Russian language at Langley, geography of the major cities was included.

Think, think! Saint Petersburg!

In a far-flung brain cell inside Louise's foggy mind, knowledge forged some lightning. *Kresty* was the prison in St. Petersburg. Translation *Cross,* for its distinct cross-shaped buildings. She became fascinated with it in the language labs because within the prison's 1730s roots was an infrastructure that was once the town's wine warehouse. Since she had moved to Burgundy her knowledge of wines had grown exponentially every year, so it jumped out at her. Expansion of the prison was completed in 1890, adding buildings creating a complex in the shape of a cross. After another century of Russian change, the prison was officially closed by Putin in 2006.

They are taking me to Kresty. It makes sense. It can still function as a prison, but clandestine forces could control who is brought there. Louise strained to hear the conversation in front, aware that Raskalov was occasionally glancing back at her to make sure she was still sedated. She needed to know if her premonition was correct. Finally, the confirmation she needed came.

"У них ещё рабочая кухня в «Крестах»?" the driver asked, *do they still have a working kitchen at Kresty?*

Kresty! sang Louise's synapses.

"Что с тобой и с едой? Успокойся, ладно?" retorted Raskalov, half in jest.

What is it with you and food? Be cool, okay? Louise translated to herself. Again, food gave it away. It was a secret prison, a spy novel cliché of historic absurdity. Putin had been a KGB foreign intelligence officer for sixteen years. If there was anyone who would allow enhanced interrogation…Louise had to leave those thoughts. She must stay 'fake sedated' for as long as necessary. She went into a meditative state, aware but in a deep relaxation.

The van suddenly pulled to a stop. An electric gate, heavy in sound, rung in her ears. The van continued.

From the sky Kresty is two distinct cross-shaped buildings. When they were built, as Louise recalled, the religiously symbolic cross design encouraged penance from inmates while also allowing observation by guards of all corridors from a single point. There was no way she could know which building, historic or not, they were taking her to, but the very atmosphere was thick with over 280 years of desperate trapped souls. *And now I'm one of them.* In her relaxation mode, sometimes Louise's thoughts were of the gallows variety.

The van lurched to a stop. They had arrived. After fumbling and stretching, Raskalov and the driver opened the back door to retrieve their captive. The October winds were cold and heavy, the layers of stench and sweat trapped in the buildings seeped beyond their boundaries. Louise felt her gag reflex tightening, but again her meditation allowed it to relax.

Her driving companions deftly got her gurney to ground level. She noted that the vehicle was efficiently equipped to move and deliver its cargo. She was so focused on figuring out where she was, she never noticed the syringe that was shot into her IV, taking her from relaxation to slumber.

THIRTEEN

Saint Petersburg, October 12, 2012

When she awoke the next day, Louise was off the gurney and in a bed in a somewhat modern prison cell. She seemed to remember that Kresty prison was overcrowded in its last days of use, and there was a term they used for the prisoners, 'pre-trial detainees.' *They loved that descriptive at Langley,* Louise recalled. Her captors either had modernized the secret part of the prison or spiffed up whatever was left behind. There were no dramatic stone walls of the old prison, she awoke in a bed that could have been in any 'Club Fed' in the United States. What startled her, as she adjusted to her surroundings, was the gentleman – yes, a man – that was in the adjacent cell. He was awake, on the edge of his bunk, and both his back and front were visible, the latter through a reflection in a small mirror on the wall. By the look of his flaccid face, he also obviously was a practitioner of the meditative arts. That, or he was stoned.

He sat shirtless, seemingly proud to display his abundant prison tattoos. Discretely, Louise shifted to a position where she could get a better look. From a certain angle, she was able to admire his entire torso covered in tats. He had distinctive shoulder art that he seemed to flaunt. Through the fog of her sedated dream state, something was beginning to click about the shapes and symbols on his taut skin. A recent conversation regarding prison tattoos, the mafia, and their meaning, but in the haze of two days under sedation she couldn't remember with whom. She really had to pee and shakily got to her feet, checking for the IV needle. It had been expertly inserted and removed so she could barely detect the hole. She placed the only threadbare wash towel provided over her lap while sitting on the toilet, but her neighbor never moved.

She wore the same clothing she had been captured in. The residue of the journey was all over her, and she craved a long hot shower. As she sat on the edge of her bunk, she felt the energy shifting, and saw two ambling figures shuffle toward her cell. One was obviously the guard, and the other, if this were a prison movie, would be the prison matron. They mumbled to each other in unintelligible Russian while the guard disengaged the lock.

"Пойдем со мной, я тебя приведу в порядок," the Matron said.

Louise couldn't let on that she understood, but her inner self was relieved to hear her say, *"Come with me, I will get you cleaned up."*

Recalling the Langley field guide for such a situation, she said in her flattest American Midwestern accent, "I don't speak Russian."

"She wants to take you to get cleaned up!" her prison mate exclaimed, startling everyone, especially Louise, with his Russian-accented-but-fluent English.

"You speak English!" Louise said too loudly.

The guard and the Matron were having none of it. The stocky woman grabbed Louise by the shoulder, more to guide her than to rough her up, and Louise feebly followed. They hadn't even bothered to cuff her.

"Keep your eyes open, podruga," her bi-lingual companion said as she was led away. *Podruga* was cynically inflected, meaning *girlfriend*.

She was now clean and dressed in the loose garb of inadequate prison clothes, which could best be described as doctor's scrubs with attitude. They were unadorned. Louise was hoping for a 'Property of Kresty' label so she could keep them as a souvenir and wear them down a catwalk at home, in a meta statement of the moment. *When is this stuff going to wear off?* she thought, referring to the sedative's punchy aftereffects.

She was now cuffed. During the last half hour or so, the Matron had put her through the paces of the classic woman's prison shower. The water was lukewarm but refreshing, and had odd smelling soap, but it did the job. She wasn't sure if the man standing guard wasn't sneaking a peek. She was appalled that she had to trade in her comfortable but cute underwear for small men's briefs, which she hoped were clean. The Matron gave her sports bra back, indicating with hand signals that Louise could wash it in the sink in her cell.

Then, the guard led her to a room which could qualify as a Central Casting archetype for a Russian interrogation scene. Akari Raskalov entered with another stoic bureaucrat behind him. They were followed by a mousy babushka lady with a tray of what looked like reconstituted powdered eggs and canned fruit cocktail. The guard un-cuffed Louise and they allowed her to eat. She was so starved it all tasted like heaven, even the bitter coffee seemed divine. When she was done the Mouse took her tray.

She remained un-cuffed, but knew the guard had an eye on her. *He had to be looking in the shower,* she thought, *he's got that male gaze going.* Her revelry was interrupted by a file slapped down on the table by Raskalov, no doubt her dossier.

"Louise Moscow, born 1962." Raskalov paused from the standard reading of the dossier in his soft accent. "Mizz Moscow, you look extraordinarily younger."

"I was even younger when I first got here," Louise said wearily.

Raskalov ignored her and continued. "Only daughter of George and Mary Moscow. Undergraduate Princeton, Harvard MBA, first job at J.P. Morgan. Impressive.

"Yes, I talked widows out of their pensions."

Raskalov glared at her. Then continued. "Worked for BCCI in the 1990s, but later turned state's witness against that bank. I seem to remember an incident in Paris causing a collapse of its assets."

"You mean a pyramid scheme," Louise corrected.

"And then there is a seven-year gap, before you re-emerged in 2001. Tell me, Mizz Moscow, so we can update your dossier, who were you hiding from?"

"90s fashion. I thought the coast was clear."

"Enough," Raskalov said dryly. "In 2001, you helped solve a years-long sex trafficking ring tied to string of familiar names, all while working with the CIA, the FBI and Interpol. You'd think someone in U.S. intelligence would have recruited you after that flashy display of law enforcement."

Louise assumed she was being tested. *Do they know I'm CIA?*

"But you chose to be a restaurant owner and raise lavender at your Burgundy cottage," Raskalov continued. "Yes, we know about the local farmer's market." Raskalov smiled at Louise's reaction. Some of his intel must have been pulled from confidential tax records but some had to have been gleaned the old-fashioned way, being followed. Either one made her sick.

"Have you ever been to Magali's Cafe? Best escargot in France," Louise purred.

He shrugged. "Yes, everybody goes to Magali's, I suppose."

"That makes me a citizen of the world!" Louise said, like she'd won a competition.

"Yes, you're *back in the game,* so to speak. We all seem to have ended up in Siena."

She paused. "Were you there for the horse races, too?"

Raskalov started talking faster now. "Why would a restaurateur and part-time flower farmer have such an extreme interest in Banco Monte dei Paschi? You even met with an executive, Mr. Dario Rossellini, who I believe you worked with at BCCI? Is your passion for researching the financial world upon you yet again? Some would call it snooping."

"Can't a gal take a vacation?"

"Now I'm going to make myself very clear, Louise." He spit out her name as if it were vinegar. "We need certain information from you. That is *my* business. Information. I obtain it, process it, and use it either for myself or my clients. My clients have a vested interest in control of the MPS, which goes higher than you could possibly understand."

"Try me. I love a good dictator-rules-the-world story."

"Listen to me!" Raskalov was just below his boiling point. "You were specifically brought here to provide the story of how you, the restaurateur and lavender farmer, came full circle to your passion, the world of financial snooping. You've been all over Siena on and off the grid. Yes, we monitored your phone. What were you doing in Siena?"

Louise began fantasizing about a shiv hidden in her waistband, like some James Cagney character, waiting for the exposed throat of the irritating Russian to get close. "I've always wanted to visit Italy," she said cheerily. "What passionate financial historian wouldn't want to go to the town of the oldest banks in the world?"

Raskalov grunted, then got up and stood with his full bearing over Louise. "This is a secret detention center. There are over 280 years of voices lost within this compound, people like you who wouldn't cooperate. According to legend, the architect, Antony Tomishko, told Tsar Alexander III upon completion, 'I built this prison for you.' The Tsar replied, 'No, you have built it for yourself.' Some believe Tomishko died here and haunts these walls to this day."

"Well, maybe he can tell me what I'm doing here." Louise was getting sick of this conversation.

"You like movies, don't you Mizz Moscow?"

Louise stared blankly at Raskalov, wondering where this was headed.

He continued. "You know the line, 'Vee haf vays of making you talk?'" It was bizarre to hear a stereotypical German accent through a Russian accent. "It's an often-paraphrased line first uttered in the 1935 film, *The Lives of a Bengal Lancer.*"

No kidding, Louise thought.

"The actual line in the film is, 'We have ways of making men talk.' We don't get many women here, Mizz Moscow, but I doubt the 'ways' of obtaining information change due to gender. The guard will take you back to your cell. I'd like you to think about those 'ways.' Your theories may cause some sleepless nights."

He paused and oddly said, "Your prison cell is not bad, right? Our apologies for putting you next to Dimitri Novikov. He once worked on the United States President's detail, known as the *Translator.* He also liked to talk to Western journalists. You may have noticed his mind tends to drift. I wonder why? Perhaps due to a lack of cooperation?"

Louise's head was spinning as the guard forced her up. She thought about interrogation training at Langley. She thought about the expression on Dimitri the *Translator's* face when she first saw him. Raskalov added one more thing as she was being taken away.

"Yes, Louise, we have ways of making men talk."

Saint Petersburg, November 12, 2012

Head searing in pain, Louise opened her eyes to the recurring nightmare. The migraine was due to lack of potable water. Over the years of her investigations, she had been locked in a castle dungeon in Belgium and the underground graveyard of the Paris Catacombs. These prison conditions were somewhere between the two. She faced the wall, lying on what had served as her bed for the past month, a lumpy mattress, with broken springs that jabbed and prodded.

Out of habit, she picked up the remaining pencil stub. The eraser had long been rubbed to oblivion and she used the aluminum ferrule for many purposes, from cleaning dirty fingernails to lancing a blister, to digging dirt that she used to scrub the putrid, uncovered toilet in a futile attempt at sanitation. In this case, she used the side of the ferrule that she had fashioned into a point to scratch one more line next to the many. It added up to exactly 30 days, this line crossing out four other lines in the sixth of five sets. Math had helped keep her brain from rotting.

By the second week, she had begun to feel her health failing due to lack of wholesome food and water. Her daily Tai Chi, yoga, and meditation had helped to maintain her physical and mental health, but the water provided was impure and the food lacked nutrients. With no access to sterilizing fire, she had to find ways to get nutrition, stay hydrated, and maintain some standard of personal hygiene.

The *Translator* in the adjacent cell had received fresh fruit daily, a good source of vitamins and hydration. She had also noticed him watching her while she did her daily Tai Chi, sometimes even quietly mimicking her postures in the shadows. Early mornings, the only direct natural light of her day came from the sunrise letting a single beam into the cells. At one point he began following along in a silent lesson, in exchange he would offer her some of the fruit.

After scratching her line on the wall, Louise got up from the cot and stretched her arms over her head. The *Translator* had started peeling an orange. But she turned deliberately to face him and put her hands together in a prayer pose and bowed toward him. He put the unpeeled orange down and stood, mirroring her stance and returned the bow. She began with Tai Chi warm-up movements, repetitive stretches, ranging from reaching up on tiptoe then down, to punching motions alternating sides, to forward bends, all simple movements repeated for about twenty counts each.

In the beginning, he had followed along a little shaky but steadily. If she saw him struggle, she would stop and started over. This practice recurred every morning, at the end of which, he tossed whatever fruit he could spare over to her. She had collected enough fruit to retain at least three at a time in case she need energy or felt dehydrated. She also used the fruit to maintain her agility by practicing her juggling. A college friend who had originally taught her said, "If you know where the balls will fall, you can control your life." In college, she had gotten good enough to juggle up to fifty consecutive counts. Now, in prison, she was almost a circus act. Her cellmate watched her like a fishbowl.

He often went shirtless giving her the opportunity to discretely study his tattoos, taking mental notes and placing them in her *Memory Palace*. She recalled the conversation with Kostas about the mafia messages in the tattoos. He had distinctive shoulder tattoos or *épaulettes* that he seemed to flaunt in front of guards. She thought he must be an honored prisoner of some sort as the guards appeared to be respectful.

As a sort of complicit courtesy when a guard approached, they stopped all friendly activity, and pretended to be estranged prison mates. But they both improved from the mutually beneficial relationship. A new sparkle in his eyes brightened his grizzled and worn face. She retained some muscle tone and healthy vigor. She didn't want to let on that she spoke Russian, and they both assumed the walls were bugged, so they never spoke. But she listened carefully.

Saint Petersburg, November 15, 2012

It had felt like eternal hell in that cell, so she had taken to sketching his tattoos on the scraps of paper her prison mate had kindly given her. She picked up a sketch she had started from the tidy stack and continued to define the tattoo from memory. But today something finally changed in her routine. A new guard approached but not to bring food or water.

"Ты слишком здоров. Ты пойдешь со мной," he said gruffly, unlocking the cell. She was *too healthy,* and he was moving her to another location.

She studied him carefully as he unceremoniously used a waist-chain system to cuff her ankles and wrists together in front. She made a mental note of his neck tattoos, a bow tie containing a dollar sign in the center knot. This focus helped distract her from the fear of whatever the new aggression meant. He grabbed her by the elbow and forced her out, scattering the small stack of sketches on the cell floor, and escorted her away.

"Where are you taking me?" Louise demanded, catching a glimpse of her prison mate, the *Translator,* who eyed her intently. She thought he gave her an almost imperceptible reassuring nod, but as she gained distance seeing him alone in the oubliette inspired little hope for him to help her.

The guard led her down a warren of doom and they approached a massive steel door presumably leading to an outside courtyard or a transportation area. She would never see it because a hood was placed over her head. Based on the sounds, her second guess was correct. She was forced into a van that started driving as she sat unsecured on a bench in the back, being tossed about. She rolled onto her stomach and moved to the floor where she sat in lotus pose. Fearing the farther she was taken, the less chance anyone looking would find her. She began breathing, counting ten breaths, and starting over. She knew from her practice that every ten breaths added up to about one minute. After just five sets of ten the van pulled to a stop. They had driven no faster than 20 miles per hour so less than two miles, probably another site within the prison complex. Voices speaking Russian, barking orders, chiding, laughing. The van doors opened, and she was dragged out.

"Come on, smart lady!" she was told, in the almost caricaturist broken English with heavy Russian accent of so many James Bond films. "We see how strong you will be!"

She remained silent, listening intently as she was brought into a musty damp chamber. A chair was dragged, and she was shoved down onto it, the hood yanked off. She focused and saw a man sitting on a chair opposite her.

"Impressive, Mizz Moscow," Raskalov said. "You are very strong-willed."

"What do you want? You have no grounds for detaining me."

"Ah, yes. Typical American thinking that laws can protect you."

"You hold me in prison for a month and never even tell me where I am or what for? So, you can collect more *kompromat* on innocent people for some devil's ledger?"

His eyes flashed at the words she used, *Devil's Ledger*, not sure if he liked it or hated it. "You will talk. These methods have worked for centuries," was all he replied.

Louise began to shiver from cold and terror. Up until then, whoever was detaining her must have feared repercussions because of who she was. But she had the feeling that they had found a work-around.

"Just tell me what you want," Louise said, trying to stop her teeth from chattering.

"You think you're trembling now..." He waved to his cohort.

FOURTEEN

LaFontaine was in his private 'nerve' center on his floating home the *Vague-A-Bond*. But paradoxically, it was here that he was most relaxed, around the state-of-the-art banks of monitors expressing all kinds of information. *Information. That's what this network constantly feeds us*, LaFontaine thought. He was so relaxed, that if someone who had known him in his former life were to walk in, they might have recognized the secretive eyes of their old pal Wendell Jarvis, a coding genius who had invented the *Kingdom of the Keys*.

Wendell Jarvis was LaFontaine's birth name, and he was American, not French. His superhero persona made him laugh. His nickname in financial circles was *Bruce Wayne* because of his reputation for fighting corruption. Little did they know, *Frédéric LaFontaine* really was a secret identity, and he really had been an orphan. But his parents had not been brutally murdered in the street. They died in an ordinary automobile accident. He was raised by his Uncle Larry and his Aunt Carol, both physicians, busy people who had been childless. Carol was somewhat cold but made sure Wendell had whatever he needed. Larry was the one with the big heart. He was a urologist who had the jokey nickname *The Plumber*. He was always trying to create joyful childhood memories for Wendell, who was fourteen years old when his parents died.

In 1975, on the first anniversary of his parents' accident, which he chose to spend boarded up in his bedroom, he heard a loud thump outside his bedroom door. Wendell waited a few minutes, then opened the door to find a large package, no doubt delivered by Uncle Larry. Inside the package was an MITS Altair 8800 computer kit. He became completely smitten with the box of magic circuitry, and it launched his lifelong passion. Over the years he had assembled and disassembled this humble machine over a hundred times, like a soldier breaking down and reassembling his rifle. It was the seed where it all began, the origin of the real *Vague-a-Bond*. LaFontaine always kept the Altair 8800 in sight, above the monitor that tracked financial news.

Like the legends of Bill Gates and Steve Jobs, Wendell Jarvis was as close to being the third legend as one could get. His specialty became financial software, with built-in security measures that no one could duplicate. The entire algorithmic invention came from him. Wendell's original investor, Dugan Golder, set up through Uncle Larry, created a holding company through which all the licensing and patent rights were owned by the inventor. Golder exited the initial million-dollar investment with a 100x return, in 1988.

Wendell Jarvis eventually got tired of being Wendell Jarvis. The year his uncle died in the early 1990s, his aunt had already passed, and Jarvis was being threatened by the very financial system he had helped to secure. He was also worth close to a billion dollars. So, he came up with a solution. Sell the company, establish several readily available offshore financial shelters, and disappear. He executed the first phase of the plan perfectly.

For the second phase, telling no one his time of departure or destination, he escaped on a private jet, then a puddle-jumper, to an unincorporated Caribbean Island. After the initial disappearance he found relative peace. But within a couple weeks the tabloids and paparazzi found him, and he became a post-modern Howard Hughes in the media for a hot second. Two months after the leeches had arrived, most departed. But a few lingered to hunt the contemporary Hughes like an exotic animal be sold to the highest bidder. With his undying desire for peace, he concocted a new plan. It was idiotic, but if executed perfectly, would be permanent.

Setting up the financial structure and transition of funds for the new plan had been relatively simple. His proprietary software, which he called the *Kingdom of the Keys,* provided a backdoor to the nine largest bank and financial systems in the world. They didn't know he had them. If he was going to use them for leverage, he had to keep it that way.

Most of his physical transformation came from losing weight. He paid for a very expensive and confidential *fat farm* that guaranteed a certain amount of success. He signed up three more times, until he felt confident enough to lose the last bit by himself. And he did. His scraggly beard, the trademark he borrowed from the young Steve Jobs, was the next to go. He added some airbrushing plastic surgery. All the best in the world. And these transformers never cared about a person's identity, just their willingness to pay the bill. All the while he was trying to figure out how to 'kill' Wendell Jarvis.

The solution was utterly unethical and bereft of morality. Suffice to say, the body of Wendell Jarvis was found near a lava flow in Hawaii, burnt beyond recognition. It was in fact a body double who had taken the dangerous hike and disappeared replaced with a procured corpse with dental records. This corpse procurement service never cared about who used their 'product,' just their willingness to pay the bill. *It will be the last immoral thing I will ever do* the newly christened *Frédéric LaFontaine* had thought back then. He had pulled off the identity switch. And his financial shelters had done their job, the cash reserves were enormous.

Buying LaFontaine's backstory proved easier than expected. He sent an agent to one of the better current novelists, Buck Chasen, and paid him an outrageous sum to create a modern finance Horatio-Alger-in-France story, which would become LaFontaine's biography. The only plot point and similarity between the two identities he insisted upon was that Wendell and Frédéric were both orphans. The rest of the story made the musical *Annie* seem like a story about a nice home.

The reinvented LaFontaine had grown his already enormous wealth exponentially through wise and timely investments in Google and other dot-com era winners. It was so subtle, and surprisingly easy to get the world to completely accept LaFontaine's existence. Wendell had always easily picked up languages, so LaFontaine's maternal language of choice was Parisian French, disguising his very American English with a pronounced French lilt. His was fully accepted as one of the tech industry nouveau riche, with the media presumptive about his financials and benefitting from his many ostentatious junkets playing up a self-mocking *bourgeois gentilhomme* character, a Jay Gatsby, but without the bittersweet ending.

The new persona complete, when LaFontaine announced his intention to build a spectacular yacht, and live on the seas, the tabloid press had a field day, and sold a lot of supermarket rags and clickbait headlines. But like the first time he disappeared, he told no one of his departure nor destination. This time his advantage would be leveraged to remain untouchable on the seas. The press coverage died down after he disappeared, occasionally referring to him by his new nickname, *The Seafarer*.

One of LaFontaine's monitors buzzed, a distinct alert, like the red bat-phone. He welcomed the secure-channel face of Michael Fuentes, his CIA recruiter. Even *they* didn't care about identity, it turned out. LaFontaine's lawyers negotiated his participation in *The Company*, which was heavily influenced by his ability to gather intel. Every waterlogged branch of law enforcement was caveated to lay off the Vague-A-Bond, since he joined up, an additional advantage of his leverage.

"An agent is missing. And *this time it's personal*," intoned Michael.

"Louise!" La Fontaine exclaimed immediately recognizing the code phrase.

She had insisted her code of capture be a movie line, the worse the better. She opted for the tagline of *JAWS: THE REVENGE, this time it's personal.*

"She was captured in broad daylight," Michael explained. "They covered their trail. Some how they got her out of the hotel, the staff recalled nothing out of the ordinary. When we played security tapes the service area cameras were conveniently disconnected."

"My Cypriot friend Kostas asked about her. The hotel told him she left a message that she had to go back to Burgundy on emergency business. Whoever took her must have checked her out via the room key drop-box and returned her rental car," he surmised.

"You remember your CIA training. Well, her captors did something that we hadn't experienced before. The front desk at the hotel read me a note from her, saying she went back to Burgundy. Shortly thereafter I received a text with our rendezvous code phrase, *the Devil's in the details*, specifically designated for *this* mission, from *her* phone. Our protocol was to text the same code word back, but no further contact, and meet at her Burgundy cottage." Michael then paused, gathering his thoughts. "That bought them two more days. By the time I arrived with my clearance to go into her coms room, there was an envelope on which was written, ATTN: NEXT OCCUPANT. Inside was her mobile phone. Split perfectly in two. The precision of that slice fucked me up."

LaFontaine felt the hairs on the back of his neck stand up. "Where is she?"

"How is your relationship with the apparatchik[19] at the Great Port of Saint Petersburg?"

"Помогает, если вы говорите на этом языке," LaFontaine replied. Meaning, *it helps if you speak the language.*

FIFTEEN

Saint Petersburg, November 21, 2012

As days of interrogation blurred together, Louise used every ounce of her CIA training to delay what might be her inevitable demise. Every scenario of capture is imagined, all possible outcomes are studied, and instruction is given on how the agent can control the direction of those outcomes. One tactic is to always tell the truth under questioning but stretch it like a storyteller. Yes, she was in Siena to study the landscape of the bank, but only for historical purposes.

"I kept looking for connections between the various money changers," she insisted, after engaging Raskalov's interrogation flunky on a deep dive into the bank's history. That only satisfied them for about a week, and then Louise really began to shovel it deep.

One of the *ways of making her talk* was solitary confinement. She had lost the camaraderie of her prison 'suite mate' Dimitri Novikov, the *Translator*. At first, the only other torture was the length of the interview session, but beyond that there were no *enhanced* techniques. Yet.

Her captors had taken away her relatively posh cell and moved her to one of the cross-shaped buildings, presumably the old female side, if they had any sense of history. She had an irrational fascination with the history of the cell. Who had been there before her? Also, the cell number 525 made her laugh. It was the date of her birthday, and it was also considered lucky.[20]

But this change of location did require a change of techniques. It was here that they commenced sleep deprivation tactics. Again, Louise relied on CIA training with a bit of invention. Her use of meditation allowed her to have *micro-naps*, an intense connection to cellular rebuilding. When the inevitable jarring event to force her awake occurred, of which there were many types, she had enough time rebuilding to keep a reserve of calming energy.

The CIA had also authorized a second phase of truth in advance for extreme interrogation. She endured thirty-six hellish wakeful hours before ending it by offering up details of her life after bringing down BCCI. The years of witness protection, the randomness of being a saloon-keeper-in-paradise, even her fake name Karen Baker. This information was acceptable to them, strangely, and she was allowed to finally rest.

How much time will this buy me? she wondered, before succumbing to slumber.

The North Atlantic, November 22, 2012

Michael flew in a military helicopter. Or what he assumed was military. There were no markings, and the paint job was black as night. He shrugged it off and thought only of the time they had lost. He had gotten back on Louise's trail through sheer luck. The *Translator* in Raskalov's detail was still in Siena and willing to sell information. He was a somewhat quiet junkie with many addictions to nurture and had heard through the inevitable grapevine that the CIA was seeking information. The *Translator* could probably buy a poppy farm for the amount he was asking, but the intel was iron clad and of extreme value.

First, he had admitted that he was the hotel-key and car drop man, because of his language skills. He also disclosed that sometimes his employers thought he wasn't listening to them, because he had an actor's demeanor of disinterest. But what he had heard over the past year had served his pocketbook well. Still, even The *Translator* was shocked when he found out where they were taking Louise.

"The Kresty in St. Petersburg," he told a handful of CIA agents, including Louise's allies Michael and Vladimir. Hanging back in the shadows, was Jean-Philippe.

"But that's been closed since 2006," said Vladimir.

"I'm just telling you what I heard," the *Translator* said. "The only reason I even know about Kresty is because I got ripped off in St. Petersburg once when my girlfriend and I were offered a 'tour' of the prison. It was only a tour of the outside. No refunds."

Back in the chopper, Michael looked at Jean Phillippe, who looked like a demented prophet. Without his undercover monk's robes, dressed in fatigues that Michael insisted they both wear, with his ample beard and head shaved *high and tight*, he was the Che Guevara of Europe, the strangest looking Interpol agent in the territory. After Michael had pointed this out, mostly in jest, Jean-Philippe attempted his own joke, replying, "Have you seen some of your recruits lately?" He was dour most of the time and would break into prayer meditation to handle the stress of rescuing Louise.

"We have a visual of the vessel, sir," the helicopter pilot squawked into their headphones. It was the Vague-A-Bond. They were about to land on LaFontaine's helicopter pad and put into motion one of the most absurd plans Michael had ever heard, a real outside-the-boxer with inexperienced specialists. It was LaFontaine who had suggested it, even recommending team members. He already had an ex-Navy-Seal named Charlie, whom Michael had met when Louise was on the island. LaFontaine got CIA and Interpol approval for the entire rescue mission just by sharing the front end of the plan, along with assurances that he would take responsibility for the cost and the lives of the men. Like 'Mission: Impossible', the CIA and Interpol would be given plausible deniability for the infiltration, if something were to go wrong.

Saint Petersburg, November 23, 2012

Louise awoke from a fourteen-hour sleep, back in her original cell, once again adjacent to Dimitri's the *Translator*. He was in his meditative state, she was unharmed. It was a bit weird that they had moved her back there where Dimitri still was. More than ever, she was in *trust no one* mode. But she was grateful to be in the more sanitary place. She shook off the cobwebs and assessed her situation, another Langley lesson: *Constantly assess your situation, look for ways to exploit a moment when you can weaken a captor's offense.*

Maybe she could leverage some info from Dimitri. Perhaps about the tattoos. She had learned from Kostas and her research that Russian bodyguards and even translators who were employed in protection detail were often ex-Russian-mob muscle, the type that would be inked with ancient designs that could bring favorable treatment upon capture. The shape of the designs *held a key to a lock*, at least that was the legend.

"Я восхищаюсь твоей преданностью медитации," she stage-whispered to Dimitri.

This immediately startled the prisoner. He was shirtless despite all fluctuations in temperature, as if he wanted to keep displaying his leverage, wielding it like a weapon or a shield. He thought he had just heard his old Pedruga, or girlfriend, tell him in a perfect Russian, with a proper dialect, *I admire the dedication to your meditation.*

It was Dimitri's turn to answer, under his breath but loud enough. "You speak Ruskey?" He paused as if weighing the next sentence. "Has it come in handy?"

Louise moved closer to his prison bars to inform him quickly. She suddenly trusted him, although she was not sure why.

"It helped me to understand the information they were looking for. Knowing what they were saying helped me to embellish until they were satisfied. Raskalov had no problem speaking his mother tongue in front of me."

"Они думают, что у них есть вся власть." *They think they have all the power.*

"Where did they keep you for the past weeks?" Louise asked.

"In another part of this hellhole. They are, as you Americans say, fucking with me."

They ended their conversation when they heard a stirring in the corridor. It was her old buddy *The Matron*, delivering lunch. She spoke in guttural Russian to Dimitri, which Louise translated as, *I see you both have returned.* Dimitri just stared dumbly. Lunch was a thin gruel of a broth with a potato and bread, no butter.

She had felt her health fading through the inadequate nourishment during the torture phase. The water that came from the small sink was discolored and impure, but she maintained decent enough hydration without ill effects. She lustily consumed her *lunch* and returned to Dimitri. She was fishing for that moment to exploit.

"Whaddaya in for?" She tried affecting a gangster voice, like a 1930s prison movie.

"Translators are privy to many conversations," Dimitri began in startlingly good English. "Whether the speaker knows it or not. Let's just say I heard one too many, and three more that were too sensitive. They are sending me home soon, or so they say. I admitted all I knew, and somehow I think they believe me." Dimitri laughed like a villain in a melodrama.

Now Louise had to go for it. "Have you heard anything about why I'm here?"

Dimitri didn't even look surprised. "I do have a little bird that occasionally sings." He imitated The Matron's guttural Russian. Despite her circumstance, Louise managed a smile.

"They think you have some kind of knowledge about the Bank of Siena, and some sort of secret and ancient stash." Louise was not happy with that news. She was *pursuing* knowledge and suspected the note that Rossellini had given her was like a treasure map. Dimitri the *Translator* just unwittingly confirmed her suspicions. But she was distressed that Raskalov both knew about a treasure *and* knew that she might know about it.

"Anything you'd like to tell me, pedruga?" Dimitri batted his eyes like a silent movie star.

"Если бы я сказал тебе, мне пришлось бы убить тебя," Louise joked. *If I told you, I'd have to kill you.*

Their conversation was interrupted by a new contingent of the guard, Louise swore they were interchangeable Russian peach fuzz types. Also, the return of The Matron, her growling voice said something to Dimitri, which Louise interpreted as bath time. She could use a wash.

Tell her she has another meeting after her shower, Louise interpreted to herself.

Dimitri turned to Louise and repeated the instruction in English, a twinkle in his evil eye.

Every time she left any *accommodation* at Kresty, she never knew if she was coming back to the same place. *There's no place like home*, she thought as they led her away.

Saint Petersburg, November 23, 2012

LaFontaine, Charlie, Jean-Philippe, and Michael were gathered inside LaFontaine's impressive room of monitors. It gave a whole new meaning to *Control* Room, Michael thought, having a feeling of omnipresence. *The Seafarer* had commandeered one of his monitors to review the plan outline. He showed photos and gave an overview of their inside man.

After they had determined that Louise was in Kresty, the CIA and Interpol worked together to establish a mole inside the prison. Vladimir had scanned some likely candidates at Kresty and was able to establish the *Peach Fuzz* guard as a plant through back channels. It was *Peach Fuzz* who had escorted Louise on her last bathing trip. He could keep tabs on Dimitri Novikov aka the *Translator* and Louise simply by volunteering for the job since none of the other guards liked *The Matron*.

It was *Peach Fuzz* who had deftly recruited Dimitri, the larcenous *Translator* in Siena. Akari Raskalov had kept a tail on the *Translator*, as he did all his operatives, never leaving anything to chance. Although the CIA had been stealthy in gaining access to the *Translator*, Raskalov knew he had been compromised and locked him up strategically in the cell adjacent to Louise.

After *Peach Fuzz* mentioned the Louise Moscow connection to Dimitri, along with a promise of freedom, a trust was established. *Peach Fuzz* also arranged the return of Louise next to the cell of Dimitri, informing his superiors that they had in fact been talking and that Dimitri could get her to speak freely to him. Ballsy *Peach Fuzz* knew he was overpromising, but *freedom has many definitions*, according to an old Russian proverb.

Michael and his three operatives, like schoolboys in a high school revue, rehearsed the mission particulars for hours. Michael had taken on many roles over the years as an FBI and CIA agent. Although he hadn't directly worked undercover with the rest of them, he gathered from the meeting they were also well-versed in roleplay. But the success of the mission depended on how well they performed. It was both opening and closing night.

"As an additional incentive." LaFontaine held up a bottle of his famous Privilege La Reserve du Prince, a cognac known for its unique history and exquisite taste. He had acquired the very limited and rare historic reserve that had been hidden from the Germans during the invasion of France and sold for $5,000 a bottle. "On our return, we'll toast the person we're about to bring home."

"I'll finally get to try your famous cognac?" Charlie said. "I'd love to have some now to toast Louise, but no alcohol before diving."

LaFontaine had arrived via the Baltic Sea then the Gulf of Finland and was docked at his usual spot with the Vague-A-Bond anchored in viewing distance of the Great Port that led to the Neva River. Twilight had come and gone, and the group agreed that everyone was on the same page, and they were ready to go.

The four aspiring rescuers gathered on deck in diving dry suits and scuba gear, just as the last twilight gave way to inky darkness. They were going to take a swim toward the Great Port at the mouth of the Neva River, on the banks of which stood Kresty Prison, with the help of small but powerful propulsion vehicles à la James Bond. Charlie, the ex-Navy-Seal, would lead when under the waves, but each of the other men had done enough leisure and training dives to rise to the necessary level of competence.

"Let's say a prayer, shall we?" Jean Philippe said with a soft French accent. He bowed his head and recited a prayer in Latin.

"Amen," they all said in unison.

"Fuck it, let's go!" Charlie ordered. They lined up on the gunwale, their backs to the water, then one by one flipped backwards into the frigid Port's Bay. They each gave the okay signal, and the deckhand distributed one propulsion device to each from the beach deck. They descended to twenty feet and followed the thin beam of light Charlie held that pierced the abyss.

They made landfall and gathered behind a fisherman's warehouse Charlie had scouted earlier that day. It was closed for the night, and he made himself at home, unpacking his small dry bag containing their communications equipment. With his experience in covert operations, Charlie would remain there as the communications hub, making sure their escape in approximately eighteen hours lined up perfectly. It was a foolproof plan if perfectly executed, and he was simply going to continue monitoring conditions and be available when the rest of the group returned, with the additional cargo of Louise.

When the three took off their dry suits and gear, which Charlie carefully hid, they were dressed in what would best be described as hip business casual. Blending in with the comings and goings of the busy port, LaFontaine pulled out his satellite phone and spoke into it in Russian. He knew of a discreet car service in Saint Petersburg and had secured transportation. They weren't going to Kresty just yet, first they needed some leverage.

SIXTEEN

Saint Petersburg, November 23, 2012

As the private chauffeur drove the three Saint Petersburg interlopers to their destination, LaFontaine turned his thoughts to the first time he had met Louise Moscow.

Frédéric LaFontaine knew people. He had carefully cultivated relationships over his years as *The Seafarer*, mostly to hold corrupt players of the international banking and financial systems accountable. This gave him a certain mystique in the Intelligence community, resulting in Louise Moscow becoming one of his fellow crusaders for that justice. Shortly after he had launched the Vague-A-Bond in the mid-1990s, he was determined to connect with the woman who had brought down the corrupt bankers of BCCI. His research in the early Internet years was not difficult, the yacht having always been equipped with state-of-the-art computation, as he continued to invest in the innovators that advanced it.

His interest in Louise Moscow had turned into obsession. In a synergistic twist of fate, LaFontaine reached out via confidential channels to the Intelligence community just as the FBI had been tracking the enigmatic *Seafarer* as a potential ally. LaFontaine had pieced together connections by obtaining some Princeton yearbooks from the time Louise was an undergrad. He spotted her in a casual campus photo with Michael Fuentes, when the caption, 'Spring Fever Brings Students Together,' caught his eye. After further research, he found out that Michael Fuentes was involved in the BCCI case through his position with the FBI.

LaFontaine initiated contact with Michael via a risky exchange of information through confidential FBI informant channels. Michael was intrigued, having heard of LaFontaine. The Bureau had kept a file on him since he had suddenly emerged and took to the sea. Michael also questioned why the file was marked *person of interest*, while also observing that LaFontaine's comings-and-goings were virtually untouched by official scrutiny on the waters.

Michael reached out via the confidential channel and LaFontaine told him of vital intel on some banking irregularities that would later result in the murder of banker Ekram M. Almasi. That case would eventually bring Louise out of exile.

"I will tell you whatever you want to know," Frédéric told Michael in his soft accent. "If you connect me with Louise Moscow."

The silence at the end of the phone told *The Seafarer* that he had contacted the right man. Michael learned that LaFontaine had leverage, in a roundabout sense, and LaFontaine learned of the Caribbean Island where Karen Baker, AKA Louise Moscow, posed as the owner of a Tiki bar. LaFontaine explained to Michael that he wanted to help get Louise out of exile and expand her powers as a financial expert to expose corruption.

"I have a vested interest," *The Seafarer* told the FBI man. "You understand."

Their new alliance became a mutual exchange of information, LaFontaine keeping Michael informed of any interaction with Louise, and the FBI informing LaFontaine of any interesting Ports-of-Call banking irregularities. Frédéric LaFontaine's concern for Louise's safety would grow to match that of Michael Fuentes' concern for his former college girlfriend.

After that, LaFontaine had his Caribbean business connection, Charlie, make initial contact with Louise and he recruited her for the investigation into the mysterious murder of internationally renowned philanthropist, Ekram M. Almasi. And the rest was history.

LaFontaine, Michael, and Jean-Philippe arrived at their Saint Petersburg destination, the Four Seasons hotel on Lion Palace Street. After having lost himself in his memories, LaFontaine snapped to and went over the plan yet again with his companions. They all knew what to expect in their ruse, but they couldn't guess what would happen if something went wrong. *We'd all be dead,* thought Michael.

LaFontaine had arranged a rendezvous, with a high-level official in Putin's governing body, Gleb Sokolov, who was doing some pre-planning himself. Sokolov had just been installed as the Russian Minister of Finance in 2011 and oversaw a major Saint Petersburg Economic Forum that took place every June.

Having recently met Sokolov at that Economics Forum five months ago, LaFontaine had a valid connection. Michael and Jean-Philippe would play the role of his bodyguards. Michael had to keep his mouth shut. Although he was fluent in Spanish and Italian, he only knew pidgin French and Russian and would have trouble hiding his American accent. Jean-Philippe assured LaFontaine that he would be the one to speak if any French came up.

Michael always had admired LaFontaine's gut instincts. His wealth was secondary to his purpose, which was unauthorized oversight of runaway international finance corruption. Michael had already switched to the CIA when the 2008 crash occurred, and it was LaFontaine who used his nimble traveling status to become a ghost negotiator between governments. After picking up a report about the steering of helpful resources by *The Seafarer* to poorer countries and noting that his general file was interestingly void of details, Michael convinced his superiors to promote LaFontaine as an informer with Agent status.

"The intel he can gather would be as vital as any field agent," Michael concluded in his proposal. LaFontaine was hesitant, but when he heard Louise had been recruited to the CIA, his reluctance dissipated. He then sent his lawyers to negotiate the terms of his participation.

Jean-Philippe, the only non-American agent, was meditating in silent prayer. The background of his conversion to spirituality began with his undercover work in a monastery, during the BCCI case that Louise helped to break, and as he later found out, LaFontaine had helped to finance. He'd do anything for this odd faux fellow countryman, and for Louise, so he was ready for anything. He busied himself by scanning the room that the Minister's aide had led them to, a large suite in a discreet location in the hotel.

"*Nice to see you again, my VAGABOND friend,*" the finance minister, Gleb Sokolov, said to LaFontaine in Russian, making it clear that Russia knew the name of his floating home.

"*You've moved up in the world,*" LaFontaine replied in Russian. He had followed his career since the late 1990s, when Sokolov was leading the Budget Office in the Ministry of Finance and formulated policy in their banking division.

Jean-Philippe had properly reckoned the situation. He knew the Minister from photographs, but he looked more like a *tête d'oeuf*, or *egg head*, than he expected. Silaunov had three bodyguards, and Jean-Philippe knew that they were undoubtedly ruthless. He also knew that Sokolov spoke no English, and LaFontaine would not be interpreting for their benefit.

"You know why I'm here," LaFontaine said in his unerring Russian.

"But of course, considering the last time we met," Sokolov answered.

"Have a seat," LaFontaine said in Russian, sitting down at the table where a man in a tuxedo was already sitting.

The man reached into his pocket and one of Sokolov's bodyguards approached. Michael and Jean-Philippe stiffened instinctively. But the tuxedoed man pulled out a deck of cards. He was there to deal *Texas Hold'em* poker. The dealer opened an ornately decorated box, revealing an impressive set of poker chips.

Sokolov sat across from Frédéric. *"I hope you've been practicing, Frédéric, I'm always happy to separate you from your fortune,"* he half-joked.

LaFontaine had set up the game when he learned that Sokolov was in Saint Petersburg, as part of the plan. He had last sat at a poker table during the Economic Summit with the most powerful finance representatives in the world. The group had included three women who had the hottest cards initially, but Sokolov kept chipping away. LaFontaine fought back with his usual conservative play. When they went *all-in*, betting all their chips, the potential win was substantial, and it was Sokolov who produced a pair of aces to combine with the community ace, to the sorrow of the rest of the players. LaFontaine had a pair of aces when combining his hole card, but obviously lost. He found it interesting that they had both used the fourth ace, and the Russian Finance Minister admired his poker skills.

"We must play again," he had said to Frédéric as they said their good-byes.

Texas Hold'em had become a popular variant of poker all over the world because it was the most dramatic, and the most group oriented. Players are dealt two secret *hole* cards, then five cards are dealt face down in front of the dealer to be used by all players, combined with their hole cards. The dealer turns each card over, beginning with the *Flop*, which is the first three cards, then the *Turn*, when the fourth card is flipped, and then the *River* when the fifth and final community card is flipped. Bets are made before each of the three card-flipping stages, building the excitement.

With only two players, the game was quick and nimble. Sokolov, with his flair for theatrics, was taking LaFontaine's chips on the River card. But

The Seafarer was finding luck on the Turn. After two hours, the chip stacks were about equal, and Michael was beginning to wonder what the endgame was to this plan. LaFontaine had indicated that something would happen during the meeting, and for his bodyguards to *be on alert*. They were to listen for one Russian word in an exchange when someone announced *all in*.

It was the Russian Finance Minister who made the big move, pushing his chips to the center of the table on the Turn of a crucial hand. LaFontaine followed with his chips. The dealer was about to flip the River card, when LaFontaine interrupted, making the observation, "*The Minister is an exceptional player.*"

Michael and Jean-Philippe braced for aggression. Years of training through their respective agencies, the FBI, the CIA, and Interpol, had prepared them for this moment. The Russian word *igrok*, meaning *player*, was the word they had been listening for.

Before the dealer could expose the River card, LaFontaine stood up. He produced five cards out of his own pocket and dealt them right on top of the poker cards. Each individual card had a series of algorithmic symbols, incomprehensible in any language.

Gleb Sokolov lost the color in his face, turning as white as an egg.

"Все должны немедленно покинуть эту комнату, кроме Фредерика!" shouted the finance minister. Michael and Jean-Philippe looked at Frédéric in confusion.

LaFontaine translated to French for them. "*He wants everyone to leave, except for me.*" Michael looked at Jean-Philippe who nodded in approval. Sokolov's men escorted them along with the dealer out of the room.

LaFontaine had used his leverage. A Russian clock chimed midnight.

SEVENTEEN

Saint Petersburg, November 23, 2012

Louise was again sitting in the stereotypical Russian interrogation room. It had been her second home at the Kresty going on 41 days, according to the marks she had now scratched into her forearm. She wasn't sure anymore, which went against her training. The CIA emphasized keeping time accurately while incarcerated in a kidnapping scenario. She felt refreshed from her lukewarm shower and noted that the new guard kept his eyes away from her ever-shrinking body. *I must have lost at least ten pounds,* she thought to herself, on a frame where even one pound made a difference in skin and bone. She was malnourished, exhausted, and may have a UTI due to the fetid water in the prison. But she was alert. The Matron and the peach-fuzzed guard were her ever-present company, but as usual she was not cuffed while in this room. Her old friend Raskalov walked in.

"We have a surprise for you," he said.

"My birthday was six months ago, and Christmas isn't for a month," Louise snarked. The door opened, and two guards were flanked around a figure she at first couldn't see.

"Hello, Louise."

The figure revealed himself. It was her father, George Moscow. Apparently, he had flipped completely to the Russians. Louise again had to resist an urge to scream. She readjusted her feelings. *Constantly assess your situation, look for ways to exploit a moment when you can weaken a captor's offense.*

"Hello, dad," Louise chirped in mocking fashion. "Fancy seeing you here. Wouldn't mother be proud?"

George's face flushed red. Recovering, he said, "Louise, this is not personal. You're lucky they called me. I had been trying to call your Burgundy home for weeks."

"Yes, I'm sooooo lucky." Louise affected a fancy tone to her voice. "Well, as you have surmised, I've been the guest of this fine establishment and this charming gentleman." She indicated Raskalov with her chin.

"I am here to facilitate your release," explained George.

"You're trying to get rid of me, Akari?" Louise said mock-lovingly.

George persisted. "They just need to know certain things. Simple things."

"I've already told them about my alias Karen Baker. What more do they want? Now I'm a saloon keeper and a lavender farmer."

"They want to know why you're in Siena. They know you've been using the library at your hotel, and they know you are a finance expert. They know you met with Dario Rossellini. Just tell them what you're looking for."

"It seems like everybody knows everything, except me. I know nothing." Louise noted that The Matron was shifting uncomfortably nearby, close enough to create an exploitation, or at least a distraction.

"Louise, please…" George was now pleading because she was his daughter.

Suddenly Louise stood up, and deftly slid her chair into the solar plexus of the guard behind her. Creating that distraction, and with two swift motions, she was able to sweep The Matron off her feet and put a Krav Maga chokehold on the hapless bureaucrat.

"I'm two seconds from breaking her neck!"

The room of men looked at the two women. George's eyes were as wide as saucers, as he did not recognize this side of her daughter. Raskalov was signaling to the two guards, including the one who had escorted George into the room and was now rubbing his upper rib cage. Unfortunately, Louise did not notice that Peach Fuzz had moved quickly and struck his rifle butt solidly between her shoulders. It hit the targeted nerve and loosened her grip on The Matron, who rolled away. The other guards swiftly intervened. Louise didn't know it, but Peach Fuzz had saved her life in that moment.

"That was a stupid move, Mizz Moscow," Raskalov bellowed, as a semblance of order was restored. He looked at George with pity. "I'm tired of this negotiation. I'm tired of *information-gathering techniques* that don't work." He indicated to his special guards, who along with Peach Fuzz had successfully cuffed Louise and had her up against the wall.

"These gentlemen who escorted your father into this room," Raskalov said in measured tones. "They have training in advanced methods of getting the information we need. We are not fooling around anymore."

"Give me more time, I didn't expect her to go Bruce Lee on you," George pleaded. Even Louise cracked a smile on that one, trying to mitigate her nerve pain.

"Come on, you fucking weakling," Louise spoke up. "It took three goons to hold me down. You never wanted a fair fight." A rifle butt in her stomach by one of Raskalov's goons was the reply. Although she'd trained herself to tighten her muscles, the butt managed to split them. Louise struggled to regain her wind.

George was mute. There was a sense of defeat to his demeanor. *Maybe they expected a touching reunion, and a shower of words,* he thought. George knew better but hadn't tipped them off. He had savored her blackbelt moves, as if watching some 1970s chop-socky movie with his daughter in the lead. But on Russian soil he was in too deep, his hands were figuratively as tied as those of Louise.

Raskalov spoke again, breaking the tension. "I want the three of you, yes, you too hero." He pointed to Peach Fuzz. "Escort Mizz Moscow to the next phase of our negotiations."

"I didn't sign up for this," George interjected. "She is my daughter!"

The contemptuous look that Louise gave George after his pitiful performance drove home the end of their relationship, Freudian sensibilities, and all.

"You…" she said, still catching her breath, "are not the father I knew."

As the security entourage led her out, Louise gave her feckless father one last glance.

"Не стоит ее недооценивать. Она умная," The Matron said in her guttural Russian.

Louise turned to Raskalov. "Yes. Never underestimate me, you son-of-a-bitch."

Now it was Raskalov whose face turned red.

"You idiot," George said. "She speaks perfect Russian."

For perhaps the last time, George looked at Louise as she was led away, and the door of the room slammed shut.

EIGHTEEN

Saint Petersburg, November 24, 2012

"We are not out of the woods yet, my friends," LaFontaine said to Michael and Jean-Philippe over the squealing tires. "I don't know what is awaiting us at Kresty."

LaFontaine's hired car raced through the pre-dawn streets of Saint Petersburg. The negotiation with Sokolov had been more protracted than he thought it would be. The Minister of Finance had to roust officials in several different offices after LaFontaine had showed him, in the flourishing of his cards, the algorithmic formula to Russia's digital safe, the *Keys to the Kingdom*. Realizing that, short of threatening LaFontaine's life, he had to act quickly, the Minister of Finance called his Minister of Technology.

It would take hours to change the codes, was the first answer he received.

As added insurance, LaFontaine disclosed to Sokolov that he had already notified Ukraine that he had important financial information about Russia. He knew that would get under the skin of this Putin lackey. Sokolov was desperate to keep this negotiation out of Putin's hearing range, fearing harsh reprisals, so LaFontaine pronounced his terms in cutting Russian.

"You will release Louise Moscow from Kresty." Sokolov's face went egg white again. *"And you will allow my vessel safe passage out of Saint Petersburg."*

"Согласовано," replied the Russian Minister of Finance wearily. *"Agreed."*

LaFontaine watched closely as Sokolov called the proper authorities, waking them up over all eleven Russian time zones. He knew that Michael and Jean-Philippe were sweating wherever they were. Reuniting with them and getting out of the hotel was his next demand. Within minutes of Sokolov's men returning his *bodyguards* to him, they were in the hired car.

He was confident they would be given secure passage the orders having come from the highest level. But he also didn't know how long it would take for the Minister of Technology to change the codes. They were dead men if that happened. It was a race against the clock.

Louise had been beaten badly by Raskalov's goons after being dragged into one of the cross buildings of Kresty. The strategy of this interrogation was to keep her conscious but beat the information out of her. She figured correctly that it was part of a drugging operation that included a syringe of unknown effect. Her brain was both hazy and compliant, as if she were having an out-of-body experience. The blows were expertly placed on strategic nerve endings, like the rifle butt that Peach Fuzz had delivered between her shoulder blades.

She remembered her CIA training. The information was coming out in drips, enough to pause the blows to her nervous system, and relieve the compliant fog that was inside her own head. Hours had gone by, she guessed, and she didn't know how long this would continue, or how long she could hold out.

Louise wanted to scream and kick and tear her hair out. But, somehow, she remained still and resumed counting breaths, eventually falling into a trance. Often in her work, she had used a similar method to solve forensic accounting problems. She would let the problem go, floating in her mind's universe, turning over and over, until out of somewhere deep within, the answer would appear matching up with the riddle, like a spaceship docking to a fuel station. She had no idea how it happened, but it seemed to come from a metaphysical place.

She focused on the images in Rossellini's note. They spun turning into coordinates. But none of the coordinates made any sense. Coordinates would be readable to almost anyone with training, so that wasn't it. Or was it? The symbols started to look like DNA genomic data. She knew nothing about DNA, except that it had been used to solve murders. Did Rossellini mean for her to use someone's DNA as the key?

Another strike to her nervous system. Amazingly, the last incident had inured her body against feeling the pain, numb, perhaps she was paralyzed? She remained in the trance and realized the sound was music. The fucker was blasting heavy metal into the chamber. It was unbearable, but she embraced it, letting it flow over her. The pulsing beat becoming part of her

DNA. *That was it!* Her eyes flew open. She was certain she had cracked the code. But she remained silent. She closed her eyes and continued counting her breaths, the number becoming symbolic, 2,222 breaths, about 3.7 hours. Her life would soon be ending. No one could survive such physical abuse. So be it. Rossellini's secret would die with her, unsolved, stuck in a book on a crammed shelf.

It was preferable to go this way, not knowing what the alternative horrors might be. She felt dizziness, hunger, cramping, sorrow not being able to say goodbye to her childhood friends, Renée and JoAnn. She was grateful they had been able to celebrate their fiftieth birthdays together on a girls' trip that year. Or her friend Big Steve whom she hadn't seen in over two years. Others she would never see again, Michael, LaFontaine, Jean-Philippe. But it was her time. She could *see* light against the outside of her eyelids. Was this the afterlife beckoning? She was at peace. Like waters through ancient aqueducts engineered by Romans that still ran through Europe to this day an eternal reminder of the flow of life. She was a Faraday shield, or Feng Shui allowing energy to dance and calm the spirits.

"Is she alive?" The voice sounded different, alarmed, kind, caring.

It was the last thing she heard.

Balakin was having a pre-dawn snack when his phone rang. He had always considered himself lucky, his name meant *very talkative*, and throughout his life he was able to talk his way into the most advantageous situations for himself. His latest sweet spot, second shift warden at Kresty, had come through his brother-in-law Levedev, who worked at a high level in the Russian Federal Penitentiary Service. He had breezed through the *top-secret* ramifications of his job interview, having worked in military intelligence in the old Soviet army. It just happened to be the most desk-oriented job, no infantry work in hot spots for him. Nobody bothered him here, so long as he kept his mouth shut, except for now this unusual ringing phone at 4 a.m. He knew he had to answer.

"*It's Levedev!*" He heard on the other end of the line.

His brother-in-law was calling him? He thought he'd never hear from him again after he had been named Director of the Federal Penitentiary Service, or FSIN. Kresty was off the grid, and the detainees they brought here were under a special security designation, which officially had nothing to do with the FSIN.

"*What can I do for you?*" Balakin asked, using his most formal Russian greeting.

"*Some men are coming for the detainee Louise Moscow. You are to let them in and allow them to escort her out of the grounds.*" Levedev was speaking very fast, and Balakin was freaking out a bit.

"*I have orders from Raskalov that she is not to be moved.*"

"*I have orders from Putin's Minister of Finance that she will be released. And that aces our friend Raskalov, as you well know.*"

Balakin felt a chill run through his body. *What am I in the middle of?* he thought, as he hung up the phone. As he was contemplating his fate, the intercom buzzed from the front gate.

The gatekeeper was of the lowest peasant order who spoke with a mumbling delivery.

I can understand that bitch prison matron better, thought the now very nervous Balakin.

"*There are men here,*" said the gatekeeper. "*They insist that you let them in.*"

Balakin erred on the side of caution. "*What are they saying?*"

The gatekeeper was direct. "*Two words. Moscow and Levedev.*"

Balakin was now sweating. "*Have them brought to me. I will take them to Moscow.*"

The gatekeeper did as he was told, although he was confused as to why everyone was going to *Moscow.* He hoped it wasn't to close the place down. He needed the job.

Balakin was suddenly in a moody silence. He knew he would have to confront Raskalov, and he hated that guy. He decided to wait until the men charged with retrieving detainee Moscow got there so they could all confront him together.

It was only minutes later when the security escort and the three men burst into his office.

"Где Луиза Москва?" the foreigner shouted. *Where is Louise Moscow?*

Jesus, he speaks Russian, Balakin thought.

"*The prisoner is being detained by Raskalov,*" he said. "*We will go straight to him.*"

"*No, you will call him now and have him take us to her.*"

Now Balakin was flop sweating. Would he lose this job? He dialed Raskalov's mobile and prayed that the *procurer of information* would pick up.

"*What do you want?*" said Raskalov in an angry tone.

"*There are people here, and they have come to retrieve Louise Moscow.*"

Now it was Raskalov's turn to sweat. And he never sweated. "*By whose authority?*"

After Balakin explained, Raskalov was in the office in minutes. The only authority he answered to was Putin, and the code word for a presidential order was *Levedev*. That bureaucrat's name spoke for the top of the ladder, and now that ladder was being pulled out from under Raskalov.

LaFontaine was now in charge. Raskalov and their original security escort led them to the cross building where Louise was being *interrogated*. LaFontaine was speaking Russian rapidly to their security escort, and most of it was angry. Michael thought his eyes were playing tricks on him, they had been awake for too many hours. He thought he caught a glimpse of George Moscow in a hallway. *Can't be,* he thought.

The three rescuers swept into the noxious cell where a bruised, bloodied, and unconscious Louise was lying on a filthy cot. Raskalov's two goons were in the corner, almost cowering. Their boss had tipped them off that people were coming, but they hadn't had time to leave. Michael saw that Jean-Philippe was about to lose it.

"Espèce de salauds!" he said in his maternal language. *Fucking bastards!*

Michael thought quickly and lunged at Jean-Philippe's hand disarming him of his weapon. He implored him. "Let's not start something that will prevent us from completing our main mission. We're here."

LaFontaine was already at Louise's side. Michael and Jean-Philippe joined him. Jean-Philippe took her in his arms, so fragile and small as he carried her almost in the fetal position.

The security escort that had brought them to Balakin had been ordered to take them back to the exit gate. Raskalov and his goons had disappeared.

During the bumpy transit vehicle ride to the front gate Jean-Philippe assessed Louise's injuries. She was most likely concussed and had been subjected to a particularly brutal nerve torture.

"She is going to need medical attention, right now!"

"*My personal physician is part of the ship's crew,*" LaFontaine said in French. He didn't want the guard to be tipped off to anything.

The drive to the front gate of the Kresty seemed to take forever, as a sliver of dawn was beginning to come over the horizon. Michael recalled the *Translator* who had felt ripped off never getting to tour the inside of Kresty. Michael would never come to this horrid place again.

As if on cue the gates opened when they approached, and LaFontaine's hired car was waiting. LaFontaine sat in front with the driver, Michael sat in the back with Jean-Philippe who still held Louise in his arms, closely monitoring her breathing.

"We're not out of this," LaFontaine said cryptically as the driver gunned the car to the Great Port.

He then called Charlie and hoped he had completed the instruction he gave him before they left port for the poker game. He was to get a boat, and LaFontaine had handed him a fat envelope with the means. They needed to get Louise back to the Vague-A-Bond as fast as possible. There were various scenarios and timeframes to change the financial codes, and they had to be out of Saint Petersburg before any of them could happen. They were just approaching the first time frame the Minister of Technology might be able to figure it out by.

Fortunately, I'm one of the few people who knows how to figure it out, Frédéric-Wendell thought. They'd soon find out.

"There he is," Michael said, pointing out Charlie. He was waiting in a crisp white jacket and had managed to get a stretcher, although it looked like military surplus from the siege of Leningrad. The car screeched to a stop, and LaFontaine had another envelope for the driver who would have to ditch the car and buy a new one. The two men nodded to one another.

Jean-Philippe and Michael carefully moved the inert body of Louise to the stretcher. The rescue team managed to form a cluster around her as they carried her to the boat. Charlie's white jacket was a medical coat, and he mimed that he was in charge as they loaded her onto the *bucket-of-bolts* he had purchased. Charlie got behind the wheel and fired up the engine.

Nobody noticed that the name of the small craft was SPASENIYE, which translated to SALVATION. Louise was going home.

NINETEEN

She awoke and opened her eyes, this time in the opposite of a nightmare. It was heaven. She felt warm for the first time in months, peaceful, there was even the sound of the birds singing. *Am I dead? Is this paradise?* She focused. Like Dorothy back from Oz, familiar people coming into view. Michael, Vladimir, and was that Jean-Philippe? Everyone except Auntie Em or her mother. Her mother was dead, she sadly remembered. The only one not there and who seemed in need of a brain, courage, and a heart was her father, the fucking traitor.

"Where am I?"

"In the hospital in Burgundy," Michael said.

"How…" The beeping of the heart monitor drew her attention to the intravenous tube in her arm. "How did you find me?"

"We *bought* some information," Michael said, his tone suggesting not to ask any more questions. But he added, "Remember that guard at Kresty right before your torture? We placed him there as well. Vladimir was responsible for all our Russian reconnaissance."

"Why did it take so long to find me?"

"Raskalov was very shrewd. He somehow got you out of the hotel, then got his translator in Siena to make it look like you had checked yourself out, putting your room key in the box, and even returned your rental car." We got the *Translator* to tell us your whereabouts. Then Raskalov must have gotten wind of it and put him in Kresty prison next to you.

"How did you realize I was missing?" asked Louise.

"Since you were supposed to stay off digital communication it wasn't unusual not to hear from you. But after LaFontaine received no word from you via his horseman for a whole week, plus another chase-of-the-tail back to Burgundy, we put the word out that we needed intel."

"The *Master of the Dark Arts,* in the library, with the tea," Louise blurted.

"Yes, that's the most likely explanation of how Raskalov kidnapped you," Michael said, resuming his briefing of the rescue.

Louise was having a hard time focusing, Jean-Philippe was no longer in the room and Louise was not sure if he had been a dream or reality. She focused on Michael's fascinating tale of how her rescuers had gotten her out of Kresty, the false flag in Burgundy, his contact with LaFontaine…

"LaFontaine!" Louise exclaimed.

"If it weren't for him, you wouldn't be here."

He omitted minute details from the rest of the story, simply telling how LaFontaine came up with the plan, and how they got the intel from the *Translator* within the prison. Then he explained LaFontaine's handpicked team including himself, Charlie, and…

Michael stepped aside with a flourish of his hand to reveal Jean-Philippe as if he was the *Big Deal of the Day*. But he was gone. Michael shrugged, understanding Jean-Philippe's reticence. When they were bringing Louise home on the Vague-A-Bond, he wouldn't leave her side, even after LaFontaine's physician put her into a medically induced coma to reduce the swelling from her concussion. Once she was stable, they called in a military-grade Medivac that took her to a transport jet, with Michael and Jean-Philippe in tow. They eventually got her back to Burgundy, still unconscious, but much more responsive to examination.

"She will wake up soon," the attending physician had said that morning. Ten minutes ago, when she woke up, it had just turned noon. Jean-Philippe had waited to make sure she came to, and then left to get back to Siena.

"How did you get into the Kresty?" Louise asked. "Did you know it's a secret Russian interrogation prison?"

"We do now," Vladimir said.

Michael explained that LaFontaine was able to negotiate with the Russian government to secure her release. He was sorry they hadn't gotten to the prison before her torture. LaFontaine's on-board doctor was stunned how her nervous system seemed unharmed from the beatings Raskalov's goons had administered. He'd fill her in on the details of the poker game and the 'wild cards' that LaFontaine had up his sleeve. That story needed a couple drinks at least, and possibly LaFontaine's presence.

Louise paused, taking it all in. Then, in a sudden shift, she locked eyes with Michael and, almost in panic mode, tried to get out of bed.

"I must get to Dario Rossellini, now. He's in danger!"

Michael pushed her gently back into the bed. "You need at least a week of rest. You're severely dehydrated and undernourished." He went over and opened the small closet, revealing one of her carry-on bags. "I took the liberty of going to your house and packing a few things for you including a change of clothes for when you're cleared to leave here."

"As soon as you're better we will need to get your full statement," Vladimir said. "As much as possible about who and what you saw. Identifying characteristics and such."

"I'll help you if you promise to let me go back to Siena to help Rossellini."

Michael could see that Louise had made up her mind and there was no changing it. He stared her down, searching for the solution most likely to sway her.

"Okay. In one week if the doctor gives you a clean bill of health, you can return to Siena. However, you will be accompanied by Big Steve. He'll need to take a leave of absence from the Tiki Bar and resume your security detail. That's the deal."

Louise's eyes brightened at the thought of having her friend again. "All expenses paid?"

Michael took a breath then exhaled, thinking of the paperwork. "Fine, all expenses paid."

Vladimir spoke up. "Louise, do you remember the guard that was paired with the prison matron toward the end of your stay at Kresty? Kind peach fuzz?" he said, moving his hand down his face and up on his head.

"I noticed he was different than the one I started with, but they seemed interchangeable."

"Whatever LaFontaine showed them that convinced them to let us take you, we were also given brief access to your *boyfriend*," Vladimir said.

"Dimitri, the *Translator*? What for?" Louise perked up, suspecting Dimitri had some special prison ranking.

"Our inside guy called him *Tattooed Man* for a reason," Michael said.

"We had just enough time to take a couple photographs and he gave us a cryptic note for you," Vladimir said, handing her the paper.

It was just one line. Louise read it aloud. *"Love is the only thing that can save this poor creature, Pedruga."* Louise had to laugh. "He was my boyfriend!" she said, doing a groggy imitation of Cloris Leachman's Frau

Blücher in the Mel Brooks movie *Young Frankenstein.*

Vladimir and Michael looked at each other, silently acknowledging her punchy exhaustion. "Well, your *boyfriend's* whole body was an information archive," Vladimir said. He showed her the pictures on his device. It was a frontal and back view of Dimitri Novikov's body tattoos, the same view Louise was privy to on her first day at Kresty.

"Those tattoos are bad-ass," Michael said, impressed with the seriousness of the conditions Louise had survived.

Vladimir analyzed their meaning. "These shoulder tattoos, or *épaulettes*, signify that the criminal was high-ranking and had a negative attitude to the system."

"Interesting," Louise said. "The guards often addressed him as *glavnyy*, or *major.*"

Vladimir pointed to one of the *épaulettes*. "These three stars signify three things: *I am not a slave to the camps; the strong win, the weak die; and Horses die from toil.* The rose on his chest means *Bitches robbed my freedom.* He earned high-ranking respect, somehow."

"The word *suki,* meaning bitches, has a double-entendre," Louise said, thanking the universe for her ability to speak Russian. It was instrumental in saving her life.

"Correct," Vladimir agreed. "It also means rat, like ratting someone out, or dying like a rat." Vladimir then pointed to the tattoo of Madonna and Child. "This, his most prominent tattoo, is a thieves' talisman signifying acting as a *guardian from misfortune and misery.*"

"Maybe he was my guardian, besides being my *boyfriend.*" She recalled more tattoos and took the pad on her nightstand and drew them. "These were the tattoos on the first guard. The one who kept staring at me while I showered." She handed the pad back to Vladimir.

Vladimir cleared his throat at the possibility of Louise in a prison shower. "The bow tie on his neck is often forcibly applied to pickpockets who have broken the thieves' code and sided with authorities. A *snitch.* His bow tie contains a dollar sign in the center knot, signifying that he was a money launderer."

"The Devil's in the details," Michael said, winking at Louise.

"So, you got my message," Louise said.

Michael took the pad and tore the page off, folding the sketches and putting it in his pocket. "Vlad will be by later in the week to get your full statement. Maybe when you have some time you can write down everything you remember."

"Including my perfect Krav Maga takedown of the prison matron?" Louise offered.

"That's a good start," Michael said, shaking his head in amazement. He kissed her cheek and Vladimir followed suit.

"Were there any other women prisoners in the shower with you?" Vladimir asked seductively. Louise shot him the middle finger in reply, and they both laughed. "There is armed security outside. Get some rest." They left her alone.

Then, she suddenly remembered something. Dario Rossellini's note that she had hid on the hotel library shelf inside the book, right before Raskalov drugged her. She picked up the pad of paper and sketched the pictogram on Rossellini's note from memory. She folded the sketch until it was very small and held it tightly in her fist and dozed off.

Burgundy, France, December 18, 2012

Louise fixed his gaze, eye to eye, defiant, hopeful.

"Physically, you are one hundred percent good to go." The doctor spoke English with a pronounced French accent, for Michael's benefit.

He switched to French for Louise's benefit. "Mentalement, pas tellement." Using the French hand gesture, he splayed his fingers next to his ear and tilted his hand back and forth, indicating she was *nuts*. Then he winked. He had known Louise almost since the first day she had moved into her Burgundy cottage after a health scare prompted her to make an appointment. It turned out to be perimenopause, giving Louise a reality check. After defying her age all her life even she wasn't immune to the effects of aging.

"I've never been sick a day in my life." Louise sounded like a Polish grandmother.

"You are the picture of health." The doctor nodded to Michael and left them alone.

"I'm outta here," Louise said, throwing the covers aside revealing that she was fully dressed in the very clothes Michael had packed for her. She opened the small closet and took out her bag.

"You don't waste any time," Michael said, shaking his head.

As if on cue, Big Steve entered the hospital room.

"Éti!" Louise called Big Steve by the shortened version of his undercover name, *Étienne,* which was French for *Steve.* She put her arms around her old friend, his six-foot-four two-hundred-fifty-pound stature dwarfing her.

He held her by the shoulders at arm's length shaking his head as he looked at her. "It's good to see y'all too, *Karen,*" he teased, using her undercover name. "A sight for sore eyes." He was stoic but his eyes glistened with emotion.

"Thank you for coming all this way to protect me."

"I'd go to the moon and back for y'all, Lulu. Anytime, anywhere."

"Good. Because we need to hit the road today. Where'd you park?"

Michael rolled his eyes as Louise kissed his cheek then ran out the door with Big Steve and Michael following.

Louise gave directions as Big Steve drove them to her cottage to prepare for the trip. Between driving instructions on where to turn she interrogated him on the latest.

"So, how's the Tiki bar holding up?" Louise asked. "No Island Fever?"[21]

"Nah. I stayed busy, protecting your investment like it was Buckingham Palace."

"Not too lonely?"

"No way. It a *destination.* After Snoop Dogg was there that last time, he told everyone. Yachts stopping off every week to party. Charlie is one of our best clients, too."

"So, he keeps you in the loop," Louise surmised.

"Y'all ain't the only one with a private communications hub, Lulu. We got high tech." He flexed his arm. "And I stay in shape, still give your free Gin Ginger Baker drink to anyone who does a sun salutation, but I switched it up a little and, also offer some Tai Chi classes and my special drink a Black Crushin'. Get it? Black Russian…"

"Aah, nice play on words, fantastic homophone."

"Y'all know I ain't no homophobe. Them's my bros."

"No, homo-*phone,*" she said, emphasizing the last syllable. "A word that sounds exactly like another word. Your drink sounds just like Black Russian. Very clever."

"Got that right," he said proudly and left it at that.

On the flight from Burgundy to Florence, they discussed the mission.

"I'm so happy you're here Steve. Not just because I missed you. It also makes much more sense than me working alone."

"I'm here to protect y'all, Lulu. That's my only mission."

"That's fine. But we need to use surveillance tactics. I have reserved a separate rental car for you and booked you a room at my hotel but let's try to play down our association."

They arrived in separate cars at the Hotel in Siena and checked in separately. As a large man of color, Big Steve stood out, but at the same time, he didn't generate the kind of institutionalized bigotry he experienced daily in the States. It was freeing. He relaxed in his hotel suite. That evening, at a table in the corner of the hotel restaurant, he ate a quiet meal alone while observing Louise and Francesco having an intimate dinner together. They were obviously thrilled to be reunited. Louise seemed to have eased right back into her Siena lifestyle.

In the morning, Louise went to the coffee bar next door for her favorite foam art. Big Steve stood outside reading *USA Today*, observing every interaction. The café was a small space called Bar Bazar, just a counter and a few chairs indoors and two tables with chairs outside. Most patrons ordered and drank at the counter, as did Louise that morning. After her ordeal, the one thing she had been yearning for was the café latte, the barista crafting the most intricate bouquet of flowers for her in the foam atop the flavorful dark roast. For breakfast, the crispy cornetto stuffed with dense handmade whipped cream. Pure decadence. It tasted better than ever after the putrid prison gruel. Louise dunked the last bite into the remaining café and delighted in the soggy crunch. She thanked the owner and made for the door. As she reached to open it, *Smarmy Guy* held it ajar and waved her through staying a respectful distance.

"Ciao, signora." He was more behaved now, wary that someone coming out of nowhere to punch him in the nose again.

"Buongiorno." Louise smiled politely and walked toward the hotel. She gave Big Steve a subtle nod indicating the *Smarmy Guy* was someone to keep an eye on.

Kostas had gotten word from LaFontaine of Louise's return and flew to Siena that morning. They met in the hotel library, determined to pick up where they had left off, before being violently interrupted, this time with Big Steve as Louise's personal security guard. For the next few weeks, they went about daily life. Louise resumed her research and the tortuous forensic accounting work of recreating the Monte dei Paschi financial structure in Excel from the public quarterly and annual financial disclosures, and additional financial statements provided by Dario Rossellini. Kostas had already spent a lot of time creating a marketing and investment plan, pitching a potential private offering to wealthy clients to fund Monte dei Paschi's restructuring. This was the only time they used their computers, being careful never to be logged on to any Internet connection.

She stopped working only for a simple but beautiful holiday season in the historic town with Big Steve, Francesco, and Kostas. They spent a quiet but unforgettable New Year's Eve on Francesco's farm, toasting with the animals all getting special treats.

Siena, Italy, January 25, 2013

Finally, after weeks of preparation, Dario Rossellini invited them to meet with the Monte dei Paschi Board of Directors during an emergency meeting called by the CEO and CFO the following day.

Louise and Kostas consolidated their work into an easy-to-follow and compelling PowerPoint presentation. Kostas had created an impressive marketing strategy including some of the biggest investors on the planet, and Louise had summarized the financial structure of the company with a projected clear path to solvency.

The next morning, they waited for Rossellini to call for them to make their presentation.

Finally, the months of work that Louise and Kostas had done to save Monte dei Paschi bank would be taken under consideration. They waited nervously for Dario to contact them once the board of directors meeting concluded and was ready for their presentation.

Behind the closed door of the large conference room, the Monte dei Paschi Chief Executive Officer, Fabrizio Viola, addressed the board of directors.

"To pay back this loan and avoid government takeover of Monte dei Paschi, I have decided to raise the bank's offering from three billion to five billion euros."

There were murmurs of concern from the board. Viola turned to the bank's Chief Financial Officer, Bernardo Mingrone, to explain in Italian.

"The increase reflects pressure from the asset review and stress test that the European Central Bank is conducting with major European banks," Mingrone said. "For MPS to remain among the top quartile of Italian banks by capital and assure passing regulatory tests we have adjusted the public offering to reestablish the right capital position for a bank this size. In the words of the manager of the Rome football team, 'We have to put the church back in the center of the village.'"

"How small will the village be?" one of the board directors asked.

"This turnaround strategy will shrink our securities portfolio, and our overall balance sheet," Mingrone said. "We must shrink the size of our footprint because banks in Italy are over branched and overstaffed. MPS will closed 450 branch offices and shutter another 100 more in the next two years. We are cutting staff by 31,500. We are also getting out of consumer finance, which is a high-cost business. We will sell a five-hundred-million-euro package of nonperforming loans to Fortress Investment Group, the New York private equity firm. Italian banks aren't the best managers of these turnaround processes because of the commercial relationship with our debtors. We have not been as tough as we should be."

The meeting concluded and board members filed out, leaving Dario seated alone at the large table in the now empty conference room that overlooked the Piazza. He dialed his phone.

"The meeting is over. You can come to the conference room now."

Louise and Kostas now sitting at the large conference table did not hide their shock.

"So that's it? No new investor offers will be considered?"

"The board raised the offering from three billion to five billion euros. That means you and Kostas will fall short of raising the five billion euros needed immediately from private investors to cover the bank's exposure to legal liabilities," Dario Rossellini said.

"But we have anchor investors from Qatar," Louise said.

"Time has run out and we must accept the Italian government's bail-out funding," Rossellini countered.

"Will the non-profit Foundation MPS lose its majority shareholder?" Louise asked.

Rossellini looked defeated. "Unfortunately, yes, it's just too late"

"Am I missing something?" Louise asked.

"We are so close," Kostas added.

Rossellini waved his hand indicating the historic headquarters of Banca Monte dei Paschi di Siena. "The devastating secret loans that you found in the vault sent shock waves through Italian financial circles. I made them public in October 2012, while you were missing, Louise." He stood. "Follow me." He led them to the same office Alessandro and Francesco had taken Louise and pointed to the dust-covered vault that contained the documents Louise had photographed leading to that fateful disclosure.

"This was the office of the bank's former general manager, Antonio Vigni," Rossellini continued. "Officials accessed this safe and found the documents you photographed. They had been hidden there by former MPS president Giuseppe Mussari and were never disclosed to the bank's board, auditors, regulators, or shareholders." Louise could tell Rossellini was having difficulty with what he had to say next. "Mussari is a childhood friend of mine, we grew up here in Siena. He became the bank's president through his political connections here. He had no financial experience before taking the reins of MPS in 2006. When he was forced out in April 2012, he admitted that banking was not his forte, and he was going back to being a lawyer. But by then the damage was done."

The sound of a creaking floor drew their attention and they turned to see the CFO Mingrone closing the door to the chamber.

"How long has he been there?" Louise asked.

Rossellini shrugged. "It doesn't matter. I have nothing to hide. Now you know almost everything. MPS was *740 million euros* in debt because one incompetent manager, my friend Giuseppe Mussari, tried to cover up a *71-million-euro* loss."

The numbers were astounding. Mussari had incurred an additional *670 million euros* in debt because of a *71-million-euro* mistake.

"1000% interest," Louise said. "That is some mafia level usury right there."

"As they say," Kostas added. "If you have to hide it, you shouldn't be doing it."

Rossellini took them back downstairs and out of the building, where Big Steve was waiting.

"Thank you for all your work," Rossellini said, giving Kostas a warm and sincere handshake. Rossellini moved closer to Louise and whispered, "Do you still have my note?"

"Of course. But to be honest, I'm having trouble understanding it."

"You can do it. I believe in you," he said, the look of shame returning to his eyes. "I was never able to crack the code. Another failure of mine." He gave Louise a kiss on each cheek. "I'll be in touch." The look in his eyes telling her there was much more to discuss.

They went back to the hotel and Kostas decided to cut his losses, stopping in the hotel lobby to bid Louise farewell. "We did everything we could. The important thing is that you are safe, Louise." He gave her a big hug and they became emotional.

She stepped back and said, "Forget it, Kostas. It's Siena," paraphrasing the iconic line from *Chinatown*. "Shall we have a consolation dinner? On the Agency?" Louise offered.

Kostas declined. "I think I'll just pack my things and catch the next flight for Cyprus." He turned to Big Steve. "Take care of our girl," he said, shaking his hand. Then he left.

Louise and Big Steve had an early dinner.

"I'm exhausted, Steve. I'm going to my room to meditate and try to get some sleep." He accompanied her to her door. "I'll be up early, see you in the morning," Louise said.

He listened for her to double lock the door, then went to his own room.

PART III

TWENTY

Siena, Italy, February 14, 2013

Louise was not the kind to just *forget it.* There were still too many loose ends, and she didn't want to spend another ten years pondering all the Russian mafia and banking connections that remained unresolved like her last case. Couple that with Dario Rossellini whispering to her about the note, she was not going to let that go. She decided to remain in Siena and decipher the cryptic epistle, if only to honor the ancient town she had become so attached to.

Since the scandal broke and the hidden Monte dei Paschi losses made public, the residents of Siena were outraged. She read the local paper while having her morning café latte at Bar Bazar. The headline article was about MPS former CEO, Giuseppe Mussari, having been subpoenaed to appear that day for questioning about the derivatives investigation.

"Let's go for a walk," Louise told Big Steve who had been sitting at the outdoor table on surveillance. Louise headed toward Piazza del Campo, Big Steve trailing at a safe distance. To witness the public sentiment in person, she made a detour past the Siena Prosecutor's office. As they approached, a surreal scene was unfolding. A crowd had gathered awaiting the arrival of Mussari. She approached just as he was getting out of his car and entering the building. The crowd heckled him and pelted him with coins. The metallic currency, a mix of euros and now-defunct liras hitting the cobblestones creating a discordant accompaniment to the public chants.

"Ladra! Ladra!"

"What are they saying?" Big Steve asked.

"*Ladra.* It means *thief.*"

They resumed walking to the Piazza del Campo where Louise took a seat at her usual table on the terrace of Fonte Gaia café. The anger and frustration of the residents was evident. But despite her valiant efforts with Kostas and Rossellini preparing, negotiating, and networking, they failed to solve the Deutsche Bank problem and salvage Monte dei Paschi in its original form, with the non-profit Monte dei Paschi di Siena Foundation retaining a majority ownership.

The marketing plan that Kostas had prepared represented all that was beneficial about offshore banking, a bold and ambitious rebranding of the concept. Many international businesses made sense having revenues flow offshore, provided proper public disclosure and accountability.

The report that Louise had created restructuring the bank's complicated capital showing how the losses from the derivatives had affected the value of the bank included a relatively easy-to-follow chart. But in an ironic twist, the discovery of the hidden debt had only increased scrutiny of the bank prompting the authorities to raid Rossellini's home, searching for anything incriminating, taking boxes of files. She felt partly to blame for Rossellini's plight.

All efforts to restructure seemed to have been thwarted, at least for the time being. But Louise was not ready to concede defeat. She ordered another café latte and took out the pictogram of Rossellini's original note that she had since retrieved from the library. If she guessed correctly, there were riches, in the form of *Il Monte*, or *The Mount*, within the ancient ruins of the under-bank, upon which the palace headquarters had been built. If there were a secret *Monte,* the value could far exceed the debt and make Monte dei Paschi whole again. But there were two major concerns.

First, if there is a secret *Mount* treasure trove, how would she prevent it from falling into the wrong hands? After experiencing the ruthlessness of the Russian prisons and the brutality of the Russian mobster mentality, Louise fully sympathized with billionaire banker Ekram M. Almasi who had been infamously paranoid with constant former Mossad security detail, only to die in a mysterious fire. Even now, accompanied by her own personal armed secret security detail, Big Steve, Louise was still on high alert.

Second, if found, how would she ensure that the treasure trove remained a secret. The bank by all accounts should remain the rightful owner of *Il Monte*, and no one, within the current management was above suspicion of trying to benefit from it. To that end, Louise decided not to reveal her hunch about *Il Monte* to anyone, not even Big Steve. She had to continue her research in the ancient archives of the hotel library and follow any leads. Big Steve provided her with the added sense of security to take more risks. But she had to keep secrets even from him, for now.

Siena, Italy, February 28, 2013

It had been two weeks since the raid of Rossellini's home and Louise had come up with almost nothing. She sat in the hotel library reading nook completely crestfallen.

"Y'all look so sad, Lulu." Big Steve sat in a chair near the door, reading glasses slid down his nose, catching up on his studies in his Layman's Bible Handbook.

She inhaled deeply, then exhaled fully, bringing unshed tears to her eyes. "I'm totally blocked." She stood and stretched her arms upward. Steve knew the routine and he had faith Louise would figure it out. "I need some water," she said.

Water was the answer to everything. This was her creed. She sat down and poured a glass of room temperature Acqua Panna Toscana bottled water and drank gratefully, feeling an immediate almost dizzying positive effect. She set the glass down but caught it on the edge of a book she hadn't noticed. Her juggling reflexes kicked in and she grabbed the glass before it spilled, sparing the book, an old text she had pulled from the archives.

She cracked it open and was astounded to read that it was all about Siena's ancient underground aqueducts and tunnels, called *bottini* that dated back to 394 A.D. What intrigued her was the fact that the word *bottini* in Italian meant *booty* or *plunder*, such as a treasure trove of gold and jewels. But the word according to the book was believed to be of Etruscan origin for the barrel shape or inverted V shape of the tunnels' vaulted ceilings in the illustrations. She read with great interest about the maze of underground aqueducts had been crucial to the development of Siena for hundreds of years, without which the town would have had no access to a water supply.

"Lulu…" Big Steve said.

She held up a hand as if to say, *don't bother me for a bit,* and continued to devour the writings. One tunnel was associated with the medieval myth of the River Diana, which was believed to flow under the city of Siena. This reminded Louise of the Arthurian legends of her adopted home of Burgundy, Diana being the goddess of healing. Then Louise read about the Fonte Gaia bottini, which supplied the Gaia fountain in Piazza del Campo and the namesake of the café where she had met Francesco.

Closing the tome with a thud, Louise rubbed her eyes.

"S'up?" Big Steve asked.

"Let's get some air." She stopped at her room to put on a coat and boots, and they headed out toward Piazza del Campo. Unbeknownst to Steve, it was a reconnaissance mission, so she needed an excuse to separate from him. As she approached the Piazza del Campo, she saw a stray cat dart into an opening near the Gaia fountain.

"I'm going to help that kitty," Louise said.

"A cat? What the heck?" Big Steve followed but stayed back to make sure no one trailed Louise. She tracked the cat to a café behind the fountain where it seemed to have disappeared. Looking around she noticed there was a trap door under a table. She crouched down and shined the light of her phone through the crack and saw stone steps leading to a tunnel. It must have been the underground Bottini. No one was near that area of the terrace, so she gently moved the table aside, pulled the handle of the trap door and it opened. She descended the steps about five meters down, her phone light revealing a vast tunnel with walls that had been carved out to form an underground structure. The walls and ceilings of inlaid brick created barrel-shaped vaulted ceilings like the illustrations in the book. In this tunnel were three rectangular pools of crystal-clear water, a small canal between each allowing water to flow.

The cat sat nearby lapping up the fresh spring water, peaceful, cozy, and dry in the spa-like setting. Louise shined her phone light on the walls to look for markings. As she had expected, she saw engravings of crosses as well as a terracotta Madonna carved into the wall, believed to have been crafted by workers during the tunnel's construction, according to the book, *to ward off spiteful scary creatures.*

During the Middle Ages, engineers solved the water problem by carving twenty-five kilometers of tunnels beneath the town. The Bottini aqueducts channeled rainwater and natural springs that followed the line between porous upper limestone and lower clay of the hills surrounding Siena. Until 1914 the Bottini River was the only source of water to Siena. Two main tunnels were the result of a painstaking process of manual labor using rudimentary instruments from the 12th to 15th centuries. One tunnel carried water to the large Fontebranda fountain. The other fed the Fonte Gaia pool in Piazza del Campo and other smaller fountains. It was fascinating but offered no clue to *Il Monte.*

"Lulu!" Big Steve's voice echoed.

"Coming!" The kitty rubbed against her leg, so she bent down to pet it. "So skinny! Poor baby." She picked the cat up and she noticed what appeared to be a lever to a hidden door behind a rock wall. The lever could have been a natural rock formation, but it looked man made. She would have to leave it for another day.

"Lulu! Don't make me come down there. Y'all know I hate the dark."

The kitty purred in Louise's arms as she climbed the steps back up to the rainy street and closed the trap door.

"I'm going to bring this kitty to my friend Francesco's animal rescue."

"We gonna walk?" Steve asked.

"No, let's take the car."

The windshield wipers were set on low to intermittently brush away the drizzle. In the cool wet weather, Francesco's animal sanctuary looked even more peaceful and welcoming. The kitty purred in Louise's lap as Steve parked.

"You think they'll take that cat?"

"I hope so, this would be a nice place for her to live."

They got out and Big Steve followed Louise around to the side of the property where she heard sheep and goats braying and Francesco speaking Italian to them. They watched in silence as he addressed each animal while he filled their feeders.

"He's crazier than you, Lulu," Steve said. The kitty gave a brief meow seemingly in agreement with Steve and snuggled deeper into Louise's arms.

"Don't worry, Ginger. You'll love it here," Louise told the cat. "There's another male ginger cat here. It's much better than that smelly old tunnel."

"Y'all named the cat already?"

Francesco saw them and came over with a welcoming smile. He opened the gate, and they entered the corral.

"Ciao, bella!"

"Ciao, Francesco. *This is my friend, Steve*," she said in Italian.

"Ciao, ragazzone," he said, meaning, *hello big guy*. They shook hands.

"Yes, *Big* Steve." Louise showed him the kitty nestled inside her raincoat. "*And this is Ginger Cat*," she said in Italian.

"Ahhh! Gatto rosso. Che bella! Le femmine gatto rosso sono rare."

"He's saying female ginger cats are rare," Louise told Steve. "He has a male ginger cat which is more common. Males are also more affectionate so I was thinking she would be accepted here." She kissed Ginger Cat's head. "You are special, Ginger Cat."

"Vieni." Francesco welcomed everyone inside, including Ginger Cat. He signaled for them to sit in front of the fireplace then put his arms out to hold the cat.

Louise handed Ginger Cat to Francesco, and she snuggled in his arms, purring loudly.

"Well, will ya look it that?" Big Steve said.

"Dove l'hai trovata?" Francesco asked where they found her, putting some food and water to the bowls he had already set out for the other cats. Ginger Cat ate ravenously.

"*She was in the tunnels.*" Louise explained in Italian how she found the cat in the tunnel under the Piazza del Campo fountain.

"Gatto di bottini!" He sat on the chair and petted the cat. This was exactly the response Louise had been hoping for.

"Yes! Bottini cat. *Would it be okay to leave her with you?*" Louise asked in Italian, putting her hands together in prayer. "*No cats allowed in the hotel.*"

"Certo, con piacere! Benvenuto gattino."

"Well, goodbye." Louise got up to leave and Steve followed her. Then in Italian she asked, "*Meet me at our café at noon tomorrow?*" hoping Big Steve wouldn't understand.

"*I'd love to,*" Francesco said, getting up. The kitty jumped into his chair, and they laughed. "*Go to Rome, lose your throne!*" Francesco said in Italian.

Louise translated for Steve, "Move your feet, lose your seat!" She gave Francesco cheek kisses. "Ciao, grazie mille."

"*See you tomorrow,*" Francesco told her in Italian. He shook Steve's hand. "Ciao, ciao."

"Ciao, bello," Big Steve said. Having learned to speak fluent French from Louise while on the island, he was pretty good at picking up languages.

TWENTY-ONE

The next morning continued their usual routine. Coffee at Bar Bazar then back to the library. After a couple hours, Louise gave a big sigh.

"I need a break. Maybe meditation will help. I'll be in my room," she lied. "See you in an hour or so, okay?"

"Okay." Big Steve accompanied her to her room and waited until the door locked. She looked through the peephole to see Steve guarding her, sitting in a hallway chair in view of her door. She put on her rain boots and raincoat, then darted to the closet and entered the code to the room safe, took out Rossellini's map and put it in her bag, which she slung securely across her body. She dialed Steve's room number on the hotel phone, set the earpiece down and looked through the peephole to watch Steve dash into his room. She hung up the phone and quietly ran out of her room and down the stairwell. Steve was gone no more than thirty seconds and resumed his post oblivious to her escape.

A few minutes later, approaching Piazza del Campo just before noon, Louise saw Francesco waiting for her at a table under the awning sheltered from the drizzly weather.

"Ciao, bello." Louise gave him cheek kisses, genuinely happy to see him.

"Ciao, bella regazza."

"*How is the kitty*?" she asked in Italian.

"*Fantastica! All the animals love Ginger Cat,*" he replied.

Louise ordered a hot tea with milk and the server Fabrizio left to place the order. She pulled Rossellini's note out of her purse and handed it to Francesco.

"*This is a map, I think,*" she whispered in Italian, holding her finger in front of her mouth signifying, *shhhhh.*

He jokingly whispered in Italian, "*A secret treasure map?*

Louise didn't laugh. She nodded once for yes, very seriously. The tea arrived and she sipped, the warmth giving her a chill. She gently took the paper from Francesco's hands and rotated it. *"I think it's the Bottini."* She whispered in Italian, pointing to a line that could be an underground river. Her finger traced the line to a square. *"Banca Monte dei Paschi?"*

Francesco's eyes widened. He looked like he was about to burst. Then he began speaking quickly, startling Louise.

She put her finger over her lips. "Shhhhhh!"

He lowered his voice and explained more slowly that he had spent his whole childhood exploring the underground rivers and never once saw any kind of treasure. Louise looked disappointed. "Te lo mostro," he said.

"You'll show me?" She gulped the rest of her tea, put some money on the table, took Francesco's hand and they walked briskly through the piazza toward the Fonte Gaia.

Having ditched Big Steve, Louise used evasive tactics to make sure no one was following them. Taking a sharp turn, then stopping to look in a storefront window, Francesco dutifully following along. They resumed walking but she thought she saw *Smarmy Guy's* reflection in a window. She quickly pulled Francesco by the arm, slammed her back against the building, grabbed him by the collar and kissed him deeply. Their passion flared. She stopped kissing him, her pupils dilating as they stared into each other's eyes. Then she discretely scanned the piazza and saw the coast was clear. Francesco was about to move in for another kiss, but Louise interrupted him.

"Fonte Gaia." She took his hand and resumed walking to the *Fountain of Joy.* Convinced there was no tail, Louise passed by the Fonte Gaia and headed straight to the table with the trap door entrance to the Bottini.

"Clever girl," Francesco said in Italian, only half surprised.

"Clever cat," Louise replied. *"Ginger Cat showed me."* He opened the trap door for her, and they descended the steps into the dank dark cavern. Louise turned on her phone light and pointed to the spot where the kitty had been drinking from the river. *"I followed Ginger Cat to here."* Then she raised the light, shining it on the area she thought she had seen a handle or lever. "What is that? Che cos'è?"

Francesco climbed over some rocks and took a closer look. *"It's a water spigot."* He waved his hand to indicate the whole underground aqueduct network. *"They're all throughout the Bottini."*

"Not a secret door to the treasure?" she asked.

"Non una porta segreta."

She pointed to the square on Rossellini's note. "*Can we go here?*"

"Seguimi." Francesco walked and she followed.

After they wound through the tunnels for about twenty minutes Louise became concerned. Monte dei Paschi by street was only a ten-minute walk. "*Where are we going?*"

"Dai." He simply waved his hand forward. It was like he was a kid again, running, turning mid skip to smile at her. She shook her head and smiled. *What a charmer.*

"Big Steve is going to start worrying and come looking for me," she nervously said to herself. "He's afraid of enclosed spaces, so he won't come down here. But you never know."

She let go of her worries and started to feel the magic of the place. Then they came to a narrow tunnel that did not have the same *spa* feel the rest of tunnel had. It was literally a hole roughly carved through the granite leading to another pool. But they went through and came out to an even more spectacular pool.

"La Fonte delle Monache!"

"*The Nun's Spring?*" Louise asked. She remembered from the book it was supposed to be the most beautiful and pure spot in the Bottini, a completely underground hot spring.

Francesco took off his clothes, his rippling abs, bulging thighs, and pronounced lats, stunning her into momentary awe. There was nothing stopping Louise. This was one of life's moments one does not think. She undressed and they plunged into the pristine water like a baptism, healing and cleansing.

They frog legged around, then floated on their backs, the steam rising, letting their bodies soak up the minerals through every pore. They circled each other, closing the distance, Louise wrapping her legs around him, his strong arms effortlessly keeping them afloat. His hands gripped her slim waist, then he cupped her soft yet firm breasts, and squeezed her tight buttocks, sparking her libido, which seemed to be even more intense since perimenopause. They kissed, passion flaring again right where they left off on the street. Louise suddenly stopped. A shudder of trepidation coursing through her body.

"Cosa c'è che non va?"

"*It's nothing.*" She leaned back looking toward heaven for reassurance.

"Un uomo," he said, placing his hand on her heart. His eyes were intensely comforting and compassionate. "*A nail drives out another nail,*" he said in Italian.

She didn't need to speak the language to understand the imagery. As a rule, Louise never enjoyed water sex, but there are times when things just inexplicably work. This being one. They trembled together in a uniting of forces beyond the physical. After they finished, even getting out of the water was pleasurable. The dirt and stone floor dried them and absorbed their kinetic energy, it was steadying. They got dressed, the purity of God's earth on their skin feeling natural. It would be washed away eventually, and it seemed okay at that moment. Francesco's lips reassured her that he felt the same and they resumed their giddy gambol through the caves.

"Cos'è questo?" Francesco suddenly stopped, stunned at the sight before them.

It was a crudely dug tunnel that had fallen completely into disrepair. Stalagmites hung down from the ceiling and a mound of calcification had built up from the ground, which was flooded with murky water. It seemed impassable but they had come so far, turning back was their last option. Louise gave Francesco a telling look meaning, *should we go for it?*

"Andiamo!" Francesco shouted.

They held hands and charged through the dank tunnel laughing and screaming. It reminded Louise of recurring nightmares that had recently returned to her sleep. The settings of the dreams changed, sometimes a luxurious Paris apartment, other times, her grandmother's house in the Chicago suburbs. Always, homey in the main areas, but deep in, attics, or basements, haunted by incubus and succubus spirits. In the dream, she would be drawn to that part of the house, knowing the danger, wanting to remain in the safe livable areas, but difficult to resist exploring the bowels. She had been trying to understand the dreams, which seemed to be about tempting fate, the danger of going too far, or maybe it was shame?

Francesco seemed to know where he was going. The tunnels became darker, danker, less frequented by humans, more conducive to protective spirits…or *evil sprites.*

"*Where are we going, Francesco?*" Louise asked.

"Di male in peggio."

"*From bad to worse?*" Louise winced. "*Are we almost beneath Monte dei Paschi?*"

"*The time comes for those who wait,*" he replied. The Italian version of *all good things come to those who wait.*

Francesco stopped and stood still, trying to remember something. Louise did the same, closing her eyes, inhaling deeply, exhaling slowly, in hopes that meditation and freeing the mind had universal effects on others.

"Ecco," Francesco said.

She opened her eyes as he moved toward a shadowy corner. He signaled for her to shine her phone light, revealing a lever.

"*Is it a spigot?*" Louise asked.

"*No, it's not a spigot. It's a puzzle,*" he said.

"*Do you know the solution?*" she asked, very intrigued.

He shook his head pensively negative. Then he touched his temple, remembering. "*It is two-sided. Someone needs to be on the other side.*"

"*What is on the other side?*" Louise asked. "*Monte dei Paschi?*"

He shrugged. "No. Andiamo." He waved for her to follow.

They arrived at another set of stairs and climbed up. Francesco pushed up on the underside of a trap door. They emerged into the daylight, albeit gloomy and drizzly, burning their corneas. As their eyes adjusted Louise realized they had exited the Bottini in another neighborhood or *contrada* of Siena. She had that dazed surreal feeling. Big Steve stood there, leaning against an Italian off-road vehicle. Next to him was *The Librarian* that she suspected might have been one of her tails.

"Ciao, Benedetta!"

"Francesco! Ciao, bello!" Her beaming smile, which Louise had heretofore never seen, made her even more beautiful and likeable, but also inspired a twinge of jealousy. Francesco joyously approached her, and they gave each other cheek kisses.

"*Louise, this is my childhood friend, the famous historian Benedetta Bargagli Petrucci,*" Francesco said excitedly.

"*It's nice to meet you,*" Louise replied in Italian.

"It's nice to meet you too, Louise. I've heard so much about you from Big Steve. You speak Italian very well."

"Crash course," Louise said, pointing to Francesco.

"Eccellente studente," Francesco said, proudly kissing Louise on the cheek.

"*Why aren't you speaking English to her?*" Benedetta asked. She put the tips of her fingers together, shrugging, hands in the air, as Italians do, meaning, *what the heck?*

"Yes, why aren't you speaking English to me?" Louise repeated, growing suspicious.

Francesco grinned like a child who had been found out. "How else would you learn to speak Italian so beautifully?" he said in very good English with a charming Italian accent.

"He played y'all, Lulu!" Big Steve laughed.

"I didn't play *you*, apparently, Steve," Louise said. "How did you find us?"

"Y'all snuck out of your hotel room like a criminal. But yesterday I heard you ask Francesco to meet you in that café at noon and I knew y'all wanted to check out that tunnel. So, I went and found an authority."

"Andiamo," Benedetta said, pulling her collar close to her neck against the chill. "It is customary to have a nice vino after exploring the Bottini. There's a café close by." They piled into the camouflage painted SUV and Benedetta put the stick shift into gear.

"What kind of car is this?" Louise asked.

"Iveco Campagnola Alpina," Francesco replied. "It's the Italian competitor of the Range Rover Defender, built exclusively for the Italian Army's Alpine Training Center sports department." Francesco's Italian accent while speaking about Italian military vehicles made him even more attractive.

After just a few blocks, they parked in front of a café, got out and went to the terrace. The owner of the café greeted them warmly.

"Ciao, Benedetta! Ciao, Francesco!" He seated them on the terrace and turned on a heater. They chatted in Italian for a few moments as he served them Chianti and local appetizers without taking their order. Louise sipped the wine, breathing in the aromas.

"No, grazie," Big Steve said, turning down the glass of red wine. "I'm on the clock."

Francesco raised his glass. "To Nicchio contrada!" The owner joined them in the drink.

Louise couldn't help but notice several symbols of scallop shells in the neighborhood reminding her of the ubiquitous scallop shell symbols all around Burgundy.

"It reminds me of the Saint James Way where you see a lot of the symbolic scallop shells." She pointed to one of the images of a scallop shell.

"This is the Nicchio contrada," Benedetta said. "Their symbol *is* the scallop shell."

Then Francesco returned his attention to Louise. "Nicchio is my favorite contrada."

"Contrada?" Steve asked.

Benedetta explained further. "In Paris you have districts called *arrondissements*. Manhattan has *boroughs*. In Siena, a district is called a *contrada*. Siena has 17 contrade with very specific borders, most are passionate rivals. Torre, or Tower contrada, at Piazza del Campo is the only neutral contrada."

"The city center, where the famous Palio horserace takes place," Louise added.

"Brava, excellent student." Francesco continued. "The contrade are all named after animals, except for two, the *wave* and the *forest*. The only contrada named for a man-made thing is the *Tower*, at Piazza del Campo."

"So, the *Scallop Shell* is your favorite contrada, because you are like Saint Francis of the animals and the coquille Saint-Jacques is symbolic of the Saint James Way?" Louise asked.

Francesco braced himself knowing Benedetta would have a long answer.

"You must realize," Benedetta began, "The pilgrimage on Saint James Way was not originally Christian. It was a Pagan ritual just like other pagan rituals borrowed and repackaged as Christian traditions like Christmas and Easter. Pagans would walk across northern Spain to follow the sun to the *end of the world* in a *born-again* ritual, long before Jesus was born."

"Oh? I didn't know that. How interesting," Louise said, visibly disappointed.

"Benedetta is a world-famous historian, so it is her job to tell the facts," Francesco said.

"It is a *fact*, that the pilgrims would finish their journey at the peninsula called Fisterra, which is Italian for *the end of the world*," Benedetta continued. "It symbolized a pilgrim's death and rebirth. They would finish at *the end of the world*, burn their clothes, and watch the sun fall into the sea. Eventually, Christians claimed to have brought the remains of St. James to *Santiago de Compostela* and encouraged Christians to follow the well-beaten pilgrimage path in the name of Christianity. But they rarely finish the real pilgrimage route. *Fisterra* is another 88 kilometers past Santiago de Compostela, and it is not even the western most point of Europe. That is further south near Lisbon in Portugal."

"That *is* interesting." Louise looked like a child that just learned Santa Claus wasn't real.

"Well, this might make you feel better. You Americans have your own *interesting* story about *Fisterra*. One of *your* presidents walked the pilgrimage in reverse. In June 1779, three years into the American Revolutionary War, after crossing the Atlantic to seek help from France, John Adams' ship was leaking and about to sink. Fisterra was the first land mass available. Adams came ashore and ran on foot from Fisterra, over the Pyrenees, through France, all the way to Paris. Once he arrived, he begged the French for money and weapons to fight the British. He returned to America a hero, became Vice President to George Washington and then second President of the United States. France helped save *The New World*, creating a bond between America and France. That is why the U.S. returned the favor and helped liberate France from the Nazis 165 years later."

"Is that true?" Big Steve asked.

"It must be," Francesco replied. "Benedetta is an expert."

Big Steve had been silently listening. It was rare that Big Steve showed anger or judgment. But there was no question that he was unhappy about Louise ditching him.

Sensing the tension, Louise reached out to him. "Thank you for finding us today, Steve."

"Not gonna lie. Y'all scared me, Lulu."

Her association with Big Steve had always been a kind of mutual protection detail. He had been her bodyguard while she was in witness protection, during which she had learned about his struggles growing up. When he was fifteen, he had contracted shingles of the brain after a rabid dog bit him. The illness had put him in a coma causing him to speak erratically and quickly, so he had to do speech therapy. The result was that he tended not to enunciate his speech.

But he was a survivor. His young adult years were extraordinary, growing up with soon-to-be-famous and infamous people like Magic Johnson, or his own cousin who had founded the Crips in South Central Watts, home of Dr. Dre. Rival gangs including the CC Riders in Compton, home of Ice Cube, and PyRules, a division of the Bloods, with Chris Brown. The gangs had started out with no weapons, just fist fights. But then big weapons arrived in the 1980s with drug gangs from south of the border, and it became a war zone. Living in *the hood* had led him to doing some jail time, but he had turned his life around, making a career protecting others. Knowing the workings of the justice system, he became a powerful asset, and worked his way up protecting celebrities such as Michael Jackson, until he was recruited by the FBI.

"Don't you trust me?" His question crushed her. It was time to fess up.

"Of course, you're my best friend, Étienne." The little dig on the French version of his name, Étienne, broke the tension.

"It's Éti! I told you, *Étienne* is too girly." They laughed. "What were y'all tryin' to do? Sneakin' out on me like a teenager."

"It's top secret, Steve. I'm not sure we should discuss it here."

Francesco's eyes went wide with an idea. "Benedetta and Steve can be a big help with the treasure map," he whispered.

"What's going on?" Benedetta asked.

"It's a caper," Francesco said.

"A heist?" Big Steve asked.

Louise cringed. "It's not a *caper*. It's not a *heist*. It's a *treasure hunt*."

"Count me in!" Benedetta replied.

"Where you go, I go," Big Steve said.

Louise took a deep breath and thought for a moment. "Benedetta, you know that I thought you were following me. I kept seeing you on the street and thought you were a spy."

Benedetta shrugged as though saying *that makes sense*. "I can see why you might have pegged me as following you. But you will learn that I am omnipresent in Siena."

"She is the most important guide of the *Bottini*," Francesco said proudly.

"That's why Steve contracted me," Benedetta said. "Maurizio your concierge arranged it."

It all made sense. In fact, with Benedetta being the foremost authority on the Bottini, it was perfect. "We have to plan it in strictest secrecy," she said.

"Breakfast tomorrow at my house!" Francesco offered.

"Nine o'clock tomorrow morning at Francesco's," Louise seconded.

They all toasted. Steve bumped the air with his fist.

TWENTY-TWO

Siena, Italy, March 5, 2013

The birds singing, sheep and goats braying, cows mooing, mingled with the scent of espresso, an Italian paradise. Benedetta entered through the back like a neighbor who knew her way.

"Ciao ragazzi!" she said.

"Ciao, bella!" Louise and Steve said in unison. They were already enjoying the warm caffeinated brew with foamy milk.

Benedetta sat down as Francesco steamed up more milk, poured in a large shot of espresso and served it to her.

"A small miracle," Benedetta said. "Turning water into coffee. Did you know cappuccino came from the Capuchin friars? Another gift from God."

They enjoyed a breakfast of fresh bread, cheeses, fruits, and nuts. Ginger cat was curled up on the floor purring. The conversation became animated as Louise gave a detailed report of the situation with bank Monte dei Paschi and fielded questions. Then, she took out Rossellini's note with the pictogram. Ginger cat's ears danced and flitted in sync with the excited exclamations. Finally, Ginger Cat came over to see what the commotion was, jumping up onto Louise's lap.

"Ah, she remembers her savior," Francesco said.

"Maybe Ginger Cat will lead us to the treasure," Louise said, scratching behind her ears. "She's the one who led me to the Bottini." Ginger cat curled up in her lap.

Benedetta looked at Rossellini's note. Her eyes opened wide. "Ecco!" she shouted, slapping the table, making Ginger Cat stretch her legs in protest.

"Ecco, cosa?" Francesco asked.

She leaned in for emphasis. "All my life I have been taught that *fate* is the main player of the Palio Horse Race. Each jockey wears the colors of the contrada for which he is riding. But the horses are assigned by *lottery*. The race only lasts ninety seconds. But it is wild, people losing their minds over something that has taken place for over seven-hundred years. What is the prize for this madness? It is a *drappellone*. An embroidered banner of the Madonna di Provenzano on July 2nd and Madonna Assunta on August 16th." One banner depicts the apparition of Mary near the houses of Provenzano Salvani, which became the site of an annual pilgrimage, and the other is of the Assumption of Mary."

"What's the connection?" Louise asked.

"Our seventeen contrade all know each other, some are lifelong friends, some are lifelong enemies," Benedetta explained. "We all know which is which. Also, if you were not *born* into a contrada, you will never be completely accepted, beyond the work you do. Each contrada is its own state with its own church and center. But most important it is a microcosm of how the world works. Don't forget, modern banking was *invented* in Siena."

"She's right, it's a very intense system," Francesco confirmed.

"So." Benedetta looked intensely at the cat. "I think I just realized the key. The Noble Contrada del Brucco, or CAT-erpillar." Benedetta stressed *cat* pointing at Ginger cat.

"*Cat*-erpillar. I get it. But what's the key?" Louise asked.

Benedetta picked up a pen and notepad that Francesco had put out. She began drawing a map of Siena, but Francesco got up and rummaged through a drawer. He unfolded a map of Siena's contrade, each district designated by its colorful flag, and placed it in front of Benedetta.

"Grazie!" Benedetta splayed her hands over the map. "Okay, pay attention!" Benedetta pointed to Siena's northern district. "This is Caterpillar, a *very* special contrada. Not only does it have the *most* allies, *three*, Nicchio, Porcupine, and Tower. It is also the only contrada with *no rivals*." She pointed to the southern part of the map. "This is the Tower Contrada, which is considered the center of Siena. The *heart* of Siena is banking." She marked a large X just north of Tower Contrada. "Bank Monte dei Paschi is right here." She drew a line down, "Here is Tower Contrada," then she drew the line to the right. "Then we go east to Francesco's favorite contrada, Nicchio." She continued turning the line up to the north. "Move north, to Caterpillar, then all the way west to Porcupine."

Louise was paying attention but also distracted by Ginger Cat. Then she looked down at Ginger Cat who was now curled up in her lap making a perfect circle like a shrimp. She looked up at the map and something struck her.

"It's a golden ratio!" Louise shouted, tracing the shape with her finger. "Here is the bank, then down to Tower in the widest part of the city in the south, then spiral counter-clockwise one rotation up, ending in the narrowest part of the city in the north."

Benedetta stared in disbelief. "You're right! Bravissima! A Fibonacci golden ratio! Francesco, do you have a map of the Bottini?" Francesco fished in the drawer for another map, this time of the underground river tunnels, and placed it next to the map of Siena's districts. Benedetta drew the same line linking the Bottini under the districts. "You see this same shape goes with the tunnels of the Bottini. There is an offshoot of the underground river to Nicchio, another offshoot to Bruco, and the main Bottini starting from Fonte Gaia all the way north." They were all speechless. Then Big Steve broke the silence.

"So, y'all *are* planning a bank heist through the tunnels." He shook his head and folded his arms, in about the biggest display Louise had ever seen him being upset.

"It's not a *heist*, Steve. We aren't planning to *steal* the treasure. We just need to find it, to protect it. There was a reason Dario Rossellini gave me this note."

Steve calmed down and leaned into the map. "So, what's the key to the treasure?"

Benedetta shook her head. "It's too difficult to explain. You must *see* it. Andiamo." They all went out to Benedetta's SUV and drove to the North-western point of Siena and parked. They got out and walked up the cobblestone streets as Benedetta gave a tour. "We start here in the Caterpil-lar Contrada. To get a sense of how special it is, this is Dario Rossellini's contrada. It is also the contrada closest to Porcupine"

"Porcupines can hurt, y'all," Big Steve said.

"You are absolutely correct, Steve," Benedetta said. They arrived at a shop that sold colorful flags and costumes of all the districts and Benedetta stopped. "All 17 contrade of Siena participate in this biannual Palio horse race. They dress in these elaborate costumes." She indicated the shop window with traditional folk costumes on mannequins. "Seems quaint, right? But they aren't just play acting. These are not just *costumes*. These are *uniforms*. These residents are trained and ready to defend against any enemy, just as we have had to do for centuries."

Instead of going inside the shop, Benedetta continued walking west. "Each contrade is self-governed with its own center, main street, and church." She turned down a small road and approached a gate. Pointing to Louise she said, "Because Dario Rossellini trusted you with his secret, the members of the Caterpillar will trust you with theirs." They entered a secret garden that was well kept and inviting. "If I had not taken you here, like the average tourist, you would never have known it was here."

She led them back out to the street and turned down another small alleyway. Checking that no one else was watching she reached down and opened a trap door. She waved them all down to the Bottini, except for Steve who refused to descend, saying he would stand watch. Once they were in the underground tunnel, Benedetta turned on her phone light.

"Over the years, the contrada members have lost their military function, since Italy is now united, and we don't have other territories invading to overthrow our leadership. But there is an unspoken protection of our assets for which we will fight to the death. It is not about greed. On the contrary, it's about *fighting* greed. Each contrada has its own slogan."

"The word *slogan* originally came from the Scottish Gaelic word sluagh-ghairm," Louise said. "It's a rallying-cry, or in times of war, a battle-cry. Sluagh meaning people or army, and gairm meaning call or proclamation."

"Yes, correct, excellent," Benedetta said.

"So, what are the slogans of the contrades?" Louise asked.

"This information is too privileged even for you and Steve, Louise," Benedetta replied. "However, if you go to Dario Rossellini and ask him, you might gain that privilege."

"What should I ask him, exactly?"

"There is a reason Nicchio is Francesco's favorite," Benedetta said.

"It's true. My family are members of Nicchio," Francesco confessed.

Benedetta continued. "And I am a member of Porcupine. Tower Contrada is neutral. Dario Rossellini is a member of Caterpillar. You need to convince him to tell you the Caterpillar slogan."

"You don't know each contrada slogan?" Louise asked.

"No, it is the most secret of all Siena secrets," Francesco said. "Only the Tower contrada motto is public knowledge: *Beyond strength, power.*"

"And to solve this puzzle of the hidden treasure we may need all three slogans."

They went back out of the tunnel where Big Steve was standing watch.

"It's been a long day," Louise said. "Let's regroup tomorrow morning this time at my hotel library.

"Yes, it is a fantastic library at your hotel," Benedetta said.

"Exactly," Louise confirmed.

They drove back and parted ways.

Back at the hotel, Louise called Dario Rossellini to arrange a meeting.

"Could you come by MPS tomorrow evening?" Rossellini asked. "I'll wait for you by the entrance to let you in, 21:00."

"Okay. I'll see you then," Louise replied.

TWENTY-THREE

Siena, Italy, March 6, 2013

The team spent the day researching in the library, taking notes, putting together a plan. Then they dispersed and Louise put on her boots and coat and headed to meet Dario at Monte dei Paschi, Steve trailing close behind.

Having worked in banking for so long, some habits were hard to break. As always, Louise had arrived a few minutes early. As she approached, she looked at her watch, 20:57, three minutes before their scheduled nine p.m. meeting, so she slowed to a leisurely pace lingering in the shadows between the back alley and the front entrance of Monte dei Paschi, Big Steve waiting a few meters back. A couple minutes later, she heard male voices speaking Italian, as two men exited the alley walking toward her. She locked eyes with each of them as they silently passed. She stood her ground as one of the men shoved his shoulder against hers, but they kept walking. She looked down the alley behind MPS from where they had emerged and saw a body lying on the ground. She raced into the alley and recognized the victim. She knelt by his side as Steve ran up and stood over them.

"Dario!" Rossellini focused his eyes, Louise being his final vision in this world. "Dario!" Louise repeated. "Please hang on!" From his injuries and positioning, he appeared to have fallen from his office window.

With his last dying breath, he said, "Trova il monte." She didn't try to resuscitate him for fear of further damage to a possible broken neck or back. She held his hand. *Trova il monte? Find the mount?* Louise dialed the Italian emergency number 1-1-2.

As she waited, still holding Rossellini's hand, she tried to recall his exact dying words. *Trova il monte. Find the mount.* That was what she had already been trying to do! It must have been why she was imprisoned and tortured. Dario Rossellini knew about something perhaps only one or two other people in the world knew, and it may have cost him his life. If his only dying words were *find the mount*, how would she find out the Contrada Bruco slogan?

Another thing made no sense. If the secret deals between MPS and Deutsch Bank had already been made public, why kill Rossellini now? Was it just the rule of the Russian mafia? Did Rossellini have to die *because* the crooked deals were made public? Or had he felt personally responsible for the demise of the world's oldest bank and taken his own life to end his inner turmoil? She looked up toward the window of his office. *But he did not seem suicidal.* His dying words, *trova il monte* meant at least she had correctly understood his note about there being a *Mount.* Her quest had only just begun. Not knowing where to even start, her greatest resources were Benedetta and Francesco and Rossellini's note was the key.

"The police are here, Louise," Big Steve said, interrupting her thoughts. "They want us to stay for questioning."

Louise and Steve gave their statements to the police, their accounts of the two men leaving the scene and finding Dario Rossellini on the ground.

"Grazie," the officer taking their statements said. "We appreciate your cooperation. If you think of anything else, please contact me." He handed them each a business card. It read, Detective M. Mastroianni, Direzione Investigativa Antimafia.

"You're with the *Anti-Mafia* Investigation Department?" Louise asked.

"Yes, organized crime division, in cooperation with all five police forces."

"Five police forces?"

"Yes. These cases can involve departments of State, Finance, Military, Prisons, and even the Forestry police."

She couldn't help but notice his name befit his appearance, a prominent forehead, arched eyebrows, sparkling brown eyes, and graying temples. He was a more grizzled version of the legendary Italian actor, Marcello Mastroianni. He squinted, reading her mind, almost daring her to ask. She did.

"Are you related to the actor?"

He shook his head and smirked. "Not that I know of." He left it at that. "Thank you for your help. Grazie. Arrivederci."

"Prego. Arrivederci."

Working on her own investigation, Louise, tucked his business card in her pocket, for possible future reference.

❧

Siena, Italy, March 7, 2013

The next morning, Louise contacted Francesco and they arranged to meet in the hotel library to discuss Dario Rossellini's apparent murder or suicide. Big Steve stood sentinel by the door while Louise, Francesco, and Benedetta buried their noses in periodicals.

"Ugh! I've read so many news articles. We must be missing something," Louise said in exasperation. She sat back and focused. "Dario's final words were, *trove il monte*. That confirms I was correct about the note. But did he mean something else?"

"It's almost four o'clock," Benedetta said.

"I could use *un po' di fiato*," Francesco said.

"Good idea. Let's take a breather," Benedetta said.

"I'll order tea," Louise said. "Steve why don't join us?"

"Y'all work your way, I work mine. Bad things happen to the unprepared," Steve said. "But I'll take one of those Orangini's."

"Comin' right up," Louise said, calling room service.

At four o'clock, room service served them a full high tea service and a bottle of Orangina with a glass of ice for Big Steve. They ate at the large reading table, giving their brains a moment to rest. But Louise couldn't stop trying to solve the puzzle. She took the notepad and pen.

"Okay, the day when things took a turn for the worse, January 25th, an extraordinary meeting was called during which the MPS Board of Directors requested a government bailout and the shareholders overwhelmingly approved. That was the day that Kostas and I were supposed to meet with the board to present our restructuring plan with investors lined up. But the board had already voted for the government bailout. January 25th…" Louise searched for the financial trade magazine on that date and skimmed through the numbers and images. Suddenly she stopped and pulled the magazine toward her for a closer look.

"What is it?" Big Steve asked.

"Steve, look at this!" Louise waved him over. His agility defied his imposing size, and he was by her side in a split second. "Do you recognize these two men?"

"No doubt about it. Those are the guys who walked past us in the alley."

Louise pointed to the names captioned and read out loud, "Giancarlo Filippone, a manager at Monte dei Paschi. Bernardo Mingrone, Chief Financial Officer of Monte di Paschi."

"They were in the alley where Rossellini died?" Benedetta asked.

"They just left that poor man there to die," Big Steve said, shaking his head.

"What the hell is going on here?" Louise said.

Francesco sipped his tea pensively. Then he went to dial his cell phone, but Louise stopped him. "No emails, no mobile phones. I have a feeling because I called Dario, that might be why he is now dead."

"Ah, dimenticavo," he said, tapping his temple. He gathered his things. "Louise, tomorrow you go to Monte dei Paschi and wait outside, eight o'clock, before the bank opens."

"What for?"

"Someone will be there to meet you. Fatto?"

"Got it."

"Ciao tutti." Francesco bolted.

Siena, Italy, March 8, 2013

Louise stood in the Piazza Salimbeni in front of the Monte dei Paschi headquarters. A large white banner emblazoned with *Verità Per Dario*, or *Truth for Dario* had been hung on the front of the building. The banner had been signed by hundreds of residents to show support for the truth behind Rossellini's death.

Louise stared up at *Monte dei Paschi* engraved over the arched entrance, a light glowed just inside the entrance. She felt the answer was right in front of her. But the harder she looked the farther away it seemed. By habit, she had already been standing with her hands raised as though holding an imaginary basket of apples. Her Tai Chi master had instructed her even when standing idly, to always be in ready pose. It was also a meditation pose, so she closed her eyes and cleared her mind.

"You have a holistic approach to banking."

Louise recognized the voice and the distinct French accent. *Could it be?* She opened her eyes to see the silhouette of a monk in Franciscan robe, the golden light of the sconces in the passageway behind him.

"Only when I'm looking for answers."

"What is the question?" the monk said.

Louise approached him and saw that it was Alessandro, the singing monk, but he spoke with Jean-Philippe's voice.

"Who are you?" was all Louise could think to ask.

He waved for her to enter. Big Steve approached and *Alessandro* put his hand out in a request for him to stay outside.

"I'll be out here if you need me, Lulu," Big Steve said.

Louise followed Alessandro inside. Instead of entering the main bank, he took her through the secondary door where he had taken her before. But this time he led her down an ancient stone staircase. They arrived at a section of the premises filled with antiquities and historical documents spanning the centuries of its existence. He stopped and turned to her, the unmistakable gamut of emotions in her eyes, confusion, fear, disappointment. At that moment, for the first time since she'd known him, Louise felt her love for Jean-Philippe extinguished. His transformation was so complete, there seemed to be nothing left that drew them together. On top of that, his deception brought back her bitterness about her father.

"You're quite the master of disguises," she said, her voice cracking.

"Francesco introducing me as the singing monk was key. It refocused your mind."

"The beard, shaved head, tinted contact lenses, and perfect Italian accent were a nice touch, too," Louise said. "How did you get so well embedded here?"

"Michael recruited me several years ago when the first warnings of Monte dei Paschi and Deutsche Bank were flagged."

Louise nodded as if to say, *figures.* "My trusted friend, Michael."

"It was a brilliant move that allowed me to infiltrate this place. Only one monk is granted exclusive access within these walls at a time, a lifetime appointment. The last had just died and Michael knew the replacement was being chosen. It was a once-in-a-lifetime opportunity."

"How convenient."

"Louise, I beg you to set your disappointment aside for now. You can be angry with Michael and me. We will not fault you and will always be there for you. But now we must work together on this important mission."

His words suddenly lifted her spirits to rise above her ego. She realized it was an honor to be included in this inner sanctum. "Of course. You're right. What should I call you?"

"Please continue to call me Alessandro. You are the only one who knows my identity. He led her through a doorway to a stockpile of riches. "This collection is not open to the public. This area of the palace is original construction combining medieval and ancient Etruscan stone floors and walls." As they entered, motion detection bathed the room in golden light. "This is a custom state-of-the-art lighting and temperature control system calibrated to preserve historic artifacts. There is also a state-of-the-art fire prevention system." He directed her to a gold-plated panel painted in muted pigments depicting the Virgin Mary. "This is the most recent acquisition of art. It is by the early 1300s Italian painter Segna di Bonaventura of the Sienese School. It cost the bank nearly one million Euros. This is only a tiny example of the treasures held under Monte dei Paschi's protection on behalf of its residents."

He opened another door and entered what appeared to be an expansive private library. She noticed a stained-glass window high in the south facing wall.

"This is the library depicted in the book I showed Francesco!" Louise said.

"Correct." He approached the medieval bookshelf containing thousands of books. "This is a collection of the most important books out of the 3,000 donated by the economist represented by the statue in the piazza outside. All very rare and priceless. But that's not the most impressive thing about this room." He approached the center portion of the sprawling bookshelf. "There is a secret chamber behind here. The key to opening it died with Dario Rossellini."

"I have the feeling Dario didn't really know the key," Louise said. "I believe that is why he asked me to help him to figure it out."

"Over the centuries those of us monks with privileged access have tried to figure it out. But it is a dual-sided system. Even if someone found the correct lock and knew the key to opening it, someone on the other side must also know the key. It was handed down from generation to generation through the Caterpillar Contrada. But somewhere along the way, it was lost. Monte dei Paschi being in the Tower Contrada cannot side with any of the other Contrade. For centuries, the Tower Contrada's role has been to keep the 17 bickering children of Siena in a state of harmony, through equitable distribution of largesse. The elegant Piazza Salimbeni was created by the bank as a gift to the city, as officially neutral ground. Monte dei Paschi will never sell its art collection, even in these dire times. The works are inextricably linked to one another, to the palazzo, to the people of Siena."

"May I?" Louise asked, indicating the meticulously organized books on the shelves.

Alessandro nodded. "Go right ahead. You may take out and read anything, but it must remain archived here."

As she had become accustomed to doing, she stood still and took in the energy. Her eye was drawn upward toward the stained-glass window then down to where prismed sunlight touched antique mahogany spiraling library steps, five steps spiraling halfway around a central shaft to rest flush against the shelves, the treads inset with gilt-lined leather, on castors. The steps were parked under *M*. She noticed a hole where a large book had been removed and turned to see Alessandro sitting at the reading table.

"You're reading my favorite French philosopher," Louise said.

"Michel Eyquem de Montaigne is your favorite?" He knew she knew that he knew.

"Bonne lecture," she said, then turned back toward the shelves. Sliding the rolling steps all the way to the left, she started from the top moving down and to the right. She had a feeling but couldn't be sure what she was looking for until she found it. After a while she became completely consumed by the impressive library, the monk now sitting quietly reading Bible scriptures. There were original editions of everything, including one of the three original Bibles commissioned by Abbott Ceolfrid, and original writings from Italian philosophers Niccolo Machiavelli and Saint Thomas Aquinas. Louise passed over them with breathless admiration.

Finally, out of the corner of her eye, a ray from the stained-glass window drew her attention to her lower right, the steps now at the center of the massive shelving system. She glimpsed a title in English. It was a leather-bound version of The Numismatic Chronicle and Journal of the Numismatic Society. Louise wasn't sure how she knew, but this book was the key. Still sworn to secrecy about the treasure hunt for *Il Monte*, Louise needed to meet with the others to discuss Alessandro's involvement. She rubbed her eyes feigning fatigue.

"Would you mind if I came back tomorrow to search more? Steve is waiting."

"Of course, just have Francesco arrange the time." He led her out to where Steve stood, steadfast beacon of security.

"Let's head back to the hotel," Louise said.

"Hungry?"

"Starving. Lunch in the hotel library."

As soon as they arrived at the hotel, Louise sent word to Francesco and Benedetta to meet in the hotel library, via the horseback messenger, who now made the rounds past her hotel every hour, at LaFontaine's request, after the daring rescue.

Louise ate ravenously, the book she was reading safe from food stains at a slight distance to her left, but her eyes glued to it. Big Steve finished his meal and resumed his position at the door, Francesco and Benedetta enjoyed some of the local delicacies and chatted quietly.

"Sorry, we were starving," Louise said, finishing her food.

"Buon appetito," Francesco said.

Louise cleared the table of the food onto the cart. "Thank you for coming. I had a very interesting meeting with Alessandro."

"What did you find out?" Benedetta asked.

"Well, I need to go back to make sure. But I didn't want to give away anything to him, he's not really part of this." Louise placed one of the books she had been studying in the center of the table. "This is a history book about the *Codex Amiatinus* bible that Ceolfrid carried with him intending to give as a gift to Pope Gregory II, but he died en route to Rome September 29, 716, at Langres Burgundy. The book later appeared in the 9th century in Abbey of the Saviour, Mount Amiata in Tuscany."

"The Codex Amiatinus is the basis for the Latin Vulgate," Benedetta said. "The Latin version of the Bible prepared by Saint Jerome in the 4th century, adopted as the official text for the Roman Catholic Church."

"Exactly." Louise moved another to the center of the table and opened to a page. "This is a leather-bound edition of The Numismatic Chronicle and Journal of the Numismatic Society *Its Ancient and Modern Laws*."

"The journals about ancient coins?" Francesco asked.

"Exactly. I saw one just like this in the bookshelf of the secret Monte dei Paschi library where Alessandro took me. I have skimmed through and there are chapters on a *Treasure-Trove* for each territory." They all gave her blank stares. "Don't you see? *Treasure-Trove*. *Trove il monte*. That's what Dario Rossellini meant."

"Is it that simple?"

"Absolutely. Rossellini's dying words, *trove il monte*, was a simple play on words hinting at a *Treasure-Trove*. He wasn't hinting at the actual treasure of Monte dei Pachi but rather how to get to the treasure. Alessandro told me that there is a key somewhere in the giant bookshelf. Many have tried to find it, but it is dual-sided and must be struck simultaneously with someone else on the other side. Just as you said in the Bottini Francesco."

"So, you think the Numismatic Society book is the lever or something and someone needs to be on the other side and coordinate pulling it?" Benedetta asked. "But that doesn't explain the rest of the Fibonacci." She thought for a moment, then had an idea. "There must be levers at all points of the Bottini along the Fibonacci path that we must coordinate. One of us in each of the entrances. Me in Porcupine…"

"Me in Nicchio," Francesco said.

"But Dario is not here to go to Caterpillar," Louise said.

"That's why it must be *you* in Caterpillar," Benedetta said.

"Okay. But who's in Tower?" Louise asked. They all slowly turned to Big Steve.

He began to vigorously shake his head. "Lulu, y'all know I hate to be in close spaces."

"This is a good time to master that fear," Francesco said.

They all stood and surrounded him like the savior.

"We need you," Benedetta pleaded.

He pondered the idea. Louise knew his fear started after serving jailtime, but her look reassured him. Finally, he said, "As long as it ain't no heist, you can count on me."

"Bravo!" They patted him on the back and Louise kissed his cheek.

"All right. Here's the plan," Benedetta said. They all gathered around the reading table. "First, we need to synchronize our watches."

"Hold on," Louise interrupted. "There's already a flaw in your plan."

"You haven't even heard it yet."

"How did anyone access *Il Monte* in the past without synchronizing their watches?" Louise pointed out.

Benedetta rubbed her chin. "You're right. It's time to go back to the drawing board and by drawing board, I mean the Bottini. I have a theory. What's the weather like tomorrow?"

"It should be sunny but chilly," Francesco said. Everyone looked at him. "I check every day for the animals."

"Perfetto," Benedetta said. "We leave tomorrow before sunrise. Dress warm, pack a snack and drink to last eight hours and bring something to write with. Francesco, I will pick you up at 5:30 tomorrow, Louise and Steve be out front by 5:45."

"That reminds me," Louise said. "Let's start fifteen minutes earlier. We will need to use evasive tactics to make sure no one is following us."

"How do we do that?" Benedetta asked.

"I'll show you tomorrow. Pick us up here at 5:15 and we'll show you on the way to Francesco's. Tomorrow we'll also go over evasive maneuvers on foot."

They all went their respective ways to get to bed early and wake up before sunrise.

TWENTY-FOUR

In the predawn darkness, Louise navigated as Benedetta drove, teaching her never to drive directly to the meeting point, but instead take a long meandering *surveillance detection route*, or SDR. Benedetta arrived at Francesco's by 5:30. He got in and they did another SDR to arrive at Nicchio Bottini where Francesco would be dropped off. Before they left, Benedetta went over the details of the plan one more time.

"If my suspicions are correct, the Bottini are designed to let in a very small amount of natural sunlight at the exact same time in each tunnel and in the Monte dei Paschi secret library," Benedetta said. "Over the years, I have noticed the phenomenon, but didn't think much of it."

"Do you recall what time of day?" Francesco asked.

"Wouldn't it depend on the time of month and time of year?" Louise asked.

"Those are both the right questions. That is why we are here." Benedetta resumed her theory. "The sun rises fairly late this time of year so I believe it will be closer to noon. It might be later, in the afternoon. Let's synchronize our watches now." She studied her watch. "In ten seconds, it will be exactly six-fifteen. Five, four, three, two…" She pointed to them, and they all confirmed their phones and watches were in sync. "Francesco, you go down the Nicchio Bottini now. Next, Louise and I will take Steve into Tower Bottini, then I'll drop Louise at Caterpillar, and I will take my place at Porcupine."

"What about the Monte dei Paschi library?" Louise asked.

"Last night I met with Alessandro to synchronize his watch," Francesco said.

"So, he's officially part of our secret plan now?" Louise asked. "We can trust him?"

Benedetta and Francesco looked at each other in agreement. "I trust him with my life. But that's a story for another time," Benedetta said, checking her watch. "The second you see any natural light entering the Bottini, write down the exact time, try to pinpoint where the light is coming in and where it strikes the surface of the tunnel. I expect us all to see the light simultaneously. But we must carefully document it. Let's go."

Once alone in their respective Bottinis, they each dealt with the long wait in their own way. In the Caterpillar Bottini, Louise took advantage of the hours to practice her standing Tai Chi meditation, but keeping her eyes open so as not to miss the light. She stood with her arms up in front of her as though holding a basket of apples. She felt her feet connecting to the earth. With each inhale she imagined pulling energy up from the earth through her feet. Then as she exhaled, she imagined returning the energy to the earth, with a sense of giving and taking.

The time passed quickly, and after a couple hours she saw the light trickle in. It happened during a moment she was experiencing particularly high lucidity. As Benedetta had hinted, it was like a *natural phenomenon*. Almost as though the light were alive, reaching into the tunnel, like a finger pointing down through an unknown opening in the ceiling, then it *touched* one of the stone plaques on the wall. Louise jotted down the exact second: 11:11. She also noted the proximity of the entrance point of the light and where it pointed to.

Big Steve tried to handle his fear of enclosed spaces the best he could. Lying on his back his head propped up on his folded jacket in a relaxed position, counting his inhales and exhales, as Louise had coached him to. But mostly he repeated his favorite prayer to himself.

Then it happened, a finger of light reached into the obscurity, pointing to a stone plaque on the wall. He checked his watch and wrote down the time, 11:11. Then he did a quick sketch of the location the light source entered and where it pointed.

Alessandro knew from daily experience almost exactly when and where the light source would enter and point to. He had noticed the light, like the hand of God, many times over the years and had anthropomorphized it as a personal blessing. About the time he expected, 11:11, the finger of light shone gracefully through the stained-glass window and illuminated the Codex Amiatinus bible. He pulled the bible from the shelf but found no plaque.

Meanwhile, Benedetta waited peacefully, with a general idea of when it would happen, writing in her journal. Having spent years as a private tour guide of the Bottini, she had a sixth sense about it. When she felt the hour was nearing, she set down her writing, leaned back against the wall to watch the phenomenon she had seen only a few times before, suspecting but not sure if it was something special. Now she could confirm it meant something very special. When the light appeared through a crevice in the ceiling, it entered almost exactly where she had predicted. What surprised her was where it pointed. One of the stone plaques.

Francesco's experience was very moving. While waiting, he explored the Nicchio section of the Bottini examining every nook and marking, recalling his childhood days exploring in the same place. The 19th century *plaques* carved into the walls were relatively recent in the history of the tunnel. Francesco perused the engravings for names he recognized. Just as one of the names caught his eye, he saw a change in light and turned just in time to witness the miracle. A single ray of sunlight reached through an overhead crevice and landed on the very plaque with the name he had just noticed. He quickly noted the time, 11:11, and wrote it down along with the point of entry and the location of the plaque.

Then, as planned they each emerged into the daylight and waited for Benedetta to drive from Porcupine to pick them up. Finally, they arrived at Tower Bottini to get Big Steve who hopped into the SUV with everyone else.

"How did it go, Big Steve?" Louise asked.

"Well, I ain't afraid of closed spaces no more." Big Steve smiled, holding up the sketch. "I drew a picture for y'all."

"That's a very good drawing!" Francesco said. "You're an artist!"

Steve smiled, humbled, and surprised by the compliment.

"I agree, Steve," Louise said. "I didn't know you drew so well." Not wanting to embarrass him anymore she added, "Okay. Let's all go to Francesco's house."

Benedetta sped off to the farm sanctuary.

Francesco's large farm table was cluttered with maps, books, their notes from the tunnels, and a large desk calendar with a large square for every day of March 2013. Francesco placed a charcuterie platter and libations on the sideboard, and they served themselves, snacking and discussing their findings. The conversation became very animated as Ginger Cat lay by the fire, her ears twitching with the crescendos.

"Now that we know exactly the time, should we try to unlock the library entrance right away?" Louise asked. "The light will keep changing and we'll miss our chance."

"Let's not be too hasty," Benedetta said. "There must be something more to it. Today it happened to be 11:11. But tomorrow it will be something else."

"That's right!" Louise acknowledged. "It will change every day, and therefore the light will shine on a different plaque."

"There was no plaque behind the book the light touched," Alessandro said.

"Which book did it shine on?" Louise asked.

"The Codex Amiatinus Bible," Alessandro replied.

"Then we know what book it will shine on for you," Louise said.

"How do you know?"

"The Codex Amiatinus bible was very close to a three-book leather-bound collection of the *Numismatic Society* journals," Louise said. "Dario Rossellini said *trove*, which is what those journals discuss. There should be a plaque behind that collection."

"What do those plaques mean?" Big Steve asked.

"It's an accounting system," Benedetta replied. "Over the centuries, private citizens had tired of carrying water from the wells and fountains and demanded their homes to be connected to the Bottini water supply. This indelible accounting system was created, carving the plaques throughout the Bottini marking who would receive how much water, based on a payment rate of one *dado* to about 400 liters every twenty-four hours."

"A general ledger written in stone!" Louise said.

Benedetta fell into deep concentration, staring intensely at the large desk calendar, which was now covered in handwritten notes. "Ecco!" She suddenly slapped the table so hard that Ginger Cat ran over and sat on the cushioned chair in the corner. Benedetta pointed at the calendar. Louise immediately understood, Francesco caught on a moment later.

"What is it?" Big Steve asked.

"Spring Equinox!" Benedetta, Francesco, and Louise said in unison pointing to the date.

"Spring what?" Steve asked.

"We don't wait for the sun to hit the same plaque. We wait for wherever the sun hits at exactly 11:11 on March 20th. That is where we must activate the locks that open the treasure trove," Benedetta explained. "We must be ready!"

"To make sure we are in the right place on March 20th, we should go a few more times to track the trajectory," Francesco said.

"We know where it will be for Alessandro," Louise said.

"We know where you *think* it will be," Alessandro and Francesco both said.

"I'm almost one hundred percent certain it will be the *Numismatic Society* journals," Louise said defiantly. The tension flared between Louise and the two men. Often, her survival instincts overpowered her equanimity, and she lashed out. "I'll bet you a bottle of Privilege La Reserve du Prince cognac." Her friend Frédéric LaFontaine happened to be the owner of the famous brand that sold for $5,000 a bottle so it was an unfair wager. They backed off.

"We should go a few more times and triangulate one or two more locations the sunlight hits," Benedetta finally said, agreeing with Louise and diffusing the tension. "Is everyone okay returning to the Bottini between now and March 20th?" They all emphatically nodded yes.

"The big question," Louise said. "What are we going to do when we find *Il Monte?*"

"Louise is right. This is the most sacred treasure in the world. Perhaps more sacred than the treasures of the Vatican," Benedetta said. "Keeping it secret is a matter of life and death."

"There's something I don't understand," Louise said. "If the *Monte dei Pietà* was initiated to help the poor, the collateral given probably wasn't really very valuable. The needy wouldn't offer great historic art pieces or gold or precious jewels. So, what if there's really nothing of value, just a lot of folk art and sentimental family heirlooms?"

"I think I can answer that," Alessandro said. He continued explaining in English with a delicate Italian accent. "You must understand that the Franciscan monks were fundamentally opposed to *interest* banking, which had only been practiced by the Italian Jewish banks at the time. In the early Renaissance period, trade and commerce flourished, but also created an inordinate amount of poverty in the lower classes."

"Not much has changed in the respect," Louise said.

"Back then, charging interest to the poor and suffering was met with scorn by the Franciscan religious order, founded on the vow of poverty, and acting on behalf of the poor to improve their standard of living. Those monks invented the idea of pawn-based money lending to offer a charitable safety net. These *pawn shops* flourished throughout Italy and soon became known as *Monte dei Pietà*. *Pietà* means *pity* or compassion. But the underlying *Monte* did not consist of items pawned by the poor."

"That's right!" Benedetta said. "It was the collection of money and other donations by the wealthy to be distributed to the needy. But there had to be a compromise between the Franciscan monks and the Italian Jewish bankers. The Franciscans' wanted to eliminate the interest-bearing loans of the financial institutions. But those same Jewish financial institutions ended up lending most of the money for *Il Monte*. The two institutions co-existed, having two different clientele."

"The *only* example of the poor receiving monetary help during the Renaissance period happened here in Siena," Alessandro added. "The Franciscan monks formed *Monte di Paschi*, which was a play on words from *Monte di Pietà*. The new Monte di *Paschi* was funded through revenues from the pasturelands or *Paschi*."

Benedetta's eyes were wide with the realization. "Historical records show that the clientele included the City of Assisi, the San Pietro Abbey, and the friars of the Monastero di San Franscesco themselves! If those entities put up collateral for banking purposes, or even for safe keeping, it could very easily have been stored in this very Monte dei Paschi secret vault!"

"There would be centuries of municipal and monastic treasures," Alessandro said.

"Francesco is right," Louise said. "It could be the most important treasure in the world."

"So, what's the plan?" Francesco asked.

Benedetta thought again. She shoved everything aside, then tore off the large calendar sheet, and turned it over to have a big blank page.

"Here's the plan." She drew a spiral line and four X's representing the four Contrade: Tower, Nicchio, Caterpillar, and Porcupine. "On March 20th, we each take our respective places at least one hour before 11:11." She drew another X near Tower Contrada. "We will assume that *Il Monte* will be under the Tower in the Fonte Gaia Bottini because that one is connected to the two-sided door in the Monte dei Paschi secret library." She traced her finger along the line between Monte dei Paschi bank to Fonte Gaia. "The distance between MPS and the Fonte Gaia Bottini where Steve will activate the plaque is about 350 meters or the size of three soccer fields. The vault holding *Il Monte* could be anywhere in between, or even that entire size."

"That raises a very important question," Louise said. "We've been assuming the sun's ray will hit on one of the plaques to be pressed in or something. But do we really know what to do?"

"That will be the ultimate leap of faith," Benedetta speculated. "If nothing happens or if we don't figure out how we're supposed to activate the vault door, we will miss our chance. Presumably it will only occur every Spring Equinox, but we really don't know. That is why we must agree on what to do at exactly one minute after 11:11." She fell silent, thinking.

"What's the plan?" Louise asked.

"A rehearsal. We go to our spots in the Bottini two more times, and mark where the sunlight hits the plaque at 11:11 to get a sense of the trajectory."

"What if it doesn't hit right at 11:11?" Francesco asked.

"Then we're completely wrong and we start over." Benedetta speculated further. "Also, we still don't know for sure what will trigger the lock and open the vault. But let's assume there's a switch where the sunlight hits that we must all press, and the vault opens revealing uncounted riches. The first thing we do is secure the area. Therefore, immediately after 11:11, we press the switch and run through the tunnels to Tower Bottini where Steve and the vault are. If there's nothing in the vault, Monte dei Paschi will be worth no more than its current assets minus crippling debt. If there is a treasure trove, we seal it back up and the secret goes no further than us. The appraised value of the vault's contents would be priceless. The most crucial thing is that we keep secrecy on our side."

"But if we reseal the vault, how will the value of the contents be assessed as the value of MPS?" Louise asked.

Alessandro replied, "As the ultimate gatekeeper, my word stands."

"Your word is enough?" Louise didn't mean it to sound as skeptical as it did.

"The same way Benedetta is the foremost authority on the history of Siena, Alessandro is the foremost authority on art, antiquities, and other objets d'art in Siena," Francesco said.

Louise looked impressed. "Is that true, *Alessandro*?"

He humbly bowed his head. "My training and accreditation go back decades."

Louise was impressed but not that surprised. The persona that the old Jean-Philippe had relinquished to become Alessandro was quite accomplished. Before Louise had met him, Jean-Philippe had been widely known as a somewhat eccentric national hero in France. He came from a very old lineage of the French aristocracy, including a long line of commandants with the French Royal Navy, dating back to Napoleon I. He had fought with the French troops against Gaddafi when Libya invaded Chad, earning him the title of *Chevalier*, which is the French equivalent of knighthood. Believing he should honor that title he devoted his life to his country. It was not uncommon to see him riding his horse through the Paris Tuileries Garden. In fact, that is exactly how Louise had met him for the first time.[22] It did not surprise her that he would continue to develop new skills over the years. After all, so had she.

"That's correct. Alessandro's authority carries enough clout with Italy's Central bank that if he were to assure authorities of the treasure trove, they would take him at his word," Benedetta said. "Now we have to determine where the triggers for the vault are." She picked up Steve's drawing of the tunnel and placed it over the map she had drawn. "Without a compass in the tunnels it will be difficult to know what direction the sun is moving."

"But it won't really matter," Louise interrupted. She leaned over and put a pencil on the point where Steve had drawn the sun's ray entering through the ceiling. Then she drew a line just above the line Steve had drawn to represent the sun's ray and marked a spot where the sunlight might touch next time. "This could be the sun's ray the day before or after today. She drew another line below Steve's line ending at another spot below where Steve had marked the sunlight hitting the plaque. "No matter what direction the sun is moving, we should be able to extrapolate from two more points of light where the next sun's ray will land. We take a piece of chalk with us, and mark where the sun hits for the next two visits."

They all looked at Benedetta, who finally said, "It makes sense."

"Okay, what days do we go back?" Louise asked. "Today is March 10th. That's 10 days before March 20th. March 14th is *Pi Day*. That would be a good day to see if anything mystical happens." Benedetta, Francesco, and

Alessandro all nodded their heads in agreement. Steve just shook his head in confusion.

"*Pie* day?" Steve asked. "Y'all thinking about *pie* at a time like this?"

"March 14th is Pi Day because it's Albert Einstein's birthday and the first three digits of the mathematical constant known as Pi are 3, 1, and 4. The 14th day of the 3rd month, 3-14."

"Okay, sis. If you say so," Steve said.

"Pi Day doesn't exist in Europe because the month goes before the day, so March 14th is actually 14-3. However, March 15th may be more meaningful," Benedetta said. "The Ides of March in the ancient Roman calendar is the first full moon of the new year.

"Pi is much more ancient dating from 1900 BC," Louise said.

"But Pi is purely mathematical," Benedetta countered. "The Ides of March from the times of Julius Caesar in 44 BC is not only a very religious date. It was also notable for the Romans as a deadline for settling the *debts*."

The room went silent. This was very convincing.

"You make a great point, Benedetta," Louise said. "We should go on the 15th and then once more on March 17th which will be three days before the Spring Equinox March 20th."

"It's a brilliant plan," Benedetta said. "It will also give us the opportunity to rehearse running through the Bottini to get to Steve right after we press the lever at 11:11."

"Okay, it's settled. On March 15th, the Ides of March, we mark where the sun hits, then run to Steve's spot under the Contrada Tower," Francesco said.

"Maybe we should all meet in the Monte dei Paschi library where Alessandro will be?" Louise suggested.

Benedetta contemplated. "It makes more sense to meet where Steve will be in the Fonte Gaia Bottini under Contrada Tower. On the off chance that the vault opens on March 15th, it's better to be in the underground tunnels."

"Bravo!" everyone shouted. They poured chianti and raised their glasses.

"To the Bottini team!" Benedetta said.

They drank then everyone calmed down to contemplate their mission. Ginger Cat came over to Louise, who picked her up and set her in her lap.

"I think the animals are hungry," Francesco said.

"Okay, we better go," Louise said, standing up and giving Ginger Cat a hug.

Francesco came close and said, "Mi manchi."

Louise noticed Alessandro look away, respectfully. "I miss you too." Louise petted Ginger Cat and added, "I miss you *both*." She handed the cat to Francesco. "We'll spend some time together when this is all over." They kissed good-bye. "Come on, Steve. Let's head back."

"I'll drive you," Benedetta said.

They all departed together, leaving Francesco to feed the animals and Ginger Cat relaxing in front of the fireplace.

The Ides of March. Ever since the team meeting, for the next few days Louise obsessively researched the vast ancient archives of the hotel library. She could write a dissertation. Could the Ides of March be a clue into Dario Rossellini's death? Had he been beholden to someone, or did he have a dangerous secret? Was there really a vault containing a treasure trove? Or possibly crucial information? Louise read and reread newspaper clippings, public filings, and documents that Rossellini had given her.

After the January 25th Board of Directors meeting, Rossellini had told Louise that he had been a close friend of the former bank president Giuseppe Mussari, who was the driving force behind the bad investments. One particular investment that started the downfall was the fateful purchase of a Spanish bank, Banca Antonveneta from Spain's Santander. Monte dei Paschi grossly overpaid, and the transaction was financed by Deutsche Bank leading to the even more disastrous refinancing of the debt with derivatives.

Being closely tied to Mussari when he did the botched deals could justify Rossellini's anguish and decision to commit suicide. But that was the only plausible reason, all other evidence pointed to murder. What Louise found very curious was that there was no available information about Dario Rossellini's origins. According to Benedetta, he was a member of Caterpillar Contrada. That meant he was born in Siena. Yet, she found nothing about him in any of the archives. She suspected the Internet had been scrubbed of him too.

While reading one newspaper, a photo caught her eye. She dug in her bag for the business card of detective Mastroianni and called the police station.

TWENTY-FIVE

Siena, Italy, March 14, 2013

Sipping coffee in her hotel room, Louise dreaded the day ahead. Detective Mastroianni hadn't returned her call and she hated losing hope, but it was clear that she had reached a dead end in her investigation into Rossellini's death and the dealings with Deutsch Bank. She rubbed her temples in frustration. Then her cell phone rang.

"Pronto."

"Signorina Moscow, this is detective Mastroianni. Could you and your colleague Steve meet me at the station for a follow-up interview?"

"Of course." Louise looked at the detective's business card for the address. "We can be there in fifteen minutes." She hung up and knocked on Big Steve's door. Their routine had not changed, he tailed her on surveillance and protection as they walked to the police station. They entered and were immediately escorted to Mastroianni's office.

"Thank you for agreeing to meet with me," Mastroianni said, shaking their hands.

"We are very anxious to know the status of the case," Louise said.

"Please, have a seat."

Louise appreciated how tidy his office was. They sat at two chairs facing his desk. He sat and picked up a notepad and pen, poised to write.

"A witness confirmed the autopsy report that Rossellini had been lying in the alley for at least an hour after jumping from his fourth-floor window," Mastroianni said.

This revelation was jarring and nauseating to Louise. "That's horrible," she said. "The autopsy report says he *jumped*? Isn't Dario Rossellini's death suspicious?"

"Yes, it is suspicious. That is why the investigation into Monte dei Paschi dealings with Deutsche Bank has kicked into high gear. His death came at a time when the bank was pushed to the brink of collapse. An international scandal involving hundreds of millions of euros lost through risky investments."

"How can we help?" Louise asked, not revealing any insider information.

"Security camera footage showed two shadowy figures appear at the end of the alley, apparently checking that there was no chance Dario Rossellini could survive the fall. We would like you to view the footage to confirm if they were the two men you saw, according to your statements. Your witness testimony could be key to the investigation."

"We are happy to cooperate, but..." Louise hesitated. "As you know, we will be putting ourselves at great risk, so I'd like to request something in return."

Mastroianni raised his eyebrows. "I make no promises."

"Dario Rossellini was an old friend. I would like more information on how he died, anything from the autopsy report, forensics, findings about the financial crisis."

Mastroianni didn't say no. "Follow me." They got up and he led them to a soundproof media room with a monitor. "Please have a seat. The footage is queued up." He started the video which was of the empty alleyway just behind Monte dei Paschi under Rossellini's office window where Louise had found him. The video showed several seconds of empty alleyway. Then suddenly Rossellini's body fell, landing with shocking impact. Louise recoiled and Big Steve put a calming hand on her shoulder. The footage continued as a sped-up time lapse, showing the banker lying on the dimly lit cobblestones for almost twenty minutes, occasionally moving an arm and leg. Then Mastroianni slowed it to half speed at thirty-three-minutes after Rossellini fell.

"As you see, Rossellini fell or was pushed from his office window at exactly 19:59:23 on March 6, 2013, landing with brutal force in the dark alleyway," Mastroianni said. "He appears to be moving for at least 22 minutes." He rewound and replayed something Louise had noticed too. "Rossellini's fall and impact are very strange. Why would he fall *facing* the building? If someone jumps to his death, why would he jump backwards? Also, at this time, phone records show that a call was made on Rossellini's mobile phone. At the same moment..." he paused the video and pointed, "an object fell onto the ground landing a few feet from the body. It was Mr. Rossellini's watch face, without the strap." He resumed the slightly sped up video to the fifty-three-minute mark when the two shadowy figures appeared. Mastroianni slowed the video and zoomed in on the faces. "One of the men walks over and examines Rossellini but offers no aid and doesn't call for help. He turns around and calmly walks out of the alley." Mastroianni paused the video showing the faces of the two men walking away.

"That's them," Louise confirmed, looking shaken. "The two Monte dei Paschi executives who I saw in the newspaper..." She searched her mind for their names.

"Giancarlo Filippone and Bernardo Mingrone," Mastroianni said.

"Yes, that's them."

Mastroianni looked at Steve who nodded in agreement. "I seen 'em too."

The video resumed to normal speed until Louise and Steve made their appearances on screen. Mastroianni paused at the precise moment the man's shoulder struck Louise's.

"Ms. Moscow, in your statement you said they threatened you during this interaction?"

"Not verbally," Louise replied. "They didn't say anything. But as you see, he struck me."

"Did you say anything?"

"No, I just waited to see what they would do."

"Did they appear panicked or frantic?" Seeing the video of the two men, Louise remembered something. "Ms. Moscow, we expect you to be 100% candid. In Italy we also have obstruction of justice laws."

"No, they were calm," she recalled. "At the time, I didn't know who they were."

"But now?"

Louise nodded. "We recognized their photos in a newspaper article I found."

"Can you identify them from photos by name?"

"Absolutely. I can testify as to who they are." She hesitated. "But I would like more privileged information from your investigation."

Mastroianni considered this. "If you continue to cooperate, I'll tell you what we know."

"Then we will tell you everything we know, as soon as we know it."

Mastroianni opened a dossier and peered down his nose through his reading glasses at a report. "The post-mortem determined that Rossellini killed himself," he read aloud. "However, his family strongly suspects that he was murdered because he knew too much about Deutsche Bank's questionable financial deals. Prosecutors ordered the trajectory of his fall to be simulated. It also ordered his body to be exhumed to determine exactly how he died."

"Did they do an additional autopsy?" Louise asked.

"Yes. Further examination showed that Rossellini had bruises and scratches on his arms and wrists suggesting that he may have been restrained forcibly before being pushed out of the window. On the back of his head was a deep, L-shaped gash suggesting he may have been hit with a blunt object before falling from the window. Three suicide notes were found crumpled in a bin in his study at home. But his widow, Antonia Rossellini, said they contained phrases that her husband would never have used. One of them said, *Ciao, Toni, my love. I'm sorry.*"

"He called his wife Toni?" Louise asked again interrupting, taking mental notes.

"That's just it," Mastroianni replied. "His wife, Antonia, said," he read from the transcript, "'He never called me Toni, he always called me Antonia.' She insists that her husband was murdered. A handwriting expert analyzed the suicide notes and found they had been written under duress."

"Are the two bank executives under investigation?" Louise asked.

"They were interviewed in the first phase of the investigation," Mastroianni replied. "We have decided to bring them back in for questioning as part of the new investigation." Mastroianni replayed the video of the two men. "The first man wearing the padded jacket is Giancarlo Filippone, a colleague and friend of Dario Rossellini. The other man, Bernardo Mingrone who was the Monte di Paschi Chief Financial Officer, appears to stay in the background."

"Did they make statements?" Louise asked.

"Yes, we have both their statements." Mastroianni found the first statement in the dossier and read aloud. "This is Mingrone's statement: 'I came from work at 18:00 and later I was contacted by the wife of Dario Rossellini who had not heard from her husband and begged me to go and call him. I sent him a text message at 19:41 and got no response, so after waiting a bit I went to the office at 20:30 and when I entered the room, I saw the window open, I looked below and saw Dario's lifeless body.'"

Louise listened in shock. "What did the other one say?"

Mastroianni flipped to another page. "Filippone's testimony was also recorded, stating: 'At 20:40 on my way out I was talking on the phone, and just as I was in the hallway on the ground floor of the building heading towards the main exit, I met another man gesticulating dramatically and confused.' He was referring to the building concierge," Mastroianni clarified. Then he continued reading. "'The concierge mouthed the words, *Dario Rossellini* then *window*, then after hanging up the phone I met with Rossellini's colleague,' again Filippone, 'who told me that Dario Rossellini was thrown from the window. I asked the two where Rossellini's office was located and to accompany me there asking if they had called an ambulance. I entered the office and I looked out the window seeing the body on the ground; at that point I called 1-1-8, since I had been told that no one had called previously.' That's the official version," Mastroianni said.

"But when I saw them," Louise countered, "as you can see from the video, they showed no panic, no distress. They were calmly walking away."

"This is why we are now involved," Mastroianni said. "The public outcry has been intense. The public prosecutor's initial review of the evidence we collected found none of the circumstances suspicious. He determined there was nothing alarming about the two men you saw in the alley where Rossellini was either pushed or had jumped. Since then, some confusion has emerged. According to his wife Antonia, Rossellini called her at 19:02, one hour prior to the deadly fall. She said he did not sound like someone who is going to commit suicide. To the contrary, they were making dinner plans." Mastroianni checked the dossier again and read. "According to her statement, she quoted Rossellini as saying, 'I will be home at 19.30. I already bought everything you need. But first I need to pick up the meatballs that I ordered for dinner. See you later.'"

"He never made it home," Louise said.

"His wife's statement clearly contradicts the initial reports and puts the entire investigation into question. To add to the confusion, upon further investigation, I found his phone records showed that after his fall a number was typed on his cell." He showed Louise the number on the phone record: 409909. "Antonia Rossellini's attorney said it may have been a computer access code."

"Filippone and Mingrone could have forced the code out of Rossellini. That's where the bruises and scratches could have come from. It could be access to a bank account," Louise said, clearly shaken. "I knew Dario Rossellini and I considered him a friend."

Detective Mastroianni decided to wrap up their meeting for her sake. He placed the report back into the dossier and closed it. "Rest assured, Signorina Moscow, I will not stop until this murder is solved."

"Neither will I." Louise and Big Steve stood, and they shook hands.

"Is there anything else you would like to know at this time, Signorina Moscow?"

"Yes." She flicked his business card against her fingertips. "What does the M stand for?" referring to the initial instead of first name.

"Let's just say, it does not stand for Marcello."

TWENTY-SIX

Siena, Italy, March 15, 2013

Benedetta picked up Louise and Steve at eight-thirty and they took the drive to Francesco's using evasive tactics arriving at nine o'clock. Over breakfast, they reviewed their plan one last time and headed out by ten o'clock.

"We are all synchronized, and Alessandro is at his post. At 11:11, everyone is to record any observations, as well as new or unusual activity, when and where the sun hits and marking where it hits with chalk. No photos for security reasons. At no later than one minute after 11:11 we all leave our posts and run through the tunnels to Steve's position at Font Gaia Bottini."

Confident they weren't followed Louise got out of the SUV and went down to her post under Caterpillar Contrada. Then Benedetta dropped Francesco at the entrance to Nicchio and Steve at the entrance to Tower Bottini. She drove back to Porcupine, parked, and descended to the Bottini by 10:45.

For Louise, time went by both quickly and excruciatingly slowly. It was the most fascinating combination of finance, corruption, and historical events she had ever encountered, which was saying a lot. Her mind raced, even as she tried to relax in a meditation pose. Could this case be the culmination of centuries of institutionalized banking corruption? Could it finally resolve the mystery of the dark underworld of international banking? Perhaps their efforts will reveal a network of criminals, and maybe even restore a more chaste, honest, and equitable distribution of natural resources originally intended? Like a caterpillar's metamorphosis into a butterfly, could banking fundamentally change to its original divine purpose?

She had set her phone alarm to 11:00, and the crystal windchime sounds began to tinkle. She sat still and focused until the sun's rays entered the cavern right on time, 11:11. It was truly magical and ghostly, pointing the way. It landed just a few inches above what she remembered last time and she marked it with the chalk. Disappointed that nothing else happened to indicate a relationship to the Ides of March or the full moon, at exactly 11:12 she turned and headed back down the tunnel toward the Fonte Gaia Bottini. Suddenly, she felt the earth trembling beneath her feet. It was unmistakable but it ended almost immediately.

As Louise approached the Fonte Gaia Bottini under Tower Contrada, she saw the look on Steve's face. He had grown up in Southern California and knew what an earthquake was.

"Did you feel that one, Steve?" Louise said, making light of the trembler.

"My heart nearly burst through my chest, Lulu. That was nothin' compared to our earthquakes back home. But this is not where I want you or me to be during The Big One."

Francesco approached. "I think there was an earthquake!" he said, visibly shaken.

"Where's Benedetta?" Louise asked, checking her watch.

"It's been fifteen minutes," Francesco said, looking at his watch. "Porcupine is the farthest Contrada. I'm sure she's on her way."

"Should we go look for her in case she was hurt in the earthquake?" Steve suggested.

"That was not an earthquake, my friends," Benedetta said from a short distance.

"What took you so long?" Louise demanded.

"After the tunnel shook, it didn't seem like an earthquake to me, but they have been known to happen in this region. So, to make sure, I surfaced and called my friend at the Seismological Research Center. He confirmed there was no seismic activity."

"Then what was it?" Francesco asked.

"I'm not sure."

"Benedetta," Louise said, not hiding her disapproval. "You could have compromised the team by ignoring your own protocol to meet here immediately."

"You're right, I should have waited until we were all here before going out to make the call. I apologize. Please do as I say, not as I did."

"Apology not accepted," Big Steve said in a rare display of disapproval. "You could'a been hurt. We were about to come looking for y'all."

"He's right," Louise added. "We would have unnecessarily endangered ourselves to come after you if you had been gone much longer."

"Agreed." Benedetta put her palms together and moved her hands emphatically, sincerely contrite. "Please, I beg you, trust me, it will never happen again."

Louise and Steve looked at Francesco who also appeared suspicious of Benedetta. But then his expression changed, and he nodded reassuringly to them. "I've known Benedetta all my life and I think she means it."

"Okay," Louise said. "From now on, no matter what, no one breaks protocol." She put her hand out, palm down, and said, "Team pact." She waited for others to join in. Francesco and Benedetta didn't understand until Steve placed his hand on top of hers.

"Bottini Team pact."

Francesco and Benedetta stacked their hands on top and all said, "Bottini Team pact!"

"What now?" Steve asked.

"Alessandro is waiting for us in the library. There may be more clues about the ground shaking there," Benedetta said. "Let's go."

Alessandro greeted them at the entrance of Monte dei Paschi and led them swiftly to the secret library. They gathered around the large mahogany reading table where the three leather-bound Numismatic Chronicles were still sitting.

"In light of this morning's events, it is critical that we make a thorough record of everyone's experience," Benedetta said. They all took out their notes. "If there are no objections, we should have Alessandro give his observations first." All eyes moved to Alessandro who seemed relieved to be able to discuss his tale.

"Thank you, Benedetta. As you may know, I have devoted my life to my home of Siena and its residents. I take pride in knowing every bird, dog, cat, and person who frequents these cobblestone streets. This city is my heart and soul and I feel attached on a molecular level. This project has enraptured me. It seems to be a final revelation of something that I have always sensed existed. Something magical beneath the very ground we walk upon. It is a truly miraculous place. So, this morning, with great reverence of purpose, I took my place fully prepared for any eventuality. As agreed, I stood here awaiting the sunbeam through the stained-glass window, as it does every day, this time landing on these three books, which I then removed from the shelf to see if there was a plaque. It was a magical moment. The ground literally shook." He gathered his composure.

Louise, pen to paper, fastidiously recorded every word. "Did anything else happen?" she asked. "Anything that you might have taken for granted but could be important? We must record every detail while it's still fresh in our minds. We need to write down everyone's experiences in detail, now while our memories are still fresh."

"Louise is correct. This is very important," Benedetta echoed. "Louise will write down everyone's recollections from today and going forward. Even going backwards. If you remember any detail at all no matter how insignificant, please speak it now."

"After the sunshine touched on the middle book of the Numismatic Chronicles at 11:11, I took them from the shelf to see if there was a plaque behind them," Alessandro said. "It was at that moment the ground shook. But as you can see, there is no plaque behind the books."

"Perhaps the bookshelves themselves contain the trigger," Louise said.

"You must be right, Louise!" Benedetta said. "There may be a system of weights and balances in the shelves. There's no plaque behind the Numismatic Chronicles because they *are* the trigger and simply must be removed to trigger it."

"That must be it," Alessandro agreed.

"Okay, Steve, did anything unusual happen to you?" Benedetta asked.

"There was something that I don't know how to describe."

"Just say anything that comes to mind," Louise said, still writing.

"That sunlight. It was...*alive*."

"Yes!" they all said in unison.

"For me too," Louise said. "It was like a finger pointing, almost in slow motion."

"What does it mean?" Big Steve asked.

Louise shrugged. "It's hard to say, but it was mystical." She resumed writing. "So, to clarify, everyone saw the light as though in slow motion, reach into the Bottini, or in Alessandro's case, into the library. We all marked the spot the light touched with chalk. On March 17th we'll see the next trajectory of the sunbeam and extrapolate where the next point will be on Spring Equinox."

"In English please, Lulu," Big Steve said.

"March 17th is the last time before March 20th that we will mark where the sunbeam lands," Louise replied. "But from what I saw today, the sunlight already landed twice on the same plaque. My chalk mark today was slightly off the center of the plaque, and the sunbeam on March 20th will probably be right in the middle. Does anyone think there were any other clues? March 20th is our last chance for one year. We need to make it count."

"The most surprising to me was that it wasn't a surprise," Alessandro said.

"Yes," they all agreed.

Louise finished writing down this response and then sighed. "For me too, it was awe-inspiring but at the same time, not surprising. It seemed natural, friendly."

"I can't speak for Alessandro," Benedetta said. "But, for me, after seeing that sunbeam in the Bottini for many years, it was not unexpected. But maybe that is a clue in and of itself."

"Great point," Louise said, literally punctuating what she had just written with a period. She put her pen down and rubbed her temples. "I just don't see how we can predict what will happen on March 20th. We are completely speculating here. The Ides of March historically means the repayment of debt. I thought today would have been more conclusive. There should be no question about our next steps."

"Perhaps on March 17th we'll get more clarification," Francesco said. "It will become clear at some point. We must have faith."

"That's it! Faith!" Benedetta stared at the small stained-glass window of the library. "I think there's a connection with the Ides of March and Monte dei Paschi. The early Roman Calendar celebrated the first full moon of the new year and then counted back from three fixed points in a month instead of numbering the days of the month. The word *Ides* is derived from the Latin word *Idus* which refers to the middle day of any month in ancient Roman calendar. Instead of March 15th, it was the *Ides* of March. The Romans also marked the Ides of March as the deadline for settling debts, along with other religious observances. The months marked specifically with the Ides as the 15th are March, May, July, and October. It is the date for settling debt and Roman empire included the seven days preceding the Ides for this purpose."

"Meaning?" Louise asked.

"Debtors who could not pay their debts considered the Ides to be *unlucky*," Benedetta said. "This answers the question that has been bothering me. Seven days before March 15th is March 8th. Rossellini died March 6th only two days before the 8th but within the timeframe. The original Ides could be from the 13th to the 15th. It works within those parameters."

"That's a bit of a stretch," Louise said. "On the other hand, there is definitely a theme of settling debts here."

"Another connection is Jesus's final words when dying on the cross, *Tetelestai*," Alessandro added. "Many translate it to mean, *It is done*. But, in Jesus' day, the word *Tetelestai* was commonly used in debt collection. When a person finally paid off a loan, they were issued a receipt that was stamped with the word *Tetelestai* meaning their debt was *paid in full*."

"It is also believed that Jesus died on April 3rd in the year 33, at the age of 33," Louise said. "Perhaps April 3rd is another important date?"

"If we keep going down the pagan rabbit hole it could go on forever," Benedetta admonished. "Christian scripture fastidiously integrated pagan rituals. The number 3 used there is considered by many to be symbolic, not real."

"Before modern civilization, humanity was very in tune with celestial and earthly phenomena," Louise argued. "It was a pure existence, being connected to nature, looking for guidance from Mother Earth. We must thoroughly examine every possibility. This library with so many resources, the key may be in these shelves." She turned to Alessandro. "Are the books organized using a numbering convention, or is it just alphabetical?"

"The collection has been carefully inventoried, in alphabetical order by title. After years reading in here, I'm very familiar with the entire archive. What did you have in mind?"

"The other day I noticed several books of interest. Perhaps the Codex Amiatinus bible will give us a clue."

He walked to the Bible she referred to. "This is only a replica, but a very accurate facsimile," Alessandro said. "It is a direct transcription from one of the three originals." Alessandro removed the replica Codex Amiatinus Bible from the shelf, placed it on the table with a thud, and opened it at the middle page.

"The only known surviving original is in the Laurentian Medici Library in Florence, not far from Mount Amiata in Tuscany where it was found," Benedetta explained. "Hence the name Amiatinus. That is the only remaining original copy and the oldest known manuscript of the Latin Vulgate, which is the 4th-century Latin translation of the Christian Bible that became the Catholic Church's official Latin version during the 16th century still used today." Benedetta moved closer to examine it.

"May I?" she asked Alessandro who nodded yes.

"This is a beautiful reproduction. 1,040 pages of sturdy smooth vellum, most likely made from local calves. It contains the same illuminated manuscript with decorated initials, borders, and miniature art with a lack of insular Northumbrian, Anglo-Saxon or Celtic style, a clear indication that the Amiatinus was copied from the Late Antique originals."

"Do you read Latin?" Louise asked.

"A little," Benedetta replied. "But our friend Alessandro is quite the scholar."

"Is there anything about debt, forgiveness, things like that, in the bible?" Louise asked.

Alessandro pondered her question. Then he leafed through the Old Testament to Chapters 12-26. "The *Deuteronomic Code* written between the 7th and 5th centuries BC is very clear." He translated aloud. "*At the end of every seven years you shall grant a release. And this is the manner of the release: every creditor shall release what he has lent to his neighbor. He shall not exact it of his neighbor, his brother, because the Lord's release has been proclaimed.*"

"*Every seven years,*" Louise repeated. "Again, in the United States, the IRS only requires financial records be kept for seven years. Seven years ago, in 2006, Mussari initiated the disastrous transaction and hid it from the board in his office vault. How Biblical."

"The Siena residents are very upset," Benedetta said. "When Mussari arrived for questioning in the prosecutor's office the crowd pelted him with coins and called him a thief."

"Yes, we were there that day," Louise said. "It was quite a scene. What is the significance of throwing coins?"

"This is not the first financial scandal of Italy, and it probably won't be the last. The first coin throwing incident was during the *Tangentopoli* bribery scandal, perpetrated by the former Italian Prime Minister, Bettino Craxi, about twenty years ago."

"I remember that very well," Louise said. "In English it was called *Bribesville.*"

"Yes, a clever translation of *Tangentopoli*. Craxi was sentenced to prison, but he fled to Tunisia and died in exile."

"How does all of this connect to the Ides of March?" Louise asked.

"Or Spring Equinox?" Francesco added. "We are back to speculating."

"There must be something in here," Louise said, looking at the bookshelf and bible.

Big Steve's stomach growled loudly.

"Okay, we can take a hint," Louise said. "Let's take a break for today."

"We have more to go over before the 17th," Benedetta said.

"Okay, let's meet at my hotel library nine o'clock tomorrow morning," Louise said.

Siena, Italy, March 16, 2013

Louise had ordered breakfast and they met in the library. After they ate and went over the final plan, Louise stood to make an announcement.

"We're ready for tomorrow, except for one thing," Louise said. "Steve?"

Everyone looked at Big Steve who was now on the hot seat. He stood up and placed a box on the table. "As y'all know, my number one priority is Louise's safety," he began. "Especially after Benedetta went AWOL that one time." Benedetta looked appropriately contrite. "That's why I have to insist we all stay connected." He opened the box and pulled out five small spy headsets with Kenwood Radio. "Wire up!"

They all tried on the earpieces and tested the equipment from different spots throughout the library. Then they gathered at the table for one final word.

"These headsets work great here," Benedetta said. "But tomorrow we will see if they work underground."

"These are state-of-the-art designed for official government business," Steve said.

"Okay, we'll find out tomorrow," Louise said.

Siena, Italy, March 17, 2013

They finished breakfast at Francesco's and Ginger Cat watched as they geared up.

"This will be our final day to look for any additional clues about opening the vault," Benedetta said. "Make a note of anything new. It's still three days before March 20th, so if we need another day to rehearse, we still can."

They got in the SUV and Benedetta dropped them each off at their respective Contrada Bottini entrances then went back to Porcupine. Alessandro sat in the secret library, solemnly awaiting the sunbeam, feeling more at peace than he ever had in his life. It was like everything he had ever done had led to what they were doing. He *knew* it.

Once in position they each tested their earpieces. Then, at 11:11 they all marked where the sun's ray landed on the plaques with chalk and headed down the tunnels to Steve's position in the Fonte Gaia Bottini under Tower Contrada. Alessandro was there too.

"Anything new?" Benedetta asked everyone, leaving it an open question, not wanting to influence their replies.

"I wrote down the name and other information on the plaque," Louise said. "The ray of light didn't hit where I expected. It wasn't in the middle of the plaque. After taking a closer look, I saw three circles."

"Great observation, Louise," Benedetta said. "I noticed that too."

"I didn't notice," Steve said.

"I'll shine my camera light and see if the markings are on Steve's plaque too," Louise said. Steve showed them the chalk marks where the sunlight hit the plaque. Louise shined her light on a spot close to where the sunbeam hit her plaque.

"I don't see the circles," Louise said. "But there's something written on it."

"It's Latin, something to do with *onus*. What does it say, Alessandro?" Francesco asked.

Alessandro came closer and translated. "He who enters, exonerates all before." He pointed to one of the Latin words. "This means *absolved*."

"Absolution is a two-sided transaction," Benedetta said. "That confirms it, to open the vault, there needs to be someone on both sides."

Within the few minutes they stood there, the ray of sun moved almost completely off the plaque, reaching the upper corner revealing another inscription.

"Those are the circles I saw on mine too!" Louise said.

"Those are ancient representations of the positions of the sun," Benedetta said.

"This circle in the middle represents the sun in Vernal Equinox." Benedetta pointed to circles above and below. "You can see the summer solstice above and winter solstice below."

"That confirms it!" Francesco said, trying to contain his excitement.

Benedetta rubbed the circle in the middle. "You can tell, this one is not just an embossed symbol like the other two. It appears to be a button." She pushed on it but there was no response. "It must be triggered with the vernal sunbeam. At 11:11 on March 20th, the sunbeam will show us where to press on the plaque. It will likely be that circle depicting the sun in Vernal Equinox."

"What do we do then?" Louise asked.

"Our original plan," Benedetta said. "We run to Fonte Gaia and secure the area."

"Okay, we all agree," Louise said. They all nodded yes.

"For the next two days, I'll continue my research in the library. Since I never found out the Contrada Caterpillar slogan from Rossellini, I will not rest until I find that and the truth about Rossellini's death. The slogan might be a key."

T W E N T Y - S E V E N

Siena, Italy, March 20, 2013

It was the big day.

Friar Alessandro Brustenghi, formerly known as Jean-Philippe de Ville-neuve, was master of his domain. When CIA agent Michael Fuentes had arrived by helicopter at Amarnath Cave Temple in Kashmir almost three years ago, he found himself assigned to an undercover role in the monastery that he seemed born for. The exclusive access to all corners of the Monte dei Paschi palace headquarters with its history had felt like coming home. Every day, he strolled the medieval roads to MPS and immersed himself in all that it offered. His preference was the library, where he spent most of his days, but he became a scholar of every room and archive.

Alessandro had become enamored with Monastic life during his last assignment. He embraced this new role with vigor, studying everything he could get his hands on, learning how monastic life had begun in Egypt in the third century spreading through Europe, where in monastic circles the eremitical life of the Egyptian monks became the ideal form of religious living. Starting with *The Rules* of St. Augustine of Hippo from 354 to 430 and *The Rules* of St. Benedict from 480 to 547, the Order of St. Augustine had been formed in 1256, uniting several groups of hermits into one Order. As part of his initiation, *Alessandro* had visited the Augustinian monastery of Lecceto about eight miles west of Siena with its depiction of eremitical life in frescos by 15th century artist Nanni di Pietro further encouraging his ultimate life purpose.

Even fellow monk Father Gregory from Jean-Philippe's previous monastic life, who had imposed himself on the mission three years earlier, had taken to the life of solitude, although he had segued into a completely unrelated and confidential assignment.

But what really converted Jean-Philippe to Alessandro was learning that the problems his family had endured years earlier were caused by the *Master of the Dark Arts*, Akari Raskalov, himself. Two of the longstanding under-pinnings of Jean-Philippe's family wealth had been energy and agriculture. Their forward-thinking leadership had embraced renewable energy and organic farming early on, both of which had becoming a threat to Russian fossil fuels and agriculture. Russia had increased gas exports more than four-fold to meet the EU's demand. Russia's agriculture had become the most steadily developing sector of the national economy. Undermining major EU-based fossil fuel and agricultural resources was highly motived by Russian oligarchs and Putin himself.

Enter, Akari Raskalov. It hadn't taken long for his corporate spies and hackers to penetrate the de Villeneuve family organization and expose trade secrets and even give the appearance of illegal insider trading and market manipulation leaving the company steeped in legal battles. The ploy worked and weakened their position in both renewable energy and organic farming markets.

It was also Raskalov who had leaked false information to Jean-Philippe's father that Louise may have been a corporate spy or double agent, which had caused the great rift between his father and him. When Michael Fuentes told Jean-Philippe that Raskalov had been behind his family's troubles, and that this operation could potentially take down the criminal who had destroyed the reputation of his centuries-old nobility in the 1990's with no way to fight the seemingly invisible enemy, his peaceful monastic life could also exact an element of revenge.

The Church of St. Augustine in Siena remained a peaceful sanctuary almost unknown to tourists that he now called home. Today, so as not to invite questions, *Alessandro* followed his usual morning routine, taking breakfast with his fellow friars. The Monastery of the Order of St. Augustine was only 800 meters from Monte dei Paschi and he headed out on his usual trek.

"Going to MPS?" Friar Gregory asked, a glint in his eye, as Alessandro quietly left the breakfast table and cleaned his plate.

"The critters will be expecting me," Alessandro said. "I don't want to disappoint."

This caper with his relatively new lifelong friends Benedetta and Francesco was the culmination of years of preparation. Alessandro had become close with Benedetta, the world-famous historian. There had been moments of temptation, but that was no longer part of his life. The mission was the most important. They had trained meticulously in preparation for the eventual moment when they could make their move to save Monte dei Paschi. All his life, *Alessandro* AKA Jean-Philippe had worked to help others in whatever capacity, playing the hero behind the scenes. Now he had a cause that felt like his own.

After feeding the monastery's cats and birds in the garden, he made his way up hill toward Monte dei Paschi by nine o'clock, dressed in full cassock. A journey normally less than a kilometer, but a winding two kilometers following the evasive trail, and stopping to greet parishioners or to give a handful of kibbles from his pocket to a stray cat made it longer. After a final discrete scan of the area, he entered the antediluvian gate of the Monte dei Paschi entrance and took the familiar walk to the library. It was 9:30 by the time he took his seat at the large table. He put his earpiece in and waited.

Benedetta picked up Louise and Steve and drove to Francesco's for breakfast. Although it had been so long since they had seen any questionable characters, they still followed the evasive protocols, being extra cautious taking the long route, making unexpected turns, and other evasive maneuvers, but it appeared all prior surveillants had moved on.

"Ci sono quattro gatti!" Francesco said, greeting them as they entered.

"*There are four cats?*" Louise asked.

"It's an Italian expression," Benedetta explained. "Normally it means no one showed up, like to a party. He's making an ironic joke. All four of us who were invited showed up."

"Oh, I get it. Happy first day of Spring!" Louise said.

"Oh, now I get it. The Spring Equinox is the first day of Spring," Steve said, finally making the connection. "Y'all sho' love to complicate stuff."

"You're not wrong," Louise said. "But it's important to make the connections between our current rites and rituals to our pagan past."

Steve just shook his head. "I hope I don't let you down on this thing. My job is to keep y'all safe, Lulu. So, I'll try my best to help with the Monty thing."

"Monte dei Paschi," Louise corrected him, with a chuckle. "You're doing great, Steve."

"To make sure, let's go over the plan one more time," Benedetta said. "I will drop each of you off at your respective contrada and wait."

"Only now we have our earpieces," Big Steve said.

"Let's make sure our frequencies are synched," Benedetta said.

"Roger Wilco," Louise said.

Big Steve tested each earpiece starting with Francesco and ending with Alessandro.

"Okay. Good to go." Louise checked her watch. "It's 9:00 o'clock. Shall we?"

Benedetta drove an evasive route to town dropping them at each Bottini. Once they were dropped off, she spoke over the radio to confirm. "Is everyone in position?"

They each replied consecutively with *Roger*, plus their respective Contrada.

"Let's synchronize our watches again just in case," she said. "It is exactly 10:39."

Everyone confirmed their time except Big Steve.

"Testing, Big Steve. *Over*," Louise said.

There was a momentary static and it seemed the message wasn't coming through. But after a minute, his reply.

"Roger. *Over*," Big Steve's voice was heard.

"Over and out," Louise said.

Louise stood in Tai Chi meditation pose, eyes open, alert, waiting for the vernal sun. Suddenly the earpiece buzzed, and she thought she heard Steve's voice.

She pressed the talk button. "Big Steve. Do you read? Over." No reply. *He probably just hit the button by accident.*

The sun's ray pointed exactly to the image of the sun button in Vernal Equinox. She pressed it and the ground began to shake.

"It feels like it's going to cave in! *Over!*" Louise shouted into the earpiece.

"Run to Fonte Gaia! *Over!*" Benedetta shouted.

Louise took off running toward the Fonte Gaia Bottini, a sense of overwhelming dread igniting her pace.

Louise, Francesco, and Benedetta converged in Fonte Gaia Bottini, just as the gaping vault door became visible through a cloud of settling dust. Louise had been right to be afraid. Just inside the entrance perpendicular on their right was the other entrance, both with an identical massive stone door, opened by identical pulley systems. They saw the library where Alessandro stood at the entrance, frozen with fear.

Louise's heart sank. Her friend Big Steve was on his knees, hands behind his neck, head hanging in shame.

"I'm sorry Lulu, I tried to warn you..." But his captor struck him on the side of the head with the butt of his Avtomát Kaláshnikova rifle knocking him unconscious. Louise tried to run to him, but Francesco and Benedetta held her back as the man holding the AK now pointed it at her.

"I owe you a debt of gratitude," Akari Raskalov said, emerging from the shadows accompanied by three more henchmen. One of them held up a lantern and Louise immediately recognized him as *Smarmy Guy* who had been ubiquitous in her daily life.

It figures, all the other tails worked for our side, except this guy, she thought, sneering at him. He gave her his signature sexist smirk in return. But she was distracted by what his lamplight revealed beyond him, the depths of the treasure trove. It seemed to go on forever into the obscurity of the massive vault.

"Not a bad day's haul," Raskalov said, smugly.

"I'm surprised you'd show your face again, Akari," Louise said. "From what I understand, my rescuers humiliated you in your own private Russian prison."

He turned and his lackey shone the lamp over the space revealing mounds of riches gathered over the centuries. They appeared to be meticulously organized by family or institution name. Engraved plaques designating ownership could be seen all the way down along the walls and on the floor, treasures in stacks, creating two aisles with three wide rows of artifacts. Raskalov casually walked over to one of the stockpiles and picked up an object.

"A stunning and rare example of one of the original in a series of fifty Imperial Easter Eggs created for the Russian Imperial family at the turn of the 19th century by Peter Faberge. As I suspected, this was not just a cache for worthless items the poor pawned for pennies at the *Mount of Pity*." He spat the words. "It is a massive safety-deposit-box."

"I thought you only dealt in influence and didn't care about money,"

Louise said.

"I don't care about money. I care about control. This is the most important find in the history of the western world not only for its value but for all its many secrets."

"You won't get away with this," Benedetta said. "There are redundant security measures in place to protect this vault."

"Spare me your penny-ante academia," Raskalov said. "You don't think I would attempt this heist without meticulous planning, do you? Dario Rossellini was the last banker with knowledge of this vault. Now that secret will die with the five of you." Steve groaned, rubbing his head as he began to come to. Raskalov kicked him. "Get over there! All of you!" He pointed to the corner between the stone vault doors. The four of them helped Steve and reluctantly moved into the corner as a team. Raskalov said something in Russian to his henchmen, and they trained their weapons on them.

"Not you, Louise Moscow. You will have the honor of sealing your friends inside and accompanying me as added insurance. This is a hermetically sealed room. The oxygen will be depleted within days."

"I hate enclosed spaces, just shoot me now!" Steve bluffed, stalling for time.

"And waste valuable ammunition?" Raskalov grabbed Louise by the arm and pulled her toward the exit into the Bottini. Three of the henchmen stayed until they exited. Once they were out, two of the armed men exited the same door and another by the door to the library, their guns still pointed at the three men and one woman.

"Now, Louise, be a good girl and trigger the lock." But there was a strange sound behind him in the Bottini. He turned and raised the lantern illuminating the tunnel. There in military rows, a squad of armed locals dressed in their respective Contrada colors stood at attention awaiting orders of *their leader*.

Louise recognized his face and couldn't believe her eyes. She looked in amazement at Michael Fuentes, whose eyes were glued on the *Master of the Dark Arts*.

"We have machine guns," he said, his men aiming their rifles on the motley, but determined ranks. "You fools are no match for us."

"We outnumber you and have no fear of dying for our legacy," Michael said.

"We have four of your friends inside with a guard ready to shoot,"

Raskalov countered.

The lone henchman still in the vault couldn't see what was happening and grew impatient. "Чего мы ждем, сэр?" he shouted. *What's taking so long?* As he spoke, he took his eyes off the hostages for a split second and Steve seized the opportunity to pounce on the man, setting off a burst of artillery.

Raskalov ducked and barked the order to his men, "*Kill them all!*"

But the three other henchmen didn't move. He turned to see Big Steve standing behind him with the AK pointed at his head. The guard was on the ground unconscious, or dead. Raskalov nodded for them to stand down, and the henchmen lowered their weapons.

"Great work, Big Steve," Michael said into his earpiece and winked. "Now this is my kind of operation. No bloodshed." Michael gave his dimpled smile. "Cuff them!" Five of the Sienese residents took out handcuffs and detained the five Russians.

Louise looked at Big Steve. "This mission was supposed to be top secret."

"Lucky for you, it still is," Michael said.

"But how?"

"You knew I was half Italian," Michael said. "It turns out my family were members of the Caterpillar Contrada. Alessandro was my inside man. This had to remain a stealth operation. Tight enough to capture one of the world's most renowned criminals. He has been very difficult to indict but these charges of attempted murder and theft should finally do the trick."

Louise was so happy to have helped put the *Master of the Dark Arts* Akari Raskalov away for a long time, tears of joy welled in her eyes. But she was fixated on this new intel.

"So, do you know the Caterpillar slogan?"

Michael revealed nothing in his expression. "Does it matter?" he replied.

"It matters because of Dario."

"You solved his murder, Louise. You fulfilled his wish."

They spent some time sifting through the treasures, while Alessandro took a visual inventory assessing for valuation purposes. But it was priceless. It was priceless of course, but if he had to estimate an overall value, it would be at least one trillion.

Louise stood back taking in the incredible treasure trove to get a solid visual in her mind, when a tiny sunbeam in the distance reached down like a finger. No one else seemed to notice it. She casually walked through the ancient cavern, scanning some of the priceless artifacts and appreciating the Etruscan craftsmanship of the structure.

She finally reached the sunbeam just as it was fading, and what she found had a visceral effect on her. It was a stunning example of an ancient Egyptian scarab necklace in dazzling cerulean blue, glimmering among many other jewels. It was almost identical to the scarab necklace that her father had given her long ago, a bittersweet memory as she toyed with the one on the chain around her neck.

She left the piece untouched and walked back scanning the treasures for something symbolic from each Contrada, like the child's game *I Spy with My Little Eye*. She smiled seeing a hand-carved wooden Caterpillar in honor of Dario Rossellini, simple, weatherworn, noble. Then pieces representing each Contrada seemed to jump out at her. A stone gargoyle eagle, a jeweled dragon, a primitive giraffe, a fossil scallop shell bed that must have been 20 million years old.

Alessandro drifted toward her carrying a lamp and yet another treasure caught her eye, as though the lamplight revealed it. It was an identical to the replica Codex Amiatinus in the library. *Could it be one of the lost originals?* She looked at Alessandro who acknowledged the find with a twinkle in his eye. It was recorded in the vault of his mind.

TWENTY-EIGHT

The team regrouped for a farewell meal and a day together at Francesco's farm. Louise was returning to Burgundy, Steve back to the island, and Michael back to New York. The conversation grew animated while the three kitties relaxed together.

"It really was the most important find in history, I think," Francesco said.

"I'm surprised that the Holy Grail wasn't in the vault," Michael said. Everyone gave a knowing look. "What? Did I miss something?"

"The Francs-Maçons or Freemasons believe that the words *Sang Royal* or Holy Blood, were misconstrued as *Saint Graal* or *Holy Grail*. They believe that Mary Magdalene was *the vessel* carrying the blood of Jesus Christ, meaning she was pregnant with his child and brought the baby to France. The Freemasons consider themselves descendants of that blood."

"Oh. I learned something new," Michael said.

"It's very telling that *the* Holy Grail wasn't in the vault from a Christian standpoint," Louise said. "It is potentially explosive and another reason it must remain secret."

"Absolutely," Benedetta agreed. "The vault could be considered the vessel carrying the mysteries of all cultures and religions."

"That's correct," Alessandro said. "It holds precious artifacts from ancient Egypt, China, Japan, the Middle East, India, most everywhere in the world."

"Best of all, it's as though nothing ever happened," Louise mused. "The local community seems to know something lifechanging has taken place, and yet it has remained completely unknown to the world."

"We care about the meaning more than the wealth," Benedetta said. "The treasures will remain the collateral of Monte dei Paschi. Italy's Central Bank will continue to negotiate with the European Union keeping the impression the bank is struggling. But the underlying wealth will remain a secret forever. It may even involve the cooperation of the other countries to protect their artifacts. We can never be sure."

"The greed and lust for power of these criminals is always shocking to me," Louise said.

"That's because you're an amazing person," Francesco said, kissing her cheek.

"I second that," Michael said.

"It's sociological," Benedetta said. "There are predictable patterns of human behavior that occur in the same sequence every time a given stimulus is introduced. They apply to any individual, and spy recruiters take advantage of them. When a recruiter approaches a target and offers a small favor of service, once the target has been helped, he or she feels obligated to reciprocate and help the recruiter, which may lead to a series of exchanges with escalating consequences. This cycle of helping is automatic and built into the structure of human interactions. As such, the responses would operate beneath the target's conscious awareness."[23]

"It's truly evil to manipulate the good in human nature," Louise said. She suddenly had an epiphany. Her mother had always lived humbly, instilling in Louise a lasting example of indifference toward the accumulation of wealth. Having chosen finance as her career, Louise had always regretted her lack of materialism, as though it had held her back, in the sense that her motivations were never about money. She had always teased her mom about her *reverse snobbism*. But that same insouciance about wealth may have protected Louise from her own vulnerability to corruption.

"Are you looking forward to going home, Louise?" Benedetta asked.

"Home suddenly has a whole new meaning," Louise said. "Siena has felt like home for months and now I'm sad to be leaving you all."

"It has been an honor to work with you," Benedetta said.

"Thank you for another wonderful meal, Francesco. It was the perfect send-off before we leave," Louise said.

They all got up and hugged. Then they gathered their things and went outside in time to see the sun setting behind the hills on the horizon casting a golden hue.

Alessandro offered these words. "The meaning of life is not to be rich, or popular, or even highly educated, or perfect. It's about being real, being humble, being able to share our selves and touch the lives of others."

"Amen."

EPILOGUE

May 25, 2013, North Atlantic Ocean

With the wind in her hair and twin Caterpillar C18 engines under the hull, Louise was back in her element. She had always loved the sea. In this case, the Strait of Gibraltar, where the Mediterranean meets the Atlantic. LaFontaine had business in the transshipment hub of Tangier Med, Morocco, the largest port in the Mediterranean. He had picked Louise up at the Tangiers Ibn Battuta Airport and whisked her off to the Royal Yacht Club near the ancient medina and launched out to sea.

It was her birthday. Another year older. Somehow, she felt younger than she had when she was in her teens. After two months at sea, immersing herself in the hundreds of pages of notes she had gathered during the investigation into Monte dei Paschi, making a comprehensive report, piecing together the timeline, and connecting the events and the players, she was starting to sense that her involuntary hiatus was coming to an end. As a birthday present to herself, she closed the document she was working on and turned off the laptop.

"Alors, tu te plait bien ici?" Frédéric LaFontaine asked. *You like it here?*

Louise turned to her old friend, knowing she'd find his irresistible smile. "Comme un poisson dans l'eau," she replied. *Like a fish in water.*

"Very poetic." Frédéric handed Louise a coupe de champagne and they clinked glasses. Heading west on the azure waters, with Gibraltar, Spain to the starboard, Louise finally felt she could clear her mind. Being at sea had a healing effect, a *blue state of mind.*[24]

"I feel like a novelist writing this intelligence analysis about the mission," Louise said, putting her laptop aside. She leaned back and sank into the lounger, the firepit warming her, the scent of burning wood eliciting primal comfort, the golden glow of the magical sunset. She sipped watching the sunbeams glinting off the horizon ahead, while casting fantastical colors and shadows on the horizon behind them.

"Yes, these grueling hours at *the office* writing your report can really take it out of you," Frédéric quipped. "Thank goodness for the view."

"We joke about it, Frédéric, but this case really got to me. The vast corruption from the very top is so insidious. What's the point of counterintelligence?"

"The point will always be to win small battles, keeping most of the innocent protected. Can you imagine the world if we did *not* do counterintelligence?"

"Somehow that is less reassuring."

"This is not even the most shocking point about the money laundering," Frédéric said. "The truth will eventually come out."

"Can you tell me?" Louise asked.

"It's related to Syria. Think of WMD's and Iran Contra," was all he would offer.

"You mean Putin is developing weapons of mass destruction? Michael suggested the same thing when he was briefing me, which seems like a lifetime ago." She took a deep calming breath, but the anxiety was always lurking.

"Your spy training of the past few years should have helped you manage the stress, no?"

"Can you imagine if I did not have my training at Langley?" Louise said. "It's just that…" She paused, looking for the words. "I'm getting that sinking feeling."

"Would you mind using another expression while at sea?"

As if on cue, Frédéric's reconnaissance officer approached and silently gave a hand signal that Louise did not recognize. But she did recognize the look of alarm on Frédéric's face. "It seems your instincts are accurate, Louise."

"What's wrong?"

"Come, let's get to the AIC." They dashed below deck to the ship's *Action Information Center*, his state-of-the art warship-grade tactical center. The array of surveillance including a Plan Position Indicator (PPI) and other advanced reconnaissance equipment served as an additional command center to the vessel's main helm console. Louise hadn't been privy to this space before, which had served LaFontaine and her rescue crew very well when she was trapped in the Russian prison.

Louise was nonplussed. "Don't tell me this thing can submerge."

"You're close, this is submarine tactical equipment. But, alas, this baby does not have deep-diving capabilities." He gave her a Cheshire grin and added, "Yet."

Suddenly a blaring siren sounded.

"Capitaine!" the Electro-Technical Officer (ETO) shouted. "The fast attack craft has armed torpedoes."

"Frédéric, what's happening?" Louise tried to remain calm.

"There is no need to be alarmed," LaFontaine reassured her. "We have been counter-surveilling a Russian military vessel that has been tracking us since we left the port of Tangier and have the advantage. There is no way they are aware of our defensive capabilities."

Louise was skeptical. Her CIA training had also focused on maritime law and tactics, and she knew government surveillance technology had the ability to monitor, analyze and even disrupt another vessel's tactical capabilities, and his private ship was no match for the military. Or was it? LaFontaine and his boat may well have reached another realm of capabilities as far as she knew. He had created an empire in banking technology and used it as a stepping-stone to develop more and greater technologies in all fields. Most of his technological advances in surveillance, encryption, tactical hardware, and software were unknown to the commercial industries or government authorities. He could make massive fortunes selling to the porn industry alone, but more wealth was the last thing he needed.

Louise held her breath as the ETO pinged the mystery craft quickly approaching abaft.

"Enemy is closing in on 3,600 meters at 16 knots, captain."

"A torpedo can go up to 50 miles per hour and is well within range," Louise said, more to herself, aware she was among experts in torpedo boats and anti-ship missiles. Although torpedo boats had disappeared from the majority of the world's navies, they remained in use in a few specialized areas, mostly in the Baltic.

"They won't want to risk missing us from that distance," LaFontaine said.

"Shouldn't we try to outrun them?" Louise asked.

"No need," LaFontaine said with a wry smile. "Wait until the enemy is 1,800 meters before initiating evasive tactics," he commanded to his crew.

"Isn't that cutting it a little close?" Louise asked.

"I'm going for maximum shock and awe," LaFontaine said, never taking his eyes off his high-powered binoculars. "Watch this."

"Enemy at 1,900, flooding torpedo ballasts!" the ETO said.

LaFontaine gave the command to his evasive ops. "Arm Vessel System!"

"*Vessel System?*" Louise muttered.

"That's what I call my cloaking device," LaFontaine replied. Louise's eyes and mouth opened wide. "That's exactly the reaction I'm going for."

"This I gotta see." Louise grabbed a pair of binoculars and watched the craft running at full throttle gaining on them, creating an impressive wake.

"Vessel System evasive measures activated!"

"Arm!" LaFontaine ordered.

"Arming, 10, 9, 8, 7, 6, 5…" As he counted down, the enemy craft slowed then veered to the starboard then to port, until it completely slowed to a near stop.

"They backed off!" Louise shouted. Her heart had been racing, and she realized she was perspiring. The crew cheered in victory. "So, what happened? Are we invisible or something?"

"As far as they can tell, we have disappeared." He fluttered his fingers as if to say, *poof!* On cue, a champagne cork popped.

"Was this the first time you used this *Vessel System?*" Louise asked.

"Indeed, this was the trial run. We were going to put a manned Zodiac at sea to test it ourselves, but this unexpected attack gave us the opportunity to try it." A deckhand gave them each a glass of champagne and poured more for the rest of the crew.

"That was very risky, don't you think?" Louise said, clinking his glass.

"Perhaps. We have other tactical maneuvers we could have tried first. But I had a feeling." He raised his glass to Louise. "To my good luck charm."

Louise smiled humbly and drank to herself. "Your secret is safe with me."

"Speaking of secrets, this is the top-most of top secrets."

"So, now you have to kill me?"

"No, because if you tell anyone about it, I won't have to. It's that dangerous."

Louise shrugged. "I'm trained to withstand torture."

The ETO returned with a bottle of champagne and topped off their glasses.

"The enemy ship has retreated to its own territorial waters," he said with a slight French accent. "Chief Officer would like permission to resume course to Iles Purpuraires, Capitaine."

"Permission granted," LaFontaine replied. Then he dropped the formalities and said in French, "Bravo, Stephane, excellent travail."

"Merci Capitaine. Toutes nos félicitations sur le *Système Vaisseau.*"

"I could not have done without all of you, Stephane."

"Passez-une bonne soirée." Stephen bowed politely. "Have a lovely evening, Miss Louise." Then he headed back to celebrate with the crew.

"What a team," Louise said.

"You'd be amazed, we have world-class expertise in all disciplines on board."

"Amazed indeed, but not surprised."

On course for the overnight trip to the Iles Purpuraires, Louise had forgotten all about her last assignment and finally relaxed, looking up at the Milky Way, so thick it smudged the inky sky like metallic paint. "So, what territorial waters did the enemy ship go back to?"

"Let's just say that it's Alaska adjacent."

Louise understood that to mean Russia.

After a restful sleep, Louise awoke feeling more relaxed than she had allowed herself to be for many years. She lay on her stomach enjoying the sunrise over the Iles Purpuraires. Her curiosity got the best of her, and she left the comfort of her luxury stateroom and went above deck where she found Frédéric sipping coffee and reading a chart.

"Do you ever sleep?" Louise asked, groggily.

His familiar laughter echoed. "Sleep the right amount and you will never be tired."

"Where are we?" Louise asked, sitting down at the table. A crew member served her continental breakfast of café au lait, croissants, butter, and jam.

"This is a set of small islands off the western coast of Morocco. We are near the bay of Essaouira." He pointed. "The largest island there is Mogador. These islands were settled by the Phoenicians and later Roman occupation of western Morocco to exploit marine resources, principally a royal blue dye made from marine organisms. Indigenous people of western Morocco fished in this locale between 3000 and 2000 BC. The color purple is believed to have originated here. Purple is generally used to symbolize royalty and spirituality." He took a vase containing a small bouquet of flowers and placed it in front of Louise. "Purple can symbolize sorrow and forgiveness. That is why a purple hyacinth is a good flower to give someone who not only deserves one's respect but one's gratitude."

"You're giving me a purple hyacinth in gratitude?"

"Consider it a birthday gift."

"It is I who should be expressing gratitude to you," Louise said.

The boat approached the docks of Slaver's Bay, on Mogador Island, and dropped anchor.

"Do you have business here?" Louise asked.

"Come on. Get dressed. We're going ashore. I have a surprise for you."

"You can see that ancient color throughout the village," Frédéric pointed out as they walked down the docks. Louise admired the ubiquitous bluish-purple hue that seemed to have been painted on every wooden boat that fished the *Purple Islands* each morning. "As a birthday gift, I wanted to take you to the island of this early civilization."

Louise had a feeling that Frédéric was referring to the ancient manuscript she had found in a hidden chamber of her Paris apartment. It had enticing, albeit very cryptic, clues to the whereabouts of The Lost City of Atlantis.

They arrived at the end of the dock where two teenagers, a boy and a girl, delivered two mopeds. They got on and Frédéric gave Louise a tour of the island. The noise from the mopeds precluded conversation as they puttered up the ever-climbing shoreline. It felt like flying and Louise was a smiling child again. They reached the highest point and parked. Walking to the cliff's edge, Louise had the distinct sense of déjà vu, but it was as real as the ground under her feet.

"Many scholars have obsessed about the Lost City of Atlantis for centuries," Frédéric finally said, breaking the ethereal silence. "It has been my greatest obsession since I was a child. It is what drove me to develop my original banking software. Many years of research have led me here. My group of esoteric friends believe the ancient Phoenicians may have been descendants of the Lost City."

Louise had a sudden sense of metaphysical lucidity. "The Ancient Celtics were also believed to be offshoots of the Phoenicians," Louise said. The subject was something she had been researching since she first found the hidden manuscript in her Paris apartment during her first investigation into BCCI. Later she learned of the ancient Celtic history of Burgundy, France, where her second investigation into a sex trafficking ring had taken her. If it turned out the ancient manuscript was directly related to Celtic history, it would be magical.

Frédéric's eyes sparkled. It was a transcendental moment. They had both spent their lives traveling the world, appreciating its wonders, studying ancient cultures, fully respecting power of pagan spirituality and its connection with nature. Louise sometimes felt like she calmly walked back and forth between the past and the present.[25]

"My group of esoteric friends have generally accepted that the Lost City of Atlantis was located off the west coast of Morocco. Hanno the Navigator was a Carthaginian explorer of the fifth century BC best known for his naval exploration of the western coast of Africa. The only record of his voyage is a *Greek Periplus*, which means *sailing around*. The Periplus manuscript lists the ports and coastal landmarks in order, with approximate intervening distances that a vessel could expect to find off the western coast of Africa. It was a type of log that served the same purpose as the later Roman Itinerarium of road stops, that became part of Greek geography."

Frédéric went silent for a while as their minds seemed to soar over the panoramic view. Louise went into an awake dream-state, envisioning the earthquake and ensuing tsunami that washed over and decimated the great City of Atlantis. It was like she personally witnessed the horror, heard the shouts of terror and despair, and could do nothing to help. Was it a past life that she saw in the recurring water dreams she had had most of her life?

Frédéric turned to Louise who was visibly shaken.

"You uncovered one of the greatest discoveries in the history of the world. But no one will ever know about it. Some things are best left unknown."

This somehow comforted Louise. She liked anonymity.

"So, what's next for you?" she asked.

"I'm fascinated by this new crypto-currency, Bitcoin," Frédéric said. "The blockchain technology has potential for other uses like securely sharing research, healthcare records, supply chains, and other industrial uses because of its amazing security."

"Yes, the technology is amazing. It's a massive debit and credit ledger, with constant checks and balances in real time," Louise said.

"You've been doing your homework," LaFontaine said.

"Always." She stared at the sea, Frédéric seeing the perpetual wheels of curiosity spinning in her mind.

"We make a good team." He nodded toward the crew. "All of us."

"I agree. Thank you, Frédéric. I haven't felt so at ease in…well ever."

"Then why do you look so sad?"

"It's not over. I have to deal with my father."

"For all your accomplishments, there's one thing that you have yet to learn." Frédéric wasn't lecturing. He was prophesizing. "The reason you feel at ease now is because you are beginning to understand that you can only control what is within your immediate ability. Your work, your preparation, your training, and your education. You have done so much in your life you are finally beginning to accept that you can get results. It's a magical feeling."

She took her backpack off and opened it. She pulled out Mary's journal that she hadn't yet decided what to do with.

"What's that?" Frédéric asked.

She inhaled deeply, contemplating her options. Then she exhaled. "Just some unfinished business." She returned the journal to her backpack, and they got on the mopeds. "Is there a post office nearby?"

May 25, 2013, Moscow, Russia

George Moscow knew he would get Hell from all sides. It went against his every instinct. He knew it was wrong. He tried to convince himself that even corrupt foreign entities had a right to a fair trial, whether from an enemy state or an asylum seeker, unless deemed a terrorist, in which case, Guantanamo. That was the law. His client's alleged financial crime was borderline, and many of those involved were respected finance industry leaders, or so he told himself. His illustrious reputation as a hard-nosed New York State District Attorney, had been besmirched. The acclaimed *Master of Argument*, the word *argument* meaning *to make clear*, could never convince the one person that mattered most, himself.

He had carried out his own investigation and found what he dreaded.

His client, Myloden, had indeed received proceeds from the crime that Sergei Magnitsky had uncovered. He had found the smoking gun. The Russian scam had been an example of low-hanging fruit, a fraudulent $230 million tax rebate, $20 million of which Myloden had laundered. George told his client what he had discovered, and in response Russian officials made him an offer he couldn't refuse. He was married to it now, and Mary was his ex-wife, for all intents and purposes.

Mary had not taken the change well. George Moscow had been her *Knight in Shining Armor*, literally saving her from a horrible fate of shame, loneliness, and trauma immediately following her escape after being kidnapped by a sex trafficking ring while working as a post-graduate interpreter in Burgundy, France. After 50 years of marriage, she no longer recognized her husband. He came home late, was more secretive than ever, and shunned close friends, even FBI agent and Louise's former boyfriend, Michael Fuentes. The stress from George's estrangement was too much and one day Louise called to tell him Mary was gone forever.

Now, in his self-imposed exile, in a modest Moscow apartment, performing legal duties for corrupt Russian oligarchs, he was wretched. He considered ending it all. There was nothing left for him to live for.

The doorbell rang, or rather the old brass buzzer that hadn't been updated since the building was built in the 1940s made a clunky chiming noise. He opened to a postman holding a package. It was a plain manilla envelope about two inches thick. He took it and the proof of delivery. He signed and handed the clipboard back. Then reached into his pocket and pulled out three crumpled 100-ruble notes, equal to about $10, and handed them to the postman, who grinned widely, rotting blackened teeth and all, which was all George needed to know it was rubles well spent.

He closed the door and returned to his desk. He sat down, the backrest breaking his weary backward momentum. He adjusted his reading glasses and examined the outside of the envelope. He smoothed his fingers over the front and back checking for any fuses or other irregularities. It just seemed to be filled with documents. Probably of the legal or banking kind. The point of the letter opener did its job, and the contents were freed, the journal with pressed flowers lacquered to the cover slid out. The raw paper label was handwritten, *Mary Moscow.*

Three hours later, George lay on the bed, alone, staring at the rustic journal, the careful elegant handwritten name, his eyes red from uncontrollable tears. The homage she had crafted, extolling their love, had made it all better, and all worse. She was gone and had left him something he had no right to.

The vile aftermath of his betrayal was all he had left. He curled into a fetal position and held the journal close in his arms, Mary's perfume sending him off to sleep.

END

A NOTE FROM LORRAINE EVANOFF

Thank you for reading *Louise Moscow Book 3, Devil's Ledger: An International Banking Spy Thriller*. I hope you enjoyed reading it as much as I enjoyed writing this amazing adventure. It would mean so much to me if you could take the time to leave a review, whether on Amazon or Goodreads, best of all on both! Be it short or long, reviews help others find my books.

Feel free to post all over social media that you have read *Devil's Ledger* and what you thought of it. Just don't give away the story in your excitement!

Also, please let your reader groups and friends know how much you enjoyed the book. Word-of-mouth is still the best marketing there is. Another great way to spread the word is by recommending the book on BookBub.

More than anything, thank you for being an avid reader. You're my favorite kind of person!

ABOUT THE AUTHOR

Former Hollywood finance exec Lorraine Evanoff is the award-winning author of the popular Louise Moscow spy thrillers. Originally from Chicago, Evanoff earned her degree in French from DePaul University. After working in Paris for seven years as a film producer, she returned to the States, settled on the West Coast, and became a Certified Financial Manager. She has since worked as a finance exec in dot-com-era Silicon Valley, and for various Hollywood film companies, notably as CFO of National Lampoon.

Stay connected with Lorraine and keep updated about special deals, GIVEAWAYS, new releases, and other reader perks, by signing up to her exclusive newsletter and following her.

Newsletter lorraineevanoff.com/newsletter
Facebook LorraineEvanoffAuthor
Twitter @LorraineEvanoff
Amazon Lorraine-Evanoff/e/B019G8QGHM
BookBub bookbub.com/profile/lorraine-evanoff
Instagram lorraineevanoffauthor
Goodreads goodreads.com/author/show/14612911.Lorraine_Evanoff
LinkedIn linkedin.com/in/lorraine-evanoff-0970166
LorraineEvanoff@gmail.com

BOOKS BY LORRAINE EVANOFF

AN INTERNATIONAL BANKING SPY THRILLER
A LOUISE MOSCOW NOVEL

FOLIAGE

LORRAINE
EVANOFF

AN INTERNATIONAL BANKING SPY THRILLER
A LOUISE MOSCOW NOVEL

PINOT NOIR

LORRAINE
EVANOFF

AN INTERNATIONAL BANKING SPY THRILLER
A LOUISE MOSCOW NOVEL

DEVIL'S LEDGER

LORRAINE
EVANOFF

NOTES

1. While held at the KGB's Lubyanka Prison in 1945, Solzhenitsyn had befriended Arnold Susi, a lawyer, and former Estonian Minister of Education, who had been taken captive after the Soviet Union occupied Estonia in 1944. Experiences that he had committed to memory while detained and wrote upon release, Solzhenitsyn had entrusted to Susi. Copies had been made of the finished work, the original typed and proofread manuscript, on both paper and on microfilm. Arnold Susi's daughter, Heli Susi, subsequently kept the "master copy" hidden from the KGB in Estonia until the dissolution of the Soviet Union in 1991.

2. https://en.wikipedia.org/wiki/Amarnath_Temple.

3. https://wayofmartialarts.com/what-is-the-best-martial-art-for-womens-self-defense/.

4. Dark Towers by Daniel Enrich.

5. Jonathan Beaty and S.C. Gwynne, *The Outlaw Bank: A Wild Ride into the Secret Heart of BCCI*, (Random House, New York).

6. https://www.theguardian.com/business/2016/dec/22/monte-dei-paschi-the-history-of-the-worlds-oldest-bank.

7. Honeypot: (espionage) A spy who uses sex to trap and blackmail their target.

8. From the author's first novel in the Louise Moscow series, *Foliage: An International Banking Spy Thriller*.

9. https://litemind.com/memory-palace/.

10. *Dépaysement*: The feeling of disorientation, of not being home, in a foreign place; change of scenery.

11. https://www.foodandwinegazette.com/4676.

12. From the author's second novel in the Louise Moscow series, *Pinot Noir: An International Banking Spy Thriller*.

13. Disloyal: A Memoir: The True Story of the Former Personal Attorney to President Donald J. Trump by Michael Cohen.

14. *Schrödinger's cat* is a famous physics thought experiment, which presents a paradox in which a cat in a box is somehow simultaneously both alive and dead.

15. Special thanks for quote from Robert Fairly.

16. From the author's second novel in the Louise Moscow series, *Pinot Noir: An International Banking Spy Thriller*.

17. A generalized, supernatural force or power concentrated in objects or persons.

18. https://archives.fbi.gov/archives/news/speeches/the-evolving-organized-crime-threat.

19. An apparatchik was a full-time, bureaucrat of the Communist Party of the Soviet Union.

20. https://numerologycolumn.com/525-angel-number/.

21. From the author's second novel in the Louise Moscow series, *Pinot Noir: An International Banking Spy Thriller*.

22. From the author's first novel in the Louise Moscow series, *Foliage: An International Banking Spy Thriller*.

23. Cialdini's six principles are reciprocation, authority, scarcity, commitment, and consistency, liking, and social proof.

24. A mildly meditative state characterized by calm, peacefulness, unity, and a sense of general happiness and satisfaction with life in the moment, when we are near an ocean, lake, or other massive bodies of water. https://medium.com/@ahmedmuneeb/striving-for-a-blue-mind-db26f1f6c6b1.

25. Special thanks to Scott Muench.

Printed in Great Britain
by Amazon

74270653R00170